The Good Girls Secrets

Rescue Me Series Book I

AUTUMN RIVERS

Authors Copyright

Copyright © 2021 By Autumn Rivers

All Rights Reserved.

No part of this publication may be reproduced, distributed, or transmitted in any form or by any person, including photography, recording, or other electronic or mechanical methods, without the prior written permission of the Author or Publisher, except in the case of brief quotations, embodied in critical reviews and certain other noncommercial uses permitted by copyright law.

NOTE: This book is a work of fiction. All names, characters, locations and incidents are products of the author's imagination. Any resemblance to actual persons, living or dead, or events is entirely coincidental.

The Good Girl's SECRETS
Written and edited by: Autumn Rivers
Cover Design by: Autumn R. and David O.
Formatting by: Jensen Kristyne

Paperback ISBN# 979-8-9851335-2-3

AUTHOR'S NOTE

CONTENT WARNING: **The Good Girl's SECRETS** is the first book in a series. Please be mindful, this is a work of fiction. People, places, events and incidents are either the product of my imagination or used in a fictitious manner.

The Good Girl's SECRETS contains mature themes that might make some readers uncomfortable. Including but not limited to, depictions or references to suicide, self-harm, vivid imagery, substance abuse and childhood trauma.

DEDICATION

To my loving husband. Without you, life just wouldn't be as crazy, fun and beautiful. To my awesome kids, you are the best little humans to watch enjoying life every single day. To all of my friends, beta and ARC readers thank you for showing so much love and support.

Prologue

Fresh tears quickly spill down my cheeks as I drag the jagged piece of glass across the pale pink flesh of my arm, feeling every single little sliver open me up like a ripe peach. I watch the warm red liquid trickle into a dark puddle beside me as the cool rain splatters in my window and chills my toes.

I can feel my eyelids growing heavy as the scent of copper floods the room and as each second passes, it's harder and harder not to fall into a sleep that fights to consume me. I lazily stare down at the wound that harshly decorates my wrist and it puts me in a fuzzy like haze. My body has gone numb and I realize that I'm no longer in any pain but I'm growing tired and my body is desperate for rest. I've craved this much needed release and now that I have it, I gladly welcome the quiet.

After so long, I finally got what I have been needing for years…to feel nothing. So, I let my eyelids fall, shutting out the darkness as a weak smile, spreads across my lips because I know I will never have to endure anything like this ever again.

1
Josephine

Three months earlier

The thunderous bang of the kitchen door jolts me out of a restless sleep, followed by the incessant bickering of Nate and his asshole father as they stomp up and down the hallway outside my bedroom door. The relentless arguing is getting old and it's starting to affect me in more ways than just fewer hours of sleep. The two of them never stop going at each other and by the sounds of it, it's going to be another miserable morning.

I can't remember the last time it was quiet around here. It's always filled to the brim with alcohol induced tension and I can feel the fury behind every word that erupts out of Jeff's mouth, even if he's not directly yelling at me. Before my mom left a few years ago, Jeff didn't seem like such a bad guy. He casually drank when they would go out or have people over, but it never seemed to be a problem. It had only become compulsive after he found out that she took off and left me behind. *I guess I can't blame him.* That's when everything seemed to fall apart like dominoes. Once the first piece falls, so does all the rest. He hasn't been able to hold a job for more than a few months at a time since she left and he spends more money on beer and cigarettes than anything else. Sometimes I just wish he would take off like my mom did. We would be much better off without him, but I don't think we would be lucky enough for him to just disappear after getting wasted and hopefully forget where he lived. I kind of wish he would just drive off of a cliff, to be honest. Being the kind of person he is, I'm positive no one would even miss him.

My stepbrother is always around giving me shit about not getting in Jeff's face too much and making sure I know to stay, invisible. He says

"It's better for everyone." I kind of wish he would move out like any self-respecting college-aged adult would. Especially since we don't even talk anymore, well not that we really ever did much anyway.

Nate graduated high school last year, so I was hoping he would move out and live in the dorms but, I figured I wouldn't get lucky enough for that to happen. He decided to stick around and get a job as a mechanic instead. When I heard him and Jeff arguing about money the one day, Nate told his dad that he doesn't make enough only working part-time to pay for school and an apartment on his own right now. He only goes to school part-time, so I would think he would have plenty of time that he could take on more hours. Personally, I think he just rather blow all of his money away instead of wanting to pay for a place of his own. I have no idea why he would want to stick around living here any longer, especially with Jeff always getting in his face, because I can't remember the last time that they spoke to each other without an argument or one of them getting a fist to the jaw.

If it were me, I would leave and never look back.

I have to get to school so I reluctantly drag myself out of bed and quickly gather my clothes for the day as I walk over to my closet to get dressed. It's hardly big enough for my clothes as it is, let alone moving around and having proper elbow space to get dressed, but I always get changed in here ever since Jeff '*Accidentally'* walked in on me changing a few times. Unless I were to shower that day, then of course, the bathroom it is. I wish I still had one of those nice large walk-in closets that I had when mom and I first moved in with them. That luxury didn't last very long, but it was nice while it did.

I grab my bag and go to open my window after making sure that I have everything in it that I need for the day. My notebooks, a couple of pens, phone charger, a granola bar out of the stash I keep in my room, and a chocolate bar that I bought on the way home yesterday.

I quietly drop my bag out the window and slide down the short wall enough to not make noise when I land, because I definitely don't need Jeff to catch me sneaking out, even though I'm only going to school. Luckily my room is on the first floor toward the back of the house, so I can cut through the woods behind our house to completely avoid the street. Seeing as the living room window looks out onto the street and Jeff would be able to see me from his recliner that he plops himself in every morning after working the night shift, and drinks himself into a coma with a six-pack and passes out before noon. It only takes me about twenty minutes to walk to school but I always end up leaving earlier than I have to most mornings so I can stop by the bookstore first. I work there most days, usually after school, but I started going there every day for some place to be just to get out of the house in the morning. Thankfully my school is in the opposite direction, so I don't have to worry about teachers passing by and seeing me if the mood strikes not to attend any classes that day. And the mood strikes more often than it should.

When I do get to school, I try to make sure to get there early enough that I usually don't need a late pass, but I waste just enough time at my locker so I don't have to go to homeroom anymore. My first day of school when we had moved to town was the most awful day I could have had, or so I thought. The teacher was such a bitch, and she gave us assigned seating even though it was only homeroom and we weren't going to be in there for more than ten minutes for announcements. Of course, I was the unlucky one and got stuck sitting next to Evan Parker. The biggest asshole in school, in my opinion. Most people wouldn't say that about him, because he's the popular jock and captain of the Jr. Varsity football team. He has this whole teachers' pet façade' that seems to fool everyone, even his parents, but from day one he has never shown an ounce of decency towards me. He would crowd me and push things off of my desk like I wasn't even sitting there and he would block me from getting to my desk so that I had to walk around him and his friends just to get to my seat. I eventually got fed up with him after the third time he had done it and seven months later, I haven't been to homeroom since.

"Where the hell are you going so early, Jo?" I freeze at the sound of a gravelly voice calling my name and my pulse instantly starts to race as I turn around. Nate is standing on the sidewalk not far from me with an odd look on his face.

"SHIT!" I hiss under my breath. *I regret not leaving earlier.*

Nate stalks toward me while lighting a cigarette and takes a rather long drag to fill his lungs with the suffocating cloud. He draws in as much smoke as his lungs can hold and as his chest relaxes the cloud slowly escapes through his nose. The scent of decay comes to mind as the exhaled smoke wafts towards me so, I make an effort to only breathe through my mouth. *gross*

The surrounding air is damp and the morning frost still clings to the car windows parked along the street. Nate's breath escapes like steam from the top of a hot mug of coffee in the late winter air as he stands in front of me. He's out here dressed like its summer in only a thin t-shirt, with the same old shitty '*I don't care about anything*' attitude. His boots make a loud thud on the concrete as he takes a few steps closer and his body radiates with smug confidence; giving off the impression like he just caught a criminal in the middle of robbing a bank with a water gun.

Nate sometimes scares the hell out of me. He's smaller in stature than most guys I've come across, but he makes up for it in rage. I've seen his own father cower to him many times since I've lived with them. He would get so irate over something that his dad said and then Jeff would just back off after Nate would lose his temper, time and time again. It would usually end in one of them being bloodied, so I learned very quickly how to avoid them both by making myself invisible on a regular basis.

"What do you want Nate? I have to get to school." I remind him.

"Didn't know school started before sun-up now?" He says with a questioning look. Guess he's curious why I'm leaving so early. *What does he care?*

"I have some work to catch up on if you must know and I need some notes from my locker to do it." I say with a cocky undertone.

"Right." He takes another drag of his cigarette and then flicks the butt across the street without so much as dropping the smirk on his face. *I would really like to go now!*

"Nate, I have to go, is there something you wanted?" I ask hesitantly this time.

"Don't worry. You have plenty of time, it's still early. But I'm just letting you know to be home by six tonight. Dad's bringing his new girlfriend over for dinner and he wants us both there to meet her."

"Why the hell would I want to be there for that? And by the way, he's not my dad, he's yours. Now if there's nothing actually important to tell me, I have to go!" Clearly, he can tell I'm irritated but it doesn't seem to faze him in the least.

"Sure, but you know how he gets when you don't do what he says." Nate warns.

"I don't care!" I yell, louder than I expected to. "Look, just leave me alone Nate and I'll be happy to do the same!"

"Yeah, alright. But I don't need to hear his shit because you're not there. Don't say I didn't warn you!" He snarls.

"Nate, you're an adult. You don't need to take his shit anymore. You had a choice to move out months ago. You have a job and can leave and never come back so you don't have to deal with him anymore! So why the hell do you stay? Just to torture me?" I question weakly.

I immediately feel guilty and regret opening my mouth and letting those harsh words escape. I don't know what came over me but I can't believe I just said that. I stare at Nate and wait for him to lash out, but he doesn't say a damn word; he just drops his head and looks at his feet. After a painfully long minute, he looks back up at me, and his mouth slightly parts as if he's about to say something, but then he just shakes his head, turns around and starts walking back towards the house.

I don't understand why Nate does certain things sometimes and why it frustrates me so damn much, but it feels like it will always be this way. I want to scream so badly right now and get rid of all my pent-up anger and frustration I have; but instead of waking the entire neighborhood, I decide to try and forget about what just happened and turn around to start walking towards the bookstore. I only get a few feet before I start to feel a burning pain in the palms of my hands, so I look down and notice my knuckles are pale white. I uncurl my fingers and they instantly start to tingle as I see the angry red crescent-shaped fingernail marks staring up at me and my hands begin to throb in the chilled air as the blood rushes back into the tips of my fingers.

"Jo…?" I hear Nate call to me. When I look back, I see him standing by the small broken metal gate in front of our house.

"What?!" I yell back automatically. The crack in my throat makes my voice sound so weak and it makes me that much angrier as I stand there staring back at him.

"Be careful, okay?" He says softly, void of any anger. Then he walks through the gate and disappears behind the overgrown hedges without another word. I turn around and start rubbing circles around the cuts on my hand, trying to soothe the sting that lingers on both of my palms. I'm not exactly sure how Nate meant what he said to me, but he's clearly confused me once again.

2
Josephine

I lied to Nate when I said I had work to catch up on at school. I didn't want him to know where I was going because the bookstore is the one place where I can go and not have to worry about what's going on anywhere else for a while. When I'm there, I don't have a care in the world and I'd like to be able to keep it that way for as long as possible.

Honey Bees Bookstore is only a seventeen-minute walk from my house. I'm there pretty much every day and on weekends when Mrs. Lawrence needs the extra help. I also spend most of my free time there reading every book that I can get my hands on. I have read so many novels in the last couple of years; that I could probably fill my room from top to bottom.

I see Mrs. Lawrence through the window just as she turns the light on to the cute little book-shaped, ***OPEN*** sign in the window and then comes to the door to unlock it to let me in. She's wearing her favorite oversized wool sweater and her hair is always so neatly tied up in a bun on top of her head. And not once have I come in here and seen her without a smile.

"Good morning Mrs. Lawrence." I say as I walk in.

"Good morning, dear. It's nice to see you so early again." She says in her usual cheery tone.

Mrs. Lawrence and I have a quiet, friendly relationship. I started coming here a couple of years ago every day before school, spending at least an hour in the morning and most days I would even come back after school. The weekends are when I would spend almost the entire day here and I enjoyed every single minute of it. I would spend hours browsing through the books to see what looked interesting but I couldn't always purchase them because I never had any money of my own at the time.
The one morning I had come in before school and Mrs. Lawrence asked if I could help her with some inventory that she was behind on. Of course,

I helped her catch up on everything she needed. After all, she would always let me stay here as long as I wanted and never complained when I couldn't actually buy anything. From then on, I would help around the store without being asked. I would realign the shelves, put back anything that the customers decided not to buy or didn't put back in the correct place after looking at them, and sometimes Mrs. Lawrence would even send me down the block to pick up pastries she had ordered that morning. She would always tell me to help myself to whatever I wanted as long as it was a sweet treat that I would enjoy.

After a few months she even confided in me and told me that the bookstore had been in her family for three generations, but since her husband had passed away a couple of years ago, she's left to take care of everything all on her own. That's when I decided to come in regularly and get right into a routine of completing daily tasks without her having to ask me and a couple of weeks later, she offered me a job. Of course, I happily accepted and I have been working here ever since, and I absolutely love it.

A few packages were delivered this morning before I left to pick up the pastries at the bakery, so I signed for them and brought them inside. I start unpacking the boxes and un-wrap each book, finding myself staring at the gorgeous covers. The colors are amazing and both look like they belong together, each complimenting the other. When I read the title, I realize that this is an author that I haven't read anything from yet. *Lullaby Series by Anna Monroe.* I flip the book over to read the description on the back and I am even more intrigued than I was just seconds ago.

I neatly line the shelves with all of the new copies, stacking them just right so the covers are sure to catch customers' attention. Mrs. Lawrence said these need to be put out before anything else in the stock room gets unpacked because they are the first two books of a series that will be coming in over the next few weeks to complete a display later on.

I never used to read the blurbs, but a while back Mrs. Lawrence told me to never judge a book by its cover after she noticed that I only sat down to read the ones that looked the most interesting to me. Then she handed me a book that had a dark green cover with pale yellow writing on it called Wuthering Heights by Emily Bronte. I can honestly say I would have never read it had it not been for her telling me that it was the most liberating novel that she had ever read and it was one of her favorite books to read over and over again. She told me to take it home that day and that if I liked it, I didn't have to return it.

I went home that day and read the entire thing from cover to cover. I would have never picked it up, much less read a romance novel before reading this one but after I did, it opened my eyes to an entire new world. I go to Mrs. Lawrence to ask if she wouldn't mind that I borrow a copy before I place the last stack on the shelf.

"Do you mind if I take these with me to read at home?" I ask her from across the room, holding up a copy of each to let her see which ones I mean.

"I ordered a few extra copies of that series. You go ahead and keep them if you like." She tells me. "I have a feeling you may enjoy reading that authors' work. Really quite talented that one, she keeps you coming back for more." She says excitedly as she waves her finger in the air over her head. I feel my face light up when she says I can keep them. I'll have to remember to do something nice for her to pay her back. I always feel kind of guilty when she lets me keep a book, so I try to show her how much I appreciate it. I thought I loved reading before I met Mrs. Lawrence, but she has introduced me to so many wonderful authors and I just can't get enough. I thank her as I break down the last of the boxes for recycling and gather my things up to leave for school.

"Have a nice day Mrs. Lawrence." I call back to her.

"See you later dear." She says as I walk out the front door.

3
Josephine

I'm crossing the parking lot just as the bell blares its obnoxious ringing throughout the grounds. *Great!* I hate being late and having to walk into class while everyone is already there but what I hate even more is having to go to the office to get a late pass from the secretary. I've never seen the woman be nice to anyone, come to think about it. The entire time I've gone to school here she's always been a bitch to me, so I'm pretty sure she hasn't liked me from day one. *Uh screw it!*

I decide I'm not in much of a mood to deal with people today so, instead of going to class I walk around the building and out of view from the main office. This side of the school leads slightly up hill to where a stone wall sits in the middle of two large pine trees. It used to be part of a sign with the school's name on it before they remodeled and moved the front door to the other side of the parking lot. They added a brand-new sign near that door and they never removed the stone from the old one because they said it would cost too much in labor to tear it down and that they could use the money they saved to put toward the science and art wing; which I inform you, never happened.

I find myself hiding out here more often than I use to. Before I would actually push myself to go into the building and sit through lectures that bore the ever-living hell out of me, but now I can't seem to be bothered with putting in as much effort. I do enough to get by and pass my classes but some days I just don't want to deal.

I would rather sit here all day and watch people scrambling to their cars to keep from getting rained on and then laugh when they step in a pothole that's the size of a small lake. Other days I just wonder what everyone else's life is like when I don't see them hanging around each other when school lets out. I think about what their houses look like and if they have parents that take care of them and love them? Do they care where their kids go or who they hang out with, or do they just let them do as they please and ignore them, like my family does? *Ha, family.* Does anyone here think about me or have any clue how shitty my life is by the way I look or how I act? Or do I hide it so well that I have now become invisible to everyone in this suffocating town?

I feel like the only reason I come to school now, sadly as it is, is to get away from the house. It's better having to deal with the egotistical adults and burnouts at this place than to have to deal with the mess waiting for me back home. The longer I can be away from there the better because living with Jeff has been hell, since my mom left. I originally thought about running away when she first took off, but I'm smart enough to realize I wouldn't get very far without a job and some place to stay. So, I'm unfortunately stuck here for a couple more years.

The rain starts to come down faster and harder now feeling like little pebbles every time they land on my head. I'm sitting under a large tree with a ton of branches but pine needles don't make for the best coverage under a pending torrential downpour, so I'm not staying as dry as I would have liked. *I wish I had stayed at the bookstore instead of coming here.* But it's too late for that, so I just pull my hood up over my head, nibble on my granola bar and stubbornly sit and listen to the new music I downloaded yesterday. I scroll through to find the song I want, sit back against the wall and close my eyes.

This is thankfully one of many places I can sit and be alone for a while; at least until school lets out. But on the days when the weather sucks, I can sit here and not be bothered for hours. I think people are afraid they're going to melt or something if they let the rain touch them. Being alone in a quiet place like this has its perks, but when it's too quiet, it lets my mind wander to the dark places that I try to avoid at all costs. Silence dredges up every little horrible thing that I could have avoided if my mom had never abandoned me and left me alone to deal with her asshole husband three years ago.

I never understood why my mom was so miserable after she married Jeff. We finally had everything we ever needed since he had a good job and she could take a break from working and focus on herself for a while. Jeff was always so nice to her at least. He would shower her with little gifts and buy her flowers, even cook her dinner and take her on vacations for just the two of them while Nate and I stayed home. It was nice to see her happy for a change, so I wasn't that mad about being alone so much. But that all seemed to change after they got married, and all of the bullshit started at the very same time.

4
Josephine

Four years earlier

We're all taking a trip to Oregon tomorrow." Mom tells me out of the blue. I didn't expect this to be the news when she told me to be home right after school. I thought I was in trouble but I had no idea what for.

"Like a vacation?" I ask. She's fiddling around in the fridge, trying to scrape something up for dinner I assume. She won't find much. Nate is a better cook and even he couldn't whip up something edible from what's in there.

"Yes, a family vacation. Well, Jeff has to go there for business, but his boss is paying to rent a place down there for all of us to go and stay for the week." She explains as she slams the door shut and huffs out a long and exhausted breath. She walks over to the sink and smooths her hand over the loose strands of hair on top of her head as she turns the faucet on and starts taking big gulps of water for the next few seconds.

"Is everything okay mom?" I ask in a quiet, concerned voice; barely loud enough for her to hear me, but she does. She stands up and wipes the drops of water off of her chin with her sleeve before swiping at her hair again.

"Yes, everything is fine bean, now why don't you start packing your things for the trip? We'll be leaving first thing in the morning." She says in a distracted voice as she walks out of the kitchen, abruptly ending the conversation.

I have never even been on a real vacation before. We could never afford it when it was just the two of us. Mom worked all the time but we never had any extra money to go and do anything expensive like that.

Any of the jobs she had never allowed for time off either since she never stayed anywhere long enough to earn vacation time, so we just lived day to day, paycheck to paycheck, and did what we had to do. I can't complain, at least then we had fun when we spent time together as opposed to now.

Jeff's job is awesome though. He gets all of these free trips completely paid for even though he can afford to pay for them himself. Mom even quit her job because he said he didn't need her to work because he made well enough above what they need to be comfortable. So, when we moved in with him and his son, that's what she did. She quit her job and promised to spend more time with me. Only that didn't happen either. I think we spend even less time together now since they got married.

AFTER WE GOT off the plane, we all grab our bags and walk out into the fresh mountain air and parked in front of us sits a large white SUV that I take it is ours for the week because everyone is walking over to it. The driver gets out and puts all of our bags in the back while Nate jumps to the seats in the back. He puts his earbuds in, sprawls his long legs out across the entire seat and proceeds to cover his face with his hat before crossing his arms over his chest. He looks surprisingly comfortable for being crammed back there though. I take the middle seat by the window and set my backpack down beside me. The driver hands Jeff the keys and opens the door for mom to get in the passenger side while Jeff goes around to the driver's side. *Jeff should have held the door for her himself.* It felt like it took forever to get to the cabin we're staying in, but was realistically only about twenty-five minutes before we pull up in front of this massive gate at the end of a stone driveway. Jeff punches in a code on the keypad and the gate opens to let us through. He stops the car in front of this gorgeous building that looks like it belongs in one of those luxury magazines of celebrity homes or something and the first thing that takes my breath away is the amount of glass that makes up most of the outside walls. I was expecting something a lot smaller and maybe run down looking, since they described it as a 'cabin in the woods' so my jaw nearly hits the ground when I open the door. The railing that wraps around the front porch is made out of branches and connects to the tree trunks, acting as pillars to hold up the roof on the covered porch. I can't help but stand there in awe. I've never seen a house this huge and luxurious looking much less allowed to stay here for an entire week.

Nate clears his throat from behind me, knocking me out of the trance like state from trying to take it all in. I didn't notice I was blocking him from getting out of the car, so I move out of his way and he jumps out. He slings his bag over his shoulder and casually walks up to the porch and into the house like he owns the place, leaving the door open as he disappears into the hallway.

"So here we are, home sweet home for an entire week." My mom says, without a hint of enthusiasm.

"What do you think kid? Is it big enough or what?" Jeff asks when he comes up beside my mom and wraps his arm around her waist. I look up at them and notice the tension in my moms' jaw as she just looks straight ahead, it speaks volumes. Rightly so I guess for Jeff being a prick to her only two days ago; how convenient for him to make it up to her with a vacation again. At least this time Nate and I got to come too.

"Yeah sure." I answer, but I barely get the words out before they start to walk towards the steps, leaving me standing in the driveway with just my suitcase. They both walk in the house but I stay outside to take it all in. I can't assume I'll ever get to stay in a place like this again so I'm going to take full advantage of it while I'm here. I walk around the grounds to see what this place has to offer and when I get to the backyard, the house looks even bigger. Some stairs lead up to a large deck on the back of the house and under a small roof structure is a covered Jacuzzi. There's even a TV attached to the wall outside above the grilling area. *Wow, this place is awesome!*

It took me a good part of the morning to make my way through the house. There are four bedrooms, three full bathrooms, a huge eat-in kitchen with a walk-in pantry that is bigger than my bedroom and fully stocked with everything you could ever think of. There are things in there I have never even heard of before, like chocolate-covered quail eggs. That sounds disgusting but what do I know, I've never tried them. I don't plan to either.

There's an in-ground swimming pool, but since it's winter we obviously can't use it right now and mom and Jeff have already claimed the Jacuzzi on the deck. That's fine with me because all I want to do right now is get away from the house since a bunch of Nate's friends showed up right after we got here. I haven't even unpacked yet and there is a house full of a bunch of dudes eating all of the new food I was planning on trying myself.

I start lugging my suitcase up the stairs to my room when mom and Jeff walk into the kitchen from the deck laughing hysterically about something. *I guess I missed the joke again.*

"Hey bean, Nate. Can you both come down here please?" I hear my mom yell. She obviously didn't see me struggling to drag this damn thing upstairs, so I just let it sit on the stair while I go over to see what they could possibly want. Probably going to get read the rules of the house, or told I still have to be in by curfew even though they don't ever really care to enforce that rule at home. It would be my luck though that they do that here and ruin my entire vacation.

Nate comes barreling down the stairs, phone in hand, and quickly slips it into his back pocket before coming to a dead halt in the doorway.

"Yeah?" He questions, clearly annoyed.

"Here." Jeff holds out his hand towards us, offering up two credit cards.

"Each of you gets one; it's spending money for while we're here. And Nate…try to make it last, alright?" He tells him and Nate grabs one of the cards out of his hand.

"Yup, sure thing pops." He says and hops back up the stairs taking them two at a time.

"Thank you." I say to them. Kind of shocked since Jeff has never been nice to me and it's like asking for the tooth fairy to be real to get money for things I need, much less just getting spending money to buy whatever I want. I'm not sure they heard me since they don't say anything and they quickly go back to talking without further acknowledging that I'm still standing in the kitchen. They grab some drinks from the fridge and go back out in the Jacuzzi. So, with that, I turn around and go back to try and haul my suitcase up to my room but it's not sitting where I left it not even two minutes ago.

"What the hell?" I say to no one since everyone left. I run up the stairs and go to one of the empty rooms to freshen up, and when I open the door, I see that my suitcase is already sitting on the bed. *Thanks Nate.*

I don't understand how Nate thinks at all. He hardly talks to me but then he'll do something nice once in a while. I didn't even see him grab my suitcase, but it wouldn't have been anyone else. I rifle through my bag to find some warmer clothes and I layer up on socks and put a hoodie on over my sweater. I'm always way colder than I think I should be, but up here in the mountains it's particularly frigid.

WALKING AROUND TOWN is like walking through a giant snow globe. All the shops are lined up along the main street, perfectly decorated for the upcoming holidays. Even the street lights and the trees across the park are littered with white Christmas lights and there are kids making snowmen and chasing each other during a snowball fight.

After some time of window shopping and wandering around capturing pictures of everything new I've seen, I stop in front of a ski shop and see a bunch of TV screens along the wall, playing clips of people snowboarding, skiing, and tubing. It looks like so much fun.

The owner of the ski shop set me up with some lessons for the next two days and gave me a rental card saying what gear I have to pick up when I come in tomorrow. The gear was included in the lesson fee so that's awesome! I saved like eighty bucks. After taking a few last pictures of the mountain all lit up, I decided to call it a night. When I get back to the house and see that the SUV is gone out of the driveway, I figured everyone went out somewhere. I punch in the code to the keypad and let myself in the front door. To my surprise, Nate is sitting in the living room on the couch, eating pizza and watching a movie. I expected him to have gone out with his friends that were here earlier.

"Hey." Nate says with a mouth full of pizza dough.

"Hey." I say back and walk into the kitchen to grab a bottle of water from the fridge.

"Pizzas on the counter." He yells over his shoulder before guzzling his soda.

"Thanks." I say back quietly. I look down and see there are exactly two slices of pizza left in the box for me. So, I take a slice and warm it in the microwave before heading up to my room to eat and relax for the night. I have so many things I want to do, so I decide to crash after taking a shower. I want to fit in as much as I possibly can while we're here.

5
Josephine

I didn't know how much I would love going on vacation, but being able to do whatever I want in a new place definitely has its perks. I wake up early to make sure I have enough time for everything I planned for today. Snowboarding lessons, shopping, and finding the best-reviewed bookshop they have around here. The town is small but there are so many things to see since I haven't been here before.

I make sure to bundle up again since I'm most likely going to fall on my ass a few times given the fact that I have never gone snowboarding before. I have no idea if I'll even be able to manage to stand up with the thing attached to my feet. *I guess we'll find out.*

I slide my phone and my extra memory card into my pocket before heading down to the kitchen. No one is home, so I decide to go out for breakfast at the little café' I passed yesterday.

When I get to the café', I order the biggest cup of hot cocoa they have, a fried croissant and strawberries on the side. The hot cocoa came in a mug the size of a small boat. It's shaped like a log with a branch as the handle and topped with a mountain-sized pile of whipped cream. The hot cocoa is delicious and the food is so fresh, like it was just freshly baked, and the strawberries picked right from the garden. It's so good I can't help but to eat every single last bite and drink every drop of my cocoa before heading back out for the day.

After an entire day of being on the slopes and not falling nearly as much as I thought I would, I am exhausted. The instructor said I was a natural with how easily I caught on and I did have a lot of fun. I definitely plan on coming back a few times before we have to go back home at the end of the week. But before I go back for the night, I feel like spending some more of the guilt money Jeff gave me. It doesn't make up for all the arguments I had to hear over the last year between them, but I don't care, guilt money spends the same way, doesn't it? And if they're going to give it to me, I'm going to enjoy myself by buying whatever the hell I want for once. I decide to buy all four books I found and have been wanting for a while. '*The Lost' by: Natasha Preston, 'The QB Bad Boy' by: Tay Marley, 'Losing Hope' by: Colleen Hoover and 'With You' by: Jensen Kristyne*. The amazing reviews they all have gotten has drawn me in and I cannot wait to sit down to read them all. But for now, I will pack them safely in my suitcase in my room and wait to have more time to read them when I get back home.

The street lights have all come on already so I check my phone and see that it's past eight o'clock. I don't care about missing dinner and no one texts me to see where I was, so they're all most likely still out doing whatever. I walk up along the icy road to the house and lugging shopping bags full of books in the snow up a hill sucks, but it's totally worth it. I spent a couple of hours after snowboarding in the town's bookstore. It's the only one around apparently, so it was easy to find. The name of it is called 'INKED'. I think it's kind of a clever name. It sort of reminds me of the one back home. It's small and quiet, and has an old cottage feel to it. No matter where we move to, I always find the best bookshops.

My stomach is growling so loud by the time I reach the porch steps. It sounds as if it is echoing off every surface out here with how quiet it is. I expected the house to be loud and littered with Nate's drunken friends again. The rental car is in the driveway, telling me that mom and Jeff are probably here so it wouldn't be ideal for Nate to have a party, I guess. I punch in the numbers to the keypad 217241 and the door pops open for me. I head straight for the stairs with my bags in my arms and start walking up the lengthy staircase to my room when I notice shouting coming from mom and Jeff's room at the top of the landing. Nate's door opens just as I realize who's doing the shouting and he ambles out of his room, shutting the door behind him harder than necessary. He looks down at me standing there on the last few steps and as he walks towards me, he shrugs his shoulders and gives me a look that says *'Sorry, trips over'* before walking past me to go downstairs. I stand there for a minute, listening to what's going on behind the closed door. The yelling, them swearing at each other. *Why the hell did they have to start fighting here!* After a perfectly nice start of actually being able to get away from all of their bullshit, they have to go and ruin it, as usual! I should have known it wasn't going to last long, but I had hoped we would at least have a few days out of the week without any of this happening.

I walk up the last few steps and go down the hall to my bedroom, swinging the door open with my foot. I stomp over to the bed and throw my bags across it but they don't stop and end up sliding off, scattering the contents all over the floor. I slam my door shut and lock it before I kick off my shoes and throw my clothes off as I walk to the bathroom and turn the shower up as hot as it will go. I don't want to hear any more of their screaming and bickering so I sync my phone to the blue-tooth speakers and blare my music so that it echoes off of the tiles, surrounding me in a cocoon of angry lyrics, drowning out the noise coming from the other side of the hall.

It's quiet when I turn off the music after my shower so I get dressed in warm comfortable pajamas and decide to go downstairs to the kitchen for a snack. I haven't eaten since breakfast and the word ravenous comes to mind right now. I almost get to the bottom of the stairs when I hear someone in the kitchen. I peek around the corner and see Nate bent over, picking up broken pieces of glass that are all over the floor.

"Nate…what happened?" I ask hesitantly. He looks up and locks eyes with me for a second before letting his gaze fall back to the mess on the floor.

"Nothing, it's fine. Just go back to bed." He says, his tone is sad, but it leaves an angry aftertaste as he continues to sweep up the glass.

"Here I can help." I go to walk towards him but as I do, he quickly stands up and yells at me not to come over.

"Wait! Don't walk down here, there's glass everywhere and you're in bare feet." But it's too late. I didn't see the broken shards at the bottom of the stairs and I step right on them. I feel the sharp edges puncture my skin, so I automatically jerk my foot away and land hard on the bottom step.

"OW SHIT!" I hiss through my teeth. I grab hold of my foot to assess the damage and when I look down all I see is red. The blood is quickly running down my toes and dripping onto the hardwood floor. Nate comes over to me, takes my foot in his hands, and looks at it for a second before letting it go and scooping me up off the stairs. He walks into the kitchen and sets me on the higher counter before wetting a cloth in the sink. He seems angry by the way he moves throughout the kitchen. Hastily opening cabinet doors and shoving them closed again when he doesn't find what he's looking for until he opens the bottom drawer next to the sink and comes up with a first aid kit in his hand.

"Nate I'm sor…" I try to apologize for being such a pain in the ass. I always seem to make a bigger mess than the one I'm trying to clean up, but he cuts me off before I can finish my sentence.

"Forget it. It's not your fault. You were only trying to help." He reassures me while picking the chunk of glass out of my foot with tweezers. His hands are gentle and I notice him being careful not to touch the cut as he wipes away more of the blood before holding my foot under his arm while he puts some kind of ointment on a bandage. He places it on the bottom of my foot and gently smooths over it with his hand before wrapping a strip of gauze around it.

I don't know what to say or how to act around Nate right now. Most of the time we just coexist, but don't usually have any kind of contact with each other. He's never really been one to jump at the chance of getting into the middle of anything since the day we moved in with him and his dad. I can't remember even having a full conversation with him that consisted of more than a few words. Granted he's not talking much right now, but this is the first time in a while that I have felt like he cares about anything other than himself. Maybe even a little for me.

I sit quietly on the counter as Nate finishes taping up the bandage around my foot. He throws the cloth in the trash can and then without warning picks me up off the counter and sets me gently on the floor before he puts the first aid kit back where he found it. I stand leaning mostly on my good foot, so only my toes are touching the floor on my other foot. The pressure from the bandage is making the cut throb when I try to walk, so I'm a little hesitant to take another step. I hobble out of the kitchen, trying to walk as normally as I can while Nate goes back over to sweep up the rest of the glass on the floor. He's silent the rest of the time as I watch him walk back and forth in the kitchen, dumping the dustpan into the trash. I feel like I should still try and help but that would probably piss him off, because knowing me I would just get in the way again. I try so hard not to make things worse and the tension in the air is already so smothering every time our parents argue that I feel like it's my fault that Nate seems so miserable and pissed off all the time. There has been nothing but tension from the day we moved in with them so, I can only think they would most likely be happier if they hadn't met us at all. Nate comes back into the house from taking the trash outside and I see that his attention is on his phone. I stand there like a dumb little kid while he walks past me, intently staring at the screen, watching him as he saunters up the stairs. I finally muster up enough courage to say one last thing to him tonight before he disappears behind his bedroom door.

"Nate…" I finally say and I pause. Not knowing how to get the words out to ask him what happened tonight. Did he witness the entire argument? How bad was it? What does he think is going to happen between our parents now? But I choose not to ask him those questions after taking a second to consider his answers. It's probably better to just leave it alone. "Thank you." I tell him. His hand is wrapped around the door handle but he pauses and looks back at me over the banister.

Sadness briefly crosses his expression again and before he walks through his door he says.

"No problem." And he shuts the door behind him. A quiet click of the lock tells me he's in for the night, so I hobble carefully up the stairs and lock myself in my room for my own sleepless night, waiting to be hauled away from what I thought was going to be a paradise for a few days. I guess I got my hopes up again because it turned out to be the same as always. At least now I know not to hold my breath if we ever get to do something like this again.

6
Josephine

Not long after the wonderful blowup between our parents happened on vacation, I came home from school one day to a note from my mother that she had left in my room on my pillow. I had no idea what it was about or why she left it for me when she could have just told me whatever it was herself. But then as I read further, I realized why she wrote it instead of coming to tell me face to face. *She had left.* She had broken up with Jeff as she said in the hurried scribble, but from the broken vase in the hallway, I'm sure it was another fight and she ended up storming out. Only, I figured she would be back. She always came back after they would fight and they would be fine again for a while. They would have a few days of being nice, then each day after they would at least be civil until they found something else to argue about.

I kept reading even though I had it in my head that it was no big deal, I couldn't understand what the words on the paper were telling me until I got to the part where she said she *would be back for me.* She didn't even tell me how long she was going to be gone or exactly why she left. I didn't understand what was going on. *How could she leave me here?* Nate and Jeff aren't even my real family! My mother was all I had.

It was difficult falling asleep that night. I stayed in my room and didn't leave for two days. No one seemed to notice though or care that I hadn't come out to eat dinner, or to go to school. I was left alone, by everyone. Nothing was said about her leaving, nothing was mentioned about what I was supposed to do. So, from then on, I stayed out of the way and kept to myself and didn't ask questions. Sometimes I wish I knew where she took off too, or if she even cares about me. But today is not the day to be rehashing all of this. I don't think I'm in a good enough headspace to deal with it right now. I've tried so long to keep things in check, but suddenly it all seems too much to handle and I can feel my eyes well up, threatening to spill so many unshed tears. The heaviness in my chest makes it difficult to keep them inside any longer, so I do the only thing I can think of to try and get some relief. I finally give myself permission to let go and cry until there is nothing left.

I rub my sleeve over my face to soak up the tears that have fallen and notice a black streak when I pull my hand away. I've managed to smear my makeup that isn't waterproof like they said, so now I probably look like a drowned raccoon. *awesome.*

Sometimes I wish my mom would come back for me, so we can go back to the way things were when it was just me and her all the time, but after three years of never even getting an email or a phone call from her, I don't have much hope in that ever happening. She selfishly left me here alone, without so much as a second thought and it sucks! I hardly ever let my emotions show anymore. I'm afraid if I do, it will end up being like last time. I won't let that happen again. Luckily for me, I'm alone, far enough away from anyone that will make me feel less than I already do.

I'm starting to shiver since I'm nearly drenched and its only March. Around here, that means if Mother Nature decides to be a righteous bitch, we still get snowstorms at the end of April, even if we have already had a few days of warm weather and sunshine.

I decide to just go home so I get up to leave and of course I slip and fall right on my ass. The stones that have crumbled and fallen off of the wall litter the ground around me and are covered in slick moss. I come here so much you think I would have remembered enough to watch my step. I get back up on my feet and brush off some of the dirt and leaves from my clothes when I feel a sudden sharp sting along my arm.

I carefully roll up my sleeve to look and end up revealing a huge red scratch, reaching from the middle of my arm to my elbow. It's not too deep but it starts to bleed and surprisingly I feel this sudden wave of relief wash over me while I stare down at the fresh wound. Seeing the blood trickle down my arm is kind of mesmerizing; distracting me from the hurtful thoughts running through my mind for a few brief moments. It's like feeling nothing. No thoughts, no anger or being sad, just quiet. *Absolute quiet.*

The rain starts to come in heavier waves now. The trees above me can only hold onto so much before it dumps the water on top of me, weighing me down and soaking through everything. The cold chilling wind crawls through my wet clothes, bringing me out of my daze. I look around and notice a few smears of blood on a sharp pointy piece that once belong to part of the sign. The rain has started to wash it away, smearing the red color along the surface and dispersing it enough to quickly make it unseen. Without really thinking I lean over and press my arm hard against the sharp edge and it slices my skin open, leaving another long angry scratch. I yank my arm away from the shock of actually feeling it cut me this time and grip my arm where the fresh cut is. I feel instant euphoria as adrenaline rushes through my body and the gash in my flesh starts to sting under my fingers. I look down at my arm again, blood prickles up in little tiny droplets that start running together. The crimson color slowly melting through my fingers like a popsicle on a hot summer day.

In that second, I'm grateful for the small sense of relief it gave me and I cry in desperation wishing that it would last a little longer.

7
Hunter

My head feels like it's in a fucking vise when I open my eyes, so I slowly sit up and rub my hands over my face and I can feel the bile crawling its way up my throat. I hang my head low and breathe in a minute until the nausea subsides. I have a feeling today isn't going to be worth trying to function feeling like this but it's better than what the alternative would be if I dared to stay in this house with my parents' home this week, so I decide to just get on with it.

I get up, walk into my bathroom and look for some aspirin as I strip for a shower. I will never touch whatever the hell Kyle had me taking shots of last night if this is the repercussions of it. I've been hungover before, but nothing quite like this. I stand under the water and let last night's sweat and the scent of whatever girl I was with pour down the drain. The pounding in my head seems to subside a little under the cold water and it makes my body subtly relax.

I get out of the shower and get dressed, my hair dripping down my back already making my t-shirt wet. I notice as I walk back into my room that I must have brought the girl I was with last night home with me because there's a pair of white lace panties on my bedroom floor, but no girl to be found in my bed. *Thank God!* I'm not in the mood to deal with having to sneak another girl out of my room that's hungover and far too clingy. Not with the pounding migraine I have right now. I know I can be a real prick when I'm hungover and she would have regrettably been on the receiving end of me being an asshole if she was still here.

I can smell breakfast being made as I shuffle my dead legs down the stairs. The aroma of grease wafts its way into my nose from the kitchen and it would smell fucking awesome if it were any other day but my stomach is still turning from whatever concoction, I consumed last night. I breathe through my mouth as I enter the kitchen, letting the door swing shut behind me and I see that my parent's chef is here today, starting to set up for another party this week. *Great, just what I need.* I roll my eyes as I silently make my way to the fridge and grab a bottle of water, downing the cool liquid in seconds as it soothes the burn in the back of my throat. I notice that there's an entire spread of food on the island; all kinds of pastries and biscuits, eggs, bacon, homemade crepes, and three different kinds of fresh juice, all of different colors so bright it hurts my eyes. I would usually stay for a breakfast like this but today I head straight for the black coffee on the counter, hoping it will counteract the effects of the alcohol.

Mom and dad walk in from the back patio a minute later, talking far too loudly about yet another boring party they're throwing for one of dad's clients. I'm just trying to consume my caffeine and be invisible when mum notices me leaning up against the counter and immediately pauses giving her directions to everyone.

"Hunter." She says and I can feel her glaring at me without even looking up.

"Mother." I say into my cup as I take a lengthy sip of my coffee. Then I hear her footsteps promptly begin to walk away. She couldn't see that my eyes are bloodshot since I don't look up at her but I can tell she knows I'm hungover again from the tone in her voice. She always knows, but she stopped saying anything to me about it a few months ago. Dad doesn't say a word as he follows her out of thc kitchen, he just shakes his head and eyes me with a bitter look before leaving the room.

I quickly finish my second cup of coffee before heading to the garage. I need the extra buzz if I plan on making it through the day.

"What the hell! I say aloud. My car isn't in the garage. "Where the fuck is my car?" I pull my phone out from my back pocket and call Kyle. It rings three times and then cuts me off to send me to his voicemail. *Fucker never answers!* I know I drove to his house last night for the party but I don't remember driving back home. *Dammit!* I must have left it there. *But how the hell did I get home then?*

I don't dare ask dad to borrow one of his cars again. I rather walk the entire way to school than ask him for anything. I pull a cigarette from my pack and light it while I stand there like a moron for a good three minutes when my old bike catches my eye from the corner of the garage. It sits against the wall behind a few boxes and the matching set of Kayaks mother bought for her and Dad. They have never once seen the water. *What a waste of precious garage space.*

I'm already running late for class but I decide to unbury the old bike and take that for now until I get my car back from Kyle's. I have to fill the gas and oil but it still hesitates to start. It has been sitting for over a year. I kick and run through the clutch and after a few tries, it finally starts and stays running this time.

The rain is relentless as I make my way across the parking lot and pull into my usual spot. The only day I'm without my car and it has to be a torrential downpour. Needless to say, I'm slightly on the wet side and not at all enjoying it. I need a minute before I'm forced to endure the assholes this place seems to let in these days. A few years ago, when my brothers attended school here, it was far nicer and held the students to a higher standard than they do now. Seems like the school board just stopped caring, really. I pull my cigarettes out of my pocket, grateful that they stayed dry on the way over. *I wish I could say the same for the rest of me.* I walk around to the side of the building where the old sign that looks like it belongs to a run-down asylum sits. I flick my lighter and take a nice long much-needed drag from my cigarette and bask in the buzz that instantly surrounds my head before making my way to the back of the lot. A sudden noise, much like a whimper, catches my attention. I follow the sound around the trunk of the massive tree and see a girl sitting up against the rocks. By the way her body trembles I can tell she's crying and trying to muffle her sobs by further burying her face in her knees. The sight of her this way makes a wretched pain course through my chest as I watch the rain dancing down her hair, soaking her like a drowned cat.

I wonder how long she's been out here. I watch her for a few more seconds; wondering if she's alright and if I should approach her or not. Classes started about twenty minutes ago, so she must have been out here at least that long. I'm afraid if she sees me watching her before I can introduce myself, she's going to think I'm a major creep.

"Hey, are you alright?" I ask, as I slowly approach, trying not to frighten or catch her off guard. Her head lifts slowly, and I see the biggest most beautiful eyes peer up at me between strands of dark wet hair. The surprise is clear on her face and it takes her a minute of staring back at me before she moves to wipe her eyes with her sleeve.

"Um, yeah, I'm, I'm fine." She stands up and crosses her arms in front of her, quickly stretching her sleeves over her fingers.

"I'm Hunter." say as I look up from her fidgeting and offer her my hand but she just stares at me. Maybe debating on telling me her name or not, is my guess.

"Josephine." She finally says, but she doesn't shake my hand, so I lower mine like I'm wiping the wetness off of my palm.

"Nice to meet you Josephine…Ouch fuck!" The hot singeing of flesh interrupts me before I can say anything else and I instantly throw my cigarette to the ground and tightly clench my hand shut. *Now I feel like a tool.* I think I scared this angel before me, considering the amount of distance she just put between us.

"Oh, shit I'm sorry, I didn't mean to scare you. I just, my cigarette, it singed the hell out of my fingers."

"Oh. Are you alright?" She asks and looks down at my hand seemingly concerned.

"No worries, all good," I say as I wipe my hand across the thigh of my wet jeans. "So, why are you out here by yourself? Are you waiting for someone?" I ask, genuinely curious.

"No…I mean. I just didn't feel like going inside today. I didn't realize how much I didn't want to be here until I was already here, and then it was kind of too late."

"Why didn't you just go home?" I ask and I watch her give me the look of 'mind your business asshole'. "None of my business…sorry." I tell her quickly while holding my hands up in surrender.

"Why are you not in class?" She asks slyly. Her eyes dart toward the ground and she starts digging the tip of her sneaker in the mud, giving me another few seconds for my eyes to take her in.

"Running late as usual, but it doesn't matter anymore." I say casually as I scan my eyes down her arms that seem to be constantly fidgeting.

"Why's that?"

"Because now I'm talking to you." I say, letting a smile briefly cross my lips as she looks up and finally makes eye contact with me.

"Oh." She says in a shy tone and shifts her body away for a second time, but I'm unsure if it's because I'm freaking her out, or if she's just hypermobile when she's nervous. There's an awkward silence, but I feel compelled to admire her for just a moment longer. She's beautiful. Even soaking wet she looks amazing. Her eyes are this hazel-gray color, and her lips are full and pouty. *Stunning*! *How have I never seen you before*? I think to myself. I finally realize how creepy I'm being, so I look over my shoulder and scan the parking lot. When I look back at her she has her hands wrapped tightly around her arms.

"You look like you're freezing. Here." I take off my jacket and hold it open for her. She moves towards me with some hesitation, but she slides her arms through the sleeves as I wrap it around her shoulders.

"Thanks." She says with a grateful head nod and a slight smile that decorates her pretty mouth. My jacket swallows her small frame and she already looks a little warmer. Not to mention absolutely adorable. I can imagine that she would look amazing in anything.

"So where too then?" I light another cigarette and take a long deep drag and hold it in while I look up at the sky. The cool rain dripping from the trees feels good on my face and the aspirin has kicked in already so the much-dreaded hangover is finally coming to an end.

"Where too what?" She replies reluctantly. I take a deep breath and lick the rain off of my lips while she stands there nervously rubbing at her arms. I scan my eyes over her face and notice that her lips are scarcely colored with the warm pink shade that they should be.

"Where should we go? I mean since we're just standing here getting soaked, we might as well go somewhere to maybe dry off? You look as if you're about frozen solid and we'll both catch hypothermia if we don't get out of this rain and get dry." I assure her.

"I'm sorry, but I don't even know you." Her words are more defensive now than they were just a minute ago. She's hesitant and I can see why. I did just come up to her unexpectedly and probably gave off some stalker vibes when I didn't do much but stare at her.

"Sure you do…my name is Hunter, remember? We just met like five minutes ago. I made an ass out of myself in the first sixty seconds of knowing you and I go to this miserable place they call a school. Also…between you and me, I am extremely uncomfortable in these wet clothes, and I'd like to get out of them." I unwillingly hiss the part of that sentence, because clearly, I can feel that this girl does something to me. "Would you like to know anything else? Birthday, social security number?" I ask optimistically while grinning like a fool, urging her to respond to me.

Josephine stands there a minute, probably debating on what to say or how to maybe get out of talking to me. *I'm hoping that it's not the latter.* But then she takes me by surprise when she comes out with...

"Are you a serial killer?" She asks with the cutest, most serious look on her face.

“No. Can't say that I am. Fortunately, that’s not one of my many qualities." I add.

"You mean your flaws?" She corrects. And I just chuckle under my breath. “And you're not a sadistic control freak?" She challenges, eyeing me.

"Well, I wouldn't say flaws, so much as areas of improvement." I declare. At that answer, I see her smirk a little at the corners of her mouth, but it's gone just as fast as it appeared. "But yes, I am a bit of a control freak. Not to worry, I’m far from sadistic." I add. We smile at each other and simultaneously let out a nervous laugh under our breath.

"Alright. So as long as we’re clear on that, sure. I'll go somewhere and hang out with a completely random stranger. I have nothing better to do." She grins.

"And I take it sarcasm is one of your many qualities." I state.

"No...not really." She says with a straight face and bends down to grab her bag that's sitting at her feet. She starts to take my jacket off from around her shoulders but I quickly step forward and wrap it back around her before she can let it go.

"Wear it. I like it better on you." I tell her as I guide her over to my bike.

"What about you? You're going to freeze." Her eyes hint at her concern. *That’s cute.*

"I'm good Jo, just get on the bike."

8
Hunter

I run my hand along the seat of my bike to try and wipe some of the water off, then lean down and use my t-shirt to wipe it as dry as I can before Jo gets on.

"Hop on." I tell her as I look up at her and pat the seat with my hand, urging her to get on quickly. *She looks absolutely terrified.*

"I've never ridden on one of those before." She says to me and I can tell by the hesitation in her voice that she wants to back out.

"It's fine." I get on my bike and start it up. "Trust me, it will be fun, I promise."

"I hardly know you. How can I trust you?" She questions.

"You trust me enough to leave with me, why does what I drive change that?" I ask seriously, giving her something to think about.

She cocks her head to the side and goes quiet for a second before she puts her phone in her pocket. She places the straps of her backpack over both shoulders and then swings her right leg over the seat to get on the back of my bike. She doesn't say another word while she tries to figure out where to put her hands and I can feel her legs tense behind me as she tries not to lean up against me. I turn my body slightly to reach around and place my helmet on her head. When I do, my thumb slightly brushes along her jawline, drawing my attention to how soft her skin is.

"Here." I say, reaching behind me to gently grab her hands and wrap them around my waist. "Hang on tight." I tell her. My lips lift at the corners, spreading a wide smirk across my face as I look ahead. The fact that Josephine has no idea what she has gotten herself into, makes me enjoy the feeling of her body wound around mine even more. I can feel Jo's hands trembling as she pulls herself closer to me and she hesitates to lean into me again but she has no choice but to tighten her arms around my waist as we take off. As we turn the corners, I feel her press her body into mine more and more and I finally feel her body relax for just a second whenever we come to a stop. She moves in sync with me and with each breath she takes in, it sends an exhilarating chill down my spine.

We get to my house about fifteen minutes later and I pull up into the driveway. I have driven that route so many times, back and forth to school, and never has it seemed to go by as fast as it just did. Even though it was pouring rain and we are both soaked to the bone, I wish the ride could have lasted longer. Having a girl be that close never felt so good.

I turn off my bike and put my keys in my pocket while I wait for Jo to release her death grip from around my waist. I can feel her slowly unclench her fingers and slide her body to the side to get off the back so I do the same and turn around as she's unclipping the helmet from around her chin. She hands the helmet to me before wiping at the rain that's dripped from her hair and onto those edible lips of hers. I notice the way she's holding herself that she looks a little uneasy as she tries to find a comfortable place to put her hands and she keeps shifting her weight between her hips. I'm hoping that it was just the ride here on my bike that made her nervous and not the fact that she wants to change her mind about being here with me.

"What's wrong?" I ask as I take a step towards her.

"Nothing, I'm just cold." She says dismissively and rubs her hands together.

"Let's go inside and get you out of those wet clothes then." I suggest as I reach for her hand and lead her up the front steps of my house. I can feel her hesitate again and slightly pull her hand back as if she's about to rip her hand away from mine, but then she starts walking behind me without letting go and allows me to lead her into the house.

"Who else lives here with you?" She asks as she looks around the large open space of the entryway. Her eyes buzz with admiration as she takes in the sight of the house, before looking back at me for an answer.

"Just my parents. Well and their assistant." I let go of Jo's hand to shut the door behind me. She quickly wraps her arms tightly around her shoulders while she stands there shivering and dripping from head to toe.

"I'll be right back. Make yourself at home." I say and gesture towards the sitting room as I walk down the hallway to the downstairs bathroom that's just off the kitchen. I figured grabbing a few towels would be a good start in making her feel a little more comfortable. When I walk back into the living room, I notice Jo has already taken off my jacket and her hoodie. She has them hanging over her arm, so I reach my hand out to take them from her before handing her one of the towels and keeping the other for myself.

"Bathroom is through the kitchen to your right." I tell her, motioning down the hall.

"Thanks." She says as she clutches the towel close to the front of her and nuzzles her face in it.

"I'll go find you something dry to put on." I say and when she starts to walk past me, I catch a whiff of her hair. It smells of cloves, vanilla, and fresh rain. *She smells amazing!* Her clothes are drenched so much that they cling to every one of her curves. I can't help my eyes from bugging out of my head as she walks down the hall because I can see the shape of her body through her thin shirt and with her hair still dripping down her back, her shirt is nearly see-through. *She's so beautiful.* When I hear the bathroom door shut, I run upstairs and try to find something of my sisters for her to put on. She's built smaller than my sister but I'm sure there's something comfortable I can find for her to put on.

Maci was built like an athlete. She loved sports of any kind since she was little; always on at least two or three teams per year. I always had to drive her to all of her practices, which I hated but I'd give anything to have to do it again every day for the rest of my life. It feels strange being in my sister's room again. I never come in here. Not anymore anyway. I don't have many options though when it comes to clothes to lend her besides my mom's, and I don't think Jo would want to sport those nightmare outfits. I take a minute to look through Maci's closet and I find a sweater and some skinny jeans that look like they would fit and grab some warm socks out of the dresser before I go back downstairs. When I get to the bathroom door, I find myself standing there, delaying a second before I knock to let her know I'm on the other side. I wrap my knuckles lightly on the door twice and call her name.

"Jo?" I say softly.

"Just a second." I hear her quiet voice reply from behind the door before it slowly opens after the lock clicks and Jo's standing in front of me with only a towel wrapped around her body. I can't help but let my eyes wander down to her neck and then move to take in the sight of her bare shoulders. My eyes rake over her body and I notice a small silver chain that fits perfectly in the hollow of her neckline, accentuating her delectable collarbone as the rain glistens on her white porcelain skin and

I swallow hard. I'm suddenly aware that I haven't said anything for at least thirty seconds and I can feel her staring back at me. I'm sure my face would flush if I was actually capable of showing any kind of embarrassment, but I'm not in the least embarrassed to be caught looking at her. Just as I'm about to try and form any kind of coherent sentence, she speaks.

"Are those for me?" She asks eyeing the clothes in my hand. Her question snaps me out of the daze that her beautifully bare form put me in.

"Hey" I whisper. "Yeah…these should fit, they're my sisters," I tell her as I hand her the pile through the door.

"Thanks." She says as she takes them from me and her dainty fingers lightly brush against mine and I catch a glimpse of her smiling just before she shuts the door. I'm freezing and still dripping all over the floor, so while she's changing, I quickly wipe up the water in the hall and run up to my room to find myself some dry clothes. Not watching where I'm going, I end up tripping over my skateboard and about face plant into my desk. "OUCH! Son of a..." I stifle a bitter growl under my breath and grab my foot for a second to stop the throbbing. I angrily kick the board off to the side and go to my closet to find a dry shirt and throw it over my shoulder, unbutton my wet jeans and empty my pockets before I rip them off and I end up pulling a piece of paper out of my back pocket that's semi tucked into my wallet. I unfold it and realize what it is before I hastily crumple it back up and throw it in my desk drawer. *I'll deal with it later.*

9
Josephine

Hunter seems like a good guy. He's being really sweet and very much a gentleman. It makes me question his motives a little considering we just met, but he's the first person in a really long time to show me any amount of kindness, so I feel like I should maybe give him the benefit of the doubt; at least for now. *What do I have to lose...?*

I grab another towel from the linen closet in the bathroom and wrap it around my damp hair before trying to peel my jeans off. Wet jeans are impossible to get off and they feel like they have been glued to my thighs. I un-wrap the towel around me and finish drying off but not before accidentally rubbing the towel over the cut on my arm. “Oh, ouch!” I say under my breath and I drop the towel as I wince from the sting. I lift my hand off my arm and the fresh cuts immediately starts bleeding again. *Great!* Now I have to find something to cover it so I don’t get blood on his sister’s clothes.

This situation is not ideal. I’m standing half-naked and freezing in a stranger’s bathroom and now I’m rummaging through his cabinets for a bandage or anything that will cover my arm. Thankfully, I find a small first aid kit in the bottom drawer of the vanity, so I rinse my arm off and pat it dry with some toilet paper so I don’t get any blood on the nice white towels and use three large band-aids to fully cover the long cuts. I finish towel drying my hair so it at least doesn’t drip all over the house and then slip on the nice warm clothes. Luckily, they fit. They’re a little long, so I’m assuming his sister is quite a bit taller than I am, but the sweater is soft and cozy. It feels so good after freezing in the rain. I throw the evidence of my wounds away in the trash and bundle the towels and my wet clothes up in my arms before unlocking the door. I come out of the bathroom expecting to find Hunter waiting by the door or in the kitchen but he's not there when I look, so I call out to him a couple of times but he doesn't respond. *Weird.* Then suddenly I hear a loud thud above my head. I assume he must have gone up to his room to change. I walk up the stairs and see a lot of family pictures lining the wall. His family looks so happy in all of them. As I make my way up the rest of the stairs, I notice that Hunter was only in one of the pictures. I glance back at that one single picture and it looks as if his entire family was on vacation at the beach. They're all in swimsuits, sitting on the sand in front of a really nice house. It's white with wood-stained shutters and has a hammock in the front hanging under two very large trees. Hunter looks younger by a few years, and the girl next to him I'm assuming is most likely his sister. She's really pretty and looks very similar to their mother. *I wonder when this was taken.* It seems Hunter hates being in pictures just as much as I do if he's only in one out of probably fifty. It's incredible the number of pictures you can fit on a wall in a house this big.

I get to the first door on the right of the stairs, it's shut so I go to knock but I hear noise from another room. I walk down the hall towards another door that's cracked open and I can hear shuffling coming from inside. I lightly tap my knuckles against it, but before anyone can answer it starts to swing open unexpectedly. Hunter is standing there half-naked leaning down over his desk and has a white t-shirt slung over his left shoulder. My eyes focus on him and I can see every toned muscle from his shoulders down to the waist of his jeans that are hanging dangerously low on his hips. *He's got an extremely nice body.* I can hear my heartbeat in my ears as my pulse starts to race. The abrupt noise of the door hitting the wall makes me jump and Hunter turns around with a smile stretched across his face when he sees me standing in his doorway. I instantly feel the blood rush to my face because I'm pretty sure he caught me glaring at his naked torso.

"Oh, um…I'm sorry I just…I knocked but the door, it just… it kind of swung...." The words fall out of my mouth, not even remotely forming a coherent sentence and my cheeks heat with embarrassment again; so, I quickly turn around before he can see me frothing at the mouth like a rabid animal and make a complete fool of myself.

"Don't worry about it." He calls to me. "It would be a waste if no one got to see all this." His voice is playful and raspy, with just enough confidence to make him sound a little cocky. Hunter's voice is so much nicer sounding than all of the yelling that I hear all the time. His tone is warm and soothing. And there's not even a hint of tension in any word that comes from his mouth.

"I was just changing into something dry. Are those your clothes?" He asks. Before I could answer, Hunter reaches around me with one hand and I can feel his chest graze my back. *He's so warm.*

"Yeah." I say and let go of my clothes as he takes them from me. I look up at him and turn around to see that he still hasn't put his shirt on. *Of course, looking like that, why would he want to?*

"Get comfortable." He gestures into his room. "I'll go throw these in the dryer." He says and he walks out of the room pulling his t-shirt over his head with one hand as he carries my dripping clothes in the other. I sit down on the bed, but quickly think better of it after a minute and get up. I don't want Hunter thinking I'm the kind of girl that is automatically at ease being on a guy's bed. Hell, I've known him for under an hour and I'm already in his room; what else could he think? I don't need to add to any ideas that might be floating around in his head. I never would have stepped foot in a guy's bedroom before, but there aren't any alarm bells going off yet, telling me that it's a bad idea just being in here. Hell, why not? I've played it safe all my life and look where that's gotten me so far.

I walk over to the other side of Hunter's room where his desk is and run my fingers along the top. It looks like he uses it quite a lot. It has pen marks and sketches dug into the surface of it and lots of notebooks stacked on top of each other on the side. There are tech magazines in the corner, tons of books on a shelf above it, and an expensive-looking laptop. There's even a flat-screen TV on his wall, across from his bed and a shelf full of movies below that. Near his window on either side are two shelves with a small bench in between, covered with pillows. It looks so cozy, that I'm tempted to dive right in the middle and disappear for the night. Books elegantly line the shelves and scattered throughout them are a few trophies and other collectibles. The trophies are not your traditional sports ones except for one that says "football", but a dude is kicking what looks like a soccer ball on it. The rest have laptops and robots on them. One of them reads 1st place Honor Society for Robotics and Engineering. I scan the spines of the books that take up every inch of space there is. Reading the titles, I realize so many of these novels are ones I've read and reread because they have become my favorites. Classics I would never have guessed belong to a boy Like Hunter; not at first impression at least. Not that my first impression of him is at all bad.

Actually, it's far from it. "Wow, he's super fucking smart!" I say a little too loudly because then I hear Hunter behind me.

"Thanks!" I turn around and Hunter is leaning up against his doorway with two large white mugs in his hands, the corner of his lips pulled up in to a grin. I was not expecting him to be back so fast but of course, he would be when I say something to embarrass myself.

"You're welcome." *God, I feel like an idiot now.*

"Here, I made you some hot cocoa." He walks over to me and hands me a steaming mug of chocolaty goodness. *Mmmm.* I sniff the steam as it wafts towards my face.

"Thanks." I take a sip too quickly, burning my lip, but it's the most delicious thing I have ever tasted. He even sprinkled cinnamon on the top so I take a few more gulps until it's almost gone. I don't know if it's just because I'm freezing right now or what but I don't care, it tastes so good. The cocoa runs down my throat, instantly warming me from the inside, making me grateful for Hunter being so sweet.

10
Josephine

So, you're into computers?"

"Yeah…some I suppose. What do you like to do?" He promptly asks. "You know, besides sitting in the rain, and skipping out on your classes?" He smirks behind the rim of his mug before taking another sip of his cocoa.

"I don't know. The usual stuff I suppose." I say, repeating his neutral remark from a moment ago.

"What's the usual stuff?" He asks as he moves toward me, sticking out his tongue to lick the cocoa off of his top lip. *God, he has nice lips*. I think he catches me staring because he does it again without breaking eye contact and I have to clear my throat before I respond.

"I love to read, take pictures of stuff that I want to remember. Random things, I guess. I write a little, nothing professional but just stuff in my head." I babble out in a hurried frustrated tone. He's making me so nervous because everything he's done in the last five minutes makes me want to know what his lips taste like. I've never in my life wanted to kiss someone before, but he's making it so tempting the way he sips his drink, bringing my attention to his mouth. Oh, and the way his jaw flexes when he says something quiet in such a confident way has my mind turning to goo.

"Nice. So, what kind of random things do you take photos of?" He takes another small, slow step towards me.

"All…kinds of things." I tell him. Not being able to remember what exactly we're talking about. His presence is so distracting. Hunter's mouth curls up into a half-smirk and he wipes his hand over the slight stubble on his chin making him appear just a bit shy. It seems Hunter is anything but shy, but then again, I've been wrong before.

"Show me something." He nudges his chin up gesturing to my bag.

"I don't have anything with me to show you." I tell him truthfully.

"You don't have anything to show me, or you don't want to show me?" He suggests while eyeing me from a rather close proximity.

"Maybe a little of both." I breathe out. "They're kind of personal but I keep them in my locker at school. I don't bring them home."

"Why not?" He says and I nervously shift my weight as Hunter still doesn't break eye contact. His eyes stay focused on me as he moves a little closer with each step and he doesn't seem at all shy about it anymore.

"You know my life's not that interesting, why so many questions?" I ask him.

"I find you interesting." He reveals as he takes another slow step towards me. I feel myself blush like I'm going to pass out if I keep holding my breath, so I take another sip of my cocoa and look around his room. Trying to avoid answering any more questions he may ask so I turn the focus back on him.

"What do you like to do?" I ask breathlessly and lean back a little without moving my feet from the spot they seem to be glued to. He looks me square in the eye and lets out a surprised snicker.

"You're deflecting, but I'll play along." He answers and then proceeds to put his cup down on the desk before coming to stand directly in front of me. *I don't know what he meant by that...?*

"What do I like to do?" He says repeating my question to him this time. "Well...truthfully." He draws out the last word. "I can tell you that I would like to do anything right now, as long as it's with you." He steps a little closer to me, nothing but my hot cup of cocoa as a barrier until he reaches up between us and takes the mug out of my hands. Without breaking eye contact he reaches behind me and places it on the table next to his bed and his body brushes up against mine. Hunter's body towers over me as we stand in the middle of his room. He leans his head down and grazes his nose against mine as our lips pass each other's and I can feel his breath on my cheek; making me realize that I'm holding my own again as he gets closer. He reaches his hand up toward my face and brushes my hair back behind my ear ever so gently before nuzzling his nose into my neck and my body flushes from his touch.

"You're so beautiful, Jo." He whispers into my ear before bringing his forehead to rest against mine. I try desperately to hold my composure but his proximity is intimidating, to say the least and I find myself welcoming the new feeling. He doesn’t try to kiss me. He just stands here holding me close to him while his soft gaze focuses on my lips. *I shouldn’t be doing this, but God does it feel good.* The moment isn’t forced or awkward, it just…is. Hunter seems perfectly content to just hold onto me. I let out a deep sigh; not knowing if it’s disappointment that he hasn’t kissed me yet, or that I’m still just waiting for him to kiss me. I need to get out of my head before I do something I might regret. But being close to him is making my head fuzzy and all rational thinking is quickly being thrown out of a second story window the longer we stay like this. I take in a deep breath and softly clear my throat to catch his attention. Unfortunately, he moves his hand away from my neck and his eyes look slightly dazed as he lifts his head up.

"I'm sorry. I didn't mean to be so forward with you Jo." To my disappointment, he moves back a couple of steps and lowers his hands to his sides.

"No, I'm sorry. We just met, and I..." I struggle to find the right words but I can't seem to care that much right now. His presence is alluring and I have definitely never felt anything like this before. *I already miss it.*

"It's ok you don't have to explain." He takes my hand and gently kisses my knuckles before he walks away, giving me some space that I don’t really want right now. "So, what would you like to do?" He says in a surprisingly upbeat manner like what just happened was a perfectly normal day-to-day occurrence for him. Either that or it didn't have the same effect on him as it did me. "We could watch a movie while our clothes dry. Do you have any favorites?" He asks as he opens the glass door to the shelf below his flat screen.

"Sure." I say as I sit down on his bed in a slight daze, watching him rummage through title after title until he finally turns around with two movie cases in his hands. He sits down next to me on the bed and lays the movies down for me to choose.

"Three options. The Purge is a total cliché but the gore factor is well done. The Matrix. The effects were impressive at the time the movie was released, now fail by comparison to most new films, but nonetheless has a good theory to it.” He explains.

"What's the third option?” I ask him since he only pulled two from the shelf.

"Third option, you can stream whatever you want, lady's choice." He speaks. I stare at the titles for a moment still trying to think clearly and get past the fact that I almost kissed a complete stranger. I'm not that type of girl and I don't want to lead Hunter into thinking that I'm willing to give more than I am." So, what's your poison?" He asks again, probably because I'm taking way too long to choose from the only two options in front of me and a boatload of things, I don't want to bother looking through. I look at the covers for another second and finally just pick one.

"How about...this one?" I point to 'The Purge.' I don't care what we watch, it's just nice to be around someone who doesn't hate me and that I might enjoy hanging out with. Again, even though I barely know this boy. But this day has already been so much better than the past few years have been.

"Good choice! Perfect for getting you to jump on my lap out of pure terror." He smirks and squeezes my thigh before getting up off the bed. "I'll go get us something to eat." And he walks out the door while I sit there thinking whether I should be walking out his front door or not right now. I have never met anyone so forward before. Not in the way Hunter is. He seems to just say and do whatever is on his mind without contemplating what others will think whatsoever. I don't know how to make myself comfortable. There's nowhere else to sit beside his bed, the floor, or his desk chair. And I find issues with all three of those choices considering they are still a part of his bedroom. But I finally decide I'm far too exhausted to care about where I sit right now, so I just stay on the edge of his bed, but I move slightly closer to the TV and wait for him to come back from downstairs. Maybe by the time he comes back, I can get my head together and stop being such a nervous wreck for once.

11
Hunter

I make my way downstairs to the kitchen and grab two bottles of coke, water, and a bag of popcorn from the pantry. I throw the bag in the microwave and run to the half bath around the corner to put on some deodorant while I wait for it. When the popcorn is done, I find one of the many serving trays to put everything on and head back upstairs. When I get to my room, I look in my doorway and see Jo sitting on the edge of my bed. She looks so guarded sitting there with her legs pulled up to her chest, her arms tightly wrapped around her shins and is resting her chin on her knees. I can see her body gently move with every breath she takes in so I stand still a moment to take in the purely unfiltered sight of her. The inexplicable feeling that I get when I look at her sitting there is all too new for me, and it makes me grin, knowing that she's sitting on my bed because she willingly chose to come here with me and hasn't tried to leave, the second I closed the door.

Jo's the first girl that I haven't wanted to leave right away after spending a few sweaty hours with. The first girl I don't want to avoid and don't mind having her know where I live while I'm sober. I'm in no rush for her to go. I feel like there's something really special about her and that she's too good for someone like me, but I'm far too selfish to tell her that and risk her leaving anytime soon. I don't know enough about her yet, so I'm not ready for her to leave.

"Hey." I walk in and set the tray down on the bed between us.

"Hey." She says and turns toward me still holding her legs scrunched up into a tight defensive little ball.

"I hope you like popcorn."

"Yeah, popcorn's great." She moves over some so I sit down on the edge of my bed next to her and my heart immediately starts beating out of my chest that I swear she can hear it. We're so close, I can feel the warmth radiating off of her body. I barely know this girl but I could kiss her right now without even thinking twice about it. *Hell, I almost did kiss her.* I only hope to have another opportunity because next time I'm not sure I will be able to pass it up. Jo seems so sweet and innocent, maybe even a little naïve; but I like that about her. She's not anything like any of the other girls I've been with in the past and I don't plan on treating her like one of them either. I inch a little closer, trying not to make it obvious but of course I'm failing miserably because I see the corner of her mouth turn up into a cheeky grin. *I think she's finally warming up to me.* I don't do this kind of thing, ever. I don't have girls over unless I'm getting something from them and usually, I don't give them much in return. It may be selfish on my part, but I have to admit I'm not exactly wired right. At least I don't try to hide it. *Most of the time.* And the girls that I've been with knew what they were getting into when they got involved with me. Hell, they would clearly see how I am every day if they hung around the crowd that I always manage to end up with. I just can't bring myself to tell Jo how *awful* I am for her. I don't want to ruin this moment, and if I open my mouth; I can already see it not going in my favor.

Halfway through the second movie, Jo uncurls her legs and stretches just a bit before she moves from the edge of the bed to the middle and crosses her legs in front of her. She hasn't eaten very much of the popcorn, but she's already downed both of her drinks. I on the other hand have hardly taken a sip from either of mine when usually I would be chugging whatever cold liquid that I could get my hands on. But sitting next to her is making me nervous. In a good way…I think, but nervous nonetheless, and I don't usually get nervous.

I move back on my bed and stretch out a bit so I can lie against my headboard. A few minutes later Jo inches her way back and leans her head against the bed frame not so far from mine. I notice her rubbing her hands over her arms, so I get up and grab the blanket off the end of my bed and I can feel her eyes on me as I lay it across her legs.

"Here, this should do the trick."

"Thank you." She says in a sleepy whisper as she wraps herself up in my comforter and goes back to look at the screen. Jo doesn't seem bothered by the movie like I thought she would be. Most girls don't like these kinds of films, but she doesn't seem to react to it very much and doesn't seem to be too interested in it either if I'm being honest.

I purposely sit a little closer as I get back on the bed and wait for her to get comfortable before I fully relax on my side of the bed. The weight of wanting to feel her against me is nagging at me to reach out and caress her skin as she lies so close, but I don't move. Instead, I sit still and fold my hands to rest them on my lap while I steal a glance of her every few minutes. I don't want to scare her away by being too forward or outright obnoxious, but I'm struggling to keep myself in line and it's proving to be more difficult around a girl I hardly know than I thought it would.

I wake up to the menu playing over and over again. It's that annoying 12 seconds of the same stupid clip, on repeat and it's driving me mad. Why does it always seem louder when you wake up than when you were watching the damn thing. I look over where Josephine was sitting up against my bed and see she's now lying curled up on my pillows. The volume of the TV doesn't seem to bother her so she must have been exhausted to be able to sleep through the noise. She's wrapped herself up so tightly with the blanket but still looks rather cold, so I get up to grab another blanket out of my closet and turn off the TV. I carefully place the blanket over her body, and she quietly moans in her sleep, but thankfully doesn't wake up, so I gingerly lie back down on the bed and try my hardest to not let the mattress dip and disturb her. As I settle in and watch a calmness take over Jo's features that make the crease between her brows that was there earlier completely disappear; I watch her body finally relax a little more each time she lets a breath escape her slightly parted lips until I cannot hold my eyes open any longer and I finally drift off to sleep.

"I hope you're still here when I wake up." I whisper. *It would be nice to know what it's like waking up to an angel in the morning.*

12
Josephine

I hear a buzzing above my head and it's beginning to get really annoying. I hate being woken up by an alarm but I always get up early to try and avoid dealing with Jeff as soon as he gets home from work.

I can feel the warmth of the sun shining brightly on my face, so I reach for my phone on my bedside table to see what time it is, but my hand hits a large object that doesn't seem familiar. I quickly sit up and try to focus my tired eyes and I realize right away that I'm not in my room. I look around to get my bearings and start to panic when I can't find my phone. *Who would I call anyway?*

I freeze when I hear a noise from behind me, so I quietly slide off the edge of the bed and discreetly turn around to see what or who it was. When I do, I easily let out a pent-up breath because when I see Hunter laying shirtless on top of the blankets, I finally realize where the hell I am.

Wait. *Holy shit!* Hunter is less than a foot away from me. I really don't want to wake him and end up having a super awkward morning, so I try to be as quiet as I possibly can. I have never slept next to a guy before; especially one that I just met not even twenty-four hours ago. *I don't even remember falling asleep.* I slide my hand under the covers and feel around for my phone but I quickly stop searching when I see him move. He doesn't wake up thankfully but it tells me that he might soon, so I need to find my phone and get out of here fast. I keep my eyes on Hunter while I continue to search for my phone and my hand hits a hard object under the sheet, I pull it out and thankfully it's what I was looking for. I check the time first and see that it's already after six. I have a few messages but when I go to check them all I see is Nate's name on one of them before my battery dies. *Dammit!* Nate doesn't usually try to get a hold of me very much but he was probably texting me to tell me how Jeff was being a dick when I didn't come home last night. *I couldn't care less about what Jeff wants anymore.* I look around the room for my bag and gather the things that I can quickly see without making too much noise and I end up tripping over my damn shoes. I catch myself, grateful for the pillows Hunter must have thrown on the floor last night when he was sleeping. They made for a soft, quiet landing. I throw my phone in my bag and I decide to carry my shoes to make as little noise as possible so no one hears me leave. I carefully sneak out of Hunters room and shut the door behind me before I tiptoe down the stairs, looking around to make sure no one else is up or I at least can avoid running into anyone. The last thing I need is for Hunter's parents catching me sneaking out; it would make for an awful first impression. I don't plan on actually meeting them but I don't need anyone else judging me when they know nothing about me. I don't hear any noises coming from downstairs so I unlock the front door and open it just enough to slide through. I turn around to shut it and I let out a huge breath I didn't realize I was holding and I hear the lock click behind me. But when I look up as a cold wet wind sends a chill through me; I see there's a wall of rain crashing off of the roof and very large puddles forming in the street near the gutter. *Oh. Great!* I am going to be soaked by the time I just walk down the porch steps. It's going to be a long walk home.

I look down when I feel how cold I am and realize that I'm still wearing the clothes Hunter gave me last night and mine are probably still in the dryer. Looks like I won't ever see those again. I can't believe I forgot my clothes. Hunter also threw my hoodie in to dry since that was soaked through, so now I don't even have that to help keep me from freezing on the walk home. I am more than grateful now that he gave me a sweater to put on last night because I won't risk trying to explain why I was sneaking out without saying anything to him just to get some clothes that don't even mean anything to me in the first place. I'm more worried about getting home before Jeff does. I quickly put my sneakers on, throw my bag on my back and start making my way home. I don't bother running at first, it's too far to my house to run the entire way. I'm already dripping from head to toe so it wouldn't make a difference to get there any faster anyway. Why exhaust myself? Then I remember it's already past six, so I don't have a lot of time before Jeff gets out of work so I start running anyway to give me a chance at getting there before he does and avoid the entire confrontation that I'm sure he can't wait to have. If he doesn't see me, maybe he will just forget about me disobeying him last night and drink himself into a nice long nap. *Could I be so lucky this time?* I've never been around this neighborhood before, so I'm hoping I don't take a wrong turn and get lost, making me waste precious time. The large houses start to dwindle in size the closer I get to my side of town and I luckily make it to a street that I recognize.

"Finally. Main Street." I say out loud. I'm so grateful for living in a smaller town. It didn't take me as long to get here from Hunters' house as I thought it would. I make my way towards the route I would usually take to go to work every morning and pass the bookshop, the bakery, and the pet store; three of my favorite places in town. A few minutes later I'm in my neighborhood and my feet are grateful for only having to cart my butt down a few more short blocks.

When I get to the end of my street, my feet stop me dead in my tracks. Taking in a much-needed breath from running most of the way here. I look up and my jaw drops to the ground. I can see my house from the corner. Jeff's truck is parked in his usual spot in the driveway, but it's still too early for him to be out of work yet. *Oh no. He's already home.* My feet are frozen in place. I don't know why he would be home already. The run home from Hunters wouldn't have taken me more than Twenty minutes. Unless he got out early. He would still take his time to stop at the twenty-four-hour liquor store for more beer on his way home. I don't know what the hell to do now. I can't stand here in the rain all day. If it wasn't raining so hard, I would just wait outside for Nate to get home, and while they are having their daily spat, I could sneak back in my window and they would most likely not hear a thing. I walk past the gate and around the back to my bedroom window; push the recycling bin up against the house and reach up to push the window open. *Dammit!* It's locked. I shut it yesterday but who the hell locked it? Maybe Jeff did because I didn't come home for dinner to meet his new girlfriend; that I'm sure will only be around for a whole five minutes like the last one was. I don't even know how someone could stand him long enough to call themselves his girlfriend in the first place. My mom sure got sick of him, this one will too. I throw the bin into the overgrown weeds in the yard away from the house, grab my bag off the ground and go to see if the back door to the kitchen is unlocked. I turn the door knob, but it doesn't budge. *What the hell!* Jeff never bothers locking doors. He usually passes out in his chair watching TV with a beer in his hand before the rest of the world starts their morning. I don't have a key to this door so I go around to the front and stick my head around the corner to look in the living room window. Jeff isn't in his chair. Maybe I got lucky and he slept in his room for once. I slide my key into the deadbolt and unlock the door as quietly as possible. The door squeaks a little until you push it open past a certain point so I do that quickly to not draw out the noise. I take off my shoes and shut the door behind me. Standing there for a second, I listen for any noises coming from upstairs or the kitchen but it's so quiet. I head for the stairs making sure to avoid the creaky step at the bottom. I learned to avoid that step after the last time I came back late.

I get to the top of the stairs and just as I'm about to open the door to the bathroom I hear footsteps stumbling behind me. I turn around hoping that it's Nate, and as I do I feel a hand to the side of my face and I swiftly lose my footing and my vision quickly goes dark. I cover my head with my arms as I fall to the floor and then move one up to hold my face where I was hit. I'm afraid to even look up so, I just lay there praying that he walks away.

"Where the hell have you been?" Jeff's voice rips through my core as it echoes off the walls around us. His hand comes down on me hard again and my head smacks against the wall. "What were you doing huh, out being a little slut, I bet!" I feel a spray of saliva hit the part of my face that's exposed as Jeff bends down and spews his foul breath into my ear. "Where were you? I said to be home for dinner!" I try to shield more of my face but he starts shoving me with his foot up against the bathroom door when I try to crawl away.

"I told you to be home last night, and what did you do, you disobeyed me again! What you didn't learn your lesson from last time?! What did you think you could just come and go as you please and live under my roof, and eat my food without doing as I say?!" His anger seethes through gritted teeth and his vile words slice through the pain in my eyes. He repeatedly slaps at my arms and the longer he yells the more pissed off he gets; and the angrier he gets the harder the blows are to my body. I can smell the fresh aroma of scotch on his breath and it makes me want to retch. I almost do as I lay here in a ball and take the beating that I should have known was coming, but I won't let him see me cry this time. I won't give him the satisfaction.

Then all at once when I thought he was done, his knuckles suddenly make contact with my mouth and all I hear is a loud crunch that makes my ear start ringing and immediately the taste of copper floods my mouth and I start gagging from the sour taste. It's hard to breathe just through my nose so I end up spitting the blood out, splattering it across the floor near his feet. A hesitant breath is audible above my head and then all I feel is Jeff's boot as he shoves his foot into my ribs again and again. The third time he actually kicks me, and it's so hard that I start violently coughing again and feeling like I'm about to vomit. I try so hard to take in enough air but it makes me dry heave, so I clench my stomach with both hands and that's when he grabs me by my hair and hauls me up, forcing me to come face to face with him. He has this look in his eyes like he's not even there. Just an angry empty shell of a human and I strongly fight the urge to turn away. I know if I turn away, I'll regret it even more than having to stare into his dead eyes. I struggle to stand on my tiptoes as I wrap my fingers around my head to keep his grip from pulling my hair out and trying to relieve some of the pressure on my scalp from him holding me up to his height by it. It hurts so much and feels like my scalp is on fire.

"When I say to be home, you better be home, or next time it will be worse, I can promise you that, you little bitch!" He growls into my tear-soaked face. And I believe every word.

Jeff loosens his grip on my head, and me having no strength to hold myself up I collapse onto the hardwood floor again and slide in the wetness of my blood I spit out moments ago. As the minutes go by and I can feel him staring as he hovers over me. I'm still dripping wet and freezing from running home in the rain so I just scrunch up as small as I can and will myself not to move. Because I know if I do, I will only make it worse for myself especially when he's like this.

Jeff's breathing slows, calming to a normal rhythm while I continue to lay here waiting for him to hit me again. But after another few minutes that might as well be hours, he just walks away and doesn't murmur another word in my direction. I stay still to listen as his heavy booted footsteps make their way down the old creaky stairs and across the hall toward the kitchen. I don't want to move but I can't just lay here and risk pissing him off again just from the sight of me in case he comes back up, so I lift my head and grab the doorknob to the bathroom and pull myself up with one hand while still holding my ribs with the other. I can feel the bruises already forming under my skin and every part of my body is tender, throbbing, and stiff. Something catches in my side as I try to stand straight, so I take a quick painful breath in and hold it as I get to my feet. It hurts so much that it feels like he might have cracked a rib. I carefully snatch my bag up from the floor and walk into the bathroom to find something to clean up the blood on the hallway floor. I lean down to wipe the floor with a dark towel and I have to hold my breath again to do it. The pain is so bad it's making me nauseous, but I hold back and breathe through the excruciating pain.

Breathing in a bent-over position is almost impossible and I feel like I'm about to puke again as nausea overwhelms me; it hurts terribly but I finish cleaning and decide to dig around the medicine cabinet for some aspirin and take three of them, hoping that it takes affect soon. I'm shivering; I have dirt and blood all over my face and my hair is tangled, so I think a shower would be the best thing right now. I carefully take off my clothes and it hurts like a bitch to move around but when I catch my reflection in the mirror, my eyes well up when I see all the bruises covering my torso. The purples and blues are highlighted with awful red brush burns, and against my too-pale skin, they stand out all too well.

13
Josephine

I should have been smarter and just come home last night instead of staying with Hunter, but my stubborn idiotic brain wasn't thinking about the consequences I would have to face when I got home. I was stuck in a bubble that was all too comforting. I know Hunter's a stranger, but it's been so long since I felt like I could fall asleep and not have to worry about someone barging into my room ready to take their anger out on me just because they could. I actually felt safer with Hunter than I ever have living with Jeff. Maybe it's because he's the only one that's ever shown me any amount of kindness when he didn't have to, but whatever it is about him, I'm grateful for it.

I hate being in this house with Jeff for too many reasons to count. But how could I be so naive to think I wouldn't get some kind of punishment for not doing what he said? Nate even warned me and I was stupid enough to ignore him. I exchanged a few quiet, peaceful hours with Hunter for a painful beating that would only cause more tension between us and me to worry how bad the next one will be. It's only happened one other time that Jeff has actually put a hand on me but he was wasted then too. He always gets like this whenever he drinks too much. Which, is most days out of the week. But I have learned how to not provoke him into taking things out on me for the most part, but when he gets belligerent and blacks out, that's when it becomes a problem; especially when I break his stupid rules, then he notices I exist. Nate is home most of the time to extinguish Jeff's temper when he gets like that but I guess today I wasn't so lucky.

I DELICATELY PULL myself out of the shower and wrap a towel around my body. It was hard enough trying to lift my arms to wash my hair, not to mention painful, so I don't bother trying to dry it. After I get dressed, I gather my bag and shoes and walk downstairs to my bedroom. I wish I had my own bathroom again like when we first moved in with Jeff and Nate. They had such a nice house and everyone had their own bathroom including the guest room which became mine. It was great not having to share with anyone, and nice to have privacy. I would give anything to have even a shred of that back. Since mom left and Jeff started his obnoxiously compulsive drinking, he would always get so drunk and make a fool of himself. One day he showed up to a meeting at work wasted out of his mind that his boss had to call the cops to have him removed from the property. Needless to say, Jeff got fired the very next day. He came home and told Nate to start packing, but didn't bother explaining anything to me. Turns out the huge house that mom and I thought was his, was actually owned by his company and since he got fired, we were given thirty days to move out. It's how we ended up in this dump; a three-bedroom, one-bathroom single floor house, and it's a total shithole.

The other house was in gated community just outside the city. It was lush green lawns, cookie cutter houses and friendly neighbors. Now that we moved to a much smaller town, we have no idea who our neighbors are. I thought that would have been the opposite of living here verse a bigger city. But the day we moved in, it felt like the neighborhood already had us pegged for being the crazy house. I can't blame them considering how that day went. Jeff howling at Nate to do this and put that over there. He even threw a wrench across the driveway at him. If Nate hadn't move out of the way fast enough, he would have gotten the wrench straight to the face. My life from that day on has been a complete and utter train wreck, and anyone in their right mind wouldn't want to be a part of it.

I can feel my eyes starting to well up again, but I fight back the tears for a while longer. There's no use in crying over my shitty situation. Afterall, I have caused most of my problems by thinking I can do whatever I want. As long as I don't piss Jeff off again, I hopefully, don't have to worry about him bothering me anytime soon. I only have seventeen months until I turn eighteen and then I can finally be free of living in this hell hole and can legally be on my own. I'm smart enough to know to get anywhere in this world, I need to graduate high school first if I don't want to be a total loser. A steady good paying job doesn't hurt either. When I applied for a few part-time jobs around town there wasn't much available. Most of the businesses are family-owned and have their kids or some kind of family already working for them. Not having my own car certainly doesn't help either. Everywhere else that would hire a high school student is too far away to walk to, considering they are at least a half an hour drive away or more. There's no way it would be worth taking a bus back and forth every day because I'd be spending most of the money that I make on the bus fare and I would never have enough time to study. Lucky for me I have Mrs. Lawrence to thank for giving me a job at her bookstore. I love being there and it gives me a chance to save up some money for when I'm ready and able to finally move the hell away from Jeff.

I walk down the stairs around the corner to where my bedroom sits in a small dark corner in the back of the house. It's out of the way past the kitchen and seems like it used to be a back mudroom or maybe a laundry room that was converted to an extra bedroom. I have a small closet that's just big enough to fit my minuscule amount of clothing and two small windows. I don't have very much but I at least have the comfort of a bed and the books that Mrs. Lawrence has gifted me over the years. I also don't have the traditional home life of a sixteen-year-old. I think most girls my age wouldn't choose to climb out of their bedroom window just to go to school so they can avoid the people they live with.

I don't bother trying to sneak down to my room since I'm sure Jeff has already drank himself into a long nap. Sure enough, when I get to the bottom of the stairs, he's already passed out in his chair in the living room with an empty beer can on his lap. I walk down the hall to my room and shut the door. I don't have a lock on it anymore since Jeff broke it when him and Nate were arguing the one day and he kicked it in and wouldn't let me replace it, even with my own money. So, whenever I'm home and try to get some sleep, I have to move my dresser in front of my door now. It gives me some peace of mind, even if it's not much but I'll take what I can get.

I know there's no way I can go to school today. Looking like this and hardly being able to walk without being hunched over from the searing pain in my ribs will only draw unwanted attention. *That's the last thing I need.* I dump my bag and shoes on the floor next to my closet and painstakingly sink into bed. It hurts to move or even breathe too deeply, so I try to get as comfortable as I can and curl up in my blanket after turning off the light. I am far too exhausted to think about anything else right now so I close my eyes and quickly drift off to sleep, hoping for tomorrow to not come so soon.

14
Josephine

The ear-shattering cracks going on outside my window startles me out of a heavy exhausted sleep. It's not my idea of a good morning; especially after yesterday and something I didn't fancy waking up to. The hammering keeps vibrating through my temples, making the throbbing in my head pound along with each thud, but I don't want to move to get up and close my window because I'm afraid of how much pain I'll be in. I slowly open my eyes, just enough to peak through the smallest of slits so I can look out to see what the commotion is but an instant pain, shoots through my eyes as the sunlight floods my room. It's obnoxiously bright and now my head feels like it's splitting in two.

I bring my hands up to my face and gently rub circles along my temples, trying desperately to soothe the discomfort. Underneath my eye feels swollen as I smooth my hand across my cheek to wipe away the sleep. I slowly sit up on the edge of my bed and swing my legs off the side without thinking and the word woozy doesn't even begin to describe how I feel right now. I attempt to take in a deeper breath to clear my head but as I do, the movement reminds me how unpleasant the pain is in my ribs, and I wince at the fierce stabbing that is now traveling up and down my side. After a few minutes of trying to talk myself into moving off of my bed when I finally get the dizziness to go away, I reach over to grab my bag and notice the blood smeared across my pillowcase, so I sluggishly reach my hand to my head and feel a large bump before my fingers graze the cut beside it. The stickiness I feel dried in my hair I assume is more blood. I have to take another shower to get this blood out of my hair and I'm hoping that the hot water will feel good on my aching body.

The banging outside continues and it's not doing my head any favors sitting here listening to it, so I carefully get up to look out my window to see where it is coming from. I push my curtains aside and I see Nate in the driveway working on his car for the third time this week. *Looks like they had it out again.* Whenever Nate and his dad get into a fight, he ends up spending a lot of time out of the house...but he's never usually away for very long. If I were him, I would just drive around and not come back until Jeff was gone to work or had fallen asleep. Leaving would be the first thing I would do after having it out with someone. *If I had the option of course.*

I've noticed Nate plenty of times in the garage beating the hell out of the boxing equipment that he bought himself last year before he graduated. Sometimes he even takes a baseball bat to it if he's really irate, and it's not hard to tell when he is. He got suspended twice for fighting when he was in his senior year, so I guess he tries to take his anger out on the bag instead of getting into trouble now that he's no longer a minor. Nate has some serious anger issues, but I can't blame him considering the kind of example his father is for him. It all seems like another lifetime that things were so different living with them; when my mom was still in the picture. Sure, Nate and I were never really on friendly terms but he was usually pretty decent to me when we were around each other; after a while anyway. We didn't get along at first, but slowly we came to accept that we were in each other's lives. He wasn't home much since he seemed to have a pretty good social life because he had friends over the house a lot. Sometimes he would even be out all night and only come home in the early hours of the morning.

Jeff never paid much attention to either one of us but he and my mom were attached at the hip before they started fighting all the time. That didn't leave them much time to pay attention to us kids, I guess. Now we all just avoid each other on purpose. Jeff is a miserable piece of work and Nate....I don't know about him anymore. He's more confusing to me more than ever because one minute he's running cold but his temper can boil out of control very quickly. There's never a gray area with him. I kind of wish it would go back to us at least speaking to each other occasionally because I always feel so alone. It would be nice to have someone in this house on my side.

I try to take small breaths in and out as I walk across my room to my closet. *I need to get this blood out of my hair.* I gather my clothes and grab my bag off the floor and head to the stairs. I wish I didn't have to walk past the living room to go upstairs and shower because I don't like doing anything that would grab Jeff's attention. I walk past the living room and notice that he's not in there at the moment and the TV is still off, so I hope that means he's asleep or not even here. I quietly step past the doorway and start making my way upstairs as quickly as possible, but when I try to hurry my body reminds me of the beating that I took last night. The pain from trying to breathe deeper is making me woozy again, so I stop for just a second.

I'm relieved when I finally get to the top of the stairs and see the bathroom door open. Jeff's bedroom door is closed and Nate's is as well so I can only guess that Jeff is either passed out in his room or he left already. I can still hear Nate banging away in the garage, so it's now or never to get a quick shower and five minutes of peace. I look up in the mirror to check my head and to see how bad the bruises are on my face. There's a dark shadow of a handprint across my cheek and my lip is split and scabbed over where Jeff first backhanded me into the wall.

"I can't go to school looking like this!" I sob. My eyes begin to sting and I can feel myself on the verge of bursting into tears. *NO! I won't cry!* I think to myself as I wipe my face and turn away from my reflection. Holding my breath, I lift my shirt over my head, desperately trying to ignore the burning pain that is now radiating through my entire body as I pull my arms out. The pain is so much worse than yesterday and I can feel the tears silently pouring down my cheeks. I drop my clothes to the floor and decide to check on how bad my torso looks since yesterday. I glance in the mirror and see my ribs covered in black and purple welts. *Oh god.* I grab another few aspirin from the medicine cabinet and gulp down mouthfuls of water from the faucet before getting in the shower; willing the pills to take effect quickly. I stand under the hot spray for a few minutes waiting for the aspirin to kick in because the gentle assault of the water hardly soothes my tender muscles. My head still throbs as I wash the dried blood from my hair and I wince as my fingers graze the cut on my head. I jerk my hand away too quickly and it puts my stomach in knots as I hold myself steady, waiting for the sick feeling to pass once again. I can't take the pain on top of trying to hold all of the ill feelings I have built up right now. They have been rising to the surface for months and I just don't have the strength to hold back anymore, so I collapse on the floor of the shower and start to sob uncontrollably. My body painfully jerks with every whimper and every single tear that escapes. I don't dare let Jeff hear me cry again. I won't let him know how broken I have become because of everything he's done. So, I hide it as best I can until I can hardly bear it. The first time I had ever been backhanded was when

Jeff raised his hand to me without any warning. It had caught me so off guard I cried more from the sheer shock of it, than from the actual pain itself. I had no idea what to do or say in that moment, so I just stood there holding my face and let my eyes well up until the tears spilled down my cheeks. Jeff had the angriest most hateful look on his face until he just walked away from me without a word. I don't know why he hit me. The only thing I can think of is that I was just there at the wrong time and he was drunk. Back then I wouldn't have said I was lucky that he only hit me once, but I would have been grateful if that's all he did this time. That was almost a month after mom left and a month of me wondering if she was ever going to come back for me. A month of being completely ignored and being alone, having no one to talk to. There was no chance in hell of ever being a family anymore; not after what he did and I had no one to depend on but myself. So that's what I did. I've kept to myself ever since that day and I try my best to be invisible until I can leave here and never have to see his face or this place ever again.

I'm completely exhausted already, but somehow, I manage to drag my ass out of the shower and get dressed. I go to grab my things off the counter and I realize that the clothes Hunter gave me to wear yesterday are still lying on the floor. I pick them up to place them in the hamper and see the red stains on them. *Shit! There's blood on them. I have to give these back, how am I going to explain this?* I run the hot water in the sink and douse the shirt with hand soap and frantically begin scrubbing the blood out of the material until my hands are raw from being under the scalding water. I wring out the shirt, checking to make sure I got whatever blood I could out of them and bring them with me to my room to hang over my chair to dry.

I finally give myself a minute to sit down, so I grab my phone and plug it in next to my bed and wait for it to turn on. I have to call the school and tell them that I'll be out again today, so I leave a message for the nurse saying that I'm sick. I lie back down on my bed and decide to just sleep the rest of the day. I can't do anything else right now so sleeping sounds like the best option. This is the last place I want to be but for now it's all I can do, it's all I have the energy for.

I sink into my pillow and try to remember what it felt like to be in Hunter's bed the other night. The warmth from his body felt nice next to mine, it was comforting and made me feel safe. Even though I hardly know him, I felt safer sleeping in a strange boy's bed than I have the entire time I have lived with Jeff. Even when my mom was still around.

My eyes finally feel heavy enough, so I let them close as I snuggle deeper into my mattress and I drift off to sleep.

15
Hunter

I hastily turn over and smash my hand down on my nightstand after being startled awake by my alarm clock and it falls to the floor for probably the fifth time this month. *The bloody thing should be broken by now.* I rub my hands over my face… “Oh shit! Jo!" I say, hoping I didn't scare or accidentally hit her. I turn over and look to where she fell asleep last night, but I only find a vacant pillow beside me. "Jo?" I call out to her, thinking she may be in the bathroom, but she doesn't answer. Just when I was enjoying the thought of waking up to a girl for once, she's the one that leaves before I get the chance to even open my eyes.

It's been forever since I have woken up without a colossal headache from drinking all night. It was nice being here in the quiet of my room enjoying her company. Not just for my own selfish reasons, I mean it is, but also out of my own curiosity that has been peaked by her. Jo didn't fall at my feet like most of the girls I’ve met do. She seemed to just enjoy the quiet that surrounded us while she was here with me.

"Hunter." Mother yells up the stairs. *Her voice could make a drowned cat sound pleasant.* Even when I’m sober.

"Yes, Mother I'm up." I growl down to her letting her know I heard her, so she doesn't send her assistant Janine up again. I grab a t-shirt off the pile of laundry that sits messily on top of my dresser, waiting to be neatly put away, but never will be and head for my shower before I have to endure whatever schedule I’ll be informed of. I plan on staying away from the house today anyway because I can't stand playing nice for clients that have a massive stick up their ass just to try and impress my parents.

When I get to the kitchen there are people everywhere. Kitchen staff from another catering company, servers wearing all-black attire, and my dear mother eyeing me from the breakfast table. I already know what she is going to say and I'm not going to let her ruin my good mood; not today. I walk over to the counter and pour myself a nice large cup of black coffee and take a sip of it as I make my way over to my mom and stand in front of her. I can see she wants to say something to me but I interrupt before she gets the chance to speak.

"I have plans for the day so I won't be around." I tell her to save her the hassle of embarrassing herself in front of all her hired help she so fondly employs on a regular basis and telling me to make myself scarce.

"Have a good day mother." I say in a sarcastically surly tone and walk out of the kitchen to the garage before she can respond with any of her snide comments. I forgot I still haven't retrieved my car from Kyle's house. I was all too distracted by someone very beautiful yesterday. I pull out my phone and text him before I light up my morning smoke. When I take in the first pull of nicotine, I remember that I haven't had a smoke since yesterday morning when I ran into Jo at school, so the buzz I get is a bit more enjoyable. My phone buzzes in my pocket so I pull it out and unlock it to see who it is.

Kyle: hey sleeping beauty

Hunter: Hey mate need my car pick me up on the way I'll give you a lift home after.

Kyle: Yeah sure see you in 20

We get to school and I can't help but look around for Jo. Kyle starts walking toward the building but I want to wait out here in case she shows up. I never did get her number yesterday so I have no way of seeing her again unless I run into her somehow. At least I know where she goes to school, or I would surely be shit-out-of-luck and it would just make it that much more difficult to find her. There are only two high schools in this town but still, that is a hell of a lot of kids to search through, but I would do it if I had to.

"Hey, Hunter…what's the holdup?" Kyle yells across the car park to me but I wave him off as I make my way around the building to check by the place we met.

"Nothing man, I'll be a minute, just got to check on something." I yell back.

"Yeah alright." Kyle says and continues to walk towards the front entrance as the sign comes into view. Of course, my luck would have it that she's not here. *Maybe she's already inside.* I can't help but to be disappointed. I would have liked to talk to her this morning without having to search the entire school first. I don't even know what year she's in, or what wing her classes are. Seems we didn't talk very much last night since I know absolutely nothing about her. *That's about to change.*

I walk to class with Kyle and scan the halls for her unmistakable long chestnut hair, but to my efforts, they don't seem to pay off this morning. I don't pay much attention throughout the day, only remembering what last night felt like being around her.

"What's wrong with you mate?" Kyle asks as he's sitting next to me so he can clearly tell I'm in a mood.

"What? Nothing…just a bit hung-over." I tell him to avoid a hundred questions I would have to answer if he knew I was thinking about a girl. One he didn't set me up with.

"Hung-over? You had a party without your best mate?" He announces and presses his hand to his chest to make like I just committed the most insulting act against him.

"No man, just a late night." I say, my annoyance with this conversation is clear on my face.

"Alright well, you might want to pay attention yeah? After all, you haven't been to class in almost a week. You missed a lot of SAT review."

"Yeah…alright." I nod my head in agreement. I do need to study if I ever plan to graduate. I may have already fucked up my life for the most part, but I don't want to be a complete loser, but that's what I'll be if I don't get into university and do something with my miserable existence.

The next two days go by and Jo is still not in school. I looked and asked around for her but no one seems to know who she is. She must keep to herself mostly if no one in this entire school knows of her. I find it odd, but what do I know, I only just met her the other day. I did go to the main office this morning to see if I could bribe the secretary to give me Jo's class schedule. Bitch wouldn't budge though. She has hated me since the ninth grade when I shattered her crystal vase all over her desk. Turns out kicking a soccer ball in the hallways isn't the best idea. I guess I'll just have to wait until Jo shows up at school because I'm fresh out of idea on where I could possibly find her.

I planned on dropping Kyle back at his house after school but he gladly reminded me that the bonfire at the beach is tonight. I'm not at all in the mood right now to deal with this shit but I have to say at least I know there will be alcohol that I can drown my sorry ass in when we get there. I might as well make the best of it and enjoy a night that I would otherwise avoid at all costs. I did promise Kyle to help him out and after all he's done for me, I would be a piece of shit if I bailed on him again.

16
Josephine

I have been to pretty much every shop around town in the last four days and I just realized that there's not a whole lot to do when you live in such a small town in the middle of nowhere. Mostly all of the shops are within walking distance and we have quite a few very nice parks around here that I can kill a few hours walking around and able to avoid people at the same time. Small towns aren't really for people who like to be left alone though. Everywhere you go, you end up running into someone that probably knows you or that you have run into some time or another. I honestly don't have to worry too much about that since I don't really know anyone around here. I've always kept to myself ever since Jeff moved us up here when my mom split.

I've had to learn how to use foundation I recently bought at the pharmacy to cover up the marks on my face so I wouldn't have to worry about anyone questioning me about them. I'm not very good at applying it so I decided not to bother with it anymore after a day of trying to smear the stuff on without it looking like my skin was melting off. Avoiding eye contact and acting like I'm far too busy to look away from what I'm doing seems to be working just fine anyway. Mrs. Lawrence has mostly been in the back of the store getting ready for her trip tomorrow while I've been checking out customers at the front. I've been sure to keep myself busy and out of sight pretty much the whole time to avoid any questions that might come up if she sees my face before the bruises become less noticeable. Mrs. Lawrence told me when I came in today that she will be out of town and closing the shop early. She said she will be back by Monday afternoon if I want to stop by after school. So now I can have the entire weekend to not have to worry about hiding the bruises from her. After I leave and Mrs. Lawrence locks up, I decide to walk around town a little and find that diner I heard her say had good breakfast food. I haven't eaten yet, so I could definitely go for something now. I walk a few blocks past the book store and make a left at the salon on the corner. The diner is right where she said. I have lived here for a few years and I never knew this place was here. It looks like a little cottage house on the outside like maybe someone remodeled their own house into a restaurant. It's hidden in the corner behind a taller building off of Main Street. No wonder why I have never seen it before, I've come down this way. The house has red shutters and large potted plants that are just starting to peek out from under the dirt. There are so many pots lined up along the sidewalk that leads to the porch, I can only imagine what it's going to look like in a few weeks when they all bloom. I walk in and sure enough, it's set up like an old-style diner with vinyl-covered booths, stools at the counter, and an old jukebox in the corner. Nothing I could have imagined given the aesthetic of the outside. I feel like I have warped back to the 1950s. It does smell amazing in here though, so the food must be as good as Mrs. Lawrence said it was. My stomach is starting to sound like a ferocious animal so, despite the worn-out look of the place, I decide to stay and give the food a try.

"Never judge a book by its cover." she always tells me. I have taken that to heart. Because working in the book shop for almost three years I have read the most amazing stories that I would have never read before I started working there. I would always look at the cover first and if it didn't catch my attention, I would never read the blurb on the back. Now I go straight to reading the back cover and the first chapter before I decide if the books not for me. I've lost count of how many books I have enjoyed since taking her advice.

I take a seat near the window and grab a menu from behind the ketchup. There are no pictures on it, it's just a piece of laminated paper listing drinks, pies, a few breakfast options and a couple of lunch menu items. I decide to go with breakfast food, which is ultimately my favorite. The waitress comes over, she's an older woman with darkish hair with gray strands peppered through it, making it look like it was white and that she just added the dark strands herself. Her red lipstick accentuates her bright look, and it seems to just match her personality to a T, even though I don't have a clue what she's like yet. But the smile on her face tells me what you see, is exactly what you get when it comes to her. Her appearance is a little modern for this small town, but it seems to suit her well. She comes up to me and introduces herself as Suzie, then places silverware rolled in a napkin down on the table. I take it she notices my bruised face since she looks concerned, but I'm sure it's more pity than anything. Her eyes flicker, trying to hide the worrying expression that crosses her eyes before she takes out her pen and pad of paper. It seems as if she may be the owner since she's the only other one here besides the cook and a couple of other customers. I'm grateful that it's not busy in here because I wouldn't want anyone making a scene if anyone else were to notice and ask me about the state of my face.

"Do you know what you would like to order, or do you need a few minutes to decide?" She asks me, with her little pad of paper in her hand, ready to jot down what I want.

"No… I've decided." I say to her. I look down at the table and point to the menu as I give her my order, trying to avoid eye contact as much as possible. "I'll have French toast with a side of hash browns and some hot cocoa with a sprinkle of cinnamon on top please." I place the menu back behind the ketchup without looking up at her.

"I'll get that right out dear." She walks away and comes back a minute later with my mug of hot cocoa and a tall glass of ice water. The scent of the cinnamon and chocolate together reminds me of when Hunter made me cocoa at his house the day we met. The memory is comforting. I thank the waitress as she walks away again and I grab the mug to lift it to my lips. The taste is heavenly. *Exactly what I needed right now.*

I finish every last bite of my breakfast. I didn't realize how hungry I was until Suzie put the plate of food in front of me. It all tasted so good. I ask for another cup of cocoa and the check and when she brings it over to me, I look at it and see it says zero-dollar balance. Suzie pats my hand.

"It's on the house dear." I try to tell her I got it, but she won't hear it and walks away with a smile on her face before I can protest. It was so sweet of her to do that, but I hate to think she did it because she saw the bruises and felt bad for me. Of course, I'm sure she's wise enough to vaguely figure out what could have happened. A guy put his hands on me and I let him, simple as that; but I don't want to be looked at as weak because of it. I decide to just accept whatever it is she thinks and leave it at that. She's a stranger, so I most likely won't be seeing her again anyway. She was nice though and the food was great. I'm just happy she didn't bring attention to my embarrassment by asking if I was alright or what happened when she saw my face. Most people would have asked, but I appreciate that she didn't. The sun is finally shining as I walk out the door. It was looking like it was going to rain again, but the sky has cleared and there's not a dark cloud in sight.

"Finally, thank you!" I say and I breathe in a deep breath of fresh warm air. The sun on my face feels good as I walk around town and I glance in the shop windows as I pass by each one. The pet store that just opened last month has a new litter of puppies that were born a few weeks ago just as they were having their grand opening. *What great timing.* They're already running around the crate in the window; most likely enjoying the warm sun shining through on them to. I decide to sit in the town square park on my favorite bench and read a while. I should enjoy the warmer weather while it lasts, because around here, who knows when it will decide to hit us with a cool blast of winter air again before spring finally makes its full appearance.

Before I know it, I'm on the last page of my book when I look up and realize how much darker it's gotten. I only just started reading it the other day so I got sucked in and lost track of time. The street lights are starting to come on and my ass is numb from sitting too long on this hard wooden bench. I pull out my phone and see that it's only eight o'clock. Jeff doesn't leave for work for another few hours so I think I'll just go down to the beach and sit there for a while. I always loved being on the beach, enjoying the sound of the waves drowning out everything else around me. It's obviously been far too cold the last few months and I've missed coming down here. Thankfully tonight is the warmest night we have had yet, it's a hint that spring is finally on its way, and I couldn't be any happier.

17
Josephine

I sit on the beach and watch the waves crash against the rocks for a while, listening to the sound of the night's tide washing over the sand and being pulled back out by invisible hands. The rhythmic breathing of the ocean brings me peace for as long as I sit here and the breeze is almost as warm down here as it was in the park earlier, but the wind is picking up a gentle mist from the ocean, so I occasionally feel the cool salty water on my face. If I never had to move from this spot ever again, I wouldn't mind in the least bit that this would be the only thing I ever see again.

The Moon is shining off the black water and there are so many stars out tonight, it looks like someone splatter painted the sky with crystals. It's rare to have a clear night sky around here. It's usually cloudy and dull and not that wonderful to look at. But tonight, it’s special and I plan on enjoying it.

It's eleven by the time I look at my phone again. I hate that the time goes by so quickly when all I want is to sit in the peace and quiet, alone and away from the outside world. I should go home soon though. Jeff should be gone to work by the time I get there and if Nate's home, well so be it. It's funny how I feel more comfortable being out here on a beach at night alone and feel completely content, but going home puts me on edge. Hell, I could probably stay here all night and maybe actually get some real sleep. Unlike back at the house, my bedroom, Jeff, all the things that make me uneasy are all in one place and they like to flood my brain with worries to keep me up at night.

Out of nowhere I hear loud music playing in the distance. I look around and notice a crowd of people around a massive bonfire. *When the hell, did they show up?* There's a truck parked nearby, blaring music and people are dancing around and yelling incoherently. They must all be drunk already or just really excited to celebrate something. I don't know how I didn't notice everyone until now. I guess I was just so off in my own head I wasn't even paying attention. I don't recognize the music but it does sound good from here and everyone looks like they're having a blast. It must be nice for them to be able to let loose and have fun with their friends. I wish I knew what that was like, but there's no use in sitting here, having a pity party for myself. That will only ruin the memories of a really nice day I had on my own.

I decide to start heading back when I see someone walking towards me from the direction of the party. I try to avoid eye contact and just walk past him, but it's too late, he's already in my path of escape. Maybe he just thinks I'm part of their group. Otherwise, why else would he leave the party when I'm the only one over here?

"Heeey!" Is the first slurred word out of his mouth. He definitely looks drunk by the way he's stumbling toward me through the sand. *I don't want to get into this right now.* I take a second look and see who it is and I'm no longer on edge of the stranger approaching me because he's not a stranger after all. Not a friend, but definitely not a stranger. I've seen him around school plenty of times; usually being loud and theatrical in the halls or the lunch room. The class clown really.

"Hi." I say back. Not really sure where this is going, but he stops just in front of me and stares for way too long, making me uncomfortable. This is extremely awkward, to say the least. "Can I help you with something?" I ask him but he just stands there with a blank expression on his face. I'm assuming from his consumption of alcohol his mouth needs to play catch up with his brain. I go to walk away after another minute of silence but then he grabs my arm and stumbles into me. "Hey…what the hell?" I shove his arm away out of reflex and he trips and falls on his ass. *Yup, he's definitely wasted.* He's lucky it's sand and not concrete. He gets up and starts toward me again when another guy comes up behind him and grabs him in a friendly bear hug to hold him there for a second.

"Yo! Devin, lay off her, she's not Lacey. Go back to the party and chill out alright?" He lets the Devin guy go and shoves him a little so he walks back towards the party, stumbling over his own feet again.

"Hey sorry about my friend, he can be a real ass when he's wasted." He motions toward him.

"Yeah, I'd agree." Is all I say before trying to walk away for the second time tonight. Mr. No name jogs up in front of me and starts walking backward, keeping pace with me rather well considering I'm sure he's been drinking tonight too.

"Where are you off too so quickly? I mean...." He stumbles and corrects himself to say. "Why don't you join the Party? You could have some fun."

"No. I'm good. I don't really do parties." I shrug. Still trying to get past him.

"Well, this isn't your regular high school party." He informs me. A playful smile shows his pearly white teeth.

"And why is that?" I ask, not really looking for an answer but I don't want to come off rude since he did just help get his drunk friend to leave me alone.

"Because, this is my party, it's my birthday." He says and lifts the bottle to his lips to down the rest of the mystery liquid in his cup.

"Oh, well Happy Birthday." I actually do mean it for him to have a Happy Birthday. *Everyone should be happy on their birthday.*

"Thanks." So, you'll come then?" He asks eagerly.

"I mean, I...." *I really don't like being around that many people but really what could be so bad trying to have a little fun for once?*

"Come on. It will be fun I promise. I don't bite if that's what you're worried about." He grins as he puts his hands into a prayer position, still holding onto the red plastic cup like he's begging me to join his party. I don't know what to do. I don't want to go home, but I also don't belong here. I don't know anyone and I have never drunk alcohol before in my entire life. I guess I'll just drink soda or water if they have it. I know that I'm over thinking it so I decide to shut my brain off for a couple of hours and agree to go over.

"Sure. What the hell?" I say, slapping my hands on my thighs and follow Mr. no name over to the crowded part of the beach. We walk over to the fire and I realize more people have shown up in the short time we were talking. Seems they even ordered pizza too because there are about half a dozen boxes sitting on the folding table next to all the bottles of alcohol. Mr. No name grabs my hand and walks over toward the bonfire to sit down around a circle. The sand has been dug out around the fire pit to make a place for people to sit on bench style seating. It's actually really cool. Looks like a lot of work went into it. I feel weird sitting next to a guy I have only seen in the hallways at school and not once has he talked to me until tonight. "What's your name?" I ask him as he hands me a red cup with an unknown clear liquid in it. I smell the sour aroma and it burns slightly as I inhale, but I lift it to my mouth and pretend to take a sip anyway.

"Cam. The wasted ass hat you met earlier is Devin." He takes a sip from his cup and squeezes his eyes shut for a minute before sucking air in through his teeth. That's my cue to not drink whatever it is he just handed me.

"Yeah, I know, he's in my economics class. He's a real ass hat even when he's not wasted." Cam's face is the look of shock and then he bursts out laughing. More dramatically than expected but he has been drinking.

"Yes, yes he is." He laughs, agreeing with me. Can't say I'm surprised there.

"So, you still haven't told me your name. I haven't seen you around school, are you new?" Cam downs another red cup someone hands him as were talking. He didn't even bother to see what was in it first.

"I'm Jo. And no, I'm not new this year. I'm a junior."

"Jo." He repeats my name then rubs his hands over his chin as if he's questioning what I just told him. Nothing comes out of his mouth for a good minute as he stares at me, making me slightly more nervous than I was five minutes ago. Then he just gets up and walks over to the table, grabs two smaller cups, and brings them over. He hands me one when he sits down. Then dumps the other small cup of his in a larger cup and tips it back to drink until it's empty. *He is so going to regret that in the morning.*

"Aren't you going to drink that? It's good if you mix them, it kills the burn in your throat." He tells me. I look up at him and see that his eyes are a little glassy as he tries to focus on my face. He's playing off how disgusting that drink really was, rather well.

"Look Cam, thanks for inviting me but I should get going." I try to hand the cups to him but he doesn't take them from me. I don't know what I'm doing around all these people, it's starting to make me really self-conscious.

"No, no stay. Look, just have some fun. Let loose a little. It's a birthday party, later there will be cake. Everyone likes cake." His drunken pleading seems sweet and innocent. What harm could it do to stay a little longer? I haven't even tried to have any fun yet. I look around at everyone here. They do seem to all be having a good time. Why shouldn't I be able to do the same? I am a teenager after all; this is what they do right? They drink and party and celebrate the freedom they have instead of sitting home alone and whine about not having any fun.

"Alright!" I yell excitedly and then I down the mystery liquid in my cup before I can talk myself out of it like any other rational human being would.

18
Hunter

Kyle man let's go already." I am not a patient guy at all, but Kyle always takes forever getting out the damn door every single time we go out. Ever since I met him, he's always the last one to arrive anywhere.

"Alright, alright. I'm coming man, don't get your panties in a twist yeah." Kyle gets in the car and throws his bag in the back seat. I roll my eyes at him and go to take off when I remember the damn paper that I threw in my desk the other night. I get out of the car and run back up to the house.

"Yo, where you going?" He yells at me with his head out the window.

"Give me a damn minute, I forgot something." I run up to my room and dig around my desk drawer for the crumpled piece of paper. Lucky me I didn't throw it in the wash with my jeans. Kyle would be a right ass about it if I did. Can't say I would blame him. I was hoping to not have to do this tonight but I owe him for saving my ass last week with the cops. He is my best friend after all. But after tonight I'm done doing shit like this.

"So, this time, I'm not the one making us late." I'm about ready to punch that asshole grin off his face when I hand him the paper.

"Shut up man, I was getting your shit. Here." Kyle takes the paper and slips it in his pocket as I drive away from the house.

"I hate having that stuff on me. I'm done with it, Kyle. This is the last time I hold that shit for anyone. I have enough of my parents on my ass to last me a lifetime, I don't need to add to it if they were to find that in my room." I'm livid. I don't know why I had to hold on to it in the first place. But I did it because Kyle is my best friend, and I would trust him with my life. "Come on, you know they wouldn't go in your room.

Besides you still lock it all the time anyway, don't you?" He questions, knowing I always do.

"Yeah well, like I said, I'm done." I repeat one last time.

We get to the beach and I pull as close as I can get to the party without actually pulling onto the sand. I won't park on it anymore. It was hard enough getting my car out of that mess last time, being drunk certainly didn't help matters but I also don't want anyone puking on it. We get out of the car and I see there are far more people here this time than I have ever seen here at any of the bonfires we've come to before. I can't help but think Kyle had something to do with that. He usually does. I go round to the trunk to pull out the case of beer while Kyle gets his bag from the backseat.

"Hey man who's property is this anyway, do you know?" I ask as we walk toward the table with all the drinks on it. I set the case of beer under it since there's no room on top. There must be like thirty bottles of liquor over here. Not that I'm complaining.

"Yeah, it's Cam's. His parents own the beach house up on the hill, but we're still on public property until we pass those rocks over there." He points to the house on the other side of the public buoys.

"Dude, I told you I wanted nothing more to do with that tool." I huff out.

"And you won't have to deal with him. Now, look how many people are here. I doubt we'll even see him." Kyle gives me a shove toward the table. "Now go get us a drink while I take care of something yeah."

He's such a dick sometimes. But I could use a drink. I sift through the rubbish options of alcohol until I find one that I can stand the taste of. *Whiskey it is.* I take a couple of swigs straight out of the bottle. No sense in wasting a cup if I don't plan on sharing it anyway.

"Hunter." Kyle yells over to me just as I'm starting to feel a slight buzz. *Dammit!* I curse under my breath.

"What is it man?" Still holding the whisky bottle, I take another swig before Kyle speaks.

"I need you to do me that favor." He eyes me to make sure I understand him.

"No man, I told you, I was just holding it for you. I don't want anything to do with that, not tonight. Besides I'm already buzzed. Why don't you go handle it?"

"Because I'm going to go see Cam, and you didn't want to deal with him tonight either, remember?"

"Alright, Fine! Fuck it! Give it to me then." I hold out my hand, and Kyle places the crumpled paper back into my palm and I throw my hands up and storm off. I could kick Kyle's ass right now. I wish he asked me to do this before I downed half a bottle of Jameson. I set the bottle on the table as I pass it and look around for a guy near the black truck parked on the beach. Kyle said he'd be around here. After a solid five minutes of looking for this dude, I give up. My buzz is going strong and I'm feeling good right now. I'm not ruining it for some dipshit that is clearly more interested in other things than what is in my pocket. I decide to get another drink when Kyle comes over and hands me the bottle I was drinking from earlier. We walk over to the fire and sit down near a few other people we usually hang around. People I can tolerate at least and I down more of the burning amber liquid. These parties are all the same. Same people, same booze, and the same god-awful music. I would rather be at home drinking my weight in scotch. I go to take another swig but the bottle is empty. *Shit.* I toss it into the fire, and it lands with a loud crash. Well, no better time to sober up if I ever want to get home tonight. I'm not sleeping on the beach again, that didn't turn out well last time.

I get up and go to grab a couple of slices of pizza, thinking it might soak up some of the alcohol I consumed tonight and I notice some commotion on the other side of the beach. Guys are running half-naked into the freezing water. Dumbasses must be so drunk they can't feel how cold the water is. I walk back over to Kyle and hand him a slice I grabbed from the table and sit back down next to him and his girl. I glance back over and see a couple looking like they're having a little too much of a good time at first. The girl takes a drink from a red cup, she laughs then takes another sip, finishing what's left and places the cup down beside her. There's suddenly an arm that comes out of nowhere and wraps around the girl's waist, pulling her closer to him as he inches his hand up her thigh and tries to kiss her, but she looks like she wants nothing to do with it, and apprehensively stands up. The guy grabs her wrist and holds her there for a second as he stands and whispers something in her ear. *Damn, what a dick!* I don't feel right just watching some asshole treat a girl like that. With the alcohol coursing through me, I decide that it's a good idea to go tell him to back off. I'm halfway over when the girl puts her hands on the guys' chest and tries to push him away and I get to see who the ass-hat actually is. *It's Fucking Cam!* I cannot believe this asshole! How is he always nearby when I try to avoid the prick like the fucking plague?

I stand right in front of where they're sitting and tap Cam on the shoulder to get his attention.

"Hey man, lay off alright. You don't need to put your hands on her like that!" The twat turns his face up toward me and speaks.

"Fuck off and mind your own damn business." As he stands up, he lets go of the girl's arm and she quickly backs away from the both of us. I turn to face her to ask if she's alright and I see that the girl that I had been watching for the last ten minutes is actually Jo. *Maybe I'm more wasted than I thought.* How could I have not recognized her? After the shock of seeing her here wears off, I realize her face is covered in bruises and her bottom lip is split and swollen. I glare back at Cam and all I can see is red. Before I know it, I lunge for him and knock his ass to the ground. We both end up landing hard on the sand, and my hands go straight to his throat to choke the life out of him.

"You son of a bitch!" I snarl as my fist makes contact with his jaw. He jabs me in the ribs, slightly knocking the wind out of me; but I'm far too drunk to care or even really feel the hit. I get up and hover over him, clutching at the collar of his shirt to make him stand up and he loses his balance for a split second which gives me the opportunity to meet his jaw with another blow. I swing again but he ducts out of the way until I uppercut him in the groin with my right hook. He falls to the ground and lands face first in the sand as he holds his family jewels. *Apparently, he didn't see that one coming.* While Cam lies there on the ground, I walk back over Jo to see if she's okay.

"Hey, are you alright?" I ask Jo, but before I can get an answer from her, someone grabs me by my jacket and pulls me away from her. The shocked expression on her face stuns me and lets the person pulling me away catch me off guard. I see stars after I feel a throbbing pain in the side of my face. *Fucker actually hit me!* I turn around, swing and hit Cam in the side of his ribs. He lunges at me, knocking me off my feet and our bodies crash back into the sand. I take one last shot to the mouth before grabbing the back of his skull and head butting the asshole. Blood immediately starts spraying from his nose and he slumps off to the side of me with his hands clutching his face. I stand up and try going for him again but Kyle gets in my way and pushes me away from him and the crowd. "Hunter, stop man, hey, stop! He's had it, he's done, enough!" Kyle gets in my face and holds my shoulders back to keep me from tearing that piece of shit apart even further.

" Get off me Kyle, I was just finishing what the dickhead started!" I growl at him as I shove his hands away but he doesn't let me near Cam again. It will only cause more trouble for the both of us if he does.

"Hey look chill, it's over." He says while he makes sure I walk away to clear my head. He then proceeds to hand me the rest of his beer and asks.

"Hunter, you okay mate? What the hell was that about?"

"Yeah, fine. But he shouldn't have touched her like that." I say but Kyle just looks at me like I grew a second head, because he has no idea what I'm talking about. The way Cam had his filthy hands all over Jo makes my stomach turn and I want to smash his face on the fucking ground again just thinking about it. I wipe the blood off of my lip with my sleeve and gulp down the rest of Kyle's beer. I hate the taste of blood. “Fucking prick!” I say under my breath as I brush the rest of the sand off my face.

"Okay well, that girl is walking away and you might want to go see if she's alright. After all, you did kick the shit out of her boyfriend right in front of her." He reminds me.

"Shit…where did she go?" I ask him. Kyle points in the direction of my car. I see her walking towards the parking lot so I hurry to catch up with her.

“That’s okay, I’ll stay here and make sure Cam isn’t planning our death anytime soon. No problem at all.” I hear Kyle yell at me as I run towards Jo and he starts to walk back to the beach. If anyone could smooth things over, Kyle would be the one to do it. I’m always the guy that does nothing but fuck shit up and makes things worse. Sometimes I think that I’m as bad as that prick Cam. Jo’s already halfway across the lot when I'm close enough for her to hear me so I yell her name...

"Jo. Jo!" She stops and turns around. I can see her face. She doesn't look that upset; considering I just kicked the crap out her boyfriend. I can’t fucking believe she would be with that tool. It's weird she just left him lying there like that with a broken nose. Can't say I blame her. It is Cam we’re talking about after all. So maybe she isn’t actually with him. Could I be so lucky? "Look, please just leave me alone ok." She says but when she makes eye contact with me her features soften and she looks somewhat relieved. "Oh. It's you." She sounds surprised to see me standing in front of her.

"Sorry to disappoint you, but if you were expecting your boyfriend, I don't think he's going to be getting up anytime soon." I tell her while I try really hard to hold back a grin.

"Wait, what?" She asks. I walk closer to her and her eyes start tearing up at the corners. I feel like a dick for making her cry but I don't regret what I did to that asshole.

"Look, I'm sorry I did that in front of you, but that's not the kind of guy that deserves someone like you. He deserved to get his ass beat for putting his hands on you and leaving all those bruises." I'm gritting my teeth right now so hard I feel like they are about to shatter. I can't stand to think about her being hit by him, or anyone for that matter. Looking at Jo with those marks all over her is heartbreaking and I'm glad I beat the shit out of him.

"Do you, you think I'm with that guy? I barely know him!" She shrieks and looks at me with those wild eyes of hers, they show so much emotion even when her words are laced with anger.

"I thought that you were... he was all over you so I just assumed you were his girlfriend. Sorry, that came out wrong, I didn't mean to say it like tha…"

"No, no." She cuts me off. "I only just met him on the beach tonight, he invited me over for a drink, said it was his birthday. I was already sitting over on the shore by the time everyone showed up. Besides, he's a real dick obviously." She looks down at her hands, rubbing her fingers over her wrist which is now red from where Cam was gripping her. "He didn't cause these either." Motioning to her face; her words trail off and she grows quiet for a moment. "Look, thanks for stepping in, but you didn't have to break his nose for me."

"Trust me, he deserved it."

19
Hunter

Listen, I'm getting out of here. Can I drive you home?" I don't want to take her home, not yet anyway. But I don't have a lot of options right now to keep her here with me long enough to get to know her.

"Haven't you been drinking?" She asks. She's got me there, so the other option is to walk her home if she still wants to leave.

"Let me walk you then." I offer. I can't drive like this anyway, even though the adrenaline from the fight sobered me up quite a bit. I want to spend more time with her and I feel like I should apologize again for what happened just moments ago, but I don't. I just stand there waiting like an idiot for her to answer me so I know what to do.

"Alright, sure." She says and then starts walking away. I jog to catch up to her and we fall into a comfortable silence for most of the way to her house. I'm itching to ask her about all the bruises but I'm clueless about how to bring it up and I really don't want to upset her again. If Cam wasn't the one who caused them, I'd like to find out who did so I can make them regret every single time they dared to put a hand on her.

"So, why haven't you come to school the last few days?" I question and she visibly tenses beside me as she crosses her arms in front of her. I know why she hasn't come to school; the evidence is all over her gorgeous face. I'm hoping that maybe I can get her to tell me what happened without directly nosing my way into her business.

"I haven't felt very well lately." *And...*

"Are you alright now?" *What a stupid question, clearly, she's not alright you idiot!*

"Yeah, I'll be fine." She says with a finality so apparent I feel like I should stop asking. The once comfortable silent walk has become tense and Jo seems more guarded than she was at the beach. So, I decide to ask her about the other night at my house instead. That should be a nice reminder that I'm not the bad guy in this situation.

"I woke up and you were gone." I say. She stops suddenly and turns around coming face to face with me.

"Yeah, I...I had to get home. I left really early so I didn't want to wake you." Her eyes have that familiar brightness in them that I saw a glimpse of the other night. But then it fades just as quickly.

"I would have drove you home."

"I just had to get home before… to get ready for school." She says but I know she was going to say something different before she thought about it.

"But you didn't come to school that day. I looked for you, but I didn't know what classes you had or anything. And I couldn't text you since I never got your number." I remind her.

"Right, well...I started to feel ill before I got home so I just stayed in bed all day." Her answers are rather vague. Her eyes show a hint of sadness and become glassy as she talks. It's killing me not to know what happened after she left my house. Clearly more happened than she's letting on.

"Fuck it!" I say as calmly as I possibly can. "Jo, what happened?" I look directly at her; willing her eyes to meet mine. Finally, she quickly glances up at me.

"What do you mean?" Her eyes grow to the size of dinner plates before she looks down at her feet, trying to hide from and avoid what I'm about to ask her.

"Why do you have all those bruises? Who hurt you?" I want to hold her, make her feel safe but I don't know how she would react. So, I stand where I'm at, for now, a close but safe distance, hoping she will let me in and tell me everything.

"It's nothing really, don't worry about it, okay? I have to go." She tries to dart away so I reach for her hand, barely brushing her fingertips with mine; she turns around to face me and silent tears start to cascade down her cheeks.

"I'm sorry Jo. I just need to know what happened. I have to know if you're alright." I step closer to her and she backs up a couple of feet. The tension in her body has grown significantly in the last twenty seconds and I can tell she's fighting with herself and trying to decide if she wants to let me in.

"Why do you care anyway? We just met a few days ago so you don't even know me or what goes on in my shitty life!" The tremble in her voice tells me there's way more that I don't know and she's trying diligently to hold it all together. I can tell whatever happened was really bad just by looking at her, but the way her voice cracked into a weak whimper makes me think that whatever happened, is way worse than I can imagine.

Her resolve weakens as she weeps hysterically in front of me but I find myself standing here thoroughly frozen because I have no idea what to do or say to her to make her pain stop. She covers her face with her hands trying to muffle her cries but it's no use. I can still hear the agony in her voice and the sound rips painfully through my chest until I can't stand it anymore. I close the last couple of feet between us in one swift step and wrap my arms around her small body, bringing her tight to my chest. Her shoulders still shake and I can feel the wetness of her tears soaking through my t-shirt. I know she's hurting and I have no idea how to help, so I do the only thing I can. I let her cry as I stand here holding onto her, hoping that she feels safe and let her decide when she feels okay enough to let go.

"I'm so sorry. I didn't mean to...to lose it like that in front of you." She breaks my grasp on her after a couple of moments and then backs away wiping her face with her sleeve. She looks embarrassed but I don't want her to feel like that. I don't know why I would care for her or her feelings as much as I do but I feel myself being drawn further in the longer that I'm around her. And seeing her like this is going to eventually kill me.

"No, Jo, it's alright really. I'm sorry I'm no good at this, I'm really shit when it comes to knowing how to make things better instead of worse, but I'm here if you need someone." I clarify. Her lips curve up into the faintest smile for just a moment and it makes my insides light up like a fucking Christmas tree to witness.

"You're sweet Hunter. But I really should go. Thanks for walking me home and..." She looks puzzled, maybe not knowing what to call what just happened between us. I am too for that matter. So, I tell her.

"It's my pleasure, Jo. But wait before you go. Can I see your phone?" I ask, reaching my hand out towards her. She reaches into her pocket of her hoodie and pulls out her phone and hands it to me. I type my own number in and save it to her contacts under H.

"There." I hand her phone back. "Now you have my number. If you decide you ever want to talk, now you know how to find me."

"Thanks." She says and puts her phone back in her pocket and turns away to start walking towards her house. I don't move from where she left me standing alone on the darkened street, void of her warmth and her beautiful smile. I just watch her walk down the block to make sure she gets safely inside her house. She finally crosses the gate in front, and disappears from my view.

20
Josephine

As I walk through the front door and lock it behind me, I let out the biggest sigh of relief. Jeff doesn't seem to be here, and it looks like Nate is nowhere to be found at the moment either. His car wasn't in the driveway and Jeff should be at work, assuming he went to work tonight. It's late and I'm grateful to have the house to myself for once. I do prefer to be alone than worry about them being home, but I hate how eerily dark and quiet the house is at night. The few street lights we do have don't do much for lighting up the dark corners of the neighborhood, leaving many places for things to lurk in the shadows. This house has given me the creeps since the day we moved in and I don’t think that is ever going to change.

My thoughts drift back to being with Hunter and it helps me to relax for a moment. Just like the other day when I was at his house, all the worry seemed to flow away from me and I was finally able to take a decent breath for once. The fight between Hunter and Cam was intense and agonizing to see Hunter get hurt. I had never witnessed something like that so up close and personal before. Whenever Nate and Jeff would fight, I would run to my room and only have to hear the awful words being spat between them. I definitely never thought it would ever be because of me that someone would be slamming their fist into another person’s jaw. I can't say it didn't make me a little happy that someone was defending me rather than taking their bullshit out on me. I'm grateful for Hunter stepping in, but I hate that he ended up taking a few hits and getting hurt because of me.

I go to my room and throw my jacket and bag on my chair. I dig in my pocket for my phone and hold it in my hand swiping to unlock it and trying to decide if I want to text Hunter. I only just left him a few minutes ago. *Would it be weird to text him already?* I feel awful for walking away and leaving him standing in the dark like that, especially after how he's been there for me. I just didn't have a clue what else to say to him. I don't like people knowing about my life or anything about me for that matter, but Hunter seemed genuinely concerned for me, given the state of how I'm assuming my face still looks. But he doesn't need to be brought into my depressing existence, not now, not ever. I think he's better off not getting involved with me, so I don't text him and I place my phone down on my desk and go over to my closet to find something to sleep in. My hooded sweatshirt and some flannel shorts are the best to sleep in on a cool yet comfortable night like this. It gets cold in my room, being in the back of the house and all. If it were upstairs, I'd have some of the heat rising up to warm the floor beneath my toes. But I don't complain, I'm just happy enough to have a door to separate me from the rest of the house while I'm trying to sleep.

I take my caddy and my clothes into the bathroom upstairs to take a shower and I realize I left my phone on my desk. I run back downstairs while the shower heats up and as I round the corner to the kitchen I run straight into a solid figure. My heart starts to pound in my chest and the knot in my stomach is tight as I scramble to find my footing. I didn't turn a single light on downstairs so it's still pitch black and all I hear is my heart thumping in my ears and the breathing coming from the person in front of me. I back up and bump against the door frame, feeling around for the light switch and turn it on, and to my relief, it's Nate standing there in the middle of the kitchen, and he's looking undoubtedly rough around the edges.

"Hey Jo." He says flatly. His eyes are glassy and he smells of booze. *Great! Just what I need!*

"Hey." I say back and turn to walk back upstairs when I abruptly feel a hand on my arm. I flinch on reflex and rip my arm out of his grasp while I back away and inch further toward the stairs.

"Sorry." He says and he hastily drops his hand to his side and looks around the kitchen before he brings his right hand up to nervously rub it over the stubble on his face and up into his hair, slicking it back for a moment, and lets out a deep, ragged breath. Against my better judgment, I stand there against the door frame waiting to see what he wants or what he is going to say. He looks awful, like he's been out all- night drinking and by the aroma coming from him, it seems like that could be the only explanation. Nate looks at me before he rests his head in his hands and covers his eyes. I'm assuming to him the room is spinning, but then I hear him quietly sob and I grasp that he's upset. He's usually angry or replying with some sort of smart-ass comment about something, so when he looks up all of a sudden and his brows are drawn together it takes me by surprise that his eyes look like they are filled with regret. He wipes his face with the bottom of his t-shirt and takes another deep breath.

"Jo..." His deep brown eyes make contact with mine and I hold in a breath waiting for him to finish. "Jo are...are you alright?" The words get caught in his throat but he manages to get them out. I've never seen him like this and it makes me curious as to what the hell happened.

"Um, yeah. I'm fine." I say, not knowing where this conversation is going or what it's even about. But then I remember the bruises on my face. *He couldn't be upset about that could he?* He wasn't even here that day. He wouldn't have any idea it was his father that caused them. Even if he did, this reaction wouldn't be something I would have expected from him at all.

"Don't lie to me!" He warns as the words explode from deep within him and he slams his fist on the kitchen table beside him. His words are laced with such animosity that it surprises me and makes me jump and back away from him even further than before. My heart starts pounding again, making me feel like Jeff is standing in front of me instead of Nate. The same feeling that I get when Jeff is about to do something horrible comes rushing through me, making me sick to my stomach.

"Sorry, shit, no Jo, I'm sorry." He stutters as he walks towards me, his hands out in front of his face. I back away into the hallway further and he stops in his tracks a couple of feet from me, the recognition on his face that I find him threatening right now. "Jo, look. I, I'm sorry." He repeats himself until his tone takes on an apologetic one.

"Yeah, I know, you said that already, a couple of times, but for what?" I ask while trying not to let my voice sound as panicked as I feel.

"I know I wasn't here. I'm sorry I wasn't." He repeats himself over and over, sounding like he's stuck in a drunken stupor, not being able to get the right words out that his brain wants to say. It's not clicking in my own head what he's even talking about. *What would he be apologizing for?* I feel for him that he seems so out of himself right now. But then again it seems like the alcohol has the opposite effect on him than it does on Jeff. I should be grateful for that fact, but I can't bring myself to feel sorry for Nate at the moment. He's Jeff's son, he can't be that much different from his dad when he's under the influence of God knows what anymore. I really don't want to get caught in the middle of anyone else's alcoholic fits. I don't ever remember seeing Nate drink any sort of alcohol the entire time I have lived with them. It's a strange thing to witness. I knew he would have friends over and they would be drinking, but I can't place ever seeing alcohol touch his lips. My mouth opens to say something to him but I can't seem to let go of the words just yet. Nate stares at the floor and his shoulders quickly rise and fall as he breathes in heavy sobs. The suspense is killing me and I'm growing more and more impatient as I just want to be left alone. I can't handle another emotionally charged conversation or fight, whatever you would call this right now.

"Look, Nate, I'm gonna go to bed, I think you should too." I go to walk away when I hear him finally clear his throat to speak.

"No, wait! Just listen please, just for a minute." He pleads. So, I turn around.

"Okay." Is all I say in response. His words have me worried now, and how can I not be curious as to what he needs to tell me. This is so unlike him, he's never really shown any emotions, and definitely not in front of me; not like this. He's a whole different person at the moment. I guess I feel like I owe it to him to hear him out, considering he's letting himself be vulnerable in front of another human being. He takes so long to get the words out but when he finally does, he says.

"I know what happened, the other night." He looks down at his hands and rubs his knuckles. I follow his gaze and see his hands are all busted up and have dried bloodied scabs all over them.

"What do you mean you know what happened?" My breath seizes in my throat.

"I saw your clothes, in the bathroom. You left them on the floor Jo."

"Oh. I, that…was just..." I stammer over my words. I don't know how much he found out but the way he looks at me makes me feel like he's thinking something different than what actually happened. His expression is resentful but his eyes are wet and full of sympathy.

"Nate, what happened to your hand?" I finally ask him. Trying to deflect the conversation away from myself, but also curious about what actually happened to his hands. His head hangs low on his shoulders, his gaze focused on his fingers that are now balled into a fist and he clears his throat before he looks up at me.

"Jeff happened."

"Jeff? What happened? Nate, please tell me." I search his face for answers but he doesn't say anything until I step towards him to get his attention. He seems to be off in his head again as he stares blankly past me. "Nate." I say louder. He looks toward me and I see there's no light left in his eyes. No matter how hateful I have seen him get before everything went to complete hell, he always had this glimmer, this brightness to him, like he was clinging onto the last shred of hope he had. But all of that seems to have been stripped tonight. He doesn't seem himself. I feel sad for him. Not out of pity, but something seems to be bothering him so much that he can't bring himself to look me in the eye. Maybe it is just the alcohol, I've seen how it changes people and it's never usually a good change. Given that he doesn't drink I'm sure it's making him not feel very much like himself either, in more ways than one, I'm sure.

21
Josephine

Nate." I say his name again to try and get his full attention and his eyes shoot directly to mine, letting me know he's finally back from wherever his thoughts had taken him.

"Did he hurt you again? What did he do?" He successfully asks even as the pain accentuates his question. The look in his eyes plead with me to tell the truth and I know that he's aware of what his father is capable of, but I can't blame him for not wanting to hear about it.

"Nate look, I don't think this is the best conversation to have right now, given the fact tha..." I think better than to finish my thought out loud. Pointing out how inebriated he is currently doesn't seem like the best idea so I take in a deep breath to give myself a second to gather my thoughts. "Look, why don't you take a hot shower, the waters already running upstairs and you could most likely use some real sleep. It will help." I try to convince him to just leave this conversation where it is and forget it ever happened. He runs his hands roughly through his hair and grips at the ends out of frustration I assume because I'm deliberating trying not to tell him about the other night.

"Look, I know you probably don't feel like talking to me about this but I think I have a right to know what happened, given the fact that this is because I found the clothes you left on the bathroom floor the other day." He holds his busted and bruised hand up towards me and tries to hold it steady, but it just doesn't stop shaking. I can see the blood starting to bubble in little droplets from under the scabs that speckle his knuckles and they start to turn pale from him keeping his hand balled into such a tight fist. He's angry and acting like it's my fault he got into another argument with his father. I guess maybe in a way it is.

"Nate look, I don't want to start anything, I just want to go to bed, it's really late." My voice pleads with him to just let all of this go. It's over and done with and rehashing it with him won't make a damn bit of difference.

"Yeah alright, fine. But next time you decide to ignore what I say, you're going to have to deal with Jeff yourself. I'm tired of his shit and ending up in a bloody brawl with the asshole is not my idea of fun anymore! I won't be like him Jo!" His voice breaks at the end as he slams his fist on the kitchen table, sending the empty glasses scattering across the surface and they shatter as they roll off and hit the floor. We both stand there, semi hovering over the broken glasses, and I see Nate's body tremble as he comes down from the adrenaline rush and mumbles something under his breath. Silence overtakes the emptiness we both feel right now and I'm ashamed that any of this ever had to happen. The misery I'm causing to everyone around me is bullshit and I don't deserve any amount of their sympathy. Especially Nate's, given the fact that he's only this way because of me and my mom. We never should have appeared in their life, because if we didn't, he wouldn't have to be going through all of this right now. It seems lately when someone gets close enough to me, they end up getting hurt. That must be a record for one night. Even for me.

I bend over and try to get him to look up at me. I'm no longer concerned about him knowing what happened with Jeff the other night, he knows what kind of person he is, and he's begged me to tell him, so I do.

"Nate...I'm so sorry; you shouldn't have to fight my battles for me, okay? I already got what was coming to me from the second I decided not to come home the other night. You even warned me and I didn't listen. "So, if you really want to know…" I stand up and back a couple of feet away. My voice was so low when I said those last words, but he heard me and he looks up as I point to the bruises on my face.

"He did this." My eyes fill with tears as I lift up the side of my shirt, exposing my torso just enough for him to see the purple and yellow patchwork that climb up and around my rib cage, showing off the broken blood vessels that slither up my tender white skin. His eyes frantically buzz around as he looks along my torso before settling back on my face, the look in his eyes is unreadable. I can't tell if he's more shocked that I showed him what Jeff had done to me, or the fact that his dad actually did something horrible enough to leave this kind of evidence behind. *Has*

Jeff ever done this to him? "He…did that to you?" The quiver in Nate's throat sends a wave of grief through my heart. His eyes are searching around as he seems to be gathering what happened. By the way his body slumps and his shoulders cave in a little he knows it's true, but I still confirm it to him anyway.

"Yes." I pull my shirt back down. I'm actually kind of relieved that Nate now saw what his father is capable of. That he's seen it with his own eyes. That I didn't just make it up, or make what happened seem worse than it actually was. The evidence is all over my body. I didn't think he would even care, not this much, and no way did I ever think he would go after his own dad for putting his hands on me. But by his reaction right now it seems that I was completely wrong. I hear him take in a shallow breath as he stands stock straight and squares his shoulders.

"Well don't worry. Jeff got what was coming to him." Nate's entire demeanor has changed from him being curious and agitated to downright hateful when he said his dads' name.

"Nate..." I say just as he starts to walk past me out of the kitchen. He stops to listen but doesn't look at me. Instead, he hangs his head low, his gaze towards his dirty un-laced boots.

"Thank you." I tell him. "Thanks for sticking up for me." He subtly nods his head and continues to walk past me and up the stairs to his room, abruptly ending the conversation. I stand in the brightly lit kitchen. Contemplating what just took place in the last ten minutes. I breathe in a sigh of relief and walk over to the sink to get the dust-pan and broom to clean up the broken glass. I wouldn't want to give Jeff another reason to lose his temper on either one of us again. I clearly did not expect to run into anyone tonight and never in my mind did I think that kind of conversation would ever happen between the two of us. I actually feel better with Nate being aware of what Jeff did. Selfishly I'm really glad he stood up for me. Maybe Jeff will leave me the hell alone now. I may not know exactly what went on between the two of them but seeing the way Nate's hand looked, tells me I might be better off not knowing.

As clear as it was that my step-brother was drinking, he still had a calm and caring disposition. Even when Jeff isn't drinking, he's still an asshole and Nate is nothing like his father, he proved that to me tonight and I feel that much more of a horrible person for thinking he was turning out to be like his father in the first place. I don't know how, but I hope one day I can make it up to him for everything he's done for me.

I run into my room and grab my phone off my desk after I finish sweeping the glass off the floor. I can hear Nate's boots above me shuffle across his bedroom floor. A loud thud lets me know he's plopped himself onto his bed, followed by the sounds of his boots being chucked across the room. I listen for another minute; out of habit, I guess. I'm sure the amount of alcohol he seems to have consumed tonight will make him sleep like the dead. And after that exhausting exchange that we had, I know I will too. The hot water helps relieve some of the tension in my shoulders. I'm still really sore, but at least I can wash the sand out of my hair properly and with both hands this time. I step out of the hot steam and into the cold air of the badly heated bathroom and I catch a glimpse of myself in the mirror. I don't look away when I see myself this time. The bruises that are painted across my torso don't make me want to tear up and silently cry myself to sleep anymore. I have a newfound strength that came from telling Nate what happened. Knowing he's looking out for me is comforting and I'm grateful that he’s around.

22
Hunter

The bitter and unwelcome emptiness surrounds me as soon as Jo walks out of sight. Her heated presence was comforting and now that she's gone the night has grown considerably bleak.

I decide to go back to the party to get my car and hopefully find Kyle in a somewhat coherent state. I've sobered up significantly myself the last couple of hours I have been aimlessly wondering around town after taking Jo home. The crisp night air fills my lungs and the thoughts of her swarm my head as I make my way back towards the beach.

The party has died down and stragglers are starting to take up in random cars to catch some sleep until morning. *No surprise there.* If I were still feeling the effects of the whiskey I knocked back earlier tonight, I might have considered sleeping in my car for a few hours myself; I wouldn't risk another wreck. My car is the only thing I have left that is mine and being a reckless idiot won't do me any good. I'd like to live long enough to get to know Josephine. I have a feeling that she's worth sticking around for.

The mostly populated area of the beach is around the now fading bonfire. Music still plays in the background and there are always those last few deeply wasted girls that just never give up being obnoxiously loud and dancing around while they're screaming cuss words at absolutely no one. I make my way over to the fire. I don't expect to see Cam, since I'm pretty sure I broke his nose, he should have gone to the hospital, but I scan the area anyway to make sure I can avoid him if he's still around. I stand near the fire trying to warm myself while I wait for Kyle to reappear. I was his ride home so I can't imagine he would leave without at least texting me. Just then I hear a bunch of screaming and splashing of the water. About a dozen half-naked people are running out of the ocean again and up onto the sand. It's nowhere near warm enough to be swimming in, it has to be below freezing still. They clearly can't handle their alcohol, or they are just that stupid they would willingly swim in ice-cold body of water; without a logical thought being present in their mind. I'm glad I am not one of those morons who think everything is a great idea when alcohol is coursing through my body otherwise, I would be in quite a lot of trouble on a regular basis. Well… a different kind of trouble I should say.

Out of all the people I assumed would be doing such a dumb ass stunt, Kyle didn't come to mind. But I see his stupid ass being the last one to get out of the water and come running up to me practically blue and shivering so badly that he can't wipe the stupid grin off of his face.

"Yo Hunter, where the hell did you piss off to earlier?" He stutters as he asks through gritted and chattering teeth.

"Nowhere. What the hell are you doing?" I ask him, pointing behind him.

"Just living in the moment, you know. Although I didn't realize how cold that water was until I was already waist-deep. I thought I'm way drunker than you think." He rolls his eyes and looks up for a second, a confused look on his face like he's trying to make sure that what he just said makes sense; but it's quickly lost on him and he starts shaking his head like a wet dog would flick off the dampness. *Yeah, you're definitely wasted alright!*

"Hey by the way, why don't you try it?" He says as he punches me in the shoulder. "It's fucking liberating!" He yells as he jumps up and down, I'm assuming to get the blood flowing back into his limbs. He's got to be fucking freezing. What a moron. He's more wasted than I thought.

"Yeah, I'm good man. I'll take your word for it." I slap his shoulder and feel his icy skin. It's a shock to him and he screams out as my hand makes contact with his bare shoulder.

"You ready to get out of here? I need to get home." I tell him.

"Yeah man, just let me find my clothes." Kyle runs over to the bonfire and grabs his shoes and clothes that are sitting in a pile next to it. While I wait for him, I light a cigarette and breathe in the sweet, sweet nicotine and it has my head buzzing within seconds. Kyle runs up to me half-dressed. He starts talking about the fight from earlier as he pulls his shirt over his head, still shivering from the lack of blood flow to his face. Kyle's my best friend but he sure as hell can be thick sometimes. "So…Cam's pissed." He eases into this territory knowing any talk of

Cam could set me off. Especially after witnessing me in a rage and mauling his face with my bare hands only a few hours ago.

"And why do I give a shit?" I walk to my car and take my keys out of my pocket to unlock the doors. He stops with his hand on the door, not making a move to get in yet. I look up, noticing him in my peripherals standing there peering over the hood at me.

"What?" I shout, but just stares at me another minute before saying anything.

"I heard Cam talking after you left. He was talking about that girl you took off with. He said he was pissed off that she left with you more than he was about you breaking his nose."

"Yeah well, he shouldn't have been such a dick and I wouldn't have had to break it in the first place." I state matter of fact.

"Who was she anyway?" He asks and redirects the conversation to a subject I don't want to discuss at the moment. I don't know much about Jo yet, and I want to keep her to myself for as long as possible. She isn't the type to hang around all these ass-hats; nor should she have to. I kind of wish she never came here tonight. Most of the people that come to these parties are not ones she would have anything in common with; then again, I'm lucky she showed up at all, otherwise I wouldn't have run into her tonight.

"She's just a girl." I don't elaborate any further and get into my car; letting him know I'm done with this conversation and I want to leave.

I pull up to Kyle's house ten minutes later and he hauls ass out of my car, sprinting toward his front door. He yells back.

"See you later mate." The dumb ass was freezing from his earlier display of stupidity so he blasted the heat in my car and now I am sweating so much that I'm starting to stick to the leather seats. I turn the heat off and open my window, welcoming the cool blast of air as I drive towards home.

Not bothering to turn a light on as I enter the house, I stumble up the stairs while I search for the key to my door. I quietly shut it behind me and fall backward on my bed without bothering to take my boots off. It's been a hell of a night. Turns out I had a better time going to the party than I originally thought I would. Of course, that's all thanks to her being there. I slowly start to drift off to sleep when I feel my phone vibrate against my leg. I let out a groan with my eyes still closed and I reach into my pocket to pull my phone out. I focus my eyes and see a message from an unknown number.

: Goodnight Hunter

I instantly know who it's from. I was hoping she would text me, but I didn't expect it to be tonight. I'm suddenly not very interested in sleeping just yet but it is late, so I simply text her back.

Hunter: Goodnight Josephine :)

23
Hunter

I don't expect Jo to respond. It was after four in the morning when I walked through my front door; but I stare at my phone a while longer than I should, hoping for another message to come through until I finally fall asleep.

MY ALARM SHREIKS and I immediately turn over to slam my fist over top of it. *I really need to get another alarm that doesn't sound like sirens going off in my head!* I groan and shove my face further into my pillow as I stretch. A yawn escapes my tired chest but I roll over and stretch last nights' stiffness away. Snatching my phone from the side of the bed, I stumble across my room and into the bathroom to shower when I get a text message. I'm quick to unlock my phone, but notice that it's not from Jo, it's from Kyle.

Kyle: need your help pick me up at my house in 30

Hunter: alright

I press send and chuck my phone across the room and it lands on my bed just as another text comes through. Reaching for it and ready to tell Kyle to hold his ass for a damn minute, I see her name pop up on the screen. *Josephine.* So, I open it and read it like a giddy child.

Josephine: meet me at the beach for coffee? My treat.

Son of a bitch! Why did I agree to whatever Kyle has planned? I should have ignored his ass
Hunter: see you in 15

Josephine: okay

I take a quick shower and throw a set of clean clothes on my still damp body while I dash around my room looking for my car keys. I remember unlocking my bedroom door last night but have no idea where my keys landed. I search my pants, my desk, and the bathroom. I eventually find them tucked beside the mattress and the nightstand. Sliding one arm through my shirt sleeve and snagging my jacket off of my bed, I scramble to lock my bedroom door. With one boot on as I descend the stairs, I end up stumbling on the last step as I kick the other on and don't bother to tie them as I jog out to my car so I can text Kyle to tell him that I won't be able to make it until later. *He'll understand.*

Hunter: sorry man can't make it catch up with you later

After hitting send and throwing my phone on the front passenger seat I pull out of the driveway without looking and almost back into a car passing by. *SHIT!*

Exactly nine minutes later I pull into the lot closest to the beach and scan the area for Jo. I finally spot her sitting on the fallen tree, that came down during last month's storm. Her long chestnut hair is blowing behind her in the misty breeze. She's the only one out here not bundled up from head to toe. Everyone else walking on the beach is dressed as if it's still winter. It is colder than yesterday, but the sun is out so it's at least tolerable.

I sit in my car a minute longer to take in the sight of her sitting there; unaware of my presence before getting out and walking towards her. Taking in a deep breath I finally grow a set and call to her. "Jo." She turns her head toward me and a faint smile stretches across her lips, lighting up her face like the first day of Spring. All I can do is stare at her and take in the sight of her full pouty lips, her rosy cheeks, and her beautiful fair skin.

The wind whips her hair around her head, covering her soft features for a moment before she smooths her hair behind her ears and stands up. "Hey." She says, opening up the conversation before it gets any weirder,

I'm sure. I'm not sure how long I have been standing here looking at her. I just needed to take her in for a minute. I think I do that too much, but I can't help it, her beauty stuns me every time I see her. Her piercing gray-green eyes are so vibrant that I could swear someone discovered some kind of rare precious stones buried deep within the earth, ground them into a fine powder, mixed them with the purest water they could find, and painted them on her gorgeous face.

"Hey." I repeat her words since my brain can't seem to think of a coherent response of my own.

"So…how about that coffee? I'm freezing." She holds her hands around her arms and squeezes herself tightly.

"Yeah…good idea." I motion for her to walk around the fallen tree ahead of me and let her lead the way.

We start walking towards Main Street where all the shops are located. As I walk next to her, I keep my hands in my pockets because right now I'm tempted to just put my arms around her to help warm her delicate body. Again, I don't want to be too forward as I'm sure she wouldn't appreciate being touched by someone she hardly knows. But I have to admit I would love to be able to feel her close to me again. I keep going back to the night she fell asleep next to me on my bed and her body being mere inches away felt amazing. I can't imagine how it would feel to actually be able to hold her and fall asleep with her in my arms every single night.

I think I must have been in my own head again for far too long since we're now standing outside the diner. Jo walks silently up the path to the door and holds it open for me. I should have been paying more attention because holding the door for her would have been a good move on my part. She moves a few feet inside and then stands in the doorway to scan the small diner before walking towards a booth in the far corner. It's tucked away, mostly out of view and I'm assuming that's why she chose it. She strikes me as the type of girl that likes her space to herself. I follow behind as she slides in next to the window and I move into the seat across from her. She doesn't take off the thin jacket she's wearing instead, she slides the zipper on it up even further towards her neck and tucks her hands into her sleeves, but the pink color on the tip of her nose makes her look chilled to the bone.

"Are you still cold?" I ask her. "Yeah…a little." She quietly shrugs her shoulders.

I look around for a waitress and spot a woman behind the counter talking to the cook through the little window that's between them. She turns around so I wave to get her attention. The first thing I notice when she comes over is her bright red lips. Strangely enough, it seems to suit her.

"What can I get for you two?" She says as she pulls out of little pad of paper and pen from her apron. Before I can tell her what we would like she quickly speaks again.

"Hey honey, how are you today?" I look up to see her staring at Jo.

"I'm fine thanks, just a bit cold." Jo answers her while she fiddles with the napkin the waitress placed in front of her.

"Well, that's good. How about I get you some nice fresh hot cocoa? I'll be right back." She says and scurries off behind the counter. I notice the exchange of familiarity between the two of them and it makes me wonder if Jo comes here often. She doesn't say anything about her, she just stares out the window for a minute after the woman walks away to get our drinks.

"So, do you come here a lot? That lady seems to like you."

"No. I just came in here the other day. Mrs. Lawrence told me they had good food here."

"Can I ask who Mrs. Lawrence is?"

"Oh. Yeah. She's the owner of the bookshop I work at around the corner."

"Do you like working there?" I'm genuinely curious about anything she's willing to tell me.

"Yes. When I don't have school or just don't want to be home, I go there to read a lot." Jo looks away and grabs a menu from behind the ketchup stand and hands one of them to me.

"Thanks." I take the menu from her just before the waitress comes back with our drinks and two slices of cherry pie and sets them down in front of us.

"Now these are on the house. But if you would like anything else just let me know." She walks away before we can object to the free dessert. Not that I was planning on it.

"Well, that's awfully nice of her. I've never gotten free pie before." My stupid childlike voice bursts out of me when I say the word pie and Jo laughs a little under her breath.

"Yeah, she's really nice." When I look down at my drink, I notice that the waitress has sprinkled cinnamon on top of the whipped cream that is piled high, so I when glance at Jo, I see that she's already got the mug up to her face and she's frantically sipping the hot liquid before it even had the chance to have cooled down. She's got her tiny fingers wrapped fully around the mug. *The warmth probably feels nice on her chilled hands.*

We sit in comfortable silence as we eat our pie and sip from our mugs of cocoa, feeling it warm us a little more as we gulp it down. Jo hardly touches her pie but is on her second cup of cocoa before I even finish my first.

"So, how is it that you ended up at that party last night?" Jo surprises me by bringing up what I assumed would be a sore subject for her. She was pretty upset when I walked her home.

"Kyle." I say before finishing the last of my drink.

"Who's Kyle?" She asks curiously.

"He's my best mate. He dragged me there last night kicking and screaming." I'm exaggerating of course, but inside I was cursing the heavens.

"Oh. Sounds like you didn't even want to be there I take it?"

"No, I didn't. But I'm glad I let him talk to me into going."

"Why?" Jo asks as she sips from the side of her cup.

"Because if he didn't, I wouldn't have seen you again." When it registers to her what I said, a small grin forms on her lips, making her mouth look absolutely edible. She looks away to try and hide the smirk but the sparkle in her eyes tells me she likes what she heard.

"I'm glad you were there too. I'm sorry you got in a fight because of me though. That guy..."

"No. Jo, look don't be sorry, it wasn't your fault. Cam is an asshole, he deserved what he got. And if I had to take a few hits to be the one to do it then it was well worth it." The fire in my gut is back when I have to think about that asshole. He sure knows how to ruin a guys' day.

"Well, it doesn't look like he got in any good hits at least. You can hardly tell you were in a fight." Jo reaches toward me and gently brushes her fingers across my cheek where Cam's fist connected with my face last night. Her hand lightly glides over my cheek and down across my jaw. When she looks up, I lock eyes with her for what seems the twentieth time today and after a moment she blinks and clears her throat before pulling her hand away at the same time I reach up for it to hopefully feel her soft warm touch for just a little longer. "I'm sorry, I didn't mean to..." Just as I go to tell Jo something, the waitress comes over and asks if we want a refill on our hot cocoa again or if we would like anything else.

"No thank you." Jo answers. "I'm all good here thanks." I reach for my wallet as I ask for the check but the waitress pats my hand as I take out a few bills.

"No, no dear, remember, it's on the house." She repeats.

I tip my head thanking her, and before she walks away; she leans down toward my ear and whispers. "Take care of that little Miss, you hear?" I smile at her words. She must really care about Jo, and that makes me come to appreciate her.

"I will Ma'am." I whisper back.

24
Josephine

So, what did Suzie say to you anyway?" I urge as Hunter holds open the door for me while we exit the diner. The wind has picked up from earlier, sending a chilled blast of wind whirling around my head and sending my hair into a frenzied mess. Early spring can sometimes feel like winter here. It likes to linger so long that I almost forget what warm weather feels like. I clutch my jacket closed and hastily try to zip it the rest of the way as Hunter walks beside me down the front steps of the diner. I almost trip on the last step from not looking where I was going but I catch myself in time that I don't think Hunter even noticed.

"She was just reassuring me about the check is all." Hunter speaks casually as if it wasn't a big deal, so I let it go and cautiously continue walking towards the road. No need to embarrass myself by letting my uncoordinated feet get the best of me again.

HUNTER AND I slowly fell into this kind of rhythm and found ourselves in the upper-class part of town after walking in a comfortable silence for a while. The neighborhood feels rich and crowded because the houses here are four times the size of mine. It's similar to where Hunter lives yet this one doesn't seem as…friendly, I guess? His street seems, cleaner, almost like it's programmed to be perfect. The houses here look expensive just like his, but in a creepy old vintage kind of way. They're large and a lot of them are encased with old dead vines growing up the sides. The still bare trees and the brown lawns make it look abandon more than anything and the fact that there are no cars parked in the street and no kids playing in the yards, it makes it eerie to walk Through; like time had just stopped and everyone had vanished into thin air.

"Um, I don't really know my way around this area. Do you?" I interrupt the quiet as I stop in the middle of the street. There is absolutely no one driving around, so I don't worry about getting hit by a car that could come down the road at any minute. He looks around for a second and his eyes hint at some kind of recognition.

"Yeah…actually, I do. My best mate lives around this neighborhood just a few blocks away." He lifts his hand and gestures down toward the end of the street while removing his beanie with the other and nervously runs his hand through his dark locks. He looks up and turns around rather hastily, almost as if he's in a panic. "Jo, look we should get back to my car before you freeze. I'm sorry I didn't realize how far we were from the beach. I should have been paying attention."

"Well, we have been walking a while, and you're not exactly dressed for this weather either. Do you think your mate would give us a ride back to your car since he only lives a few blocks away?" I say "Mate" in a teasing manner, since I have never used the word before in my life, it sounds strange coming out of my mouth, but it's so natural and mature when Hunter says it. I stop my thoughts right there before they can go any further. I still hardly know Hunter, but I can't help but find him attractive, he is extremely good-looking, and he's one of the kindest people that I have had any kind of contact with in the last few years.

"No, it's fine. I'm good walking back if you are." Hunter's face is red and he has on a barely thick enough jacket to possibly be warm enough. I can even see our breath as it mixes with the cold air around us. The temperature feels like it has dropped ten degrees since we met up this morning.

"Actually, I'm kind of frozen. Could we maybe, warm up a little and then go back to your car? Do you think Kyle would mind?" I ask reluctantly, but I am freezing and I can hardly feel my toes anymore. Rubbing my hands together I blow warm air into them as I wait for Hunter to reply. He looks around and to my relief, he finally says "Sure." Not that I mind walking back; I'm just so cold and I would love to be someplace warm for a few minutes before our frigid walk back to his car. After walking for another few minutes Hunter stops in front of an old Victorian-style house. It's white with black trim and dark charcoal shutters. The three-story house comes with a colossal-sized porch that stretches out in front of us along the entire front of the house. There area set of double doors in the middle, that I'm sure are leading into a grand entry hall and it seems like it reaches high up into the gray clouds above our heads. If my face weren't so frozen from the cold, I'm sure my mouth would drop to the ground from the sight.

Hunter steps in front of me and carefully maneuvers his gaze the length of my body. Kind of like when a dad would analyze his daughters' outfit before she leaves the house. It feels a little strange and I'm not sure why all of a sudden, I feel so exposed. Hunter's icy fingers softly graze my jaw-line, sending shivers right through me and when I meet his eyes, there's a serious change in his expression.

"Jo, can you wait here for a minute?" He pleads. I lightly nod my head without breaking eye contact, so he drops his hand from my face and turns toward the front steps of the house, his long muscular legs letting him quickly ascend the steps two at a time without missing a beat. *If that were me, I would have fallen flat on my face.*

Hunter rings the bell, then quickly wraps his knuckles against the door three times before impatiently ticking his fingers against it as he waits for someone to answer. The door opens and Hunter hastily steps in front of the person before I can see who it is. Their hushed conversation is low, so no discernable words reach my ears and then Hunter abruptly stumbles back a few steps. He easily catches himself, stepping forward towards the other person, but now that someone is standing in full view on the porch. He looks at me and then back at Hunter with a growing snarky grin.

"So, she's the reason you blew me off this morning huh?" This guy sounds more amused than pissed so, I'm slightly relieved by it.

"Look Kyle can you just listen for a fucking minute?" I can hear the agitation in Hunter's voice as he grumbles at Kyle, and I notice the tension growing in his body the longer this guy stares at me. Then I realize he just called him Kyle. This must be his mate. *So why the hell would he be acting so defensive if this is his best friend?*

I stand in front of the house as they start arguing again. Their voices low so I can't hear much. The street is quiet around us though so a few words slip out louder than were intended I'm sure, but they catch my attention. Mainly because the name 'Cam' was one of those words that came out of Kyle's mouth.

I'm not interested in getting into the middle of any more drama so, I call out to Hunter that I'm just going to leave. He peers down at me then looks back at Kyle, he just nods so Hunter takes off down the steps to me. Whatever that was, it was the strangest exchange between best friends that I've ever witnessed. It seemed more like sports rivals getting ready to compete against each other in a big playoff game or something.

"Don't go." Hunter's voice comes out calm, not at all like the way he sounded just a minute ago. "Kyle said he'd drive us back to my car after you warm up. If you still want to that is." His eyes look back and forth between mine. His voice is calm, but the intensity in his stare says something else entirely.

"Look, I didn't mean to cause whatever that was between you two, but I should just get home, it's getting late." I rub my hands over my shoulders and squeeze my numb fingers tightly around my arms.

"Alright, just a quick cup of cocoa and then I'll take you home? I wouldn't be able to live with myself if you froze to death because of my stupidity and lack of direction." He grins slightly, just barely showing his teeth. Those piercing, hardened green eyes are willing me to stay. So, I can't help myself when I concede.

"Alright. One cup. But only because I can't feel my fingers anymore." I grin.

"Here." He takes my hands, covering them with his and lifts them to his mouth before blowing warm air through his hands to reach mine. I can feel my fingers start to tingle after a few seconds as the blood starts to flow back into my fingertips. His eyes are closed while breathing on our hands and I can't help but stare at him while he's unaware I'm doing it.

"There." He says and rubs his hands once more over mine just as he looks up and catches me ogling him. He keeps hold of one of my hands as he starts to walk toward the steps of Kyle's house. I follow behind, noticing a slight increase in his grip as we get closer to the front door. Kyle pops his head around the extremely heavy looking cherry colored door and holds it open for us, smirking as we pass him and shuts it tight as we step into the entryway and out of the cold.

25
Hunter

My grip tightens ever so gently around Jo's hand as we enter the house. *I should have never brought her here today.* Had I known Kyle was going to be entertaining the idea of dealing with what I should have helped him take care of this morning; I would have just done it then, instead of having the possibility of Jo getting dragged into the middle of it now. I couldn't have known we would possibly be here today. I almost wish I had never left my bed this morning. *Almost.*

I feel Jo's hesitation as we round the doorway into the living room. *She's for sure picked up on the tension.* I hold her hand firmly and give it a small reassuring squeeze even though I don't want to be here myself at the moment. I walk around the large sofa and sit on the end closest to the doorway pulling Jo to sit next to me and this time she doesn't hesitate. Kyle sits across from us on the oversized leather chair and glances down at our hands as he relaxes into the cushions, but I don't let my grasp on her loosen as we both try to relax into each other. My grip slightly tightens while I gently tug her hand to rest between us.

Kyle's watchful glare shifts up towards Jo, and I immediately tense, curious as to what will come out of that enormous trap of his. I'm only still getting to know her, and I don't want anything getting in the way.

"So, Jo. Hunter said you go to our school. How come I haven't seen you around before?" Jo's body further nudges up against my side, our elbows and thighs touching as she replies to the question.

"Oh, well, I'm a junior. I'm guessing you're a senior like Hunter, so we wouldn't have any classes together." She replies casually. Sounding comfortable even.

"Right. Do you live around here?" He asks.

"No, I live on the other side of town, near Pinewoods Park."

"Oh. Well, I don't know the area much, but I'm sure it's nice."

"Yeah." Jo gives an awkward half-laugh and agrees with him. *I hope she doesn't feel embarrassed to say where she lives, given the fact that we're in the wealthiest part of town in probably the biggest house in the neighborhood.*

Kyle's phone rings, breaking the awkward silence, so he jumps up from the leather chair beside us to pull it out of his front pocket. His expression when he stares down at the screen doesn't put me at ease, but he motions for us to excuse him.

"I have to take this, be right back." He says nervously and takes off toward the kitchen at a too hurried pace, so I turn to Jo.

"I'm going to go make you that cup of hot cocoa. Be right back." She nods her head and I let go of her hand and place it gently on the cushion next to her and head down the hall towards the kitchen. I hear Kyle trying to talk quietly on the other side of the door, so I push it open and walk in. He turns around to see me standing in the doorway with the look of *'Oh shit'* plastered on his face.

"Yeah, I'll see you in 20 then." Kyle holds his hand up in surrender while he places his phone back in his pocket with the other.

"Look man, you should probably leave if you don't want anyone eyeing your girl. Cam is…." He doesn't get to finish his sentence before I'm in his face. The mere mention of that prick's name, and the vision of his hands all over Jo at the bonfire make me fucking livid!

"WHY? What the hell man?" I want to vociferate every profanity at my best friend right now, tell him how fucking stupid it was to agree to this bullshit, but I know it won't help. It will only make matters worse. Even more, I don't want to scare Jo off. She's seen plenty of my violent temper already. I don't want her thinking that's all I'm about. "Kyle, why are you having Cam come here, you know your parents would kill you if they found out you had that addict in their house while they're away."

"Look, I have it under control alright. I just thought I'd warn you before he got here, he wouldn't take no for an answer. And If I recall, I asked for your help multiple times with this, and if you had just gotten it done at the party, he wouldn't be on his way now, about to eye your girl again!"

Kyle's pissed, and rightly so because he does have a point. I promised I would help him with this after what he's done for me in the last couple of weeks. He's on probation for 6 months because of me. It's the least I could do. "Yeah, you're right. I owe you one man. I'll deal with Cam.

But I don't want him anywhere near Jo, so can I borrow your car to get her out of here, and then we can take care of…." Kyle's face freezes as he stares wide-eyed in front of me. I turn around mid-sentence and see Jo standing in the doorway. *Shit, how much did she hear?*

"Hey, baby." I unconsciously use the pet name, even though I have not a clue where she and I stand just yet. Given how new all…whatever this is between us. It surprises me that those words even came out of my mouth and when I turn toward Kyle, he's got a confused look on his face like he has no idea who I am right now. I don't blame him. I've never acted this way with any girl before, it's just not me. "Kyle's going to lend me his car to take you home." I quickly say to distract from the previous conversation that she might have, or might not have heard and walk over to her, reaching for her hand as I glance back at Kyle, warning him to keep his mouth shut. I know he will. He always has my back. I feel a bit guilty for being deceitful around Jo, but once this business with Cam is over, I can relax and not have to worry about bringing her into my bullshit anymore.

26
Hunter

"Yo Hunter…think you might need the keys? Or do you plan on hot wiring my car?" Kyle takes his keys out of his pocket and tosses them to me from the other side of the kitchen.

"Thanks." I say and I place my other hand on the small of Jo's back to guide her through the kitchen and out the front door.

I walk her to the passenger side of the car as soon as we step off the porch and open the door for her. As I shut it and walk to the driver's side, I hear a loud grumble coming from down the street. The sound of an obnoxious and overbearingly loud muffler; belonging to a car that I know all too well. *This is not what I need right now!* I turn my head toward the street just in time to see none other than the asshole from the other night getting out of his car. Cam walks across the street and up the pathway as the arrogance radiates off of him so much, that I feel the need to go over and punch it out of him again. I regret not leaving sooner. Kyle should have warned me that he was going to be here today.

I decide against confronting Cam again, just as he enters the front door. He must not have seen us in the driveway. Luckily Kyle's mom is obsessed with rose bushes and they are abundant in the front yard, so much so, that we are shielded from Cam's view. It's just as much my fault as it is Kyle's for this asshole being here so, I'm kicking myself for not dealing with it this morning when he asked for my help to finally be done with this rubbish once and for all.

"What was all that about in there?" I hear Jo ask as I sit down in the driver's seat and shut my door.

"What?" I heard what she said. I just want to buy myself a couple of extra seconds to figure out what to tell her.

"Why were you acting so strange? I thought you and Kyle were best friends. You were acting like he was trying to set you up for murder or something."

"Oh. Yeah, it's nothing you should worry about. Just some things we need to sort out later is all." I start the car and the engine roars to life. I forgot he had some work done on it recently and it has made it about five times as loud when you start it now. *Fucking awesome, just what I need, to draw more attention to us being here.* I quickly put the car in reverse and pull out of the driveway. Just as I shift into drive, I see Cam rushing out of Kyle's front door, his eyes locked onto us as I pull away.

We're both silent the entire way back to the beach. The air between us is thick and I can see how Jo has again become guarded; the tension in how she's holding herself makes it obvious. I should say something, anything to make her relax and forget what happened at Kyle's, but I keep my mouth shut like the fool that I am; not having a clue what to tell her. To be honest, I'm hoping I never have to tell her about any of this.

I pull up beside my car, parked where I left it this morning, and turn off the engine. The rumbling abruptly comes to a halt, making the silence all that more deafening inside the small space of the front seat. I lean back slightly and retrieve my keys from my pocket and turn towards Jo. She's sitting a few inches away and starts to reach for the door handle so I grab her other hand and gently pull her back to get her attention.

"Here." I open her palm and place my car keys in her hand, noticing her fingers feel like ice again. It makes me want to selfishly hold her close and warm her with my touch. We did leave Kyle's house in a hurry before she even had the chance to properly warm up. And I never did make her that cocoa I promised. *I am such an ass.* "I have to go back to Kyle's and take care of some things. Take my car and go to your house. I'll come to see you after alright?" I assure her. I feel like shit having to do this, but I don't see how I can keep her out of this any other way right now. She looks at me with wide, glassy eyes but just says okay and gets out much faster than I expected. I watch her get in my car and slowly pull away, leaving me here trapped in my own guilt.

I get back to Kyle's house and sit in his driveway for longer than I should. I don't see Cam's car, so I assume he left already. Kyle's going to be pissed if this shit doesn't get sorted, and soon. I couldn't risk Jo being around for the kind of mess that my past keeps bringing up, it's bad enough I got my best friend involved. I finally get the balls to get out of the car and swallow my pride as I walk up to the door. I knock a few times and wait. Then ring the doorbell and wait some more. *Where the hell would he go without his car?* I pull out my phone to call Kyle's cell, when the door starts to creak open. I push it open but it gets caught up, so I look down and see a bloody mess on the floor. I carefully push the door open enough to slide through and when I do I realize that it's Kyle lying at my feet. I crouch down beside him, not a fucking clue what happened, and immediately dial 911.

"Kyle, ay mate look, stay with me man come on. I'm gonna get help!" The call clicks over to a person and I hear someone ask "what's your emergency?"

"Yeah, look, my friend, he's bleeding badly, he needs help. Address is 22475 Willow Brook Lane." I drop the phone to the floor after enabling the speakerphone and insist to the woman on the other end that I can't find where the bleeding is coming from. She says to check his pulse and see if he's still breathing. "Yeah, yeah, he's breathing!" My hands are saturated with blood as I keep trying to look for a wound. "I need to get a…a towel or something, hold on man!" I run down the hall to the bathroom near the kitchen and snatch up as many towels as I see. He's still lying lifeless on the floor when I get back to him and as I look down, I notice the part of his face that's still visible through all the blood is pale and sweaty. He's lying on his side and it looks like it's causing him more pain the way he's all balled up, so I gently roll him onto his back. He lets out an agonizing mumble, but at least that lets me know he's still alive.

"Look is the ambulance almost here? My friend needs help, and he needs it now!" I can't tell if I'm screaming or not but my throat is rough and burning and my voice feels stuck in the back of my throat like I can't yell loud enough for them to hear me. I search Kyle's torso for wounds again now that I can get a better look and I finally come across a huge gash down his side far below his ribs. I grab the towels and press them firmly against his side to hopefully slow down the bleeding. The operator tells me that the ambulance should be here in a couple of minutes.

"They're just around the corner, okay sir?" I hear her say again.

"Yeah." I say while I press my hands firmer against the towel since the bleeding doesn't seem to be stopping. I hear sirens growing louder and louder as they approach the front of the house. Swirling lights cascade through the windows and dance around on the walls. The lights and sounds begin to fade in and out as a tall figure suddenly rushes through the front door. His mouth is moving but I can't make out what he's saying to me. The lights are messing with my head and I seem to notice wetness spilling through my fingers. I look down at my hands that are still pressed against Kyle's side and see nothing but dark red material. The once white towels are soaked through with Kyle's blood, not a spec of evidence that they use to be any other color.

Just then my hands are being moved away and someone is pulling me from where I was kneeling beside my best friend. I think they're asking me questions but I'm not hearing what any of them are. I'm far too distracted staring at Kyle's face while he lies in front of me on the floor, hoping that he opens his eyes and tells me that it's just one of his asshole pranks again. I desperately hope that it doesn't turn out to be like last time.

Again, someone close to me has been hurt because of my selfish stupidity. *When will I stop hurting people?!*

27
Josephine

I drive Hunter's car to my house and sit in the driveway for a few minutes before deciding that it's probably a bad idea to have his car parked here. If Jeff were to come home early and he sees it, I can't imagine the lecture I would get from him. Not to mention it is a really nice car and I would feel horrible if something happened to it while it was in my possession. I'm sure Jeff would retaliate for one reason or another and damage it in some way to piss me off.

I decide to go in the house and get a warmer coat from my room and change my shoes since my sneakers aren't very good at keeping my toes from turning to ice; they're still frozen solid from walking around town today.

I start the car and turn the heat on full blast before pulling out of the driveway and finally head toward Hunter's house. *I hope I can remember how to get there.*

Twenty minutes later I finally pull up to the large gate that his house hides behind. He never told me how to get past the gate, and the first time he brought me here, it was already open. I look around and find a large button on the visor above my head and push it to see if it will open the gate; lucky for me it does so, I drive up the incline of the driveway, hoping that no one is home, so I don't have to explain why a stranger is in their son's car. From the looks of it, no one seems to be here because they're no other cars in the driveway. I park in front of the double garage doors, turning the key to extinguish the soothing heat along with the sound of the engine. Hunter told me he would be over to my house as soon as he was done at Kyle's. I better text him to let him know I brought his car back to his house instead.

Jo: I thought it would be better to just drive your car back to your house

I stare at my screen for a few minutes waiting for him to reply. After a while I think about calling just to make sure he got my text. I don't need him showing up at my house, especially when I'm not there. But instead of calling I send another text because whatever he and Kyle were on edge about earlier seems important enough not to interrupt.

Jo: Hunter is everything okay?

The heat in the car has gone now and I can't sit here too much longer. It's getting darker and I don't know my way around this neighborhood all that well.

It's been over an hour after I got to Hunter's house and he still hasn't replied to my messages. I have his car so I don't think he would just blow me off. *I guess he got caught up with his mate.* The sky is now so dark, that the only light around is from the lights on the outside of the house above the door. I have to take that as my cue to start walking home. Seems weird that Hunter's parents and sister haven't even come home yet. I guess that's a good thing. They might think I'm trying to steal his car or break into their house. After all, I haven't met any of them yet so I would think the same thing if I came home and seen a strange girl just sitting around outside my house in the dark.

I leave the car keys in the center console and shut the door softly enough to not make any noise. Seems I do things like this all the time out of habit now. I'm used to being as quiet as possible so I don't get shit from Jeff. Maybe if he would stop drinking constantly, he wouldn't have a permanent headache. Or at least I'm assuming that's why he doesn't like sounds above a whisper most days. I could also be completely wrong and he just enjoys being an asshole for no reason.

I walk down the driveway and out of the gate, making sure it shuts tight before making my way home. I walk down the street, back the way I drove here so I don't get turned around and end up getting lost. I zip my jacket further up towards my chin and stuff my face inside the neck as much as I can to keep my nose from freezing off.

Since the sun has finally set, it feels like the temperature has dropped another ten degrees just since I left Hunter's house. I hate to say it but, I can't wait to get home and take a nice hot shower to bring back the feeling in my fingers again. *I'm so tired of the cold.*

FINALLY, AFTER WALKING for what felt like forever, I see the middle of the town square and Main Street. The shops are starting to close up for the night. If it were summer this place would be jammed packed with people until the early hours of the morning. Just the other day we were at the beach and there were so many others there, some were even swimming. The night was cool and it had that fresh early scent of spring in the air. Now the weather is playing games and it almost has that early feeling like winter is starting all over again. Maybe it's just because I have been outside all day with very little time at all to get warm. *Ugh, stop complaining Jo, today could have been so much worse.*

My mind wanders to Hunter and how he was so adamant about us staying at Kyle's after we got there. But when I actually agreed to stay for a while to warm up, and to that hot cocoa he offered to make me, he seemed to be on edge and ready to run out of there at any moment. I can't think too much into it, after all, I hardly know him or his friend. Whatever goes on between them is their business, not mine. I just wish he would have texted me back so I wasn't sitting in the cold all that time waiting for him. I don't need to throw myself a pity party, although I am kind of pissed at Hunter for not showing up like he said he would.

I walk past the book store and see the security lights are on. I wonder if I can pick up some extra hours this week when Mrs. Lawrence comes back; I could really use the money. After walking the shorter way home, I get to the end of my street, looking toward the house, and to my relief, Jeff's truck isn't in the driveway. Looks like he may actually keep this job longer than the last three he's had.

I head up to the front door and put my key in the lock when I hear a loud thudding and music coming from around the side of the house. I look past the porch and into the back of the house toward the garage door. It's wide open, lights are on and there's music playing from inside. *Nate's home.* To my surprise, I feel very much relieved with Nate here lately. After the exchange we had, somehow, I can't help but feel a little bit better knowing he's staying close.

28
Hunter

I can't find a goddamn parking spot in this place! It wouldn't have been an issue if I was allowed to ride in the ambulance, but as badly injured as Kyle is there just wasn't enough room for me. Still doesn't negate the fact that I should have been able to be by his side. Instead, I was forced to leave him alone with strangers as he fights for his fucking life!

I pull around to the back of the lot in Kyle's car, finally spotting a sliver-sized opening and I pump the breaks to slide into the parking spot. I'm barely able to open the door without scratching it, but I can't be bothered with something as trivial as car paint right now.

Running from the other end of the parking lot and fresh out of breath by the time I reach the emergency room doors, I hurry past a couple of people walking in and make a rather wide detour around a guy to avoid being splattered by his bloody hand that he's holding above his head. I spot the nurses' station and head directly over to talk to the woman on the phone. She's speaking so much louder than she needs to and before I get a word out, she holds a finger up to me so, I assume she wants me to keep my mouth shut until she's off the phone; but I'm impatient, so I interrupt her and start to ask her about Kyle.

"Hi, my friend Kyle Smith…he…he came in here a few minutes ago by ambulance. Can you tell me where he is or what's going on?" I'm trying to spew the words out faster than my brain can think of them. The receptionist holds up her hand again and gives me a dirty look as if I've just made her day much worse than it was thirty seconds ago. *She can't imagine how shit my day has been!*

I slap my hand on the counter out of frustration that she's making me wait and she looks at me again with a startled expression. I raise my hand and tip my head down like a wounded puppy, silently apologizing for the interruption. I don't need to get into it with her in case she decides to call security on me, so I wait until she's off the phone, and keep quiet while I stand at the counter in front of her.

"Can I help you sir?" A voice asks after a few minutes. I turn back to her after trying to see if anyone else could help me if she took too long, but there is nothing but injured and sick people taking up most of the seating across the lobby and I'm assuming all the doctors are busy behind those locked metal doors.

"Yea. My friend, Kyle Smith, can you tell me where they've taken him, or what is going on, is…is he alright? Anything you can tell me please." My voice is frantic and unsteady as I tell her why I'm here, and I feel out of breath. My eyes plead with her to tell me anything even remotely positive right now.

"Let me check, you said he came in on an ambulance, yes?"

"Yea, not too long before I got here, Ten minutes ago maybe." I impatiently tap my fingers on the surface of the counter, the seconds' tick by as I wait for her to type something into her computer.

"Alright, Kyle Smith. Yes, he's in surgery right now. Why don't you have a seat and we'll call you as soon as we know anything."

"NO!" I growl. The anger seethes from my mouth and I pound my fist down on the counter between us again. I don't mean to direct my anger at her specifically, but I just felt the need to let out the fear and frustration over not knowing what the fuck happened and if he's going to be alright. *I couldn't handle losing someone else.*

I lay my head on my interlaced fingers and rest them tensely on the counter. D*on't lose you temper in front of all of these people, I can't do it.*

"Look, Sir, you should have a seat." I hear her say after a few seconds; her words sounding uneasy. I inch my eyes up to look at her and I notice her name tag on her shirt. Bethany. I look up further and make eye contact with Bethany so I can try to apologize. She doesn't understand what I've been through today, but it's no reason to take my anger out on her.

"I'm sorry." I say, defeat in my voice and I stand up and walk away from the counter to find a hole to crawl into, while I wait to hear about Kyle. I spot a window ledge down the hall, far enough away from most of the carnage that's in the waiting room, but close enough to hear if someone were to call me. The window stretches from floor to ceiling with a bench-like seat about the height of a regular chair. I don't know if it's classified as a seat or not, but it's the only place to sit without being right next to someone bleeding or vomiting. I just need a place to sit before I fall on my face; otherwise, they'll have another patient on their hands, and I'm sure that's the last thing they need right now because it looks like they have their hands full as it is already.

I think about calling Kyle's parents but they're out of town right now. There's no sense in ringing them and making them worry until I find out exactly how he's doing. I can't very well just tell them he's in surgery and not have a clue what else to say. They would hate me even more if they found out that he got hurt because of me, so I decide to wait until I can find out more so I just lean my head against the window and feel the coolness of the night seep through the glass and onto my sweaty forehead. I need to close my eyes for a while and try to get a few minutes of peace.

"SIR. SIR? THERE are some officers here needing to speak with you. You're here for Kyle Smith, right?" I feel my shoulder being nudged as a female voice, rings through my ears. I abruptly sit up and rub at my eyes trying to focus on my surroundings. There are two officers in uniform standing in front of me and Bethany the receptionist from earlier is standing beside me with her hand on my shoulder pressing the sticky material to me, it makes me aware of how sweaty and gross I feel.

"Yes, yeah, uh, sorry, I must have fallen asleep." My voice is groggy and overused; like I swallowed a handful of gravel and it's scratching its way down my throat. *I'd kill for some water right now.*

"The officers are here about your friend. They just need to ask you a few questions."

"Yeah, no problem." Bethany starts to walk away after I stand up but I stop her before she gets out of earshot because I need to know if there's any update about Kyle. I have to clear my throat again and it gives me a few extra seconds to brace myself for what she may tell me.

"Wait, uh…Bethany, right?" I question, to get her attention again. "Is there any news about my friend yet?" I look her in the eyes and see the corners of her mouth twitch a little before trying to hide a frown. *It can't be bad news. Please, I can't take any more bad news.*

"I can't tell you much unless you're, family especially under the circumstances, but I can say he's out of critical care and stable at the moment." "Alright, can I at lease see him?"

"No, not right now, but when things settle down, I'll be sure to come to find you again." She assures me. I nod my head and turn back towards the officers that have been waiting to talk to me.

"So, you were with Kyle Smith today when this all happened then?" The older one asks right away, not wasting a single second more of his precious time.

"No, no. I was over his house for a short minute and then left to take my..." I hesitate. *Shit! Jo.* I think to myself before I finish my thought to the officer. "...my friend home, then I came back to his house and found him on the floor behind his front door covered in blood. I called the ambulance." I add, trying to assure him that I have no idea what happened.

"Can I have the name of your friend you were with?" The younger looking one asks. He sounds far more polite than his partner, but having to talk to them right now is the last thing I want to be doing.

"Jo. Her name is Josephine…"

"And her last name?" One of them says as I'm staring down at my feet. I bring my head up to answer his question and the prickly one is eyeing me, making me uncomfortable. To be honest I'm not quite sure how to answer the question since I don't actually know Jo's last name. It never came up during the times we were together. *I guess we haven't known each other long enough.*

"I don't know her last name." I tell them as they glare at me. They both quickly glance each other and the one writes something down on a small pad of paper I didn't realize he was holding until now. *Great! I bet that just made me look real fucking guilty.*

I mean, I am the reason Kyle was dealing with Cam in the first place…wait! *Fuck!* I didn't tell them that Cam was at Kyle's house before I left with Jo. But I can't, I can't tell them. If I do, Cam will fucking tell them about my past, which will make it look worse on my part. *Dammit.*

"Alright look. I was at Kyle's house and then I left to take my friend home, and when I came back, I found Kyle inside his house on the floor. I dialed 911 and held towels over his wounds while he bled through them and onto my hands. See." My voice comes out shaky and horse as I lift my hands to show them that they're covered in my best friend's dried blood. The blood that I couldn't wipe off on my shirt because there was just too much of it, it saturated everything and I haven't had a second to think to wash it off until now.

When I say exactly what happened out loud, I suddenly comprehend what it means to have Kyle's blood all over me. My eyes drift downward. The blood doesn't show on my dark shirt but I can tell where it soaked into the material from how rigid and sticky it is. I only see the dark shade of red starting to flake off of my knuckles as I ball my hands up into fists. Vigorously rubbing my hands together and scraping at my skin, trying desperately to scratch it all off; hoping that I can scrub away the images that are haunting my vision.

If I hadn't gone back, I wouldn't have found him until it was too late. If I had been to chicken shit and blown him off again, he could have bled out and died. His family could have come home and found him there on the floor, cold and pale, with no life left in him. Surely if I was any later than I had been, he wouldn't be here right now, and it would be all my fault.

29
Hunter

I've lost count of how long I've been in this fucking waiting room. The fumes from when the janitor came to mop up that guy's blood up off the floor, still lingers in the air. It smells like he used an entire bottle of bleach from the way the fumes are burning my eyes. No one has allowed me in to see Kyle yet and he's been in recovery for hours already. The only way I could see him is if his family were here and gave me permission. *This is such bullshit!*

I called my parents earlier and told them what had happened so they could let Kyle's mom and dad know. I think my mom would be better able to handle telling her best friend that their son is in the hospital. It's probably best that they hear it from her, rather than from me. Especially after the last few months and everything that's happened last year, they don't like me very much anymore. They said that I'm a bad influence on their son. *That's original.*

I sit up and stretch my back while glancing over the crowd of people, and when I do I see my parents walk in towards the receptionist desk. My mother tries to get the woman's attention, the same woman that I seemed to have caught off guard earlier tonight when I came barging through the doors. I sluggishly get up from where I have been sitting anxiously all this time and shuffle over to them, hesitantly putting my arm up to get her attention. She turns and grabs hold of me, instantly wrapping me into a tight comforting hug and she catches me so far off guard with the gesture, my body automatically tenses up as I slowly wrap my arms around her, and hold her tight for a moment. *It feels like so long since she's actually hugged me.*

"Hunter." She says, her voice thick, as she lets me go. She takes a step back and runs her eyes over me, I would assume to take in my appearance as she always does, but this feels different, it's like she's looking for any sign that would explain to her how I sounded on the phone when I called her a few hours ago.

"Mom, I'm fine." I interrupt her. "But no one will tell me anything."

"I'll go find someone." She says, and quickly walks away in the direction of the receptionist desk again; a determination in her stride.

"Hunter, I'm relieved you're alright." My dad admits in a low gravelly tone. His voice breaks slightly at the end as if he's upset. Not that his face would show it though, especially in public.

"Yeah dad, I'm fine, I wasn't even there when it happened. I just found him when I went back to his house." I clarify lowly.

"Well, I take it he's very lucky that you showed up." My father states matter of fact. The emotion in his voice is gone and I nod my head and look over to where my mother is arguing with a nurse. It's not Bethany, but this woman looks absolutely terrified, as most people do when my mother is angry. After another minute she makes her way back over to us and says that I can see him, but for only a few minutes.

"Hunter why don't you go in and see him, I'll wait here for Allison and Noah, alright. He's in room 252."

"Yeah....alright." I walk away without another word and pass the nurse's station. The nurse buzzes me in as I reach tentatively towards the metal doors on the other side of the waiting room. They creak as they swing open. I feel the need to take in a deep breath as I pass through the doors all while thinking how scared shit-less I am of what I'm going to have to see when I get to Kyle's room. I'm not ready for it, not yet, but I wouldn't be much of a friend if I wasn't afraid for him.

My feet shuffle along the floor, slowly and heavily dragging behind me as I read the signs posted above the doorways. They help direct me to the correct room, but it's hardly needed since I've been here before. The walls seem to blend seamlessly into the shiny white unmarked floors. Not like the floor in the waiting area. They were a dark gray and had black diamonds scattered throughout. Three hundred and twelve I counted before my parents showed up.

I push the button on the wall to the right side of a double set of metal doors. There's a sign directly in front of me on the wall that reads 'ICU Recovery'. When I get to the end, I take a right and walk down past a few more doors, a vending machine, and a coffee cart, meaningless things that just seem to taught me as I walk past them.

I remember the way to this part of the hospital even though it looks much different than it did then. All the plastic is off the windows to the patient rooms, the walls are painted from a dusty gray to a shiny white and the caution tape is gone from in front of the doorways. The look of it is much different from last year, but the feeling of hopelessness has never left.

I pass rooms, 248, 250, and finally get to Kyle's room, 252. Standing still a minute just staring at the numbers on the door, I wait. For what, I'm not entirely sure but I can't bring myself to open the door yet. I know I have to; I want to, but it's taking all my strength to not run out of here like a coward.

Last year I almost couldn't bring myself to walk into a room much like this one. Back then I should have known what to expect when I walked through the door. They told me as much what to expect. But absolutely nothing could have prepared me for actually seeing my little sister lying there all alone like that. Her face was ghostly pale, and when I got closer, I noticed that her lips were blue and not the shade of pink like her lip gloss that she had applied over and over again; making sure it was perfect for when we arrived at the party that night. Her hair was matted to her forehead by the red sticky liquid that coated her pale skin.

They told me she was gone even before she got to the hospital. That she had died on impact and most likely didn't feel anything.

How the fuck would they know that anyway? Liars! They couldn't have known that. I didn't want to believe that my baby sister was gone. We were just at a party not two hours before and she was laughing and having a good time with her friends.

"Excuse me, sir?" I hear someone say and I quickly wipe the wetness with my hand off my face and turn around to see a nurse in gray scrubs standing a few feet from me. The look of concern crosses her face as she studies me, waiting for me to answer her.

"Yeah?" Is all I bother to respond with. I wipe my cheek on the shoulder of my shirt and look up at her because she's still standing there.

"Do you need help with something?" She asks after a beat.

"No." I point to the door behind me and tell her why I'm here. I don't know how long I've been here before she showed up. Thankfully after looking at the door and then back at me, she carries on her way down the hall.

I finally grow some damn balls to turn around and reach for the handle, pushing open the door. I take a few steps into the room, hearing the beeping and clicking of machines. A white curtain is pulled closed over the side nearest to where I am and I know that Kyle's lying on a bed just behind it. My feet are hesitant to move but I make them carry me over closer to the bed. My shaky hands reach for the plastic curtains and pull them to the side, finally revealing that my worst thoughts had come true. *Again.*

30
Josephine

Nate's been in the garage all evening since I got home. Doing what, I have no idea, but I'm sure the noise is going to piss off the neighbors sooner or later. I text him a while after I got home that if he wanted dinner, it was in the microwave. We haven't spoken face to face since the night he came home drunk. I guess if I were him, I wouldn't want to see anyone I broke down in front of either, but I have no reason to judge him. After all, he did what he did for my benefit. He has talked to me through text though, so I guess that's something for now. Neither one of us is really great at holding a conversation, never really have been, but it's nice to know that he's sticking around more if I need him. Maybe Nate not moving away to college could be a good thing after all.

I decide to take a shower before bed, so I grab what clothes and toiletries I need and head upstairs to the bathroom. The laundry in here is piling up, so I'm lucky enough to have a clean towel to dry off with after my shower. I run the hot water and wait for the room to warm up and then double check that the door is locked before undressing. The steam fills the small bathroom, fogging up the mirror within a couple of minutes, making me grateful that I won't have to see how puffy and red my eyes are.

The soft spray of the water feels incredible as it beads off of my face and cascades down along my frigid body. I truly enjoy the rushing sound it makes as it passes my ears and it quickly warms me before disappearing down the drain. The longer I stand in here the easier it is to drown out the noise inside my head. It forces me to stay in here a little too long, to the point of the water running cold on me, so it kind of defeats the purpose of taking a hot shower if I'm frozen by the time I decide to get out. I get out of the shower and hastily dry off, wrap my hair in a towel and pull on my pajama shorts and an oversized t-shirt that

I like to wear to bed. I could wear them every night because they are the best most comfortable pieces of clothing I own. I gather my things back up and unlock the bathroom door to head downstairs and when I get to the bottom and my bare foot hits the landing, I realize that the floor is freezing; as if someone turned on an air conditioner in the middle of winter. *HA, like we could actually afford air conditioning. Maybe I just stood under the cold water far too long again.*

Not wanting to wait another second to jump in bed and get under the covers, I hurry to my room down the hall and push open the door. To my surprise I now know the source of why the entire downstairs has turned into an icebox. Everything in my hands fall and scatter across the floor and my feet feel like they're stuck in cement until I realize after a second who is sitting on my bed; and I can't do anything other than stare at the heartbreaking sight in front of me.

"Hunter..." His name a soft whisper escaping from my lips as my eyes shoot back and forth between my open window and the broken boy sitting on the edge of my bed. His hands are barely able to hold his head as he rests his elbows on his knees for support and his body achingly jerks from the sobs that he's trying to stifle back. I hear his breath catch in his throat as he looks up towards the door where I am still standing and unable to move.

I had hoped all day that Hunter would show up like he said he would, but then the time came and went with no word from him. No text, no phone call, nothing. I sat here in my room, on my bed, worried about him, hoping that he was okay. I thought he would be a decent enough human being to let me know if he couldn't make it because all I thought was that something bad happened to him. Then, that led to me being pissed off for an hour or two when I finally stopped being unreasonable, so I turned my phone off and dramatically threw it into my laundry hamper across my room, and chose to ignore it the rest of the night. I knew it wasn't a good idea for him to be here in the first place but you can't blame me for still wanting him to want to show up after he said he would.

I don't have a single clue as to why he has this effect on me. Why do I even care if he follows through with the promise that he made me? I'm used to everyone breaking their promises, why would he be any different? After a few hours, I finally got my shit together and stopped feeling sorry for myself, and decided Hunter was just another liar and that he would most likely keep letting me down like everyone else has in my life. I was going to add him to the list of people that were no longer allowed past the wall I built around myself and just another person I would eventually forget about.

But now as I stand here and see the amount of pain that he's in, as he sits crumpled up on the end of my bed, I can see how truly broken he is. Whatever happened between now and the time we last saw each other must have been bad, so now I feel like the shittiest person in the world for thinking that he was just like all the other assholes that I've come across.

"Hunter, what are you doing here?" I ask as I finally get my legs to work and step inside my room and shut the door behind me. Luckily Jeff is at work all night but I have no idea if Nate came in from the garage or not yet. I don't know how Nate would react now to a guy being in my room this late at night. Before a few nights ago, I never really cared what Nate thought, so it's a strange feeling worrying about it now, but those worries can wait until another day.

Hunter roughly rubs his hand over his face a couple of times before running his fingers through his rain-soaked hair, slicking it back before he tugs at the ends, his head hangs painfully in between his shoulders as he stands up and takes a minuscule step in my direction.

"I'm sorry Jo, I'm really sorry." He croaks. His apology sounds loaded like there's something else that he's not saying.

"What happened?" I quietly urge him to continue. He finally looks up at me and I see that his blood shot eyes are overflowing buckets of tears.

"It's Kyle." He chokes on his best friend's name as it passes his lips and he sinks his eyes to stare at the floor again. I hear an audible breath escape his chest, making his shoulders collapse forward. "Kyle's in the hospital Jo and it's my fault. I left him there alone to deal with my fucking mess!" His voice fractures at the end before he continues. "But…but I had to, if anything would have happened to you if we would have stayed, I could never forgive myself." His words come barreling out of him in a single breath like if he didn't get them out fast enough, he would break right down the middle.

Everything he's saying isn't making much sense to me. I look up and see the guilt and worry and anger threatening to burst from him at any minute, and it makes my heart hurt to see him like this. So, I do the only thing I know how. I walk over to him, closing the distance between us and wrap my arms around him and hold him as tight as I possibly can. I don't know what happened, I don't know if what I'm doing right now is even going to help, or even if it's what he needs, but just a short time ago he did the same exact thing for me. When I had no-one, he was there and he held me while I broke down and cried into his chest. He comforted me just by being there and letting me release all the bullshit that I closed up inside of me for so long. I had finally broke and let it out. Unfortunately for him, he was the only one there and so he got to witness the mess that I am first hand. So tonight, that's exactly what I'm going to do for him.

31
Josephine

The echoing of a door being slammed jolts me awake, instantly bringing a pounding to my chest. I keep my eyes closed and listen carefully to my surroundings for any other noises that might follow, but after a couple of minutes, I breathe a sigh of relief that the house stays silent.

I'm suddenly aware of the arm that's draped over me when I open my eyes, and when I look down and see Hunter's tattooed flesh lying over me, I remember last night when I found him in my room. His fingers are interlaced with mine as he loosely clutches my hand and without warning, a smile starts to spread across my face as I revel in the feeling of having his body pressed against me. *He's still here.* I carefully pull my hand away, slowly roll over to face him without lifting his arm and I settle comfortably back into the hollow of his chest. I lie as still as I can and enjoy the quiet moment because he finally looks peaceful. The sadness from last night is gone and all that shows on his face is, comfort.

I remember holding him last night while the storm raged outside my window and crashed the heavy rain against the glass. The lightning felt like it was narrating the anguish that was spilling out of him as he sobbed into my lap. It would fiercely brandish itself through the curtains and crept along my ceiling before leaving us in total darkness. Much like how I knew he felt in that moment.

I close my eyes and appreciate Hunter's warmth as I listen as our breath moves in sync with each other and it slowly starts to sooth me enough to doze off. It's difficult not to want to just lie here for the rest of the day. I would be perfectly happy to never have to move again; as long as I can stay in his arms like this forever.

Just as the sleep starts to take me under, I feel a warm hand brush against my cheek. *He's awake.* I don't open my eyes at first because then he may stop. His touch is so gentle and welcoming, I don't want him to pull away from me before I get to fully enjoy the way he's making me feel.

"Jo." He whispers my name so softly like he doesn't intend for me to hear him just yet. His hand traces my cheekbone and then his fingers slowly brush my hair away from my face behind my ear, before he rests them on my neck for a brief second. This sends chills down my body and I can feel the goosebumps start to prickle along my arms.

"Jo." He repeats. "Are you awake?"

"Mm…hm." I moan. And nod my head just enough to let him know I am in fact awake now, even though I know he's going to stop pressing his skin against mine far too soon. I open my eyes and cast my gaze into the most beautiful pair of green eyes that I have ever seen. I have to say, this… I could get used to this; because I am definitely not hating it!

"Good morning shortcake." He says with a shitty little grin on his face that appears out of nowhere. "Sleep well I hope?" He surprises me by his chipper mood when asks me. Almost as if last night never even happened. There's not a sign of hurt or anger on his face right now, which makes me happy, but also very confused. I don't want anything to put a damper on this moment, but I'm curious about what happened last night that had him so distraught. I know it was something bad and had to do with Kyle; but Hunter never said another word about it after he broke down in my arms.

"Hunter..." I start to say as I look him directly in his eyes. *They sure are beautiful.*

"Yes?" He responds as his eyes drop from mine and his thumb softly traces my bottom lip, making me forget what I wanted to ask him only a second ago. I hold my breath and try to blink away the euphoria, but his touch makes my mind run wild and I forget how to speak. *How can a boy's touch make my mind go completely blank? J*ust as I am able to somewhat gather my scattered thoughts, Hunter moves his free hand and slides his fingers ever so gently in between mine. He moves his hand still near my face into my hair and tenderly rakes his fingers through it again. I try to ask him about last night but he speaks up first; quieting my inquisitive brain for a few more moments.

"Jo…I'm sorry if I scared you last night." His voice is a strained whisper. It's sad and dull compared to his greeting only a few moments ago. "I didn't mean to just show up like that, but I... I didn't know where else to go." He veers off, stroking my hand a s a distraction then squeezes gently as he brings his lips to my knuckles giving them the softest of kisses. "Hunter, it's okay, really. I'm happy you came, but what happened...last ni" I'm cut off by the loud creaking of a door, followed by it being slammed so hard that I could feel the floor vibrate under my feet. "Shit!" I murmur. I can feel the panic in my voice so I'm sure Hunter will know something is off. I swiftly move my hand from Hunter's grasp and quietly jump out of bed and turn to him holding my finger up to my lips to silently tell him to stay quiet. I motion for him to get up and he gets off my bed, and as his feet hit the floor, I realize he still has his boots on.

God, I hope they don't make too much noise. I grab his hand and lead him over to my window. "Hunter, I'm so sorry, but you have to leave." I whisper to him. I keep close, so the sound of me talking doesn't carry past just us. My voice hitches in my throat and my eyes dart to my door, the hallway just on the other side of it, no lock on it to possibly give me another minute to explain why I'm suddenly kicking him out of my room, and why he needs to leave through my window.

"Baby, what's wrong?" He presses. I don't have a lot of time to get him out of here, so I just reassure him that it's the whole having a boy in my room thing and I don't want to get in trouble.

"Okay, I'll go. Text me later, okay?" He leaves a small quick peck on my lips before I can answer him and hops out of my window. I hear footsteps coming towards my door, distracting me from the image of Hunter leaving. A hard knock rattles the door as it hangs on the hinges.

"Nate?" I'm praying it's him and not Jeff.

"Yeah." He answers. "Jo? Is everything alright?" I exhale so hard it hurts because I thought Jeff was about to barge in.

"Yeah. I'm fine, just getting ready for school." *Lie.*

"Alright, well I have a late shift tonight, so I won't be home until after eleven. Try to make yourself scarce…if Jeff is home." The pause in his sentence gives a whole new meaning to "so quiet it's deafening."

"Okay." I confirm quickly.

"Okay." I hear Nate say quietly before he walks away from my door.

I flop down on my bed, close my eyes and let the thoughts of last night swirl around my head and fully consume me. After a few minutes, I feel the dampness seep through my thin t-shirt from the spot where Hunter was sleeping last night. I don't mind. I would lie here all day to take in his scent that he left behind, but I think the universe is telling me to get my ass up and get on with my day. *At least I get to see Hunter later.*

32
Josephine

Nate left for work already and Jeff still isn't home, so I really wish I hadn't made Hunter leave so quickly. We didn't have any time to talk about last night, and I can't get over the fact that he had stayed all night. I'm happy that he stayed. I'm also extremely grateful Jeff didn't come home. Now that I think about it, we haven't even crossed paths since him and Nate got into it the other night.

Nate still seems a bit on edge though, but I can't blame him, and with the way his knuckles looked, I can only imagine what Jeff's face looks like right now. It can't be easy knowing you had to get physical with your own father because of some girl, that isn't even your real sister. I didn't ask him to, but is it so wrong to be grateful to have him looking out for me? After all this time I thought Nate couldn't care less about me. Turns out I was wrong. Maybe he just didn't know how to show it, since I pretty much withdrew from everyone completely after my mom left. I guess I just didn't give Nate enough of a chance to be there for me.

Hunter

I walk to my car after making sure my girl was ok. I hated having to leave in a hurry when something seemed off, but I didn't want to stay if it was going to get her into trouble. Hell, I can't blame her family for being strict…Jo's something special and needs to be protected. I may not have known her for very long, but I can already tell she needs to be kept a secret otherwise, every boy in town would be knocking down her door just to be in her presence; if they had the chance to feel the way I do whenever I'm around her, they would kill to be in my position.

Josephine

When I'm done getting ready for school, I text Hunter so we can meet up.

Jo: Hunter you think we could meet at the bookstore in 20 minutes?

I go to the kitchen to make some toast when I hear my phone chirp. It didn't take long for him to reply.

Hunter: see you there

A second later another chirp.

Hunter: …Shortcake :)

I hurry to my room and grab my bag and throw on my favorite hoodie and jacket. I'm in such a good mood right now that I don't think about anything except getting to the bookstore. I grab my keys from my bag and turn around to lock the front door as I leave but when I turn to run down the steps, dread washes over me instantaneously. I see Jeff pulling up into the driveway. My limbs start to shake as I stand here on the porch. I want to run, hide, do anything other than be standing here.

Shit! We're outside, in public, it's ok…he can't do anything if people can see. At this very moment, I think I'm afraid of him more now than I was before Nate got in his face. Maybe because I know he's going to retaliate sooner or later. The worst part is not knowing when.

Jeff gets out of his truck and closes the door. He doesn't stumble or make those awful groaning noises he usually does whenever he seems pissed. I have to pass him to walk in the direction of the bookstore, so I just keep my gaze neutral and try to pick up my feet that now seem to weigh a ton, and start walking towards the end of the driveway. Jeff unfortunately notices me as he walks around his truck and I dart towards the sidewalk, furthest away from him as we pass each other. He glares up at me and I eye him from my peripherals, but there's nothing there. His eyes are not hard or angry and his mouth isn't curved up into a snarl that is usually a permanent fixture on his face. To my relief, it seems like he just can't be bothered anymore. *I can live with that.*

Hunter

I put my phone back in my pocket as I get out of the car. I'm an idiot for saying I could meet Jo at the bookstore in 20 minutes, considering I still need to shower last night's hospital stench off of me. She didn't seem to mind what I smelled like last night, but I'm sure she noticed how much of a wreck I looked. Jo being who she is, she was nice enough not to point any of it out. I walk up the driveway after parking Kyle's car on the road. His parents are sending someone to pick it up today, so I said I would leave it there in case no one was home to let them in the gate. I notice my car is parked in front of the garage when I look up towards the house.

What the hell? But Jo had my car.

"Dammit!" I bellow to no one and grab a fist full of my hair. *I am such an ass!* She must have driven here to wait for me and I never showed up, which means she had to fucking walk all the way home last night. I pull my phone back out and open the messages from Jo and as I scroll down, I see that I have two marked unread from her.

Jo: I thought it would be better to just drive your car back to your house

Jo: Hunter is everything okay?

Son of a bitch, how could I have missed those?! I run to the door while scrambling for the right key to unlock it. I slam it behind me after I enter and punch in the security code to disarm the alarm system and then break out into a full sprint up the stairs to my room. I rip off my grungy t-shirt and kick off my boots as I head towards my bathroom. I quickly shower and make sure to scrub off all the dried blood that soaked through my shirt, adhering to my torso like melted candy sticks to a child's hand in a ninety-degree summer. I wish I could stand here all day and let the weight of yesterday's bullshit get sucked down the drain, but I have a beautiful girl waiting for me out there and I won't make her waste her time on me ever again.

33
Josephine

I get to the bookstore fifteen minutes later and see that Mrs. Lawrence is already here and the door is unlocked. It's still a little on the cooler side today, so I think I'll wait inside until Hunter gets here. I'm thankful that she's finally back in town now, so I can get away from my house more during the day and have somewhere to go after school again. It's awful when she has to be away because then she has to close the store since she doesn't have anyone else to run it. I always offer to keep it open for her while she's gone but she always says that I shouldn't miss so much school, especially on her account; she just closes up for a few days a couple of times a year and then I figure out what to do with myself until she comes back.

I walk in the door and the bell rings above my head, alerting Mrs. Lawrence that someone has come in. I hear her heels clack across the floor behind the counter until she comes into view and she greets me with a smile like always.

"Hi, Mrs. Lawrence. How was your trip?" I'm very eager to find out. She went to a convention to start inviting authors to the store for book signings and had been talking about it for months. I've never had the chance to meet a real author in person, so I can't wait to see how everything is going to turn out.

"Oh! Hi Josephine. It was great! How are you dear?" She buzzes. Sounding excited and relieved simultaneously as she comes closer from around the large counter, that's really more of an antique desk that you stand at, or have to have a very high chair to sit at it with.

"I'm good. I'm glad to hear your trip went so well." I walk towards her and rub my hands together, as my fingers are still a bit cold.

"Yes, the trip was great but the crowds were awful, so many people in such a small area. But I loved it! I do wish you could have come along.

I think you would have really enjoyed yourself." She says enthusiastically as she grabs my hands and pats them between hers in a friendly gesture.

I look up at her and make eye contact for the first time since I walked through the door and she suddenly has a startled look, on her face. She still has a hold of my hands as she stares at me for a minute and then she slowly lets them drop. Her expression has gone from happy and cheerful to sullen and worried in less than a breath.

"Josephine…are you alright sweetheart?" She directs her worry on to me when her voice comes out in a whisper so gentle, she almost sounds sad.

"Yeah of course." I tell her. And I mean it. I'm genuinely confused by the sudden change in her demeanor. I don't like being the center of anyone's attention, especially when I don't know what warranted it in the first place.

"Alright, I just wanted to make sure. You do know you can always come to me if you need anything yes? Anything at all?" She assures me as she brushes her hand across my cheek before pulling me into a gentle hug and sighing deeply as her arms squeeze just a little tighter around my shoulders. She gives me one last comforting squeeze, much like I assume a mother would give her child when they needed comforting. Not that I really had the chance to experience that firsthand from my own mother, but Mrs. Lawrence's hug feels like the kind a child should know. The kind that silently says I'm here for you and I care.

She lets go after a moment and places both her hands tenderly on either side of my cheeks to look at me and smiles before she walks away with a sigh.

"Josephine, dear. I have some hot cocoa for you in the back. I'll bring you out a nice hot mug in a moment. Don't you go anywhere just yet." She waves a finger above her head as she walks towards the back.

It's set up like home back there. Truly. There's a small little kitchen, just big enough to make tea and coffee. Some counter space to prepare small snacks to go along with her tea time and my hot cocoa cravings. She always keeps hot cocoa on hand for me when I said I wasn't much of a coffee or tea drinker. And she always has some sort of baked good she buys from the bakery around the corner before she comes in to open the bookstore every morning.

My favorites are the buttery croissants she gets that are almost as big as my head. I eat one of those the mornings I come in before school, they're always flaky and warm, and sometimes they have Nutella in the middle that melts through the layers of dough as it bakes. What better than a chocolate croissant and hot cocoa for breakfast while reading your favorite book in the corner of a quiet, cozy bookstore that smells like vanilla and cinnamon?

Mrs. Lawrence comes back a few minutes later with a to-go mug of hot cocoa and a small white paper bag that's folded over at the top.

"Here, now they didn't have croissants today, but they assured me that these are just as good. They're new, so I hope you like them." She hands me the bag and the hot cocoa and I gratefully accept them.

"Thank you." I tell her. I can smell the fresh-baked treat as the scent escapes through the paper bag and wafts towards my nose. I suddenly realize how hungry I am and I can't wait to eat whatever it is because the smell is so delicious and I'm already beginning to salivate even before I get to take it out of the bag.

Just then the bell chimes above the door as someone walks in, so we both look towards the doorway to see the brown locks on top of someone's head. Mrs. Lawrence greets them before they even come from around the one shelf that sits in the middle of the store.

"Good morning." She says in a higher, louder tone so they can hear her.

"Uh…goood…morning?" The voice questions; sounding unsure how to answer exactly, and who he seems to be answering to.

I know that voice.

Hunter steps around the bookshelf and smiles when he sees me looking up at him. His eyes quickly find mine and the simper on his face grows wider across his lips. I can tell that it's a different kind of smile this time; it doesn't quite reach his eyes like it had the days before.

"Jo. Hey. I wasn't sure if you were here yet so I thought I'd see if you were waiting inside. I'm sorry I'm later than I said I would be." He hurriedly explains.

"Hi." I say back. "You're here now, aren't you?" I grin.

"Well, who is this, Miss Josephine? Would you like to introduce me to your new gentlemen here?" Mrs. Lawrence asks in a sweet inviting voice. Kind of like a grandmother would ask if you would like a Christmas cookie before dinner, but don't tell your parents kind of way. *Hunter does look delicious today. I would devour him right now if… Oh god, what am I thinking?* These intrusive thoughts need to leave my head before I say them out loud and embarrass the hell out of myself. I snap out of it when I hear one of them clear their throat. Whoever did, I don't know? I was too mesmerized by looking at Hunter like he was some sort of edible treat made just for me.

"Um, Hunter, this is Mrs. Lawrence, she owns this place. And Mrs. Lawrence this is Hunter, my uh…" *Shit, I don't know what to call him. What do I say?* I freeze.

"I'm Jo's friend, Hunter." He says as he holds out his hand and steps forward towards Mrs. Lawrence. She steps towards him, meeting him halfway and they shake hands.

"Wow, that's a strong handshake you have young man." Giving him a smile. "It's nice to finally meet one of Josephine's friends. Come to think of it, with as long as she's worked here, you're the only friend of hers that I have actually met."

"Yes ma'am. It's nice to meet you too. Jo has told me how much she loves it here. She said it's her favorite place to be."

Wow. He's good with adults too! Is there anything he isn't good at? He's so calm and collected that it's almost intimidating to watch.

"Well, it's certainly is great to see her with such a nice boy." I hear the tone in her voice that says a little more than her words did just now. A warning tone that I'm sure with as perceptive as Hunter is, he's already picked up on.

"Thank you, Ma'am." Is all he says before Mrs. Lawrence speaks again.

"Well, you two should be off before you're late for school, right? Oh! Hold on just a second, I'll be right back." She tells us and takes off into the back room again.

"Hey." Hunter's voice hits me like the waves of the ocean. I turn my head to him and my body follows before I repeat his greeting.

"Hey." I whisper breathlessly like the air has been sucked straight out of my lungs when I feel his eyes lock onto mine.

I had no idea how to introduce Hunter because I never thought about it. I know Mrs. Lawrence isn't my mother but I do respect her opinion, and she is the closest person to a mother I've ever had after my mom left. I also didn't want to say the wrong thing, I didn't want to insult him by only saying he was a friend, and I didn't want to be too forward by calling him my boyfriend either, which by the way is too soon to be calling us anything relating to being a couple. I'm glad I hadn't called him my boyfriend, since he didn't introduce himself to her that way. I don't even know if he actually feels anything for me like that anyway. *Ugh stop rambling Jo.*

We stand near each other, close enough to almost feel our fingers touch between us. I can smell him, *what is it? Cologne, soap, I don't know.* But he smells as divine as he looks.

"Here we are." Mrs. Lawrence's voice breaks our stares from one another as she comes out from the back with another to-go mug in hand and a second white paper bag, handing them both to Hunter.

"Hunter these are for you. Let me know how you like them. I can't very well eat them all myself now, can I? You two enjoy. I'll see you later Josephine. And Hunter…" He turns towards her as she pauses. "It was so nice to meet you."

34
Hunter

Nice to meet you too Mrs. Lawrence; and thanks for these." I say, holding up the bag and hot cocoa to my face, gratefully inhaling the sugary aroma of whatever is inside. She gives me a wide smile as I turn to walk away and follow Jo out the door.

"So… She's really great huh?" I say as soon as we step out onto the sidewalk.

"Yeah, she's one of the nicest people I've met since I moved here." She continues walking towards the end of the block, looking down at her feet and holding her arms tightly to her body as best she can with the cup and pastry bag still in her hands. *Is she cold?*

"Jo?" I say with hesitation. I want to ask her more about this morning and why she was so anxious, but I'm afraid she might say something that I won't like. I don't know what it could be; but after I thought about how restless she was when she heard someone else in the house, I now assume it's not anything good.

"Yeah?" She answers back as she walks down the sidewalk, not bothering to stop and look up at me, so I put the pastry bag in my other hand that clings to the hot drink and reach out and brush my hand over her shoulder to get her attention.

"Jo…did something happen when I left this morning?" Her body visibly tenses under my palm before she lets out a long relieving sigh. *Why is she always still so jumpy around me?*

"Oh that. No. That was just my stepbrother Nate. He was just telling me that he was going to be working late so…well that I would be home alone tonight." Her eyes shift nervously. There's something behind her words, something she's not telling me. I know it's really none of my business but I can't help the overwhelming need to find out what's behind those sad eyes of hers. "No, I mean, why did you seem so frightened and why did I have to leave so fast if it was just your stepbrother? Are your parents really strict?" I implore. Hoping that's all it is and that I'm just reading further into it than is needed.

"Oh." She repeats her words from a second ago and drops her head to look at her hands. "It's sort of complicated. But Nate, he's not the kind of stepbrother that would rat me out to his dad." She seems as though she's not going to give me any further explanation so I pry a little more; letting my protective curiosity get the better of me.

"Can I ask you something else then?" I nervously bite at my lip and wait for her to answer me.

"Sure." She finally agrees and her voice is clear as she looks up at me with curious eyes.

"Where did you get the bruises Jo?" My tone comes out demanding the truth from her. I really do genuinely care to know who hurt her and why. I can't even fathom that there would be any reason anyone would do anything bad to her. Jo's eyes peer into mine and it surprises me that she hasn't tried looking away this time like I thought for sure she would.

"Jeff." She plainly says. "My Stepfather." There's no emotion in her answer this time, not even a crack in her voice. She says his name as casually as she would tell me what kind of ice cream she prefers. I smash my lips together to hold in words that I know I shouldn't say out loud, especially in front of her. I'm trying my best not to lose it, after hearing what she just said, that it was a man that made her face look like that. *NO! Not a man. A real man would never lay a hand on a female, especially his own family.*

I thought it was Cam before, at the party when I first saw them. But no, it was her own fucking stepfather that hurt her and she has to go home every day to the same house where that piece of shit could hurt her again and I wouldn't have a fucking clue until I would get a chance to see her next. *I wouldn't be there to protect her from him!* Jo's staring at me. Surely waiting for me to say something, but I can't, my lips won't separate. My words are stuck in my throat every time I want to say something to try and at least comfort her in some way. I want to tell her it will all be okay, that I will keep her safe. *But how can I promise her that when I have no idea how to even keep that promise?!*

"Jo, look I…" I start to speak but she holds her hand up for me not to continue. "It's okay Hunter, really. I don't think he's going to do it again. Nate took care of it. I really don't want to talk about him, so can you just walk with me to school?" Her eyes shift nervously and the exhaustion in them over the current conversation is clearly evident in her expression.

"Sure." I agree. "But I do have my car so, we don't have to walk." I gesture towards my car a few parking spaces down from where the bookstore is and she starts walking in that direction, with me following slightly behind her as we pass a couple standing in front of the pet store. She looks through the window and I catch her smile at the brown and white puppies playing together.

I won't really let go of what she told me. I just said that so she won't think I'm being a pushy asshole. I don't want her thinking I'm trying to control her in any way but I can't just go on about my life knowing what her father did to her. *Her Stepfather, I mean!* I may not know the whole story, but she definitely doesn't deserve what that piece of shit did to her!

35
Josephine

The drive to school seemed longer than it should have. Only because I wasn't sure if Hunter was going to let go of the fact that I just told him my stepfather was the cause of my bruises. Sitting silently next to someone after letting them in on such an embarrassing secret left me exhausted. Thankfully he only saw them after they already started to heal and look a little less harsh than the morning after it happened. The ones on my body look far worse than the ones on my face so at least Hunter hasn't got a clue about those.

Hunter pulls into a parking space at the back end of the lot near the old sign; the sign where Hunter and I first met not so long ago. He seems to be fond of parking back here, as there are plenty of empty spaces closer to the main entrance. But having this nice of a car I would gladly walk the few extra yards to make sure it wouldn't get damaged by some newly licensed sixteen-year-old that thinks it's fun to do donuts in the parking lot at seven a.m.

I hear the engine turn off and Hunter unbuckle his seat belt as I stare out the windshield. The air in the car is warm from the heat vents so I hesitate to get out at first until it seems like Hunter wants to say something. I'm not sure if it's just me trying to avoid any more questions about my shitty living situation or that I truly wouldn't be able to handle the look of pity from him if I were to tell him anything else; so, I quickly reach for the handle to open the door so I can avoid the entire thing.

"Thank you for the ride, Hunter." I push the door because let's face it I am extremely horrible at holding a conversation right now. I wanted to ask Hunter about last night but then this morning at the book shop with Mrs. Lawrence put a halt to that, then him asking me about my bruises threw me for a total loop and now I can't seem to get any words to come out of my mouth. My mind is fighting with me to tell him more, but I still barely know him. It's exhausting just thinking about how complicated everything feels right now.

"Jo please, wait a second?" I stop pushing the door and slowly release the handle after deciding to stay put in the passenger seat until I hear what he has to say. I could give him that much. He has been the only other person that's cared to ask me if I was alright.

"Okay." I agree.

After another few quiet seconds, Hunter gets out of his seat and shuts his door. I watch him walk around the front of the car and he holds a finger up to me, saying to wait as he reaches for the handle on my side. He opens my door and holds out his hand in front of me. I stupidly gawk at him like an idiot not knowing for sure what he's doing when he cracks a smirk and chuckles under his breath.

"Jo, give me your hand." He tells me, not in a rude or authoritarian tone. He sounds more pleading and cordial when he says it. The adorable little dimple on his left cheek doesn't hurt either. So, I put my hand in his and he lifts me out onto the pavement and waits until I'm steady on my feet. His hand slides to my right hip as he shuts the door with the other, making our torsos come together. I flinch slightly as Hunter's arms squeeze me a little tighter, rubbing against my still aching bruises and so I take in a breath of the chilled morning air to try and suppress a painful squeal that hungers for release.

The few times that we have been this close, he has taken my breath away or given me butterflies that seem to travel all the way down to my toes. It's a feeling I can't seem to get used to, but I definitely don't mind the sensation. It's a foreign feeling but a much welcome one and the kind of comfort that just makes my body melt in his arms.

"Jo." He breathes. His arms are still wrapped around my hips as his forehead slowly comes to rest against mine.

"I'm sorry. I didn't mean to bring up bad shit earlier." He confesses.

"I..." I go to speak but he places a soft finger on my lips before I get another word out.

"Wait." He says as his thumb gently smooths over my lips and he takes another breath before he continues.

"I won't make you tell me things you don't want to, but I want you to know, that I will not stand for anyone laying another hand on you ever again." He slides his finger under my chin and meets my eyes with a seriousness I have never seen cross his face until now. His tone is powerful, caring, and sweet and I believe him as his expression screams nothing but truth.

"Okay." The word barely makes it out of my throat as I witness the intensity in Hunter's eyes. I close mine and let out the breath I had been holding the entire time he spoke. I needed to make sure what I was hearing him say to me was the truth and not some delusion I made up to make myself feel better. *Nope, he really said every word.* And I crave to hear more.

36

Hunter

Fuck this is torture!

Sitting in this god-awful mind-numbing lecture about why we need to put letters and symbols into an equation is beyond idiotic if you ask me. I rather stick a plastic fork through the fleshy part of my hand than to sit here, while this Ferris Bueller wannabe of a teacher tells me how to find the limit of (x) by inverting the exponential function of a derivative. *When in God's name, am I ever going to need to know this shit?* Let's face it. I'm not going to be a mathematician so why do I even bother?

The hands on the clock slowly tick by, mocking me with every second as I wait for it to signal the lunch bell. Each tick…tick…tick… incessantly taunts me as it draws out the seconds, making it feel like hours. I would normally sleep during trig, but right now it's impossible. Waiting to see Jo has turned my brain into total mush, and I can't turn it off long enough to sleep through this agonizing class, so instead, I find myself obsessively thinking about her for the entire period. *Three more minutes.*

Josephine

The morning with Hunter was, *intense.* And, that's putting it lightly. My mind wanders to the thought of him and what he might be doing right now. How good he smelled, and how his soft touch felt on my face. The entire morning in class has been a massive blur other than the fact that it just dawned on me; that I was so close to letting him kiss me. I'm still not sure about allowing myself to feel so vulnerable with him. The wall I built up around me over the years seems to be no match for Hunter's smokey green eyes and wickedly devilish grin. *I would hate to think that I'm the type of girl to go weak at the knees just because some guy flashes his pearly whites at me.* But it feels like there's something more than what he's been willing to show me so far; and if he wants me to bare my deepest secrets, then he's going to have to show me his.

Hunter

The bell rings and I'm out of my seat before the teachers are done talking about whatever assignment is due tomorrow, but I couldn't care less. My only thought is meeting Jo at her locker to walk her to lunch and sit by her side so I can get a whiff of that delicious coconut-scented hair of hers again. *Shit! What is wrong with me? I feel so whipped by her and we're not even officially together. At least I don't think we are…yet.*

Never have I ever managed to be a person that spent more than a night with a girl, and damn, the thought of dating has always scared the hell out of me. Now here I am thinking about that exact thing and what her fucking shampoo smells like. I walk past the vending machines and around the corner near the weight room doors. She said her locker was in the old wing by the dance room. Why this school has a separate dance room, I will never know. I've never even seen girls at this school dance for anything. And trust me I would have noticed the tight little uniforms they supposedly wear if they walked around school in them like the cheerleaders do all the time. Maybe that's exactly why they never leave the dance room wearing them.

I walk a few more feet past the doors and find the number to her locker, thinking I got the wrong hallway somehow since I don't see her yet. But no, there it is. Locker #222; right in front of me and Jo isn't here. Maybe a teacher kept her after class so I decided not to blow up her phone by texting her just yet. I'll give her a few more minutes.

Five minutes pass and the first lunch bell sounds. She's still not here. Jo seems to be the punctual type and she promised to meet me here before going into the cafeteria before class to grab a soda this morning. She said it was her daily morning ritual. I decide to text her in-case she got held up for longer than she anticipated. She hasn't been in school for a while, so she's most likely being bombarded with work that all the teachers in this school feel the need to catch her up on her first day back.

The thought crosses my mind again on why it's her first day back. The few days she was out, she was having to hide at home. Because if she had come to school with black and blue marks all over her face, I'm sure there would be some teachers raising a lot of questions about where they came from. *Shit!* Then it hits me. She still had some visible bruising on her jaw-line this morning. I knew it was there in the first place so it was obvious to me, but it was finally so faint that I thought for sure no one would notice. Maybe they would just mistake it for a shadow or makeup, possibly. I was too distracted by her lips to think too much of it at the time.

I pull my phone out of the front pocket of my jeans as I start walking towards the main office. I pull up Jo's number in my contacts to send a message and a second later one pops through, interrupting the message I already started typing to her. *Dammit!* Clearly, I'm going to ignore that one, so I start typing another message to Jo.

Hunter: Jo

Hunter: Where are you?

I wait a few minutes as I make my way down the hall and pass the security check-in by the main office. The retired police officer is eyeing me as he always does when I open the doors. He's probably wondering if I'm going to cause trouble for him today. It certainly wouldn't be the first time. *Sorry, not today. I have other pressing matters to attend to.* I probably shouldn't waste my time by mouthing off for once. Jo still hasn't text back so I'm not at all sure if looking in the office for her will do any good. She's probably not even in here; but I don't know where else to look other than the parking lot.

Josephine

I don't like being made to wait in here like this and I've never been in trouble at this school. Well, real trouble anyway. It was pretty much just an insignificant lecture by the school counselor to not miss so many days. I haven't missed that many, but she feels the need to remind me of the same thing every time I come in late. It must make her feel like she's actually doing something instead of just sitting in a dusty, closet- sized office all day until a kid, spazzes out in biology when the dissection of frog's lab, comes up out of nowhere. The teachers tend to plan it that way so the parents can't protest and keep their kids out of school to avoid the lesson altogether. I think it's absolute b.s.

"Josephine Michaels? You can come in now." I hear the school counselor say my name and I can feel my body wanting to freeze and I wish I could just ignore her. *Or run, maybe running would be the better option right now.* My reaction to being called into that awful, tiny, claustrophobic office of hers has me feeling like this may not be good. I push myself off the chair and have to will my feet forward. I hate confrontation and I hate attention. This is the absolute worst place I would have to be today.

"Have a seat, Josephine." She says as she takes a seat behind a makeshift desk of papers piled high on either side of her keyboard. *Wow, what a packrat.*

"It's Jo." I tell her. "I go by Jo." I say louder, making sure she heard me. Each and every time I speak to her, I tell her this, but she insists on calling me by my full name, and it's really starting to piss me off.

37
Hunter

I walk in and eye the secretary behind the counter. She's on the phone but she points to the seats across from her. The blinds are all closed so at least I won't have the guard burning a hole into the back of my head. I take a seat and slouch to try and get comfortable. These shitty plastic chairs are anything but comfortable.

I lean my head back against the glass and close my eyes for a second when I hear a woman's voice yelling from a back office. Both voices are muffled but whoever is screeching seems pissed. A minute later a woman comes stumbling out of the door after it violently swings open and hits the wall on the other side, rattling the windows behind me. For a minute I thought maybe it was Jo and my stomach clenched in fear that something bad happened but to my relief, it's not her. It's a woman, most likely a parent getting pissed off that their kid isn't on the honor roll or something. *Better luck with the next one, lady.*

As she walks towards me, assuming she's leaving I can tell there's something off. She's not just angry, she's drunk. I know a stagger like that has to be caused by some sort of spirits, and they were strong. She's now yelling obscenities behind her to the principal that is still standing in his doorway like a coward, eyeing her as she walks further away from him. I see him let out a held breath and turn to grab the receiver on his desk. I turn back to look at her; she's now only a few feet in front of me and she gives me a smirk before saying.

"He's the biggest asshole in this school you know." She slurs her words, but they're clear enough to understand who she's talking about. It's comical hearing those repugnant words coming out of this tiny little female's mouth, especially since she had a hellish smile plastered on her face the whole time. She finally pulls open the door and casually walks out, so I look back around the office and notice that everyone in here is now so quiet that you could probably hear a mouse sneeze.

Josephine

"So…how are you today, Josephine?" She asks while looking down at a notepad on her desk. It's just far enough away that I can't see what it says.

"I'm fine." I say in the most convincing voice I can and keep my eyes drawn to the paper that she's still staring at. Her eyes move in a slow motion back and forth as she follows with her fake brittle nail. The chipped pink polish on her thumb is distracting and I want to tell her to fix it, but I never do. *Maybe she bites her nails like I do?*

"Today you had a class with Mr. Gibbons this morning, correct?" She finally looks up from that damn paper, and now I know, whatever is written on there has to be about me. She's been reading it the entire five minutes I've been in here and she's only said ten words to me.

"Yes. I had history this morning like I do every Monday morning." She knows this. So, why do teachers feel the need to have you repeat information to them that they already know? I think it's just to see if we were skipping class and trying to lie about it.

"Where were you before you went to class this morning?" Her eyes become a little bit more serious by the time she says the last word. I've never seen her be anything but nice and bubbly and she usually has a smile on her face. But right now, her expression says she means business and I really don't like the way this conversation is headed.

I suddenly become aware of the desert in my mouth that's severely drying out my tongue, making it almost impossible to speak in a clear unwavering voice like I need to. The chair beneath me pinches at my back so I squirm in my seat and try to swallow before answering her. *Why does she care what I did before I got to school?*

"I was at home. Then I got ready for school and came here. Why?" I won't get into the details of what my usual mornings consist of. Today of all days, my morning was anything but normal. "Well..." She pauses and sighs before continuing. "The reason I ask is that something was brought to our attention and we wanted to check up on it to make sure either way that it wasn't going to be an issue." The inflection of her voice has changed again; bringing another uneasy vibe to the small space.

"What do you mean? Someone said I did something?" I'm clueless at this point. I thought it might be about the bruising on my face that everyone I passed today seemed to notice; they're starting to fade anyway. I never drew any curious looks before so I thought I could just hide in plain sight like any other day. Of course, my luck just wouldn't let that happen, would it?

"You're a real fucking piece of work you know that! I'm taking her out of this appalling place today!" I hear someone screaming from down the hall. The door muffles their voice but it sounds like an extremely irate woman. *I wonder what that's all about.* A loud bang follows the woman's bitter words down the hall and it shakes the walls of the office making the pictures behind me rattle. They don't fall off and break like I had expected them. The counselor jumps out of her seat and tells me to hold on a minute. She walks to the door and opens it to peak out; cowering behind it because a crazed lunatic is on the other side. I'm sort of grateful for whoever was causing a distraction and taking the attention off of me for a minute.

"Can I go now? I have a lot of work to catch up on." I tell her. I'm hoping she will just let me out of here so she can handle whatever is going on out in the hallway.

"No, um…actually, you should stay here until I get back okay. I'll just be a few minutes." And then she just opens the door and quickly leaves without letting me respond first.

Hunter

The school counselor comes out of her office and walks straight towards the principal's. She hurries in and shuts the door, blocking more of their whispered conversation from me. *Shit luck for being able to be nosey.* I really don't have the patience to sit here any longer. I decide to text Jo again to see if she answers this time.

Hunter: Hey Jo ru okay?

Hunter: Can you meet me at my car in like 5 min.

I hear a phone go off one after another in the office across from me as soon as I send Jo both texts. My phone alerts me that she's typing with those annoying little alternating dots. Well, they were annoying to me before, but now they're just making me anxious.

Jo: sure

I hear a chair scrape across the floor and then the door to the counselor's office opens; revealing the one and only person that I wanted to see today. She's looking down at her phone and typing something. Then my phone beeps, making her look up in my direction. I glance down and read her text.

Jo: ***meet you there***

I peer back up at her and say, "So, I take it, it was five seconds then?" I smile at her and stand up; waiting for her say something, but she just sprints over to me, grabs my hand, and quickly pulls me out the door.

38
Hunter

Jo didn't say a word to me while she ran out of the office and simply dragged me behind her by my wrist. She quickly popped open the main exit doors and hauled ass past the cameras outside the building. I don't know if the security guard even had a chance to see us leave; she was moving so fast. Even if he did, he could have thought we were let out early since we did just come out of the office where they would have seen us leaving in the first place.

"Jo, slow down. I don't think anyone is following us." I say to her from behind. She lets go of my hand and I can feel the sudden void that it has left me with. *I don't like the feeling very much.*

"I just didn't want to get caught by Mr. security douche and have to go back to class. I've had my fair share of bullshit today." She utters sounding exhausted as we approach my car.

"I take it your first day back was shit?" I assume and stop beside my car. She stops mid-stride before she reaches the passenger side of and dumps her backpack on the ground, taking a seat on top of it. I guessed as much since I know my day wasn't that great either.

"Yeah. You could say that." She replies instantly like she already knew what I was going to say.

"Then I think we're obligated to do something that will make it better. Don't you agree?" I turn and look at her, trying to judge her reaction to see if she has that little excited look in her eye. That same cute ass little grin she had the first day I met her and told her to get on my bike. She glances sideways at me and sure enough there it is.

That adorable little grin that I have come to love so quickly.

"I'd say, I would have to agree with you." She's still looking at me as her grin turns into an even more beautiful smile. *I so badly want to kiss her right now!* I would have already kissed her. God knows I have had plenty of opportunities. Jo's not just like any other girl I've been with though. She's special and she deserves more than just a quick make-out session with yours truly.

"Alright. Well, then where to?" I playfully demand.

"I'm having a small case of déjà vu." She sighs and her lips pull up into a smile and right away I know what she means by it. I asked her the same thing the day we met out here. She looked like she needed some cheering up and she gave me a great excuse to ditch school. I sit down next to her on the curb in front of my car and pull my knees up, resting my arms on them. *Damn this concrete is still so fucking cold!*

"Yeah. Seems we have a thing for this particular parking lot. I can't say that I've had many good memories of it until I met you here." I tell her. I glance over to my right and see her grin again. Her dimple just barely shows in her right cheek as her smile grows wide on her perfectly plump lips. I can't help it but they keep drawing my attention because they look absolutely edible. The right shade of pink, and her top lip, oh god, that's my favorite. It's shaped like a heart, soft, firm and begging to be kissed.

"Hunter?" She breaks my attention away from her mouth when I hear her say my name.

"Yeah?"

"What happened the other night? With Kyle I mean?" Her voice is quiet when she says Kyle's name; like she's afraid to bring it up.

"Oh." I'm not that keen on telling her what happened, but I don't want to lie to her either. But if I do tell her, I'm afraid she'll be scared of getting involved with me, since trouble seems to follow me everywhere I go lately. *Hell, lately, try all the time asshole.*

"Kyle's in the hospital because of me." I confess as my eyes fall to stare at the ground between us, I don't want to see judgement in those hypnotizing eye of hers.

"What do you mean because of you? You weren't even there." She adds that last word and it sounds like she's asking me rather than confirming that she knew I wasn't there when it happened. She knew I was driving her back to my car parked at the beach, so she could go home, but she has no idea about what happened after I left her. I was supposed to help Kyle take care of business with Cam; then a massive fucking wrench was thrown into that plan and screwed it all up when I found Kyle beaten to a bloody pulp. The image of him lying there on the floor makes my stomach twist up into a tight knot, making me feel sick.

"No, I wasn't there, that's the problem. If I had been, maybe he wouldn't be in the hospital right now." I can feel myself getting defensive by the second, so I honestly don't want to continue talking about this. I feel I owe it to Jo to explain a little more now that I know she was waiting for me that entire time I was at the hospital and didn't have enough decency to even text her to let her know I wasn't going to show up after I said I would. "Jo. I'm sorry. I didn't mean for you to get dragged into my mess. I think I owe you some sort of explanation why I showed up in your room the way I did." I look into her eyes as she spins her body to face mine. "That guy Cam that you met at the party the other night?" My insides cringe as I think back to seeing him with his hands all over her. I bite my bottom lip to keep myself from bursting with disgust. "He's not a good guy, Jo. Kyle got involved with him not too long ago because of something I did and Cam found out about it. If he had told anyone what he knew, then Kyle and I would have been in a lot of trouble."

"What did you do? Was it that bad that Kyle had to get involved with a guy like Cam?" She asks with what seems like real curiosity. Not a sign of judgment in her eyes like I expected.

"It was bad enough. Things got blown up to be this huge deal and it wouldn't have worked out so well for either one of us if Cam opened his mouth."

"You know it's okay if you don't want to tell me, but you don't have to worry about me saying anything to anyone. Who would I tell anyway?" She questions. Her eyes fall to her hands, her signature move for when she's uncomfortable or embarrassed. I've noticed she does this quite often and I wish she could see just how absolutely perfect she really is. I quickly get on my feet and take in a deep breath as I run my hands through my hair. I tug slightly on the ends as I let out a deep relieving sigh to get my head on straight. I don't need to say the wrong thing to make her think I'm officially the asshole I could have been when we met.

"Jo. Can I take you somewhere?" I'm hopeful she will agree. Even though I know she's still waiting for a better explanation than the one I've just given her. "Um…sure." Where are we going?" She hoists her bag up and brushes off some of the dirt that collected on the bottom and swings it over her shoulder.

"I can tell you but… it's probably better if I show you." I grab my car keys out of my pocket and slowly walk around to the passenger side to open the door for her. "After you." I say eagerly. She walks over to the passenger side and glances up at me, stopping with her hand on top of the door; she leans up towards me and plants a small kiss on my left cheek before she gets in the car. Exhilarated doesn't even begin explain what that did to me. I stand there a second and smirk down at her. She won't look up at me but the pink blush in her cheeks says more than words could right now.

39
Josephine

We've been driving for roughly thirty-five minutes so far and all I can see are trees beside me before the road drops off to an extremely steep cliff leading directly into the frigid water below. I may not be able to see the water at the moment, but Hunter said the river runs beside the entire length of the road all the way to where we're headed. I don't have a clue where he's taking me and I've never been this far away from home since moving here a few years ago, but I'm not as nervous as I thought I would be, or probably should be.

It's been a really peaceful drive, one that has made me close my eyes and breathe the fresh cool air that's coming in through my barely cracked window. Hunter wouldn't tell me even after asking him a million times on the way up here where exactly it is we are going. He just said it was better if I saw it for myself.

"Are we almost there, or are you just driving me out in the middle of the woods to help you dump a body or something?" I ask. Meaning for it to sound sarcastic, but it definitely doesn't come out that way. The reason I can tell is that the look of horror on Hunter's face says otherwise. All of a sudden Hunter's head tips back and he lets out the loudest belly laugh I have ever heard come from a human being. He laughs so hard that tears actually start running down his face and he has to hold his chest as he tries to inhale some much-needed oxygen before he passes out. *He has such an intoxicating laugh. Is there anything he does that isn't ridiculously hot?*

"No. Hell no! I could never involve you in such a repulsive act. You're far too adorable to get arrested." His grin is still anything but subtle and I love it. "Don't worry, we're almost there, it's just another couple more minutes down the road." He points out the windshield towards the bend up ahead. Hunter turns left to go down off the paved road and pulls onto a dirt road that's just barely covered with thousands of small pebbles. Another thirty seconds beyond that and he makes one last turn into a tunnel that has been constructed by the timber canopies. The sky opens up above our head after passing through and suddenly a vast clearing is up ahead.

Just beyond where Hunter stops the car is a crystal-clear stream and sitting above it is a red covered bridge that connects the fields on either side of it and the backdrop is laced with thousands of tall pine trees that make it look like it's cut off from the rest of the world. Like it's very own little bubble.

The woods are so thick it's impossible to see anything through it from where we are. Above the forest, far in the distance, I can just make out the rolling hills of open land. We must be so much higher up than I thought to be able to see this far into the distance. The sun is shining so bright today that it reflects off of the water, making the bridge look like it's been set ablaze.

"Here we are." Hunter says as he looks out through the windshield with an expression of longing on his face. He looks more at ease than I have ever seen him, but the slight tension in his jaw tells me maybe there's something else to him bringing me here. What that is, only time may tell. He opens his door and gets out, leaving his keys in the ignition before coming around to my side and holds his hand out for me. I take it and let him pull me to my feet once again before he shuts my door without letting go of me and starts walking up towards the bridge, gently pulling me along beside him.

Hunter

"Beautiful, isn't it?" I sigh.

"It really is." She simply replies as we walk up the pathway leading to the bridge. Her eyes stare ahead in awe, as we approach the water and I gently squeeze her hand in between my fingers, appreciating the way that it fits perfectly in mine. Her skin is always so soft and smooth, I cherish every time I get to touch her.

I lead Jo up onto the bridge and rest my arms up on the wooden railing as we stop to look out over the water. Taking her arm and tucking it undermine I rest her hand in between my palms to keep her as close as possible. She leans in towards me, brushing her side against mine, and places her elbow up on the railing, finally resting her chin in her palm. Her eyes a soft gaze as she takes in the surroundings; looking at every inch of this place like she's trying to remember every minute detail by taking a mental picture. She's looking at it the way Maci looked at it the first time I brought her up here. Her eyes dazzle at the sight of untouched beauty.

I notice the deep breath she takes in as she closes her eyes and I automatically have to stare at her as she indulges in the warm rays of the sun shining across her face. He shoulders soften, giving me the impression that maybe she's forgotten about whatever was stressing her out today.

The calming sound of the water flows from under our feet down-and splashes against the rocks along the edges. It's the only sound for miles.

"I use to come here all the time." I reveal; breaking the serene silence that seems to be so easily attainable with her.

"This place is really special to you, isn't it?" She asks as she stares down into the crystal-clear water. I subtly nod my head.

"Mm-hm."

"How did you ever find this place?" She angles her body in my direction as the breeze caresses her skin and swirls her hair away her face, exposing the side of her neck to me. I fight the urge to let my eyes wander over her body any further than her bare neck. She's just so beautiful; it's difficult to keep my eyes in my head. The sunlight just adds to her beauty by highlighting those gorgeous doe eyes of hers. They sparkle like the night sky and are so clear that I can see the waters reflection in them so perfectly. Jo looks back out over the distance in front of us, smiling, and with such excitement in her expression, she seems so happy. Happier than I have been able to witness her being since the day I met her. I would give anything to freeze this moment if it meant that I could see her smile like this every single day for the rest of my life.

"I found it the day I took my driver's test. As soon as I passed, I didn't go home and tell everyone like most people would have. I just started driving and didn't stop until I ended up here."

"That sounds like the perfect day to me." She agrees.

"It was." I say easily.

"So, are you going to tell me why this is your favorite place, or am I going to have to play twenty questions and guess?" She graciously asks, once again breaking the silence with her silky sweet voice. I can't help but to want to tell her every single detail. She just has this honesty about her that makes me want to tell her everything. *What is wrong with my brain?*

Josephine

I stand beside Hunter and wait for him to tell me more about this little piece of heaven. Not wanting to interrupt him, since he seems to finally be opening to me.

"This became the place where my sister Maci and I would come hang out a lot. Mostly when our parents were throwing some obnoxious dinner party for their friends. This became our place to just exist, however we chose."

"Do you and Maci still come up here a lot?" I ask him after a minute. And I can see the sadness appear in his eyes so suddenly that it throws me off and puts a stale taste in my mouth.

"I do." He says sadly. His shoulders draw in towards his body, making him appear smaller; more guarded. Compared to the strength I'm used to seeing in him; he suddenly looks utterly defeated. What he tells me next, I understand why…"

40
Hunter

One year ago

No Maci. Mom and Dad already told you you're not allowed to go until next year. I'm not going to be the one they rip into, if they find out that I took you to a party while they are out of town." I never raise my voice to my sister, but right now being brash seems like my only option because she refuses to listen to me.

"Well, I'll just have Cole take me then if you won't!" She shrieks at me with her hand propped up on her hip to emphasize her determined little attitude. I know her mind is set on going, but I'm hoping to be able to somehow talk her out of it.

"Look, Kyle just wants me to meet him there. We most likely won't stay long anyway. So again, it would be pointless to even take you." I reiterate to her while trying to be as casual as possible about the biggest party of the year. I obviously don't want her to know. She'll want to go even more if she finds out that there's going to be live music. One of her favorite bands is going to be playing, and I won't be able to keep her away if she finds out.

"Hunter, I'm going whether you take me or not. I'm not missing the best party of the year just because mom and dad said I can't go. I'm not even grounded; they just don't think I'm mature enough to handle a party with a bunch of drunk high school douche bags."

Shit! Cole must have told her more about it than I thought.

"Yeah, that's exactly why you shouldn't go, because all of the ass-hats that go to our school are going to be there! You know what they're like sober, why would you want to be around them when they're all wasted?" I challenge, hoping she'll give it a second thought and decide to stay home and call one of her girlfriends to come over or something to do, whatever it is that girls do when they hang out together.

"Okay fine." She says, her voice is all of a sudden calm and that can only mean one thing. She pulls out her phone and starts typing something.

"What are you doing now?" I question before pulling the phone out of her hand.

"Hey!" She squeals. "I'm telling Cole to pick me up on his way to the party." She quickly swipes the phone back from me and continues typing. "As if it's any of your business."

I weigh my options. Either I take her to this damn party and keep an eye on her, or she goes with her asshole boyfriend, that our parents know nothing about by the way and I get my ass chewed out when they get home; if they find out she went at all. Which my guess is, they will because her friends have big mouths and can't seem to stay off fucking social media. Not a great combination when you're trying to keep a secret from parents who check up on everything their kids do.

"Alright fine!" I huff out a loud defeated breath. "I'll take you." Maci looks up at me and stops texting simultaneously. Her pissy, pouty, little I-get-my-way-with everything smirk, quickly turns into a spoiled little grin fit for a princess. She runs up to me, throwing her hands around my neck, squeezing the dear life out of me as she hugs me. Knowing she has gotten her way; I have become her favorite brother again.

"On one condition…" I say as I pull away from her to look her in the eye, letting her know I'm serious. She looks up at me waiting to hear some sort of bullshit stipulation I usually spat out, but I'm not playing any games this time. Because now, she has a boyfriend, and I don't trust him a single bit after hearing his name around school. I know my sister. She has to see what an ass-hat he is for herself. She won't listen to anything I say about any of her boyfriends. And she's right, I will hate them *all* no matter what.

"Fine. What's the condition then?" She asks, crossing her arms over her chest with her phone still in her hand.

"No drinking." I tell her flat out. Her expression quickly falls, but it tells me that she understands I'm serious about it. She's underage and she knows how I feel about her being around these people in the first place. She heard me talking to Kyle about the shit that has gone down at these parties plenty of times. It's another reason why I don't drink. "Okay." She responds timidly. I know she's not lying to me when she agrees with what I said. We have always had an understanding between the two of us. I've always looked out for her as my little sister and she has always looked up to me to protect her. We're the two youngest out of the four of us siblings. Almost two years apart from each other. So naturally, I guess that's why we have always gotten along so well. Our other brothers Jason and Dylan are older than me by four and five years so they're hardly around anymore; since they have their own lives and both live out of state.

Maci starts up the stairs to go get ready for the party when I call up to her.

"Maci…" She stops on the landing and looks back at me. "Don't make me regret this, alright?" I plead. She nods her head and smiles.

"You know I can't promise you that big brother." She says with a devious smirk, and then bounces down the hallway to her bedroom.

I am so going to regret this, aren't I?

AFTER MACI GOT done changing outfits about five times, we pull up in front of a large house an hour later. We could hear the rumble of the music from a few blocks away as we drive down the street, so the party I can assume is already going strong. I pull up to park where my car would have less of a chance of getting puked on. It's between a large oak tree and an unsightly rose bush. Knowing the many thorns on said bush could scratch the hell out of my car I carefully open my door, only wide enough to get out and avoid scratching my paint. I did just get done restoring this thing and I would lose my fucking mind if anything happened to it. My sister gets out of the car and immediately has her phone in her line of sight. I swear one day she's going to walk into a tree.

"Maci." I call to her before she joins her girlfriends that are already waiting for her on the porch.

"Yeah?" She looks up from her phone and turns around to face me.

"I'll meet you back here in three hours." She looks at me and nods her head and then walks up on the porch and out of sight. I let out an exhausted breath and lock my car when I hear some moron yelling from behind me. "Hunter!" I hear myself being summoned. *Must be Kyle.* He's the only one that has the shriek of a howler monkey when he's been drinking. As I turn, I see the head of the school mascot staggering towards me.

"What the hell?" I say under my breath. "Why do you have the fucking bird head on? And where the hell did you even find that thing?" I yell across the lawn to him. He takes the head off and drops it by his feet right before suddenly bending over and puking into the rose bushes. *Better the roses than my car.* "Started without me I see." Kyle finally stands upright and wipes his mouth with his sleeve. *Gross.*

"It's so fucking hot in there. I probably shouldn't have drunk whatever was in the punch bowl." He belches out.

"No one should ever drink what's in that bowl." I say, one hundred percent agreeing with him. Especially after seeing what he just barfed up.

A WHILE LATER I finally spot Maci after looking through the crowd of sweaty drunk idiots. She makes keeping track of her almost impossible. But I always make sure to have eyes on her so she doesn't get into too much trouble. For one, there's a ton of people here I'm sure don't even go to our school since I have never seen them before tonight. So, I guess more people heard about the live band playing. Kyle is back and forth between trying to get the number of this new girl he's been stalking at school and trying to get me to have a few beers with him. I always tell him the same thing. I don't drink. I don't really see the point. The stuff tastes like toilet water and by the way Kyle looks and smells when he wakes up with a hangover, I can tell I wouldn't fancy smelling like that. I've only ever seen people regret getting wasted, and I don't ever want to be one of them.

41
Hunter

The band started setting up as soon as they got here over an hour ago. They finally start playing and as they do I whip my head over to where I just heard the most ear -piercing squeak. Of course, I knew it had to be coming from my sister and sure enough it did. She's bouncing up and down to the beat of the base, keeping up with the rhythm unlike her friends, who I'm sure are already past their alcohol tolerance, by the looks of it. Maci stops and looks around and swiftly makes eye contact with me. I freeze because the look on her face says she may be a little pissed. I can never tell if it's genuine anger or just her letting me know that she's going to kill me for not telling her about who the band was.

"Why didn't you tell me that they were the ones playing tonight? You know they're my favorite band!" Maci yells over the music and the screaming frenzy of people so I can hear her.

"Because you weren't allowed to come and I didn't want you to think you were missing out." At this time the song hits a very well-known chorus and everyone goes nuts over it. They start singing along with the band and jumping to the beat; increasing the decibel level well above what I'm sure the windows can handle for an extended period of time without shattering. She gives me a sour look and crosses her arms like she's about to rip into me again.

"You're here now, aren't you? Just enjoy the party and go crazy Maci. You can kill me later if you still want to." I playfully shove her shoulder, and she slaps me back, sticks out her tongue and saunters back over to her friends.

"Mate come on, just one drink." Kyle holds a can of what I only assume is beer because the name on it is in another language that I cannot for the life of me pronounce even sober. "Then you and I can officially say we attended the greatest party of our entire High School careers."

Kyle slurs his words a little and I can tell he's had another couple of drinks after puking his guts out earlier. A little too close to my car I might add.

"Alright fine." I finally concede and grab the drink from Kyle.

"That's it… relax a little and enjoy the party for once." Kyle tells me. I open the beer and only just put it to my lips to get the taste. If it's gross, I'm chucking it.

KYLE DISAPPEARED SHORTLY after he handed me a second drink, this time in a red cup. The first one wasn't half bad. The second was something different and tasted like ass. *I should have stuck with the shit in the can.* The band left a while ago and the music has died down significantly so I can finally hear myself think for the first time since we arrived. I checked in with Maci and she of course talked me into staying longer. I scan the dying crowd for her once in a while and take up space in the further corners of the room while I nurse my drink since Kyle gave it to me over an hour ago. If I finish it, he will just keep giving me more. I don't need anymore, so I just let him think I got my own when he was off doing whatever the hell he was doing.

"HUNTER! YO HUNTER!" I hear someone frantically yelling my name from the backyard. The few people that seem to know me look my way as I hurry through the kitchen towards the back door. I have to push past a few drunken idiots that are using the doorframe to lean on to try and keep themselves upright.

"Hunter!" Kyle comes barreling through the yard and up onto the deck. He was out of breath and looking like he was going to puke for the second time tonight by the time he was able to get out what he needed to say.

"Shit. Okay, you need to go get Maci." He gasps, bent over and bracing his hands on his knees.

"Where the hell is she Kyle?!" I demand as the adrenaline has already started coursing through my veins.

"Around the back by the creek." He points and I take off running that way as fast as I can before the last word leaves his mouth.

I can hear Kyle's heavy footsteps following behind me as we run to the very back of the property. I know I can always count on him to have my back even when he's shit-faced and knows that he can't win a fight to save his life when he is. I stop and notice the creek beyond the trees but here are still so many people out here I have to look around for a minute before I see my sister. Within seconds of spotting her, a guy's hand comes out of nowhere and strikes her across the face; making her stumble painfully to the ground. At this point all I see is red and I take off after him. I run up behind him and yank on the collar of his t-shirt, bringing my right fist around to make contact with the side of his face with a heavy thud.

It was hearing Maci screaming that brought me back. I regard my surroundings and see my sister standing above me. Her eyes are red-rimmed and her makeup is smeared down her raw cheeks leaving black tear lines behind as she cries out and begs for me to stop. Her hands are still clenching the sleeve of my shirt as she tries to pull me away and I suddenly realize that I'm sitting on top of someone and my knees are on either side of his ribcage, keeping him pinned to the ground. I look down at the guys face and I see blood spouting out of his nose and running down the inside of his ear. The rest of his face is splattered with the red substance, much like my right hand and t-shirt. I slowly look around and see everyone from the party is standing in a quiet circle around the three of us. Not one person is talking or making any kind of noise. The only sounds are coming from my little sister's sobs that are muffled by her hands over her mouth and the labored breathing of the guy that I just laid into. I finally put the two together and realize he's Maci's boyfriend. *Fuck.*

42
Hunter

What the hell is wrong with you Hunter, you could have killed him!" Maci is understandably pissed off at me. She's screaming at me as I try and coax her across the lawn to get to my car. I don't say a word while we walk over to the passenger side and I open the door and get her to sit by gently pushing her in the seat. Her words rip bitterly through the air and into my head as I shut the door and run to the driver's side to get in. She tells me what a fucking asshole I am and I take it, still not saying a word in response. If I open my mouth now, I'm afraid I may say something that I can't take back.

I slam on the clutch and throw my car into reverse. My body vibrates as rage flows though me and I don't see it letting up anytime soon. All I care about is getting Maci as far away from that asshole as I can so, I speed off down the road as Maci slaps at my arms, demanding my attention.

"Hunter!" She yells my name again. The anger just keeps building up and I don't trust myself to keep it curbed long enough to stop me from going back and laying into that prick again. I blew up once tonight already, I can't do it again. "Are you going to say something or what?!" She pauses and takes in a deep breath to ready herself to scream at me some more. I just know it.

"Damn it, Hunter! Do you know how much trouble you're going to be in now? How could you do that to Cole?! He didn't mean it, okay? It was an accident. Just take me back so I can see that he's alright!"

"Are you crazy? You think that was an accident? I saw the whole thing. He meant to hit you. And he fucking did it hard enough to bring your face to the god damn ground. You're insane if you think I'm taking you back there!" I loudly huff out my frustration that's building inside my chest. "Besides, I told Kyle to stay behind and make sure he was still breathing! I'm not stupid so don't fucking worry about it!"

"It was an accident! He's got a temper but he's getting better." She says, much quieter than she was a few seconds ago when she was blaring her attitude in my ear. When she stops talking for more than half a second, I realized that she just revealed something to me that I'm not sure she really meant to, something I should have noticed before tonight. *He'd hit her before! And I didn't have a clue.*

This makes my blood boil to recognize just how stupid I have to be to not notice my little sister's relationship was a shit show from the beginning. Now I regret having Kyle even helping the little twat. At least Kyle's smart enough, drunk or not, to get out of there in case someone from the party called the cops.

"He's fucking hit you before, hasn't he?" My words demand she tell me the truth. I know it's true. I just need to hear her say it so I can make her understand that what I did to him was justifiable.

"It's none of your business!" She screams at me with fierceness in her eyes.

"It is my fucking business Maci. And if you think I'm not going to tell mom and dad about this as soon as we get home, think again!" I warn her. I hope the threat of telling our parents will make her think twice about ever going back to being with him. "I'm sure they would have a field day knowing that their only daughter has been dating an abusive piece of shit!" I spat. She knows I have every intention of telling them and she can't say a damn thing about it.

"You can't tell them!" This time her voice rattles the windows with the amount of displeasure seething from her mouth. She stares at me again and she looks like a rabid animal losing her mind.

"He's lucky he's not fucking dead after what you just told me!" I roar! The words rush out of my mouth before I can rein in the disgust that seeps out with them. The expression on her face breaks my heart, because I know I have caused her a great deal of pain that she didn't deserve. "Your piece of shit boyfriend deserved what he got and I would do it again without a second fucking thought Maci! You can't think that I would just let someone lay a hand on you and not do anything about it!" I'm so far past pissed that I can hear my pulse hammering in my ears. I'm even more spiteful knowing he's hurt her before and I can't get why she's protecting him right now! I turn the corner faster than I should and I notice the car sliding slightly over the middle line so I gently let my foot off the gas to slow down. The street is still damp from the early spring shower we had just before the band packed up to leave.

"I'm not the asshole in this situation Maci. Your boyfriend is alright. He's the one that's put his hands on you and nearly cracked your jaw by the looks of it." I motion to the left side of her face. "Now tell me, how am I the bad guy here when all I did was get you away from that prick before he did anything else?!"

"He loves me, okay!" She cries out with such intensity, that it makes me realize she actually thinks that's true! She's blind to him being wrong for her in so many ways.

"Are you that fucking stupid Maci?! He doesn't love you he just wants to get in your pants and then he'll leave you like every other guy out there does to girls like you!"

"You can go to hell Hunter, I fucking hate y…."

Just then everything goes silent. The radio that seemed to be narrating our rage-filled brawl inside the car has suddenly become static. The sound echoes in my ears as a high-pitched ringing gets louder and my head starts throbbing. I lift my hand to the side of my face and feel a warm wetness dripping from my eyebrow. My eyes feel like they're caked with sand as I try to pry them open and search around me for whatever it is I think I need to find when I touch something soft. I carefully peel open my eyes and there, lying in front of me is my sister. She's on her side and her head rests against the steering wheel in an awkward position, so I try to move her.

"Maci, Maci wake up." I say as I nudge her arm. I shift my body closer but when I feel a searing pain rip through my shoulder, I realize that my left arm is tangled up in an uncomfortably awkward position.

I look around, grateful for what little light there is shining through the broken windshield but I don't understand what happened, all I know is it's not good when I see that there's blood now coming from the corner of my sister's mouth. The more I move, the worse the dizziness gets, but I finally get my arm free before I feel like I'm going to pass out again.

"Maci wake up." I rub her cheek as gently as possible. I know she's hurt and I don't want to make it worse but she doesn't even flinch, she doesn't blink or move at all. The worry in my gut has me frantically struggling to get myself upright as I desperately try to get my bearings.

There's broken glass everywhere and I can feel it poking through my jeans and slice my knees to shreds as I crawl out of my window. I stumble around the car, using it to steady myself until I reach the passenger's side. I bend down to reach inside the window and grab hold of Maci's jacket and as gently as I can, I drag her out onto the pavement. The pain in my shoulder weakens my grip but I manage to get her out and lay her down on the ground; checking to see how badly she's hurt. There's not much to see other than a small red and purple gash on her head and the delicate little trickle of blood drying along her mouth.

"I called for help. The ambulance is on its way." I hear someone off to the side of my car talking to me but all I can focus on is trying to get my sister to wake up. I can hear my heartbeat in my ears as my blood pumps so fast, it makes it impossible to tell if I can feel a pulse on her or not and I can't catch my breath as I plead with her to open her eyes; but she doesn't move. She doesn't, fucking move!

The longer she stays silent the more worried I get as I sit here holding her close.

"Maci please, please wake up. I'm sorry, I'm so fucking sorry. Please, I don't want to lose you. Maci, please wake up…you have to!" I cry and choke on my words as I sob into her hair, but after a while, they grow softer but even more painful as I remember what our last words to each other were. My tears blanket my vision, making it difficult to differentiate between them and the rain but I sit on the cold wet ground clutching onto my sister for dear life as she lies on top of my legs and I hold her in my arms, until help comes.

Only I know they're already too late.

43
Hunter

Silence. It's all that's left. It's all that surrounds me as I sit by Maci's side and hold her hand, feeling what little warmth that is left being slowly drained away from her with each passing minute. The machines have since been turned off that were temporarily breathing for her. The oxygen being pumped into her lungs for that short time made her chest slowly rise and fall, again and again; giving the illusion that there was some life still left inside her. The rhythm was devastating because it had given me a few short seconds of hope that she would wake up. That she would by some miracle feel the oxygen filling her lungs and she would come back to me. But that minute amount of hope was ripped away from me as soon as the doctors told me there was nothing more they could do because she had died on impact in the crash. At that moment I can honestly say that I felt my heart stop…and it so effortlessly brought me to my knees.

I haven't left her since. So many hours have been lost on me as I stay by her side. The doctors keep encouraging me to go back to my room to get some rest but I won't leave her. I can't think of ever leaving her alone for even a second in this cold and sterile room; while the harsh, unfriendly lights blind her into a forever sleep. I requested them to be turned off after they said I could stay and have as much time as I needed.

They finally understood that they weren't going to get me to leave, even if they had tried to drag me out; I was not going to move.

"Hunter!" I recognize my name as someone lets it out in a bellowing cry just outside the door. I turn my head, and bear witness to a devastating version of what once was a bright, strong and youthful woman. My mother is hardly recognizable as she collapses on the cold laminate floor in front of me. Her dress is crinkled and her hair for the first time doesn't have every single strand in its rightful place. The long flight back and the added worry about Maci had clearly taken an immense toll on her. Her saturated eyes stare through me, dark and vacant as if she doesn't see me standing right in front of her. I look down and follow her gaze to see what's caught her attention so immediately and realize that Maci's hand is still tightly clutched in mine. Her skin is pale and it's now the color of fresh snow and striking against my tanned complexion. I don't move or speak, or even breathe for as long as I stand here staring down at my sister.

Her skin has irrevocably lost the glow that was Maci. She always had this light about her that seemed to brighten any room that she would walk into; even when she was having a bad day or in one of her well-known lousy moods. You couldn't help but be happy when you were around her. And now all of that seems to have faded with her without a trace the second she was gone.

My mother is in the background, sobbing uncontrollably on the floor, and is being comforted by my father. I know I should go to her, pick her up and support her weight with mine. Let her cry on my shoulder and be strong for her, but it's not in my power to walk away yet. I haven't the strength to let go. I'm afraid if I - that's it. I'll be letting go of my baby sister forever, and I don't think I can survive that. *It's too soon.*

"Hunter…" My mother's broken cries softly call to me as my father helps her up. He's holding her as if she's going to crumble into dust if he were to let go. I turn to face my mom as she places her arms around me, pulling me into her and sparing me what little strength she may have left for me. My arms gradually wrap themselves around my mother's small frame and I can feel the immediate loss of my sister's fragile little fingers as her hand slips out from mine.

"I'm so…sorry mom." I cry out to her. The tears overwhelm me again as I let myself collapse into her arms. I feel my father embrace the both of us and tightly hold us together as he stands quietly, not one weakened sob threatening to burst out of him. He's so afraid of showing any emotions, that he can't even spare a few tears for his only fucking daughter! It makes me hate him right now.

"Hunter, please… tell me what, what happened." She sobs through the tears and it kills me to hear those dreaded words I was hoping she would never ask. I don't want to remember the last horrifying moments I spent alone holding my sister's lifeless body while the rain drenched us both; but leaving only me an uncontrollably shivering mess. I pull my head off of my mother's shoulders and look down into her eyes. I tower over her so, I feel I should be the stronger one right now, but the strength my mother needs to have; to hear what she asked of me cannot come from me. Mine, is spent, I have nothing left to give. Maci took it all with her when she left this world.

"Mom." I clear my throat and look down at her hands holding mine. Grasping them as tightly as she can to prepare herself for what she's about to hear. "Maci…" I have to swallow the lump in my throat when I say my sister's name. It's going to take everything I have to get this out. "Maci and I went…went to go see that band that, that she told you about before you left on your trip. I know, I know you said she couldn't go but…but she begged me mom, and I felt that if she went with me then I could keep a better eye on her since she was going to be with Cole, I didn't want her alone with, with him." The more I tell her, the faster the words barrel out of me, desperate to get them out so I can be free of them.

"Cole? Who, who is this Cole you're talking about?" She demands. Now more alert than she was just minutes ago. A stranger's name has brought her out of the daze she's most likely been in for hours since she found out about the crash.

"He's Maci's boyfriend." I whisper under my breath. I knew they had no idea about him and I don't want to paint my sister in a bad light but they have to know what happened. "Mom, listen to me please…please. Maci was dating this guy Cole and he put his hands on her at the party, so I got her out of there as quickly as I could. I just don't know where everything went wrong mom, I was looking out for her I promise." I whimper.

My strangled words come out in a weak cry, pleading with my parents to understand. My body starts to jerk as I try to contain every negative emotion that's now rising to the surface. It's agonizing to be telling them this but they need to know.

"Were you drinking Hunter?" My father asks. His tone harsh but as calm as I ever heard him.

"What?" I question, surprised that he would ask me that after what I just told them. He hasn't said a word since my mother came barging in the door. "Dad I…" I don't know how to tell him. I'm sure he's going to get the wrong idea.

"The truth Hunter." My father interrupts me before I could get my thoughts to make any sense.

"Yes." I finally answer him, feeling defeated. It's the only thing I say in response. I know anything I say after they simply just won't hear. Not tonight at least.

44
Hunter

I thought tonight couldn't possibly get any worse, but it turns out, that I couldn't have been more wrong.

"Dad I, I don't know what to tell you because I don't know what went wrong. I don't remember everything that h, happened." My words fumble out of my mouth and fall on deaf ears. I can tell my father doesn't want to hear any excuses. *How can I blame him?* His only daughter, the baby of the family is dead because of me being reckless! "Dad, please just, just listen to me, okay?" I plead with my father as he walks away from me and over to my mother. She's hovering over my sister and sobbing even harder than she was when she came into the room. I didn't think her cries could sound any more devastating than they already had.

I roughly scrub my hands across my face, at the tears that continue to fall that have soaked through my t-shirt, making the material cling to my skin. I stumble over to my mother and try to get both of their attention but they won't even look at me.

"Mom, dad please let me explain. It's not even what you're thinking…I promise. You know I don't drink like that. I just had one beer I swear. Something else happened at the party with Maci and…."

"*Hunter enough!"* My father's words crash off of the walls inside the tiny room, which seems to have only gotten smaller since he appeared in the doorway. He finally looks me in the eye, a straight-lipped frown of disappointment strewn across his face. But beneath the anger, beneath the disappointment, is a sadness that no father should have to feel; especially when he feels that sadness, because of his own son.

"Son…I think now would be a good time for you to go home." He speaks to me as if he's talking to someone that's taking his coffee order. Cold and distant. All emotion has been wiped clean from the energy that has been spent talking to me. It's like hearing a stranger in my father's voice so, I say nothing more to him or my mother. It's no use. All they see when they look at me now is the person that has caused them an immense amount of pain, and they don't want that reminder around anymore. I only wish they could know how sorry I am, and that they could forgive me.

I left Maci in the room alone with my parents. I still needed to say goodbye but I couldn't bring myself to do it. Not with my parents in the room. I lost my chance to tell her how much I love her and how it breaks my heart that now I have to live the rest of my life missing her every single day. I lost count of the many apologies I muttered to her in the hours I sat by her side. *Serves me right though; why should I get closure when it's my fault that she's gone?*

I WAKE UP to a loud banging coming from downstairs. I don't give a shit about a damn thing right now so I roll over and shove a pillow against my head to drown out the noise; trying my best to ignore it.

"Hunter." My parent's housekeeper yells to me from downstairs. I ignore her and shove another pillow over my head and press down as hard as I possibly can until it's hard to breathe; but I can still hear the dampened sound of her footsteps coming up the stairs.

"Hunter." She bangs a few times on the door. I let out a loud groan to signal I'm not in the mood for company right now, but she still continues to thump her fist against my bedroom door, making sure that I get up.

"You should come downstairs now. There are police officers here to speak with you Hunter."

The words 'police officer' makes my sleep-deprived brain wake up immediately as I quickly sit upright in my bed. Swirling nausea suddenly hits and I have to hang my head between my shoulders until it passes. *I hope they found the fucker that hit us last night. I'd love nothing more than to get my hands on him right now!*

I drag myself out of bed so fast that I don't give my body anytime to adjust or account for the amount of pain that suddenly hits me out of nowhere. My body aches and cries out for me to sit back down by making me noticeably dizzy. The pain killers the doctors had given me at the hospital must have worn off because I can feel every muscle in my body painfully contract just by taking in a few shallow breaths and the searing pull in my arm catches me off guard. I take a minute to catch my breath and reach for the prescription of pain killers that they filled last night that are on my table next to my bed. I pop two in my mouth and swallow them dry. They don't go down easily, but like a batch of rusty nails that scrape their way down into my gut.

The doctors wanted me to stay overnight for observation considering the scale of the accident, but I couldn't stay there any longer. I just left and didn't even sign myself out. No one seemed to notice. Not even my parents. My father told me to leave, so that's what I did.

I stand up after a minute and grab the t-shirt that's thrown over my desk chair with my good arm. It's probably the cleanest of anything that's in my room. I make an effort to move slower because my body is unusually stiff and the many cuts across my skin feel awful as I drag the fabric of my t-shirt over them. Getting my arms over my head to put my shirt on is a feat in itself, but it's nothing compared to the ache that resides in my chest when I pass a photo I have of Maci on my dresser. It glares at me as I walk past it, a constant reminder of what I lost last night.

I finally make my way downstairs. Not having brushed my teeth or my hair, so I'm sure I look like a train wreck. *I certainly feel like one.* I open the door to find two guys in formal suits.

"Can I help you, gentlemen?" I ask as I lean on the door for support to take some weight off of my back. They turn to face me, the look of annoyance clear on both of their faces from having to wait while I tried to pull myself together.

"Mr. Alistar Scott?" The one says in question. Reaching out to shake my hand; I assume.

"No. Mr. Scott is my father. I'm his son." I extend my hand to shake his. My arm feels like it weighs a hundred pounds, making a simple handshake all the more painful.

"My mistake. Is your father home? We have some information about the incident last night. We would like to speak to him in person."

"I don't know if he's actually in…"

"Detectives…" I hear my father say from behind me. I turn and see him walking towards us. Hand outstretched to shake their hands like he always does; well before he would even be close enough to. "Thank you for coming so soon. I heard you have news for me." He invites them in, guiding them over to the sitting room, as my mother calls it. He's well dressed as usual, pressed suit, slicked hair, not a single fucking difference than any other day. Almost like last night never happened

For him. I guess that's the difference between the two of us. As shitty as it feels, I still have a heart. His has frozen, leaving him no real feelings to make him look like he's shed even a single god damn tear.

"The boy was found hiding out at his girlfriend's house a couple of hours after the accident. He was pretty banged up so he was taken to the hospital for care early this morning." The dark-haired officer clarifies that the asshole that hit us was driving home from a party last night. The same party that Maci and I were also at it turns out.

"And I assume that he will be charged accordingly?" My father states.

"Yes. We also needed to inform you that he wasn't just under the influence of alcohol. He had drug paraphernalia in his car and tested positive for a prescription medication that didn't belong to him. The combination made him black out temporarily, causing him to side-swipe your son's car. He fled the scene before anyone got a chance to talk to him. But the license plate showed that the car belonged to his father, so we located his family to inform them about the situation as well." The man says all this like he discussing some casual business details, not the life altering accident that killed my sister!

"Situation! I would hardly call it a situation." My father hurriedly stands up at an intimidating pace. "Mind you, my only daughter is dead because of that boy and I fully intend to press charges against him." He's now towering above the detectives that sit on the large gray sofa across from him. They glance at each other quickly as if to say they know that my father's mind is set and that he doesn't plan on changing it. My attention is pulled away from the conversation when I hear my mother come down the hall. She walks past me and doesn't utter a single word to me as she joins my father. *I can't stand here and listen to any more of this.* I know when I'm not welcome and by my parents to not even acknowledge that I'm standing in the same room, a mere three feet from them, hurts more than if they were to tell me they hate me for what I let happen.

I start to make my way down the hall when I hear someone knock at the door again. *Doesn't anyone use the fucking doorbell anymore?*

The vibrations of them pounding makes my eyes feel like they're being pressed out of my skull, so I hurry to the door, letting out a frustrated breath, and open it for the second time this morning to see two police officers; this time in full uniform. Badges on their chests, guns at the ready on their belts and one of them has that stupid haircut you see when rookies just get out of the academy. “Can I help you, officers?” Me being sleep deprived and in a lot of pain, since the painkillers haven’t started working yet, I question in the cockiest tone that I can muster up; which I would soon come to regret.

“Are you Hunter Scott?” The older one asks. He gives me a strange look when he says my last name. *Hmm, he must know my father.*

“Yeah. What’s this about?” I question, a little less cocky than before. My father comes around the corner with my mother following behind him, and behind her are the other detectives getting ready to leave.

“Hunter, what is going on out here? Who is at the door?” My father demands. And as soon as he does, we all get the answer.

“Sir I’m afraid that we’re going to have to take your son into custody.” The balding one says. *What the fuck?!*

“On what grounds? The detectives here have already informed me of the matter that involves the other driver, not my son.”

“Sir we’re not here about the car accident. We heard what happened and we’re very sorry for your loss but this is an entirely different matter involving only your son and another boy.” I stand in the hallway, hearing my father go back and forth about this incident and the charges; all bullshit that doesn’t seem to be registering in my brain. Their voices are a distant echo to me as I remember why I was in such a hurry to leave the party in the first place. *Maci’s fucking boyfriend.*

“Hunter Scott, you’re under arrest for the assault and battery of Cole Owens.” I feel the officers grab hold of my arms and place the cold metal of the handcuffs around both my wrists. I don’t say anything, even though I am withering in pain from him forcing my injured arm behind my back. I see the look on my parent’s faces before the officer walks me out of the front door. It’s the look of disappointment. I’ve come to know this look well over the last twenty-four hours, and if I never saw it again, it would be too soon.

SEVERAL HOURS LATER and I’m sitting in the passenger seat of my father’s car. He’s been silent the entire drive back after picking me up from the holding center downtown. He didn’t even come in to speak to the officers who arrested me to find out what I had done. He just sent his lawyer in instead to handle everything. *I guess I’m not worth the effort anymore.* The officers had a lot of questions, but they informed me not to answer them until my father's lawyer was present. My father is well known in this community and lucky for me the cops in this town actually like him. I was charged with first-degree assault and battery and had a restraining order filed against me to stay no less than five hundred feet away from Cole. My father's lawyer however got it reduced considering it was my first offense and claiming that I was protecting my sister. I have to serve six months of community service and I'm on probation for the next two years until I graduate Highschool. Considering I broke his nose, shattered his cheekbone, and dislocated his shoulder, I would say it was well worth me getting charged to see that he got a taste of his own medicine. Maybe now he will think twice before putting his hands on another girl.

45
Hunter

After what I just revealed about my past to Jo, I expected her to look at me as if I'm some horrible monster that shouldn't be allowed to breathe the same air. I don't get that feeling at all while looking into her eyes because all I see is the sadness and empathy that pours out of them along with the tears that are staining her cheeks.

A few moments of silence have passed between us and I hear Jo take in a deep breath as she lets her shoulders finally relax a little as we stand only inches apart. She hasn't let go of my hands or tried to pull away from me in the slightest; her grip has only gotten tighter.

"Hunter, I'm so sorry that that happened to you and your sister. I can't imagine what that must have been like, and I can't tell you how sorry I am that I brought up something that has caused you so much pain. It was stupid of me." She sounds so dejected as her voice marginally weakens. I try to reassure her that she has nothing to be sorry about, but she doesn't let me. "Wait. Can I just say one thing?" She quickly asks as her eyes start to glisten from the tears threatening to break free again. "You have to know, that none of that was your fault. It wasn't. You can't blame yourself for what happened. It was out of your control." Her words are filled with the strength I wish I could possess, like she knows it in her heart to be true. It's giving me a sense of relief that she hasn't run away from me yet. Anyone else would have by now. Instead, she's standing by my side giving me hope without even knowing it. I move our hands closer to my chest, holding both of hers tightly against me so that she has to take a step forward, so I can plant a small kiss on her knuckles, and I feel the coolness of her skin against my lips. I'm grateful for the small moments that she allows me to have with her; and this is a moment I will always remember. "Jo." I look up at her after pulling my lips away from her delicate fingers. "You're the first person that I've ever told. I need you to know that I didn't tell you so you feel sorry for me." I gauge her expression as I confess what I have been dreading for her to find out. "I need to explain what happened. I want to be honest with you because you deserve better than me, better than what I can offer you." I notice the slight hesitation that's starting to appear on her face, but she doesn't say anything. "The day I dropped you off at my car and had to go back to Kyle's well, when I went back, I found him in pretty rough shape. Someone beat the hell out of him and left him there to die. The only one that was there at the time was that guy Cam that showed up as we were leaving his house." I start to explain.

"Oh my god! Wait, you mean the guy from the bonfire? The guy whose nose you broke?" She asks. Panic lacing her words. It's a shock to hear such a drastic change in her tone while I see the concern appear on her doll like features.

"Yes." I nod my head to confirm.

"Why what happened? Kyle seemed so nice. Why would Cam do that to him?"

"That's what I need to explain."

Two Weeks Ago…

It was against my better judgment to go home with that blonde tonight. She's Kyle's, girlfriend's, sister, I think…Kyle told me not to mess around with her because he 'knows how I am with girls' and he didn't want to get any shit from his girlfriend. Of course, me being the asshole that I am, I did it anyway. *What he doesn't know won't hurt him, right?* So, I didn't tell him about it. How can he even hold me accountable when he saw how loaded I was? He can't really blame me, she was hot.

The walk home seems so much longer than I remember. Maybe being half a bottle of whiskey in will do that. I stagger along the sidewalk, trying my best to not look blitz out of my mind so I don't draw attention to myself. I could have stayed the night at her place, she said I could, or rather I should have stayed and waited until morning to walk home but, I don't do sleepovers. *Never fucking will.* I'm starting to see double from finishing off the last few shots that were left at the bottom of the bottle. It was after midnight when I left her house, so I shouldn't have an issue running into my parents when I get home. I need to sleep off the shit day I had.

The days are starting to warm as spring will be here soon, but the nights still feel like there's frost in the air; like the sky is about to open up and turn the town into a giant snow globe all over again. I think we're due for one more big snowfall around this time, like every year before this, because it's cold and I am freezing my balls off out here. I stop to take another swig of the bottle, but I remember I just finished the lot. *Fuck!*

I look around to try and get a grasp on the direction of where the hell I'm going when a large gray SUV, sitting in the driveway in front of me catches my attention. I find it in my memory bank somehow that that vehicle, looks a hell of a lot like the one that I saw Cole and his mom get into at the police station as I was walking out. I look around to see whose house it is that it's parked at. Not that I really care but I'm drunk, so anything seems like a good idea right now. I spot the mailbox on the other side of the car and see that the last name printed across it says 'Owens.' *No fucking way!*

The cold air has been quite sobering. Especially when it's mixed with raging indignation that's been shoved down and ignored for a fucking year! I dig in my pocket for my phone and find Kyle's contact. It only rings twice when I hear him yell into the speaker.

"Hunter? What the fuck, why did you bail?"

"Never mind that man, what does Cole drive?" I ask.

"What?" He says, sounding confused.

"What kind of car does Cole Owens drive? Is it a gray Range Rover?" My voice is loud and clear this time to make sure he hears me even over all of the music and the stupid drunken howling in the background.

"Yeah, I think man, why? Where the hell are you?" He urges again. No more than 2 seconds go by and I hear him yell. "OH SHIT! Hunter, don't do anything stupid man!" I'm sure he just realized where I am and what I'm about to do; but I hang up on him before he can say something to try and talk me out of it.

"You son of a bitch!" I shout. Possibly louder than I should have but at this point, I don't give two shits who hears me. I don't give a fuck if I wake the whole god damn neighborhood! Right now, all I can think about is the memory of Cole's hand striking the side of my sister's face! And just like that my switch was flipped.

I smash my hand still holding the glass bottle onto the hood of the car, sending it shattering into a million little pieces and setting off the car alarm. That's not nearly satisfying enough, so I look around for something I can use to that will do a hell of a lot more damage and my attention lands back on the Owens' mailbox. I stomp over and kick at the wooden pole it sits on until it splinters in half, making the top fall with a thunk to the ground. I pick up the larger chunk of wood and land another blow against the driver's door as hard as I can; leaving a massive dent.

I repeatedly swing the heavy piece of wood at the car until the driver's window breaks, and then I slam the metal box down on the middle of the windshield; collapsing a sizeable hole. The glass caves in on itself and it litters the inside of the front seat. I need a minute so I bend over and lean on my knees to ease some of the dizziness and when I open my eyes, I spot a hefty stone in the garden that surrounds the other broken half of the mailbox. I pick it up and stare at it in my hand for a second, promptly contemplating my next move.

Walking up to the side of the car, I start scraping the stone along the door and listen as the alarm continues to blare into the quiet, street. After I scratch every inch of paint on the side of the car, I take a second to stand there and admire my handy work. Zoned in on the satisfaction it gives me to see what a mess I made of Cole's overpriced piece of shit! My entire body is tense and hot and my chest heaves as I rest to catch my breath. The anger still courses through my veins, feeling like it's overflowing and pouring out of me onto the concrete for all the world to see. No matter how much I destroy this fucking thing, it will never bring me enough relief from the pain I will always feel, for the rest of my fucking life.

"Hunter!" I hear someone call to me as I stand at the end of the driveway behind the carnage I've created. Their voice is a distant echo as I look down at the tears falling onto my hand. No one has come out to see what all the noise is about yet, or maybe they have and they chose to ignore the mad man destroying someone's car because it isn't theirs.

"Hunter, what the fuck are you doing man?" Kyle comes up to me and grabs hold of my shoulders, shaking me to get my attention. I'm still staring down at the stone in my hand and I notice a few wet marks that have dripped onto it, turning it a darker shade of gray. "Hunter, are you okay man? Look, you have to get out of here, you're on probation!" The panic in Kyle's voice makes me look up at him and drop the stone to the ground. He's staring at me, waiting for a response. That's when I feel a right smack across my left cheek come out of nowhere. "Dammit Hunter, snap the fuck out of it!" He yells. And I do.

His hand making contact with my cold cheek brings a fierce sting to my face.

"OW! You asshole!" What the fuck did you do that for?" I bark out.

"Because of this, dickhead!" Kyle points to the mangled Range Rover sitting smashed to bits, not two feet from where we are standing. "You need to leave, now! Take my keys and go to my house, I'll deal with this, alright." He instructs.

"I can't drive man, I'm fucking wasted." I groan. My anger is still fresh enough that I don't fucking want Kyle to be here so I can finish the job. "Besides, who the fuck cares?" I shove Kyle off, taking a few steps away from him. "It's not like I can damage my reputation anymore right! Let the prick come out and see what I did to his prized piece of shit!" I howl into the heavens, arms spread wide, a challenge to Cole; praying that he comes outside so I can finish what I started a year ago!

"Are you out of your god damn mind?" Kyle steps in between me and the Owen's front door. Trying to keep me from making anymore foolish mistakes; but it just makes me want to haul off and hit him. "Just think for a fucking minute, would you?" He says and suddenly stops square in front of me so, I try to go around him. Not expecting him to blindside me I don't look at him until I feel his right hook thwack me in the side of the face. I stumble over my feet and careen into the side of the car. Stunned, I glare up at Kyle and vigorously rub at my jaw.

"Is it like that now, Kyle? You can't let me have this one thing, can you?"

"No. It's not like that, but I'm not going to let you destroy your entire life, man. Maci wouldn't want you to do this, any of this, and you damn well know what I mean." Kyle slumps his head in defeat; doubtful that I'm going to listen to him. But there's a reason why he's my best friend; because he knows exactly what to say to bring me back to reality, and this reality has consequences that I can't face alone. Out of nowhere the car alarm chirps once and shuts off, alerting us to the chaos that's about to follow. "Alright…shit okay look just get out of here Hunter. Text Miranda to pick you up as far away from here as she can. Go to my house, no-one's home." I watch Kyle take his house key off of his key ring and shove it in my hand.

"Now get the hell out of here before we *both* get arrested!" He mumbles just as we both hear a door slam. Kyle pushes away from me and starts jogging in the opposite direction and I see him pick up what's left of the splintered mailbox and then disappear behind the car. So, I do what he says, I start running towards his house; leaving him to clean up my mess alone.

46
Kyle

"Yo, Kyle!" My name echoes through the empty street but I don't bother turning around. I know the moment I do it's just going to make my night a whole lot worse if they saw anything that's happened in the last three minutes. I focus down the street and can just barely hear the faint chirps of the sirens as they crawl closer to my location, and I have to think of what to tell the cops once they arrive.

"Kyle!" They call out a second time so, I begrudgingly turn around to see who it is. Just when I thought things couldn't suck anymore… *Ah, Jesus Christ!*

"What the hell do you want Cam?" I ask annoyed while I peer back down the street.

"I see Hunter left you high and dry again." Cam says smugly. *Fuck! How the hell do I get out of this one?* Cam's arrogant stride makes me want to dropkick him in the middle of the street. "Seems to me the asshole just can't handle anything himself these days. I mean after he got Maci killed last year, he's turned into a…" I lunge and tightly grip Cam's shirt and shove him backward, slamming him up against the back of the car, effectively catching the prick off guard.

"Don't ever fucking bring up Maci's name again, you hear me!" I jab my fists harder against Cam's throat, feeling my knuckles dig into his Adams-apple. "She has nothing to do with this, and neither does Hunter, so tell me what the fuck are you're doing here?"

"Whoa man!" He rasps. "Look, I have no problem with you. But Cole's sure going to after he finds out his Rover's been smashed to hell. Well…if you take the fall for Hunter that is." He adds. *What the hell do I do?* Cam's expression is now a devious sneer that I would love nothing more than to wipe clean off his face with my bare hands. *He's toying with me. He must have seen Hunter before I even got here. SHIT!* The sirens are closing in and growing louder the longer we stand here. *I have to get rid of Cam before he opens his big mouth to the cops!*

"Alright!" I release my grip with a shove, making Cam bounce off the back of the car. More glass scatters on the ground as he moves away from the car and straightens his collar.

"What do you want Cam, I don't have all night?" I defeatedly grumble.

"Clearly." He agrees and points down the road. The flashing lights have now come into view, ricocheting off of the windows of every house they pass. It's only a matter of minutes before I have to tell them what happened, and I can't do that with Cam butting in. *He'll nark on Hunter for sure.* "I need you and Hunter to do me a favor; that is if you want to keep this little misunderstanding between the three of us." He points out. that I only have a few seconds to decide what I should do, so he can fuck off. I bite my tongue and I say the only thing that I can think of to keep Hunter's ass out of jail.

"Name your price." I tell him, knowing full well I'm not going to like what he's going to say.

Hunter

The Next Day…

The throbbing in my head sends an ache so bad to my eyes it's difficult to focus on where that irritating noise is coming from. When I realize that it's my phone, I sit up and reach for it on the coffee table. *I have to stop drinking myself stupid!* The name on the screen is a fucking blur so I just unlock it and answer with an annoyed, "Hello?"

"Hunter Scott?" The voice on the other line questions.

"Kyle, man is that you?" I ask. My ears are ringing so badly it's difficult to hear the other person clearly.

"No, Hunter. My name is James Purcell. I'm Kyle's lawyer. He asked me to call you and tell you to come pick him up at the police station in an hour. Do you need the address?" *Fuck! Last n*ight's events are starting to flood their way back into my memory. Kyle took the blame for my dumbass mistake, even after I acted like a childish asshole. A real friend wouldn't have let him take the fall like that; but I did it anyway. "I know where it is. I'll be there. Thanks."

"No problem, I'll tell him." He confirms and ends the call.

I slide my phone in my pocket and shuffle to Kyle's bathroom. I know he always has a hangover remedy in here somewhere. I see a bottle of aspirin so I pour a few in my hand and swallow them, chugging a gallon of water from the faucet to force them down all at once. The cool liquid eases the raw burn from the alcohol-infused bile that's crawling its way up my throat. I clean up as best I can to look halfway normal for when I have to walk into the police station. Looking hungover and getting out of a car wouldn't be the best idea.

I GET TO the station less than an hour later. I had to walk to pick up my car before coming here so I'm grateful that Kyle doesn't live far from my house. I walk slowly to the glass double doors and pull the right one open. The stale air inside hits me in the face, making the nausea worse on my empty stomach.

"Uh, I'm here for Kyle Smith." I tell the officer as I stop at the front desk. He looks up from his paperwork and gives me an intimidating glare, then types something into the computer.

"He will be out in a moment. Who are you in relation to Mr. Smith? He asks.

"I'm his friend." I say quickly. The officer doesn't say anything else about it so I take a seat across the hall and wait for Kyle to come out.

Normally I wouldn't mind waiting so long, but sitting her under the eyes of the one very grouchy officer isn't my idea of fun. When Kyle finally does come out, I feel like I can breathe again, because now we can get the hell out of here. I don't like this place and my ass is numb from sitting on this shitty metal bench. Kyle sees me and just nods his head toward the exit. He walks out first and I silently follow him into the parking lot to my car. I pull out and light a cigarette as I open my door and take a long drag, holding it in until I feel my head buzz.

"Thanks for picking me up, man." Kyle says flatly. I open my eyes and see Kyle staring at me from across the hood of my car.

"No, don't thank me for anything. I owe you one. Not that this will ever make up for what you did for me last night. I don't really remember everything that happened, you want to update me on some things?"

"Well, I'm not going to jail if that's what you're worried about. I got probation and community service, and I have to pay for all the repairs on Cole's car. If I don't, then I'm going to have to serve time. My lawyer wasn't a total twat after all huh?" Kyle adds. I laugh at that last part, even though I probably shouldn't.

"I'm going to pay you back for everything man. The damage to the car was my fault obviously, so I'll get the money to you." I assure him.

"I know. I'm not worried about it. I'm more worried about what Miranda is going to do to me when I see her. I'm sure she asked you what was going on when you called her. But do me a favor…from now on; let's avoid doing stupid shit that will get us arrested. I don't think my record can take another hit if I ever plan on going to college." Not knowing how to respond as the guilt starts ripping my insides to shreds, I take another hit of my cigarette and nod in agreement and get in the car.

"You really don't remember everything from last night?" Kyle asks after a few minutes of silence.

"No, not really. I mean I remember calling you and then standing in the middle of the driveway with a piece of wood in my hand. I think it was a mailbox."

"Yeah, it was. You must have broken it off and then used it to smash in all of Cole's windows." Kyle laughs, making the situation not seem as bad as it is for a brief moment.

"Shit. I'm gonna hate to see that bill when it comes."

"Yeah, you and me both." He huffs. "Hey man…all things aside there's something else I need to tell you." Kyle's tone takes on a seriousness that makes my gut clench.

"Okay…out with it then man." I urge.

"Cam was there, and saw the entire thing." *No fucking way!*

"What do you mean Cam was there? I was alone. I may have been wasted but I would have known if that asshole was there!" I can feel the sweat bead down my neck. *He couldn't have been there, I was alone. There was nobody around!*

"He was…because when you left, he walked up behind me and he knew you were the one that smashed Cole's car and that I told you to take off."

"Son of a bitch!" I blare and slam my fist against the steering wheel.

"Hunter, chill out man, listen to me would you!" Kyle demands.

"Alright, alright." I say, taking in a few deep breaths to get my pulse back to normal. "There's more. Cam said he was going to tell the cops everything if I didn't agree to help him with something; if we didn't agree to help him." He says motioning between the two of us.

"What did you say Kyle?" I ask, not wanting to know what comes next.

"The only thing I could think of to keep your ass out of jail. I told him we would help him."

"Are you out of your fucking mind?!" I loudly bellow, questioning my best friend's sanity.

"I had to! You would have gone to jail. You're already on probation, and you violated the restraining order Cole filed against you. Not to mention you were wasted last night so add underage drinking to the number of laws you just broke. I saved your ass, so don't be a fucking dick about this!" He explains setting me straight.

"I get that, but I would have rather gone to jail than to help that piece of shit do anything except walk in front of a bus!" I spat.

"Look, it's only one favor. We can deal with it and get it over with and be done with Cam for good. Besides, we back out now, he will go straight to the cops, then I get in even more shit for lying to them."

I have to think this through, but I know Kyle's right. He did save my ass last night. I owe him big. And if it helps to keep Cam quiet, I have no other choice.

"Alright. What do we have to do?" I cave. In as calm a voice I can manage. It's difficult to do when your life is in the hands of the likes of Cam.

"We have to meet with a guy named Gary to give him something. I don't know what it is, so don't ask. We have to meet him at the bonfire later this month."

"That's it?" I question, not believing that it could be that easy. Cam is involved after all.

"That's it. I didn't ask any more questions, the less we know the better for right now." Kyle says.

"Fine. We'll do it. But after this, I'm done with him, Kyle. He can't be trusted."

47
HUNTER

"Wait, Hunter. I need a minute. This is a lot to process all at once." She sighs. Jo's eyes are now buzzing as I look at her, but I don't detect anything but curiosity in her voice. Surely, she must now think that I'm some kind of violent criminal after everything I've just told her. Hell, even I would be hesitant around someone with a past as dark as mine.

"I know. I know…I'm sorry Jo. If it's all too much I'll understand if you don't want to see me anym…" Jo presses her finger to my lips, gently easing me into being quiet.

"Hunter, please stop apologizing so much, okay? You don't have to keep saying you're sorry when you haven't done anything wrong.

"Alright." I say against her smooth finger. I don't argue or come back with a smart-ass remark like I usually would in tense situations. Being with Jo makes this all seem ok for the moment, like I can finally be free to tell someone my side without automatically being judged or written off like some horrible delinquent. *Or, maybe her touch just has this hypnotizing effect on me, making none of my past matter right now.*

"So, what was it about that night that made you go hulk on his car?" Jo's lips curl into a smile as she speaks.

"It was the anniversary of Maci's death." I somberly tell her.

"Oh." She whispers. Her playful grin quickly falls away from her lips, and it's when I notice her chin quiver for a brief moment that I wish I could take it back and tell her something that would make her smile again instead.

"I didn't mean to…I'm sor" She starts.

"No Jo. Please don't. You're not the one that needs to apologize for anything." I assure her. "I take it this is what you meant before when you told me Cam wasn't a good guy?"

"Yes. I knew the kind of person he was, I couldn't just stand by and let him put his hands on you like that. I was just trying to keep you from getting hurt is all."

"And you did. I'm really glad you were there that night." She says and she moves a little closer.

"So am I." I agree. "Remind me to thank Kyle for that later." I whisper and she lets a breathy giggle slip through her beautiful lips.

The urge to feel her lips against mine is increasingly unbearable, after what that sound did to me; so, without thinking, I reach out and caress her bottom lip with the pad of my thumb as I gingerly slip my other hand around her waist to pull her closer. She closes her eyes and burrows her cheek into my palm.

I press my forehead to hers, my hands gobbling up her warmth and I feel her hands clutch at the front of my shirt, tugging the cotton tightly against my chest, like she's bracing herself for impact. Her eyes casted down, I close my own so I can revel in her touch.

"Jo…" I hiss. "When we met that day under the trees…all I could think about was having you for myself, to be able to be with you, just like this. But this…" I wrap her hand in mine and hold it to my, chest. "This is so much better than what I imagined.

The breeze catches Jo's hair, whipping the silky strands around her face and sending the sweet aroma of coconut wafting towards me. It makes me want to bury my face in her neck to inhale every ounce of her intoxicating scent. *She feels amazing.*

The world around us starts to blur and everything slowly falls into nothing, leaving this moment to just the two of us. I've held back from kissing her too many times now, and I won't let this time be another regret of mine. I can't, I don't have it in me to deny my feelings for her anymore. It's too late, I've let her in, and even if it destroys me, it will be worth having this moment be ours forever.

"Jo…" I pull my face away from her, just enough to look into those deep crystal doe eyes.

"Yeah?" She breathes. Her eyes meet mine again. I can feel her chest rising and falling against my own at a pace that tells me her heart is beating just as quickly as mine.

"I need to kiss you." I tell her; the urgency in my voice surprising us both. "Okay." Is all she says, but it's all I need to hear. I look at her as she closes her eyes and I take in everything that is making this moment come alive. Her sun warmed skin, her sweet scent, the feel of her small frame wrapped up and protected by mine. *I don't think this moment could get any better.* I pull her tight to me and our lips finally collide. *I couldn't have been more wrong...*

Kissing her is like being alive for the first time. Everything is so vivid. The colors are brighter, the sounds clearer and the air is so refreshing it's almost impossible to breathe. I have never felt anything like this before and I just can't seem to get enough.

Josephine

I need to come up for air.

Time seemed to stop as soon as Hunter's lips touched mine. He held on to me so tight like he was afraid I would disappear, but the comfort I felt was like nothing I had ever known. The way he was clinging to my lips as he held onto me; I don't think he would have ever stopped if we didn't have to breathe.

Hunter breaks our kiss, but eagerly comes back to leave a little peck on the corner of my lips. His breathing is excited and uneven, telling me he may have needed to come up for air sooner but he didn't want to pull away until he absolutely had to.

My cheeks are flushed and I can imagine they would be hot to the touch since my entire body feels like a wave of fire has just swallowed me whole. *I never want this to end.*

"Jo?" Hunter whispers under his breath and tilts his head up.

"Yeah?" I respond and wait anxiously for his next words.

"You're so beautiful." No longer in a whisper. Just strong and confident as he consumes me in another longing kiss.

48
Hunter

I look over at Jo sitting quietly in the passenger seat as we drive back to her house. Her knuckles have turned a ghostly white from clenching onto her phone. I'm afraid if she squeezes that thing any tighter, it's going to shatter in her hands.

"Jo? Are you okay?" I ask nervously. I switch my gaze from the road to Jo and back, waiting for her to reply. She hasn't said a word since she asked me to take her home.

"Yes." She says unconvincingly. "I…I haven't seen my mom in years. I didn't expect to hear from her after so long." She explains.
Well, she sure picked the perfect fucking time to show up! "I just don't know what to expect." She adds, dropping her gaze and she starts to anxiously rub her hands together over her phone. I can tell she's stressed out, because as soon as she looked at her phone, my sweet angel seemed to shy away from me all too quickly. I reach across the seat and gently stroke the top of her hand with my thumb, and I can feel her body noticeably relax a little. Her mouth catches my attention when I glance her way and see the corner of her lips lift into a soft grin, freeing a sigh when she smiles and closes her eyes. If there's anything I can do to get her mind off of whatever this is about, even for a little while, I will. She will have to confront whatever it is she needs to deal with soon enough.

After a half hour of discussing her favorite music, I find myself pulling onto a familiar street. *Another minute and she'll be back to reality; whatever that is, I want to be there with her.* Jo's body tenses beside me as she recognizes where we are. I want to comfort her, so I ease the car over to the curb and put it in park. I don't turn the engine off just in case she changes her mind about staying. I'll gladly take her wherever she wants to go. "Thank you for bringing me home, and for today. It was really nice to get away for a while." She says timidly as she reaches for the door handle.

"Wait!" That came out harder than I meant it to, it's just that my eagerness makes me sound crass sometimes. I selfishly want to delay her from leaving for just a little longer, so I reach out to grab hold of her other hand that's still clutched around her phone. She looks at me, then at our hands that rest on the center console. A surprised expression appears and she sits back in the seat and let's go of the door handle.

"Jo. I…" I have to think of what I want to tell her before I open my mouth. If I ask if she wants me to come in with her to see her mom, then I'm almost sure she will decline my offer. I know she doesn't like to feel like a burden to anyone by asking for help, so I decide that it's better not to ask and just go inside with her so she won't have to.

"Hold on." I say and I turn off the engine. I lift her hand to my lips and place a quick kiss on top of her knuckle before I open my door and run to her side. I swing open her door and look down at her. She still seems surprised every time I do this. Maybe even more surprised the more I do it. *Has no one ever done this for her?*

"After you, My Lady." I tell her. Playfully bowing my head and offering her my hand like I'm her personal coachman, trying my best to lighten her mood. She lets out a most delightful giggle as she takes my hand and steps up onto the curb.

"Why thank you, kind Sir." She says; to keep up the modesty of our banter.

That is until we turn around and her body immediately freezes before me.

"Jo? Baby, hey are you okay?" I ask her. She's looking right through me, not even realizing that I'm talking to her. She doesn't move, or speak, she just stares straight ahead, I'm not even sure if she's breathing at his point. She suddenly has me worried, so I look up to see what could have possibly caught her so off guard, and that's when I notice a small woman with dark hair eagerly walking down the sidewalk in our direction. As she draws closer, Jo grabs my hand and squeezes it, immediately cutting off the circulation in my fingers. She has my full attention and now I know why she's reacting like this. I can only assume she's Jo's mother. The first thing I notice when she's but a few feet from us is that she and Jo have the same long chestnut hair. And when she comes to stand in front of us with her arms stretched out to embrace her daughter, I get a glimpse of her eyes. It's the same hazel gray I see in my girls. There's no denying the resemblance. No one else has those same eyes. Her mom's may not shine as brightly, nor do they have that same magnificent reflectiveness about them that I love so much. They may be the same color, even the same shape, but they seem to have lost the depth a very long time ago. Thankfully Jo's are still so unimaginably as deep as the ocean and it's impossible to not lose myself in them every time I look at her.

Holy shit! That's when the sudden realization hits me who she is. Today at school, she was the same woman that was screaming down the hall to the principal and called him an asshole. She was also very, very drunk. I think I know why Jo was so nervous to come home now. Just when I think it couldn't get any more uncomfortable, she walks right up to Jo and wraps her arms around her as if she does it on a daily basis. Which I already know, she doesn't. Jo told me that she hasn't seen her mom in years.

I firmly hold onto Jo's hand, not letting her mom pull her away from me because her grasp has only gotten tighter since she spotted her and when I went to pull my hand away to let her mom past, she wouldn't let me. The hug seems forced and unnatural and I can tell Jo wants it to end as soon as possible.

"Josephine!" Her mom theatrically throws her arms up in the air and then clamps onto Jo's shoulders; squeezing her far too strongly making her wince.

"Hi." I intervene and hold my free hand out to her mom, offering to introduce myself so she releases her death grip on my girl. "I'm Hunter." That gets her mom's attention and she reaches out to shake my hand.

"Hi, Hunter, I'm Lily, Jo's mom. It's so nice to meet you." She says slurring her highly animated words. No wonder. *She's still drunk.* Jo stands silent between us, watching our exchange. So, I take the opportunity to keep the attention away from her as best I can until she feels like saying anything.

"I hear you just arrived in town?" I claim.

"Oh, no, I've been here a couple of days. It took some time to finally find out where my little bean lived, you know since the school wouldn't give me an address." She rolls her eyes mentioning this. I can only assume that's what she was so irate about this morning.

"Hey!" She pitches. "You look familiar, haven't I seen you somewhere recently?" She asks. *Damn!* I look to Jo and her eyes are as big as saucers. I don't want to lie, but I don't want her thinking I was keeping anything from her. *I had no idea that was her mom!* I would have told her if I knew.

"Could have?" I say, acting like it's no big deal, I add. "You were in the office this morning and called the principal an asshole, right?" I remind her. Trying to make it seem I wasn't paying that close of attention for Jo's sake. Lily suddenly lets out a high-pitched laugh, making Jo jump slightly. I don't mind as it brings her closer to me so that our shoulders are now touching and she's huddled close to my side.

"So that was you in the office. I knew I recognized you. Wait, so how do you and my little bean know each other again?"

"We go to school together." I say, knowing full well she probably realized that already. I don't have the faintest idea what Jo is thinking right now and considering I don't know anything about what happened in the past with her mom, I don't want to upset her by telling Lily something she may not want her to know.

"Well yes, I gathered that, but I mean who are you to her, friend, boyfriend, friend with benefits?" She amusingly shoves at my shoulder and smirks at her daughter. At the same time, I see Jo start to approach Lily, looking like she's about to lash out at her mother from the awful comment, so I give her hand a brief tight squeeze, trying to tell her not to react just yet. I already don't like the woman by how she talks about her daughter; but I have to stay calm for Jo right now. I would rather not let Lily push her into spreading their personal business all over the neighborhood. It seems her mom likes any kind attention she can get, so I know she wouldn't give a shit if she and Jo had it out in front of everyone if it came down to it.

"Look why don't we all go inside. I make a mean cup of cocoa." I gloat and thankfully Lily agrees and starts walking back to the house.

I'm grateful I could help avoid publicly displaying how broken their relationship seems for the time being. I wouldn't want my girl to feel any more awful than she probably already does.

Tapping my finger against Jo's palm as we walk to her house, giving whatever reassurance I can to let her know that I'm here for her. Her mom is up ahead of us already walking up the porch steps and all I can think of is that I really hope, when we walk through those doors, the only thing that happens is Jo getting what she came here for.

49
Josephine

Hunter holds the door open for me as we step into the house. I feel him give my hand another squeeze as he looks at me out of the corner of his eye. I have come to love all of his thoughtful little gestures, especially this one.

Looking around, it doesn't feel like my house at all. Not even with my mom here. She's never lived here with us as a family. Although I can't say this place has ever truly felt like a proper home anyway. I'm not even living with any of my blood family.

"I'm so glad I finally caught you at home. Bean. You don't know how happy I am to see you." She says in an elated tone as she waits for Hunter to close the door before walking towards the kitchen. *She's acting like she lives here.* My stomach turns at the sound of her calling me her 'little bean' again. I use to like when she called me that. But that was a nickname she used for me whenever she was trying to suck up to me after being gone for days on end and leaving me alone in the house, or having to rely on other people who never seemed to want to be bothered with me. She's the reason why I always felt like a burden to everyone.

"It's Jo." I reply stubbornly. My first words to her are bitter as I start towards the kitchen; Hunter following closely behind me. She hasn't even noticed I've only said two words to her so far. She never did pay much attention to anything unless it served her selfish ego in one way or another. I hear my mom's footsteps behind us as she slowly makes her way to the kitchen. She rounds the table, opposite side of us, and opens the refrigerator, pulling out a clear glass bottle from the freezer. When I see what it is after she sets it down in front of us on the table, I want to shrivel up into a ball and pretend all of this isn't happening. *She's still drinking.* It's bad enough that the reality of my situation has come back to hit me in the face. That my mother is still using and even after all this time, hasn't even remotely tried to turn her life around and fix any of her problems. *But did Hunter have to be here to witness it?*

I turn to face him while my mother is preoccupied with finding a glass to poor her favorite clear beverage in; Vodka. no ice. That's how she always liked it. *I should have seen it coming.*

"Hunter." I whisper. He looks down at me. The expression on his face is dismal. His mouth is strained like he wants to say something, because I know he's figured out by now, that my mom is so obviously wasted. But if I were in his position, I wouldn't even know where to begin. I don't think I would have the courage to stick around and get involved with such a screwed-up family. *I just wish I could disappear.*

"It's okay, you don't have to stay." I tell him. But now he looks confused as his brows pull together.

"Jo. I'm not leaving you here alone." He says quietly as my chaotic mind wanders. He shifts his body to face me and holds me closer by putting his arm around the small of my back. "I'm here if you need me. I'm not going anywhere." He adds. A reassuring look crosses his face and the guilt inside me starts to get very overwhelming.

"But, I don't…" I go to respond, but of course, my mother interrupts as usual. She's never been one to let a person finish a sentence without butting in, ever.

"So, Hayden, was it?" She asks rudely. She knows his name. She's just being childish. I'm sure she's pissed because I didn't bother introducing Hunter to her when she barged in between us outside. If I had my choice, she wouldn't have even known he existed in the first place!

"It's Hunter!" I shout it at her. My voice is louder and more irate sounding than I expected. I look right at my mom to make sure she can tell how irritated I am with her and I would love nothing more than to throw her out on her ass.

Everything from the day she left, to the day Jeff hit me for the first time, and finally to the day when I was beat so badly, that I thought I wasn't going to wake up, comes to the front of my mind. I can feel my heart rate increase the longer I stare at her, she's brought back such depressing memories, and just the fact that she had the nerve to come back and act like nothing happened, like she didn't just abandon me for three years, it's enough to make me want to tell her to go to hell. But another part of me just wants to ignore the fact that's she's drunk right now, wrap my arms around her and tell her how much I missed her. I just can't bring myself to leave the comfort of Hunter's side just so she can let me down again. She's the reason my life has been a living hell these last few years, and I don't know how to get past that to let her back in my life. *I know she won't stay.*

"Sorry, Hunter I mean." She corrects herself. "Have you two been seeing each other for very long? Because you know I won't have my daughter's heart broken by some boy that only wants to see how much he can get from her." She states, sounding very arrogant. *That's it!* I rip my hand from Hunter's faster than he could blink and shove the kitchen chair out of my way and it goes sliding across the chipped linoleum. I don't know what I'm thinking I'm going to do at this point but I can't let her stand there and judge Hunter when she doesn't even know anything about him!

I guess I don't have to worry about it for long though because I feel a pair of arms lift me off of my feet and pull me in the opposite direction; while disgust radiates from every part of my body. I have never wanted to confront my mother or rip her hair out of her head so badly as I do right now, but with every word that is spewing from her mouth, I can't help but let the hatred I have for her take hold and consume me.

"Jo. Jo, stop!" I hear Hunter yell. His arms are around my waist, barely straining to hold me to the spot where he put me down. I try to push out of his arms to get him to release his grip enough so I can confront my mother face to face, but I know it's no use; he's so much stronger than I am, and it doesn't look like he's going to let me do anything he thinks I would regret later.

"What the fuck is going on in here?" Another voice loudly breaks through the commotion from the back door. We all look up simultaneously, and I see Nate standing there wide-eyed and clearly pissed off from the grimace on his face. I can't imagine how this situation looks from his perspective. Nate just walked in while I was being dragged away like a rabid animal by some guy he's never met. Now that Nate and I have gotten a better understanding of each other, I can see how this most definitely has to look bad for Hunter.

"Who the hell are you?!" Nate demands. Rushing over to where Hunter and I stand. Not even noticing that my mother is at the other side of the kitchen because his focus seems to be on where Hunter's hands are. On me! "Get the fuck off of her!" He snarls as he gets closer, trying to put himself between us; but Hunter doesn't back away from him. "Nate! Nate stop okay!" I yell and push against his chest to move him away from Hunter before one of them makes a regrettable move. *Two guys with very short fuses, Great!*

"Jo what the hell! Who is this?" He demands, pointing at Hunter.
I take in a deep breath and drop my hands from Nate's chest.

"Nate this is Hunter." I gleam at Hunter and then back to face Nate again.

"He's…he's…" *Shit, again? What do I say now?*

"He's her boyfriend Nathan!" I hear my mom's arrogant stutter. Extremely pleased with herself that she thinks she knows something before everyone else. Nate hates being called by his full name, and she knows it. Of course, that's why she said it. Most likely to piss him off because of how he always ignored her every time she called him to help with something and he never answered until she would call him Nate instead of Nathan.

The first time we met them and had dinner at their house, she called him Nathan and he rudely corrected her by saying. "The only people that ever called me Nathan are now dead. It's Nate." I know he had to have meant his grandparents probably called him Nathan. I later found out after we moved in with them that they had passed away a couple of years before. But I never did ask him why he doesn't like his full name.

"What?" He questions. The anger in his eyes swiftly changes, making him look confused as his brows pull together in the center of his face.

"I'm her boyfriend." Hunter calmly says behind me; and my jaw almost hits the floor. I can't help the smile that's creeping across my face right now, and I don't even care that my mom had said it first. The only thing that means anything to me is that Hunter confirmed it. And I love the sound of it coming from him.

I can feel the hairs on the back of my neck stand up; knowing Nate's probably waiting for me to confirm or deny it and explain everything, but before I can tell him anything; he addresses the big fat elephant in the room.

"And why the hell are you in my damn house Lily?" Nate's challenges my mother. "Better yet, where the hell have you been for the last three fucking years? You know abandoning your daughter, like that was superb fucking parenting!" He says, throwing that little blip back in her face.

"I don't think that's any of your business Nathan!" She repeats his full name again, drawing out the letters as long as she can to add fuel to the fire. She wants to get a reaction out of him, but I think she's biting off more than she can chew.

"I think it is my fucking business, you're in my house!" He gestures with his arms sprawled out at his side as the words grumble deep in his throat.

"Nate, stop ok. Please." I plead. I don't want Hunter here having to be stuck witnessing how messed up my family is. It's embarrassing enough that he already knows my mom's an addict and I haven't even known him very long. It's all too new to be revealing how screwed up the situation is that I'm stuck in.

Nate looks at me and gently pulls my arm so I follow him out into the hallway near my room. I glance back at Hunter and subtly nod my head letting him know that it's ok. I follow Nate out of the kitchen even though he lets go of my arm. He stops and turns to me, looking down into my eyes. His face is very close and I can clearly see how worried he is underneath all of his anger.

"Jo. We need to get her to leave before Jeff gets home. He's not going to take to her being here too well. You know how he was when she first left." He confirms what I was sure he was worrying about. I was thinking the same thing as soon as he called me to tell me that she had shown up.

"I'm sorry I had no idea she was even back, but I take it that you didn't talk to her before you called me earlier either?" I assume.

"No, I didn't. I had seen her sitting in a car outside the house when I got home from work. Her yelling to whoever she was on the phone with caught my attention. I called you after I came inside."

"I don't know what to do Nate." I admit.

"Look, we'll deal with it, but first, who the hell is this guy you're with, Jo? How well do you even know him?"

"Oh. Um, I met him at school. He's really nice Nate. I don't think you have to worry."

"Just be careful alright? I'll kill him if he lays a hand on you." He warns. Those words shock me into utter silence. I knew Nate and I were on better terms now, but I never expected him to take on the overprotective big brother role.

"Is everything okay Jo?" Hunter asks. I turn to see him walk out of the kitchen doorway towards us.

"Yeah." I assure him. Looking back and forth between the two hotheads that are currently staring each other down as they close the distance with me stuck in the middle; I decide to properly introduce them to each other to hopefully sort out any misunderstanding.

"Nate, this is Hunter, my…boyfriend." I hesitate to say the word. It feels foreign on my tongue. As strange as this situation is to me right now, I can't help but feel somewhat like a normal teenager for once. It's the dreaded, boyfriend meeting the family situation. Well, meeting the protective older brother anyway. We haven't been a real family in a very long time. *I'm not sure if we ever really were.*

Nate looks at Hunter and Hunter eyes Nate from the short distance that's between them. Then something even weirder happens. Nate takes a step forward with an outstretched hand.

"Nice to meet you man." He says, with a calm, neutral expression on his face; like he doesn't actually want to kill him. Hunter extends his hand to shake Nate's and responds with.

"Yeah, nice to meet you too." I can't say I have ever felt more relieved as I do at this moment, and how grateful I am that they didn't rip each other's heads off.

50
Hunter

Having to walk away from Jo tonight was the most difficult thing I have had to do since we met. Leaving her side with that vile woman there has me worried that she's just going to end up in tears, and I'm not going to be there to bring her back to the Jo I'm getting to know. I had to honor her wishes and leave when she asked me to because I know she wants to handle things with her mom without having an audience. I can understand that since we haven't known each other for very long, but I was still hoping she would want me there with her. Seeing how she reacted to her mother in the short amount of time that she's been here, I can only imagine how things will more than likely get out of hand. I know Nate is there for Jo, but I want to be the one who's there to help her fight her battles, no matter what they are. It's killing me to not know what's going on.

Josephine

After another two hours of arguing with my mother; she finally lets me call a cab to take her back to her hotel. *I have never been so exhausted in my entire life.* Trying to talk to my mother after she starts drinking is a lost cause and I really do hope she forgets everything we talked about tonight because I don't want to go and live with her and her new boyfriend. *That worked out great last time.* At least living here with Nate, I finally have someone who's on my side for once. I never thought I would say that. If I were to move back with my mom, I know that I would be completely on my own and I would have to go back to taking care of her, like I'm the adult of the relationship. I don't want to go back to that.

I feel awful for asking Hunter to leave earlier. I just couldn't deal with another good thing being tarnished by the toxic people in my life. He would probably just be better off not ever having met me. I'm sure that's probably what he's thinking right now after seeing what a mess I really am. No one in their right mind would want to deal with all of this.

After my mom left, I was alone for the night again. Nate had to go back to work to finish a job for some rich guy that paid him extra to get his car done by six a.m. tomorrow. He said he wouldn't have done it because he didn't like leaving me alone at night, but we needed the extra money. That's another thing I can't help but to feel guilty about; him having to work so many hours because he's worried about money. I feel like if I wasn't here for him to have to look after, he wouldn't be as stressed out as he is. I just wish I could pay him back somehow for everything he's done for me.

The rattle of the back door signals my brain that it's time to wake up. I crack my eyes open and begrudgingly glare at my phone screen. 6:42am. *Must be Nate.* He said he would be home before seven. My phone dings just as I set it down so I unlock it and see that the message is from him.

Nate: I'm home sorry if I woke you

Jo: Its ok I was up

Nate: You got work today?

Jo: Yeah

Nate: need a ride?

Jo: Im gonna walk

Nate: ok

I lock the front door behind me and pull out my phone, stopping on the middle step to text Hunter. After he brought me home last night, we didn't have a chance really to say if we were going to meet up today.

Just as I get ready to hit send; I see his car parked under the tree out front of my house; and there he is in the front seat. His eyes are closed and his head is resting propped up against the side of the door. *He's sleeping?* I walk to the passenger side of his car and whisper his name through the crack in the window.

"Hunter?" I tap my nail on the glass and a meager groan, escapes as he stretches. *He's adorable when he wakes up*. He sits up and blinks a few times before he focuses his eyes on me. "Hi." I say quietly.

"Hey." He clears his throat and shifts his body to sit up straighter. "Hi." He repeats and motions for me to get in so, I slide in and close the door.

"Did you sleep out here last night?" Hunter looks at me for a minute and then looks down and rubs his hands over his face, brushing the sleep from his eyes.

"Would it be weird if I did?" He searches. I glance at the ceiling, like I'm thinking for a minute before I answer and I see his eyes grow slightly larger as If he thinks I'm weirded out by him staying.

"No." I plainly say. "It wouldn't. "But…why did you stay?"

"I couldn't leave without knowing you were okay." He explains. The dimple Hunter's cheek simply dissipates as he grows more serious in his answers.

"Oh. You really didn't have to. I was fine." I tell him. I see his expression fall again "But I appreciate that you did. Thank you." I quickly tell him, since I have no intention on hurting him and making him think that I don't want him around.

"You know… of all people, I understand families can be difficult, and mine is far from perfect. You don't have to hide from me Jo." He affirms. Letting me know he understands where I'm coming from. I let out a breath I felt like I was holding since last night when he left. Knowing he understands is offering me some relief.

"Thank you." I utter.

"I'm going to visit Kyle at the hospital today. Care to join me?" Hunter asks.

"Uh, I don't think he would want me there."

"Why not? I think my best mate should know that I'm no longer single, don't you?" He grins while staring into my eyes, daring me to say otherwise. I smile and just nod, truly agreeing with him. I don't know what else to say to that. Hunter's dimple reappears on his cheek as a toothy-grin spreads across his face. *God, I so love that dimple.* "Then it's decided. We'll pick up your favorite pastries on the way. I'm sure Kyle is dying for some real food by now after eating all of that rubbish the hospital, dares to call food."

"Okay." I agree but then I remembered I have to be somewhere this morning. "Oh, wait."

"What's up baby?" He places his hand on mine.

"Sorry, I just remembered, I have to work this morning. Mrs. Lawrence needs help with all this stuff for a book signing"

"Alright, then that's our first stop. Well after the pastries of course." He says and turns the key to start the car.

HUNTER PICKED OUT the most delicious pastries the bakery had today and we sat at one of the tables outside. We ate two pastries each and drank a large cup of cocoa before he drove me back to start setting up for Mrs. Lawrence. Hunter helped to carry boxes of books out of the storage room and set them up so I could log everything in the system and stock them on the shelves. He is so sweet, no one asked him to do anything, he just started asking where things needed to go, and then we all fell into a pretty good rhythm, accomplishing everything we had to for the day.

The book signing isn't for another few weeks and we're already almost done with making all the displays that we need. Not to mention all the heavy lifting that Hunter so generously took upon himself to do, saving me a lot of hassle by not having to use that crummy old dolly.

We're standing in the corner of the store, finishing up the window display that advertises Anna Monroe's book signing when Mrs. Lawrence calls over to us. "Okay, you two love birds we're done for the day here. Why don't you two go off and have fun."

"Will do, Honey." Hunter calls back quickly. My face scrunches up in the oddest expression my brain can possibly muster up and I can feel the embarrassing heat in my cheeks.

"Honey?" I question, turning my head to look up at him.

"What? Do I have something on my face?" He asks while he feels around his mouth with his hand; rubbing the miniscule stubble that shadows his jawline.

"No. But do you realize what you just said?" I ask, hoping he actually does, so I don't have to explain it to him. "Yeees?" He says. Like he's not entirely sure if he does know what he just said, and that he's definitely questioning his own memory.

"Oh, you mean the fact that I just called Mrs. Lawrence by her first name?"

"Um, no genius…you called her Honey." I remind him.

"Yeah, that's her first name. She told me this morning to call her Honey. Said she prefers it over being called Mrs. since her husband passed away a couple of years ago."

"Oh. I had no idea." *I feel like a total moron.* "You're on a first-name basis with my boss?"

"Seems so. What can I say? She thinks I'm adorable." He admits with a smirk, casually shrugging his shoulders as he folds up the last box.

"Are you ready to go then?" He asks. While I stand there holding the last two books in my hand, Hunter walks over to Honey… *That's still weird I never knew her first name, even after all this time…*and tells her see you around. But we don't get away until she offers to pay us a little extra for today and makes us take the rest of the pastries with us.

51
Josephine

I'm nervous to go see Kyle. I guess from what Hunter said he's going to be okay, otherwise, they wouldn't let non-family members in to see him yet. He said Kyle called him last night and told him he was allowed to come up since he told the hospital staff to ignore what his parents said. He's eighteen after all, so he's allowed to have whoever he wants in his room now that he's awake.

It's not long of a drive to the hospital. Since the town is relatively small it's the only one that we have within thirty miles or so; other than the private clinic on the other end of town. When we walk up to the emergency room doors, I feel Hunter hesitate next to me. I can't imagine what he went through when he found Kyle the way he did that night. I'm just so grateful that he didn't lose his best friend, he doesn't deserve to lose anyone else he cares for.

"Hi. Can I have the room number for Kyle Smith please?" Hunter says to the woman behind the receptionist desk. She looks up at us standing in front of her and a smile starts to form as her eyes land right on Hunter. I see her name tag as I curiously stand on my toes to look over the high counter. *Bethany. She seems nice.*

"Oh my, you're back. Came to check up on your friend I take it?" She assumes. She looks quite cheery for working in such a dismal place.

"Yes ma'am." He says in a low murmur.

"Let me just look up his room number, one moment." Bethany glances at computer as she taps away on the keys. "He's in room 116. First floor, go left here around the corner and it will be the fourth door on your right."

"Thank you." Hunter says and he starts walking the way she directed us to go, pulling me along a half step behind him. "Good seeing you, Hunter." She calls and I see him nod his head as we turn the corner and walk down the hallway. There's some equipment resting up against the wall as we pass the first few doors. It's dimly lit and smells strongly of disinfectant; so much so that the fumes are making my eyes water. We're silent until we finally spot the number to Kyle's room. Hunter hesitates a few seconds before he knocks.

"That better be you Hunter or I'm going to be seriously disappointed!" We hear Kyle yell from the other side of the door and Hunter chuckles slightly, hearing his best friends voice seems to help him to relax a little before he turns the handle and pushes open the door.

"Holy shit mate, what took you so long? I'm withering away over here?" Kyle says as he fiddles around with the buttons on his bed; finally pushing the one that raises the head so he can sit up to greet his best mate.

"What the hell does that mean? Your parents made sure I couldn't get past the front desk to see you until you changed the visitor log. I couldn't get within a hundred feet of your room." Hunter squabbles. Holding my hand, he walks up to Kyle and fist bumps him with his free hand.

"I see you haven't scared her away yet. How did you manage that one?" Kyle asks, nodding his head my way.

"Don't be an asshole." Hunter quips.

"What? I'm just asking? I thought I was always the more desirable of the both of us. Guess she doesn't have as great of taste in men as I thought." Kyle playfully smirks at me, the sly grin on his face lets me know he's just messing around and giving Hunter a hard time. Hunter turns to me as I stand there holding the box of pastries from this morning. He takes the box out of my hand and drops them on the bed next to Kyle.

"Here. Maybe Jo and I should have kept these to ourselves since you keep insulting the only people who cared to bring you food that won't make you want to throw up." Hunter tells him.

"No, okay, okay, I'm sorry." He seizes the box before Hunter can take it back. "Jo, forgive my dirty mind, being stuck in here is driving me insane. It's like my filters broken or something." He explains.

"Not like you ever had much of a filter to begin with." Hunter adds. Kyle takes a pastry out of the box and shoves most of it in his mouth; dropping crumbs all down the front of him. He then proceeds to moan as he chews the massive bite, all while giving Hunter a dirty look. Making it seem like he hasn't eaten anything but sawdust for the last year, he inhales the pastry in record time.

Hunter

"You're a slob, man." I laugh as I watch Kyle inhale bite after bite, making a glutton out of himself. Can't blame him, the food here is terrible.

"Yeah, so, I'm starving, and these things taste amazing!" Kyle finishes stuffing the last bite into his trap and motions for me to come closer. I look back at Jo and she releases my hand to slowly walk away so Kyle and I can talk. She already understands some of the situation, but Kyle doesn't know I've already told her most of what happened. "Look man, in all seriousness you should keep a close eye on Jo, better yet maybe keep your distance from her until all this blows over." He warns, suddenly making the conversation serious.

"What the hell are you talking about Kyle?"

"Cam, man! Cam was the one that attacked me."

"I figured as much, but you told the cops you didn't see his face. You can't just lie like that, we're already in enough trouble as it is!" I yell under my breath, hoping Jo isn't paying much attention to us idiots.

"Yeah, well if I didn't, then we would both be in deep shit again anyway. Remember that little thing with you losing your shit on Cole's car?"

"Fuck!" I say. Hoping to dampen the sound of my anger by tightly gritting my teeth together.

"Yeah. Cam came over the day you and Jo were there. Just as you left. He said he was there to make sure we settled what we needed at the bonfire for him. To be honest I wasn't sure if you had dealt with it so I lied and said I hadn't seen you, and then he just lost it and came after me. Look."

Kyle lifts the hospital gown and reveals patterns of black and blue on the entire left side of his torso. There's also a large bandage wrapped around his lower stomach, and hiding underneath is the stab wound that could have killed him. It makes me cringe finally seeing the actual size of the wound and it quickly sends a wrenching queasiness to my gut knowing that my best friend could have died, all because of my cowardice actions.

"Fuck! Kyle, he must have seen me that day!" I tell him. "He pulled up right before I had gotten in your car to leave. I had seen him comeback out of the front door as I was pulling away. I didn't think he knew it was me since I wasn't even in my own car. That's got to be how he knew you lied about seeing me that day."

"Shit man. He wasn't supposed to be there for another fifteen minutes from what he told me on the phone. The asshole just seems to do whatever he wants."

"Yeah, no kidding. We need to figure out a way to fix this and fast, whatever he's into, we can't have anything more to do with him, Kyle."

"Woah! Okay, hold on. First what the hell was even on the paper? I never did bother to look. It seemed so insignificant I didn't put much thought into why it was so important. You know how dramatic Cam is when it comes to shit; he'll say anything to get what he wants." Kyle reminds me.

"Well, it wasn't just what was written on it, I think he's more concerned about what was taped up inside of it." I tell him.

"What do you mean? What else was in it?" His voice nervously trembles.

"I'm not entirely positive what it is, but I'm pretty sure it's some kind of drugs." I stand there waiting for Kyle to reply when his face just freezes. *He really didn't look inside of it.* Kyle's mouth opens, then closes, then opens again but he hasn't produced a single word. I'm sure he's just realized the kind of shit we are in now.

"Dammit, man! What the hell did he get us into? I don't need this kind of bullshit to deal with right now!" Kyle's pissed, and rightly so. Cam has us by the balls and I don't how to get us out of this yet. "Shit…" He mouths. Looking down he reaches for his phone and stares at the screen, scrolling through it like a mad man. "Alright!" He suddenly looks up at me like a light bulb just went on in his brain.

"What? What are you thinking?" I ask curiously.

"Tell me what was written on the paper?"

"I think a phone number maybe, I don't know for sure." I tell him.

"Okay. Look. As much as I don't want to do this, I'm going to get Cam to meet up with us after I get out of here." He starts to explain, but I interrupt him when it hits me what he seems to be planning.

"Are you fucking crazy?! Cam almost killed you, and you want to meet up with him?" Kyle shoots me a glare and glances over towards the door, warning me Jo might still be able to hear us. And when I look over, I see that luckily, she's not in the room. She must have gone into the hallway when her phone rang. "Look, we don't have a choice. If Cam is involved with this shit again, especially if it's with the people I think he might be dealing with; it's nothing to mess around with. I've seen him do a lot of sketchy shit, and it's not something that we need to be involved in. Let's just finish what we said we were going to do, and be done with it alright?"

"I hope you're right." This has gone far enough and I can't keep having him get hurt because of my stupid ass not being able to control my anger.

"I'll make some calls first and I'll see you in a few days when I get out of this place."

"Alright, man." I agree.

"Hey…no worries." He says, but the look in his eyes don't at all convince me that he's actually as confident as he's trying to sound. "Yeah, no worries…"

52

Josephine

While I give the boys some privacy to figure their stuff out, I get a text from my mom, asking if I thought any more about moving in with her. I cringe at the thought. I don't want to live with her again. Not after she proved to me that nothing has changed. If she hasn't gotten help by now, I can't count on her ever getting sober and me being able to rely on her as a parent ever again.

"Hey, you ready to go?" Hunter asks from the doorway.

"Yeah, I just want to say goodbye to Kyle." I walk back into Kyle's room and he's sitting on the bed eating another pastry. He looks fully engrossed by the food that he doesn't even look up as he talks.

"Are you and my boy off to go cause trouble, or are you the one that's going to keep him out of it?" He quizzes me as crumbs fall from his open mouth.

"No, I like to avoid it at all costs. Unlike yourself, it seems." That's what pulls his attention away from the flaky pastry. His eyes lock onto mine and he stops chewing, swallowing hard what's left in his mouth, and plops the box down next to him.

"Well, you're spunky! I like it!" He beams.

"Take it easy mate. She's too much for you I'm afraid." Hunter informs him.

"Yeah, well, can't blame a guy for trying." Kyle shrugs as he drops a hunk of pastry back in the box and brushes his hands on his shirt.

"No, but I can kick, said guy's ass if he pushes his luck." Hunter warns him.

"You wouldn't. Besides I'm injured, rain check though." Kyle snaps his fingers and points them at Hunter and then they both let out a sly laugh under their breath. "Okay, well I just wanted to say I'm glad to see you're alright, Kyle." I tell him.

"Always a pleasure seeing you doll face. Don't be a stranger." He tells me. "And make sure you take care of my boy. He needs someone to keep him in line." He adds as we start to walk out the door.

"I'll be sure to do that." I say with a smirk. I see Kyle grin before I turn towards Hunter.

"Later man." Hunter says.

"Things seemed pretty heated in there for a minute. Is everything okay?" I ask as we walk to Hunter's car.

"Yeah, everything's fine." He says shortly but his expression says he seems worried about something again. He opens my door to let me in the car without elaborating and lights a cigarette; taking a long drag as he slowly walks around to the other side of the car and flicks the cigarette across the pavement before getting in. I don't know what they were talking about in there after I left but if it left Hunter in a prickly mood, so my guess is that it's probably not anything good.

"I'm glad Kyle is okay. I guess he had you worried for a while."

"Yeah, he's obviously back to being himself now though." Hunter replies shortly.

"Did he say when he can go home?"

"Yeah, in less than a week most likely. They want to keep him longer to make sure his stitches would heal properly. I guess he didn't listen when they said he needed bed rest, so he ended up ripping his stitches already." He explains.

"Well, he doesn't seem like one that listens to authority figures very well…I mean he seems to like to do things on his own terms." I add, trying not to sound rude.

"Yeah, I'd say you're right."

Hunter

"It's about time. I've been itching to get the hell out of here all day!" Kyle bellows from across the lobby; drawing the attention of everyone that's sitting in the waiting area. He's sitting in the wheelchair, actually he's more so playing around and trying to hold a wheelie. *I'm going to laugh my ass off when falls on his face.*

"Chill out Kyle, the nurse said I couldn't come until 9. That's when you're getting released." I point out.

"Yeah, well it's…" He sets the chair down on all four wheels and pulls out his phone. …9:03."

"You're lucky I'm even awake this early to pick you up. It's 9 am on a Saturday! I should just leave your ass here you, ungrateful prick!" I crack. Probably scaring the people in the waiting area, they must think we're actually pissed off by the looks on their faces. It's comical really.

"No girlfriend today? Or are you still afraid I might steal her away from you?" He says, obviously he has a death wish.

"Dude, don't go there. If I recall, you have a girlfriend. The name Miranda, ring any bells?" I start pushing the wheelchair towards the exit doors after throwing his duffle over my shoulder.

"Yeah, not so much, she dumped me after saying she doesn't want to get involved in my criminal behavior." He says making air quotes. "She didn't even come to visit me while I've been in here being subjected to daily torture." He says humorously.

"Damn, sorry man." We didn't have much time to talk when I was here the other day, so I kind of feel like shit for not knowing.

"It's cool. I didn't think we would last much longer, to be honest. She was kind of mean."

"Well, still, keep your dirty mind to yourself around Jo. I won't hesitate to kick your ass, like I said I would." I remind him.

"Noted." He replies and jumps out of the wheelchair before we even get out of the doors, so, I roll the chair away and leave it sitting near a bench just outside the doors. Kyle stands in front of my car and stretches as far as he can, making absurdly loud grunting noises.

"Ahhh yeah! Finally, I feel like I can breathe again." He exaggerates.

"Just get in the car you tool. We're going to meet Jo for breakfast." Mentioning food makes Kyle's swivel and he quickly gives me an a hysterically enthusiastic look as I get in the driver's seat, so he opens his door and hops in as fast as his body will let him.

We walk into the diner and I see Jo sitting by the window at our booth. She's sketching on a paper place matt in front of her and sipping from her mug, so she doesn't see us walk in. Lucky for me, Kyle has a big mouth, and decides to announce to the entire diner that we have arrived. "JO!" Kyle wails across the diner. He didn't have to do that; the place isn't big enough that someone would have to yell to get attention. A second later, I see her look up and notice Kyle and his big fat mouth, before she turns to lock eyes with me. We both walk in the direction of the good booth that Jo's currently occupying. He slides in the open seat and I sit down in the one next to my girl.

"Hey." I say; sliding a little closer.

"Hey." She smiles at me.

"Heeey!" Kyle quickly mocks, making it awkward as usual. I give him a death stare so he casually holds his hands up in surrender before pretending to look around to admire the décor.

"What can I get you?" A young, tall blonde waitress asks as she comes to stand at the end of our table, holding a pen and small pad of paper.

"I'll take care of them." Another woman calls from behind the counter before any of us get a chance to answer the first girl. Suzie, the nice waitress that I had the pleasure of meeting already, walks out from behind the counter with a pot of coffee and two clean mugs. "These are my favorite customers." Suzie beams, as she sets the mugs on the table. "Kimberly, can you take care of the gentlemen that just walked in please?" Kimberly walks away, not bothered at all by Suzie's request. I look over at Kyle and see his face drop as he gawks at Kimberly and follows her with a look of disappointment on his face as he stares at her across the diner.

"Who's your new friend here?" Suzie asks as she pours Kyle a cup of coffee, leaving my mug empty because she knows Jo and I prefer hot cocoa. I'm guessing that's what Jo is already drinking.

"This is Kyle, Hunter's best friend." Jo tells her, dragging Kyle's attention away from Kimberly temporarily.

"Ah, I see." Suzie smiles as she realizes what he was staring at; or rather who he was staring at. "Well, welcome Kyle; we're happy to have you." Suzie says. Kyle slowly stands up and attentively but comically bows like a medieval Lord would do.

"The pleasure is all mine." He says in his most gentlemanly tone. *What a kiss ass.*

"Oh, aren't you a polite one?" She says to Kyle. "I'll be right back with your cocoa." She pats my arm before walking back behind the counter.

WE SIT A while and make bullshit conversation. Jo seems to be tolerating Kyle rather well, considering he's still being a pain in the ass, but it's nice because she seems to just fit seamlessly into all areas of my life. *There's nothing I don't love about this girl.* She doesn't even mind when Kyle makes a fool of himself by not bothering to hide the fact that he's drooling all over the table whenever Kimberly walks by.

"Kyle, why don't you go and ask her if you can take her out for coffee or something instead of sitting here like a lost little puppy?" Jo asks him. She's smirking because we can tell he wants to. I just think he doesn't want to embarrass himself in front of us if he strikes out. If it was just me sitting here, he would have already asked for her number and gotten a free piece of pie out of it.

"I'm working up to it." He says through his teeth; hinting for us to shut up about it so Kimberly doesn't hear us talking about her. I would love to yell out that Kyle professes his love to her, just to be a dick and get him to grow a set and ask her out, instead of monopolizing the conversation with his tragic love life.

53
Josephine

I feel Hunter gently pull on my hand so I stop walking and turn to face him.

"This is your stop." Hunter says. He looks down and takes both of my hands in his and runs my knuckles back and forth over his lips twice before he stops to leave a kiss on each hand, sending shivers up and down my body. I watch his movements, they're thoughtful and sweet, little gestures of affection that I will never stop loving. He makes full eye contact with me, never dropping my hands away from his mouth. I almost forgot that he said something. *He's so distracting in the best way.*

"Yeah, yes, it is." I stutter coming out of my head to answer him.

"Can I see you tomorrow?" He asks. Still holding onto my hands, he gently squeezes them close to his chest.

"Sure. I'll be here all day because tomorrow is the book signing, but after that, I'll be free."

"Then this is where I'll be." He says matter of fact. Suddenly he leans in, surprising me again by placing a kiss on my cheek. Only he doesn't move away so quickly after. One of his hands releases one of mine and travels up, softly grazing my cheek before tracing the lines of my ear and he pushes the stray hair away, wrapping his fingers around the back of my head to pull me close. I love feeling my body react to his touch and the way his forehead creases just a little, as if he may be over thinking things. I don't know if I'm thinking enough but right now, I don't really care.

His hand lingers on my hip while the other is still tangled in my hair and his mouth is dangerously close to mine, so close I can feel his minty breath giving me the courage to stand here and let this happen. I close my eyes so I can give all of my attention to feeling every little detail of his body that's pressed against me. His hands are warm and his nose is slightly cold from the chilled breeze coming off of the ocean. When he touches me it sends electrifying tingles through me, invigorating every fiber of my flesh that he comes in contact with. *I feel like the air has been sucked out of my very soul.*

Then it happens. I hear him take a breath and close the few inches of space between us, finally letting our lips touch. My body slowly melts into his as he holds me tight. I never thought kissing him could get any better, but every part of me feels like it's on fire. But then that feeling quickly fizzles out and is lost when I feel him pull away shortly after and ending the kiss; tearing this moment of bliss away far too quickly.

"Good. Then I'll be here at ten." He tells me and gives me a smirk along with one of his little pecks on the corner of my mouth, leaving me speechless once again.

Hunter

Walking away from Jo, leaves me feeling empty every time that I have to do it. It feels awful leaving when all I want to do is spend every waking second with her. Every time I kiss her it's like kissing her for the first time and she's the only person that has made me want to feel again. Because whatever it is that she does to me, makes me feel alive, makes me feel good again for the first time in so long. I get in the car and Kyle is already messing around with all my shit.

"Man, what the hell took you so long?" He pesters.

"Stuff it. I was barely gone five minutes."

"Yeah, well it seems like much longer when you have to take a piss." He wriggles in the seat like a toddler.

"Are you five years old? Why couldn't you have gone before we left the diner?"

"I hate public bathrooms. You should have seen the ones in the hospital. I would have rather used a dumpster!"

"Yeah, well, count yourself lucky that we're not far from your house then." I tell him. "I do. But other than that, I just got Kimberly's number while you were sucking face with Jo." He says as he waves his phone in my face, and grinning like an idiot.

"Bullshit!" I don't believe him. I was only gone a few minutes. *How the hell did he talk that poor girl into giving up her number to his goofy ass?*

"I'm not kidding. She gave me her number. I went back in and charmed my way to her digits. I had to do something while you rudely made me wait in the car like a dog."

"How do you make asking for a girl's number sound so gross, man? I guess it doesn't matter since it seemed to work. So, congrats, I thought you lost your game after being with Miranda for so long."

"Yeah…" He chuckles. "I thought so too, to be honest. But no worries, your boy is back and better than ever, it didn't take me long to convince Kim that she needed to find out for herself that we are completely right for each other." Kyle smirks and adjusts his non-existent tie and then shoves his phone back in his pocket before rolling down his window and we take off to his place.

I drop Kyle home and get him settled with the nurse his parents hired to help him around the house until he fully heals. She seemed like a nice girl and didn't look much older than either of us. I'm sure Kyle is going to be just fine with this arrangement by what his face looked like when she introduced herself. He was practically drooling all over the floor. I had to remind him of a certain waitress he just asked out not even a half-hour ago. I know he's not the kind of guy to play around with girls' heads, but it's nice to see he's back to being himself again. I thought Miranda had ruined him forever.

I pull up to my house after leaving Kyle's place and all I see are tons of cars parked down the block. I drive further up the driveway, about to pull in when I see enough cars to fill a sales lot parked around the property, and blocking my only way to the garage. *You got to be kidding me!* I take it my parents are throwing another ridiculously expensive party for their coworkers. "Who the hell has a party in the middle of the day?" *Old rich people, that's who.*

No way I'm going to leave my car on the road, so I pull past the ones that are lined up down the stone driveway and I drive my car over my parent's precious lawn and park it right in the middle of the front yard; leaving tire marks all the way up the grass next to the rose garden. It's a dick move, but I'm tired of not being able to properly park my damn car at my own house.

I get out and see a hired valet staring at me. *Looks like they went all out for this one.* The guy just stares at me in awe as I saunter toward him.

Probably afraid he's going to get in trouble if someone thinks he parked it like that.

"No worries, mate I live here." I tell him as I walk past. I'm sure he's relieved to hear it. I go in the open front door and slip past everyone just standing around talking about nonsense so I head up to my room before my parents get the chance to notice I'm home. Not that they will care unless one of their clients thinks introducing themselves to my entire family is their way to be nosy. My parents will do anything to impress the people they work with; even if it means having to endure talking to me.

After speaking with Kyle, the last few days I've been trying to figure out a way to deal with Cam and his low-life friends. But first I need to find that dam piece of paper that's been a god damn thorn in my side. Only I have no idea where the hell I put it after the night of the bonfire. I rummage through my desk and both my nightstands and come up with nothing. I check my hamper with my dirty laundry that I haven't done since I have been preoccupied with a certain someone recently and still come up empty-handed. *Shit...where the hell is that thing?*

I nearly tear my room apart trying to find what I thought to be such an insignificant pain in my ass. I finally check my bathroom and find the pair of jeans I wore the other night. I grab them off the floor and search the pockets. Sure enough, I find it. I unfold it and read what it says and see that it does in fact have a name on it, and a number. The ball taped up inside of it is so small no wonder I never thought much of it. I can only speculate what it could be, but given Cam's past, both Kyle and I have a pretty good idea that it's most likely drugs. I pull out my phone to take a picture of it and send it to Kyle. Not a minute later my phone rings and it's him.

"Is that all it says on it?" Kyle asks immediately after I answer.

"Yeah, that's it. I don't recognize the name, do you?"

"No. But whatever that number is, must be pretty damn important if Cam was willing to almost kill me to get it back." I cringe at his words. He's right, and he almost died because I didn't make sure it got to the person it needed to. If I had made sure to deal with it as soon as that paper landed in my hand, none of this shit would have happened! "What's the ball of tape?" He asks eagerly.

"I don't know like I said, I think it's drugs, it's so carefully wrapped, it has to be intentional, what else could it be?"

"I don't. But listen, I'll talk to Cam at school, and tell him to set up a day for us to meet up with that guy Gary again. That way he can't do anything if we're in public and we'll settle this shit. He won't be able to hold anything over our head anymore." Kyle says. It sounds like a loaded statement. How does he think Cam will just leave us alone after this?

"Okay, but I don't have a good feeling about this man. Look what he's already done to you. This shit should have never gotten out of hand like this!"

"Yeah, I agree." He says. "Look, I'll call you later about it after I talk to him."

"Alright man, good luck." I say and hang up. Kyle doesn't seem as worried as I think he should be about all of this. I don't have a fucking clue how this is going to play out, but I'm almost considering just turning myself in like I should have from the beginning. If I hadn't let Kyle take the fall for me over something so stupid, Cam would have never been able to drag us into this mess and blackmail us to do his fucking bidding.

54
Josephine

Using this dolly is getting on my nerves. The thing is bigger than me, and adding three huge boxes of books to it is impossible to maneuver. *This thing hates me.* It didn't give Hunter this much trouble when he used it.

"Mrs. Lawrence, where would you like me to put these boxes?" I ask. Mrs. Lawrence stands up and looks over the counter at me.

"There's a fold-up table leaning against the wall in the back room that you can bring out and put the black table cloth over it. It's sitting on top of the chair behind you." She points. "Put as many books on there that will neatly fit, and then just leave the rest in the boxes and slide them under the table until we need more." She instructs.

"Okay." I say and I quickly get back to work.

Everything is almost done and Miss Monroe will be here in the next half hour, so I make sure that all the last-minute details are taken care of so things go as smoothly as possible. I set out sharpies on the table, flip open the first twenty-five books and line them up neatly on the table like Mrs. Lawrence asked. I bought bottles of water and her favorite coffee along with snacks and pastries from the bakery down the street and recheck to make sure everything she needs and requested is in order. She didn't ask for much, just the water and a place for her assistant to sit. She couldn't have been nicer when I spoke to her last week about the details. I go to the front and flip the open sign on before I open the door. Looking down the street I see countless people standing along on the sidewalk, while more people are walking towards the crowd to get in line. *This is so awesome! I can't wait to meet her!* I think giddily. I call down the block as far as my voice will carry. "The store is open, so it will only be another five minutes until you can start coming in. Have your books ready if you already have one, if you don't have a copy yet, there will be plenty for you to purchase after you meet Anna."

I hear the tone of the line grow louder as people start to get even more excited. I know how they feel. After all, meeting your favorite author seems like a once-in-a-lifetime experience; and when I read her books, I was hooked. I couldn't put them down. Thanks to Mrs. Lawrence, Anna Monroe is my all-time favorite author, and I can't wait to meet her in person.

"Josephine?" I hear Mrs. Lawrence call me from the back room, so I set down the last few items on Anna's table and go to the back of the store. I walk through the door and see Mrs. Lawrence standing in the middle of the room next to Miss Monroe, and my jaw nearly hits the floor.

"Josephine, this is the wonderfully talented Miss Anna Monroe. Anna, meet my dear friend, Josephine." She gestures to me. I can't help it. *I…am…speechless!* I never thought I was a person to be 'star struck' as they say, but standing awkwardly in front of such a talented and beautiful creator, makes my mouth not understand how to form a proper sentence. *Now I know what they meant.*

"Oh my gosh! Hi Anna. It's so nice to meet you." I say, finally getting the words to come out after a short but awkward silence.

"Thank you so much for having me." She says. "Your town is so beautiful. I absolutely love the feel of small towns. They have such magic in them, don't they?" She beams.

"Yeah, I really love it here." *I lie.* Well, I like the town; I just don't like the reason why I live here, and half of the people I'm stuck living with.

"Well, we have everything all set for you. I hope everything will meet your requests and give you a little glimpse into our world here." Mrs. Lawrence speedily says to Anna. "We have so many people that are extremely anxious to meet you today. We have had lots of new faces come to town just for this occasion." Mrs. Lawrence's words come out so rapidly I can tell her nerves have gotten the best of her. But Anna doesn't seem to mind, because she just listens and smiles while nodding her head in agreement. "I am going to check on things upfront. Anna if you need anything, Josephine will be with you the entire day, and I will be back and forth, so if you need me just send Josephine over and I will be sure to get anything you need." She assures. I have never seen Mrs. Lawrence so nervous before. She's usually very calm and collected; but

I can understand where she's coming from because having Anna here is a really big deal, for the store and not to mention the town! Selfishly, I have to admit, it's so exciting that I get to meet her first before anyone else that's most likely been waiting outside for hours. Most of them were here before I came to work this morning. Perks of the job, I guess.

"Oh no, I'm sure everything is just great. I'm already in love with this place and I have only seen very little." Anna smiles.

"Oh well, the pleasure is all ours." Mrs. Lawrence says. "Now I'm going to be right back." She tells us before walking out to the front of the store.

"It's so nice having you here." I say to Anna, as we're about to head out behind Mrs. Lawrence. "I was so excited to meet you. When I read the first book of your Shattering Heights series, I was instantly hooked on every single little detail. And then when I got my hands on all of the rest, thanks to Mrs. Lawrence, it was so nice to find a story that wasn't just about a perfect relationship. Your characters are real and flawed and it was great to have something to read that was so raw and vulnerable, knowing that other people out there all have their own struggles gave me a new outlook on things." I explain. I have never been so long-winded before, but I felt like I needed to tell her this. I wanted to let her know she's made a difference in my life. *Isn't that what writers usually want?*

"That is the sweetest thing to hear; especially coming from such a young girl. You seem like you have a great head on your shoulders. Don't let anyone ever tell you anything different." She demands nicely.

"I won't." I promise.

"Can I give you a hug?" Anna asks.

"Um? Yeah sure." I say shyly. She comes up to me and wraps me in a friendly hug and I hug her back. *How is she this nice?*

"By the way, a little secret." She motions for me to lean closer after releasing me from the hug. "Casey in the book, is being portrayed in the movie by an actress whose real name just so happens to be Josephine, and it's set to be released next Fall." She whispers. This is news to me. I had no idea they were being made into a movie! *I am way too sheltered!* I feel like I should have known this information before meeting her, but I literally just finished reading the series like a few days ago! "Maybe this means it was fate that I come here and meet you after all." She says.

"Yeah, maybe it was. And I can't wait to see the movie. You wrote such an amazing story, Anna."

"Alright then." Mrs. Lawrence pops her head through the doorway. "If you're ready then you can follow me if you like, so we can get you set up. We'll be letting people in, in about two minutes."

"Okay, let's do this!" Anna says excitedly! We start walking out of the back room and into the main area where we arranged the shelves to accommodate a lot of people to stand in line. Luckily Hunter was here to help with that last week. Otherwise, I would have had to take all the books off before moving the empty shelf. It would have wasted a lot of time. "You know I have only ever done a few book tours so far, but I have to say, it never gets old. It's always nice to see new places and meet so many new people that I would have never had the chance to meet if this wasn't my actual job. I don't think I will ever get used to it!" Anna says in a bewildered tone, with the biggest whitest smile I have ever seen. *She definitely loves what she does.!*

As we walk to her table where she's going to be signing books and meeting fans, I listen to every word that she says. I want to remember this day forever. And when I see Hunter later, I can't wait to tell him how awesome Anna is! I may have loved working here before, but I wouldn't be mad if I got to work here the rest of my life if this is what I get to experience.

55
Hunter

I have to meet up with Jo first." I tell Kyle.

"What? Now? Won't you be seeing her tonight anyway, like you have for the last few weeks?" He asks, sounding irritated.

"No. I want to get Cam off our backs first and I don't want Jo getting involved in any of this shit." I say sharply. "Besides, I told her I would be there today to help with something and now I have to bail on her. The least I could do is tell her in person."

"Well after tonight we shouldn't have to worry about Cam again for a long time; as long as everything goes as planned." He mutters.

"What do you mean 'if', Kyle?" I ask. Because he seems like right now, he's not telling me everything. I know him well enough to see that, but I already don't have enough time to see Jo before we go do this, so I can't wait around to pry an explanation out of him that I know he won't give.

"Nothing man. I…just mean as long as he doesn't be a major prick and he sticks to his word, we can all come out of this with our heads still attached." He jokes. Probably trying to cut the tension because we're already on edge about all this, and he knows how I feel about Jo.

"Alright, then I'll see you later." I say, and walk out the front door.

I pull around the back of the store since all of the parking out front and down the block is taken up; even the lot across the square is full. Honey told me to come around back when I called since I most likely wouldn't get through the front without getting trampled by the crowd. So, I go through the back door, which she left unlocked for me and I immediately get hit in the face with the smell of Jo's favorite pastries. There are boxes full of them sitting on the counter. I consider having one but they might be for that author lady and her people that are here, so I don't take any of them; even though I could eat an entire box to myself right now. *I hate nervous hunger pains.*

I make my way through the back and watch from the doorway for a minute. *Damn, that's a lot of people.* My eyes wander through the crowd until I see Jo standing on the opposite end of the room. She's holding a large stack of books in her arms as she stands to the side of the table. Her hair is pulled out of her face revealing her magnificent neckline while her full luscious chestnut waves cascade down to the small of her back.

My eyes nearly pop out of my head when I notice the little white lacey number she's got on. This is the first time I've even seen her in a dress and I think my heart just stopped for a brief moment. A white cloth belt wraps around her small waist, accentuating her curves that she has obviously been hiding up until this point. She looks like an angel standing across from me and I can't help but stare at those magnificently edible legs of hers. The soft material stops mid-thigh and briefly rides up a little higher on her skin while she sets another stack of books down on the back table. *Holy Hell!*

I slowly make my way past everyone, never taking my eyes off of her. I can feel the dirty looks everyone is giving me, but my gaze doesn't stray in the slightest from the gorgeous sight of my girl. Jo's eyes widen as she looks up and notices me approaching, so I walk around to the corner of the roped-off area and sneak behind the banner as Jo comes around to meet me.

"Hunter!" She whisper-screams and jogs over to me, trying to not be noticed so we don't interrupt anything, and wraps her arms around my neck before she leaves a kiss in the middle of my lips.

She sure is excited! I could get used to this kind of PDA.

"Hi." She looks up at me and then releases her arms from around my neck.

"Hey. How's it going here?" I ask her, nodding my head into the crowd of people.

"It's great actually. Anna's really nice. She has so many fans."

"You're not kidding. I had to pull around back; there was nowhere left to park in the entire town."

"Yeah, people have been here all day and the line, never gets any smaller." She smiles. Her giddy energy brings on a grin because I'm loving how excited she is to be a part of something like this.

We both turn our heads towards the sudden commotion on the other side of the banner when we hear the mood of the crowd suddenly change and increase a few decibels. Jo looks concerned so she pokes her head around to see what it is. I'm curious so I do the same. A girl is crying hysterically as she's trying to ask Anna a question. Her face is beat red and she can't calm down enough to get any words out. Anna gets up from her chair and walks around the table to the crying girl and gives her a hug. She pats her back a few times and whispers something to her and she smiles. Anna grabs a sharpie off the table and signs the girl's book after asking her name. She hands the book back and gives her another quick hug before the girl walks away looking extremely happy, so Jo relaxes and we duck back behind the banner.

"Wow, you were right, she is nice." I agree.

"Told you."

"Yeah, almost too nice; I would have just signed the book. That girl almost had snot coming out of her nose, she was crying so hard." I snicker and Jo giggles and looks around the banner to check on things. *Always so responsible.* "So, I came here to tell you something." Jo immediately looks back at me; her eyes wide with curiosity.

"Okay?" Her tone questioning.

"Kyle and I have something important to take care of, so um, I can't stay and help like I said I would. I'm sorry. It just came up last minute and I wanted to come by and apologize for bailing on you and Honey." I confess. Trying to sound as sincere as possible instead of my regular brash self that I'm used to.

"It's okay." She says and her chest falls, letting out a held breath. "This isn't your job anyway. You're just nice enough to want to offer your services all the time." We have everything pretty much covered here anyway. Things are going surprisingly, smooth." She explains.

"Okay. You're sure?" I mean, I'll be back as soon as I can, but I can't promise when."

"No, it's okay, really." She assures me. I feel like a total dick for bailing on her last minute, but it's better that I do this today and I know that she's here and out of harm's way than to be with me and something possibly going wrong. I don't know what to expect when Kyle and I meet up with Cam later on. Right now, I just need to be sure Jo is safe.

"Alright then." I lean down and brush the hair away from her neck, gently resting my hand there for a moment, and lean down to leave a kiss on her flushed cheek. "I'll see you later babe. Good luck with everything here." I tell her. "Thanks, Hunter." She says, lightly smiling as she walks back from around the banner and over to Anna. *God, she's absolutely Amazing!*

56
Hunter

I rip my phone out of my pocket to text Kyle as I walk back to my car. I'm not looking forward to this, but it has to be dealt with sooner rather than later. Putting it off any longer will only piss Cam off more, and I'm not going to let any more people I care about get hurt.

Hunter: What time we meeting Cam?

Kyle: 2 hrs. just outside West Pine Hills near coaver park.

Hunter: alright meet you at ur house in 1

Kyle: see you then mate

When I get to Kyle's house, he's just coming out of the front door. After a couple of weeks hunched over, he's finally walking in the upright position how he should be. He was afraid to rip his stitches again so he purposely walked a little shorter for a while after he got out of the hospital.

"Hey man." Kyle greets me as he opens the passenger door.

"Finally got rid of that gorilla walk you were sporting for a while yeah?" I stupidly say. Grinning like an asshole.

"Yeah, yeah…you had your fun now kindly fuck off." He laughs under his breath.

"You ready to do this then?" I know I'm ready to get this over with, but that doesn't mean either of us know how this is all going to play out. "Not really man." He says distracted and he pulls out and looks at his phone to start typing something as I back out of his driveway. WE DRIVE FOR about twenty-five minutes and pull up to a small café near the water. The parking is close and there are plenty of people around, so I can't imagine Cam would try to pull much while there are so many witnesses. He's an idiot, but I don't think he's completely brain dead. *I guess were about to find out.*

"He said he would be parked near the café but I don't see his car." Kyle informs me.

"Maybe he didn't drive his car. He might have come with that Gary guy." I remind him that there's still another guy involved that we know nothing about, we don't even know what he looks like, so he could be watching us already.

"Yeah, possibly." He agrees while looking around at all the cars parked in the area. We get out and walk up to the café window outside and order a couple of drinks. I pay and Kyle finds somewhere to sit down while he continues to people-watch. I hear Kyle's phone buzz a few times, one after another and he unlocks his screen. If I had blinked, I would have missed him doing it.

"Okay." He says quietly and subtly nods his head. I know he's not responding to me because we've been sitting here for ten minutes without uttering a word to each other. We've both been too distracted looking around for Cam to give him little chance to catch us off guard. Kyle types a quick message in his phone before he shoves it back in his pocket. "He's here." Kyle finishes gulping his coke before slowly standing up, making sure to look in the direction I'm assuming Cam told him where to be.

"Where the hell is he?" I ask as I quickly search for Cam's ugly mug. We don't need any more surprises.

"He's in the middle of the park." Kyle points to a picnic table under a pavilion. I get up and look in that direction to see two guys sitting awkwardly on top of a picnic table. They're both looking this way, so I doubt they haven't seen us already. We walk across the street towards them and I notice the way Cam continues to rub his hands against on his knees, nervously fidgeting and it seems he's struggling to sit still. *He looks like complete shit.* The closer we get the easier it is to see the dark circles around his eyes that are also bloodshot to hell. They look almost as bad as they did when I broke his nose. Kyle and I walk right up to them and the guy that's with him stays seated while Cam swiftly gets up and paces back and forth asking if we had what he needed.

"Straight to the point, I guess." Kyle states dryly. "Yeah and, do you have a problem with…"

"Cam man, shut the hell up!" The guy yells, cutting him off and he promptly shuts his mouth without an argument.

"You're Gary, I take it?" Kyle states. Knowing full well he's the guy in charge by the way Cam cowers at the mere sound of Gary's voice.

"Yeah. I am. I heard you have what this little twat was supposed to get to me weeks ago." He snidely points to Cam and I glance back at him, seeing him not able to stand still. It's really starting to agitate me, but I settle next to Kyle, closely watching the tense exchange between the four of us. Cam continues to pace back and forth while he rubs his hands together, turning them red from the constant friction. *They look fucking raw.* I pull the paper from my pocket and hold it up for Gary to see. *I just want to get this over with already.*

"Well, we have it right here." I tell them, breaking my silence. Cam suddenly freezes mid-step and his eyes widen to the size of dinner plates. I can tell Kyle noticed too because he's gone rigid. I don't think he expected it. Gary on the other hand doesn't look very pleased for some reason.

"Is that it?" He asks; pointing to the paper in my hand as he glares over at Cam for reassurance.

"Yeah, man. That's what you…you, you asked for." Cam stutters and audibly swallows the golf ball in his throat.

"Well, let's have it then." Gary order and reaches his hand out like he's going to try and snatch it and run. Kyle and I quickly back the hell up. I'm not letting him take it just yet. We want to know for sure they're both going to leave us alone from now on. He's already gotten his revenge from getting his ass kicked by Gary; by taking it out on Kyle and landing him in the hospital. I don't think it can be anymore square than that.

"Hold on." Kyle firmly says. "We need you to guarantee us that you're going to live up to your word and leave us the hell alone from now on. We didn't have anything to do with this shit until Cam here, needed us to do him a favor. We don't know what this is all about, but I think we can come up with a conclusion without being told." Kyle explains; authority dripping from his words. By the way he said that and how he's holding his stance, it gives off the impression that he's not one to fuck with. If I hadn't known him most of my life, I definitely wouldn't fuck with him myself. He's even hiding the fact that he's still in pain from injuries that aren't fully healed. I give him a lot of credit for not letting them see he's slightly vulnerable. Kyle can hold his own of course. But right now, he's not healed enough to withstand another fight even if I am here to have his back.

"Well. You give me that little piece of paper, which I'm sure isn't important to you and I will happily be on my way boys. You won't ever have to see me again." His arrogance reeks of bullshit. So, I look over at Kyle. He's staring straight ahead at Gary and I see a slight change in his stance. His tightly balled fists slowly relax and his shoulders drop just enough that if you weren't looking, there's no way anyone would have noticed it. He seems almost relaxed in a way if I didn't know any better.

"Alright then." Kyle agrees without warning. "Hunter, give it to him." He tells me. *What the hell?* I have no idea what Kyle is thinking and I sure as hell haven't heard either of these dick heads guarantee anything yet. I feel like he's completely ambushed me, making me want to pull him aside and demand what the hell is going on. Luckily the intelligent side of my brain tells me not to, so I don't; because that will just make these idiots suspicious and Gary doesn't look like a guy I want to tussle with. I eyeball Kyle; questioning his sanity just a bit when he just gives me the "shut the hell up and do it" look. He's used that on me enough times I know to just listen to him by now. I've already gotten him involved in enough of my mayhem, to screw it up again. I know I can trust him, but if he's up to something, I wish he would have told me about it. I shrug my shoulders and step forward to hand Gary the paper without breaking eye contact with Kyle; until I hear Cam yell.

"No, don't give it to him!"

"What the fuck?" Gary shouts as he lunges towards Cam. "You stupid little asshole!" Gary swings his hand around, smashing his fist against Cam's jaw, knocking him off his feet and Cam thumps hard against the picnic table with a loud thud. He doesn't try to get up, he just sits on the bench and holds his hand to his face for a minute, and doesn't dare say another word. The sheer panic on his face tells us everything we need to know, and it doesn't look good for us.

I look around and notice that the four of us have now caught the attention of everyone within the park. Some people walking by have stopped in their tracks and are now staring dead at us. Others are hurrying away, acting like they haven't even noticed the heated argument.

"Look." Kyle holds up his hands a second before dropping them to his sides. "We don't want any trouble, so just take whatever this is and we'll gladly forget this ever happened, alright?" Kyle isn't showing any signs that he's worried about where this is going, while I'm standing here, internally freaking out that this may end up really bad if Gary doesn't just walk away after he gets what he came here for. Cam undoubtedly knows how to screw things up! I hesitate just a second before moving close enough to Gary to hand him the crumpled paper. He holds out his hand and roughly snatches it from me like he thinks it's going to disappear. He opens it just enough to peek inside and an evil smirk, spreads across his face before he crumples it back up and shoves it in the front pocket of his coat.

"Pleasure doing business with you boys." Gary says. He calmly turns towards Cam and eyes him from where he stands. Cam gets up and gives me a pitiful look before he turns to walk away and starts to follow Gary out of the park.

As they get further away, Kyle quietly tells me something while he stares straight ahead.

"Don't do anything stupid in the next five minutes." He warns.

I stand here dumbfounded and just look at Kyle casually standing still like he's waiting for something instead of walking away to get the hell out of here as quickly as possible.

"What the hell do you mean Kyle?" I question hesitantly, not knowing what he has up his sleeve if anything, or if at this point, we are both completely screwed as I watch Gary and Cam walk away free and clear.

"Just trust me, alright." Kyle says urgently, not making eye contact, he's just staring dead ahead. I'm frustrated as hell not knowing what the fuck is going on and I can feel the sweat running down my neck. Just when I want to turn to head to the car, I hear sirens go off as four dark SUVs pull up behind the truck that Cam and Gary got into. The red and blue lights shine brightly from inside the top of the windshield and it finally clicks that they're unmarked police vehicles. They try to pull out of the parking space but the SUVs have blocked them in on all sides, making him hit the break to bring the truck to an abrupt halt, and just barely missing hitting one of them. I look over and see Kyle grinning from ear to ear. *Did he have this planned?*

"Kyle, what the hell man?" I say through gritted teeth. He turns to me and calmly tells me to stay put.

"Look, those cops over there are going to take us down to the station. So, don't get your panties in a twist when they come over here. Just do what they say and everything will go smoothly. I promise all of this will be explained." He tells me, but I'm about to lose it when two

Officers approach us from behind, making it seem like they thought we were going to run.

"Gentlemen, if you will please come with us; we're going to have to take you both down to the station." I hear one of them say as I scowl at Kyle in disbelief. I still can't wrap my head around what the hell is going on, so I just do as I'm told and follow Kyle's lead. I hold my tongue while the officers' handcuff us both and lead us to the police cruiser. Kyle warned me not to be stupid. But all I can think right now is that we are royally screwed! *I'll have to remember to kick his ass later if we ever get out of this.*

57
Josephine

So, what did you think of today? You seemed like you enjoyed yourself." Mrs. Lawrence asks.

"I absolutely loved it! I wish we could do this every week!" I say excitedly.

"Well, you're certainly good at handling chaos, that's for sure. Her fans are really…passionate about meeting her." She says with a pause and a smile.

"Yeah, I would say so too. And thank you, for having me be a part of this. It was so fun. And the best part of course was meeting Anna."

"Oh dear, no need to thank me, I should be thanking you for all of your help; and not to mention that sweet boy of yours. Where is Hunter by the way? I thought he was going to be here today?" She questions while gazing around to see if he's here and she just missed him amongst all of the people.

"Oh, he came by this morning. He told me he had something come up that he had to take care of today and apologized for not being able to help." I explain with a longing expression. I know Hunter can't spend every second of his life with me, but it would have been nice to have him here today. Maybe it's better that he wasn't, because I was so busy that I haven't sat down once since this morning. I guess I wouldn't have had a lot of time with him and he probably would have been bored out of his mind anyway.

"Well, that's alright, we seemed to handle everything pretty well. Maybe he can join us next time if he likes." She offers before going back to sorting receipts.

Hunter

I've been waiting in here for over an hour, and no one has come to talk to me yet or let me talk to Kyle to find out what the hell is going on? They took my phone so I can't text Jo to see if she's still at the bookstore with Honey, needless to say, I'm a bit on edge wondering when I'm going to be able to get the hell out of here. I hear the click of the lock just before someone pushes it and it swings open. The echoes from the commotion in the hallway flood the small room before the door shuts and it quickly muffles the voices.

"Hunter Scott?" A well-built man in an expensive suit walks over to the table and sits down across from me, plopping a thick white folder on the surface. I answer him with a tired, "Yeah?" Not knowing who he is, since I haven't met him before and he wasn't one of the officers at the park to arrest us. I'm not too sure if we were even arrested; since neither one of us were read our rights and Kyle didn't seem too worried at the time about it either.

"Would you like a drink? Water…soda…coffee?" He asks naming a few options to choose from.

"No thanks, I'm good." I tell him. *But I sure as hell could use a shot of whiskey.*

"Alright, so I guess we should just get straight to the point then." He says, flipping over the front page of the file and skimming through it, for whatever reason. "You know someone by the name of Kyle Smith, is that correct?" He asks.

"Yes sir, he's my best friend." I confirm.

"Well, it seems your friend Kyle has been helping out our local detectives with a case for a few weeks, and it's come to our attention that his efforts just might have paid off for the both of you today." I feel like this guy is speaking in code, either that or I'm on a hidden prank show or something. I don't have the slightest idea what the hell he's talking about, so I just sit here quietly while I nervously bounce my knee up and down waiting for him to elaborate more on this whole ridiculous situation.

"Do you know a man named Gary Walker?" He asks.

"No sir. I don't." I say without hesitation. "You don't know this man then?" He turns the folder to me and points to a photo of a guy with long hair and a mustache that looks rough and zombie like. I recognize him immediately, so I change my answer.

"Actually…yeah." I say, and sit up a little straighter in the chair, my back pushed up against the hard metal support. "I've seen him before, but I'm sure you already knew that. I only knew his first name was Gary. Before today, I never even met the guy." I explain to him.

"Yeah, your friend Kyle told us the same thing. Turns out he's the one guy that our department has been looking for, for over a year. And you gentlemen have helped us finally put him behind bars today." He says as I remain quiet and he continues to explain the situation.

It turns out Kyle's dad and the head detective on the case; have known each other since college and are good friends so Kyle thought to get more information on the guy that had been dealing some new kind of drug around town for the last year. Kyle had found out earlier on, that Cam was up to no good and was keeping an eye on him when he noticed the shit that he was doing every month at the beach bonfire. He finally contacted the detective when he figured out what was going on and took the opportunity to benefit from helping the case.

Gary's specialty was selling this new drug extremely cheap to anyone that attended the high school and Cam was his first sale. After a few months Cam became his right-hand man, by selling for him directly on school grounds, and his parent's beach house eventually became the second-best location during the summer for it. Cam used the job to fund his new acquired habit.

"This uh…Cameron Jones ended up owing a lot of money to Mr. Walker. I assume since you and Mr. Smith being involved with him recently, most likely noticed that he has quite a serious drug problem." He assumes and folds his hands in the middle of the table.

"Yeah, I've noticed, especially since he nearly beat my best friend to death." I'm growing impatient and I want to know what's going to happen from here. I don't like when people beat around the bush instead of just being out with shit!

"Well, not to worry, Kyle explained everything. He even told us he would only give us the information that he has if we did him a favor in return." He pauses and looks at me; probably waiting for me to ask what it was. But my stubborn ass just stares back at him and remains silent as I cross my arms over my chest and inhale through my nose, flaring my nostrils. I'm pissed they haven't been able to catch this asshole for more than a year. If they had done their job, Kyle and I wouldn't have gotten in this fucking mess at all, even if I still ended up being a total dumb ass and letting my anger get the best of me.

"He said that he would help out the department if both of you had your records expunged of any previous charges. That means from now on as long as you stay out of trouble and stop getting involved with the wrong kind of people, you both have clean records as of twenty minutes ago." He looks at me, maybe expecting me to jump for joy and act like a criminal that was just given his freedom after ten years in prison, but I still just sit there absorbing everything he's told me with a straight look on my face. It takes me a minute to try and fully process everything. I look up and find the man grinning as he shuts the folder on the table and picks it up, neatly shuffling the papers together.

"You're free to go, Mr. Scott. If you have any more questions, I'm sure your friend will explain everything in more detail to you, but if you like, here's my card, feel free to call me if I can answer any more of your questions." He takes a business card from the inside of his jacket and hands it to me before standing up and walking to the door and leaves without another word.

I cannot believe Kyle did all of this without me knowing. I wish he would have told me, so then he wouldn't have had to do everything on his own. It was my asshole temper that got us both into this mess, so I should have been the one to get us out of it.

I get up and leave the small room and see Kyle walking out of a doorway further down the hall. He says goodbye to someone and I call his name to get his attention.

"Kyle." I holler. He turns his head and makes his way over to me.

"Holy shit man!" He mutters under his breath. "Congratulations! We're finally free!" He says and slaps me on the shoulder. "I couldn't wait to get out of that room, I'm sick of seeing this place." He adds seriously letting out a long, exaggerated breath.

"Kyle, Kyle. Listen for a minute, would you?" Getting his attention so he could shut up for a second.

"Yeah, sorry mate what's up?"

"Look, that detective told me what you did. I just needed to thank you man, for everything." I don't know what else to say. A thank you doesn't seem like enough for all Kyle has done for me. After all this, I'm just grateful that he's still my best friend. "Ahh…no worries, mate. We're in the clear now." He reminds me as he punches my shoulder. "So, what do you say we go get some grub; I'm starving!" He exaggerates by roughly rubbing his gut.

"Can I have a rain check? I need to go do something important, and it can't wait." By the look on his face, he knows where I'm going and he surprisingly doesn't seem pissed. I feel guilty as hell for even asking to bail on him again. But I can't let Jo down for a second time in one day. No matter what I do, I'm always letting someone down.

"Yeah no, it's cool. Go, we'll catch up later." He says, waving me off.

"Thanks man. I owe you one." I say seriously and give him a brotherly slap on the back.

"Yeah, don't mention it."

I start jogging down the hall towards the exit and hear Kyle yell to me.

"Don't keep her waiting."

I don't plan on it.

58
Josephine

Have a goodnight Josephine. I'll see you tomorrow." Mrs. Lawrence calls to me as I leave for the night.

"You too. See you tomorrow." I call back then shut the door behind me.

It's another cool night. Not cold, but it definitely smells like it's going to rain. As long as I get home before the sky opens up, I won't be mad if it does. A calm rain will be nice to fall asleep to after such a long day.

There are a few lights on when I walk in the door. Usually, the house is dark and uninviting but tonight it surprisingly doesn't look abandoned. I didn't check to see if Nate's car was in the driveway, but I assume he's home since I shut off everything before I left this morning. I go to my room and let my bag fall off my shoulder and onto the floor. For the first time in over a year, I don't bother pushing my dresser against my door. It's a strange feeling not being on high alert when I come home and it's a feeling I've definitely missed. Grabbing something cozy from my closet to put on, I get dressed and set my alarm on my phone and put it next to my table to charge. I haven't heard from Hunter since this morning when he came by so, I decide to text him and just tell him that I hope everything worked out with whatever he had to do today, but then change my mind before hitting send and decide to just say goodnight. *I don't know why I overthink everything all the time.* I come downstairs from freshening up a few minutes later and I hear noises coming from the kitchen as I head back to my room. I push the door open slightly and it's just Nate standing in front of the stove cooking. The smell of whatever it is, is making my stomach rumble, so I push the door open and walk in.

"Hey, Nate." I say as I cross the kitchen and open up the fridge to get a bottle of water. "Hey, Jo." He says quietly; just barely looking away from the food in the pan.

"Is everything okay?" I ask because he seems a little off. He's usually very forward when he's speaking to you and right now, he's acting like he's trying to avoid me.

"Yeah…everything's fine…why do you ask?" This time he shifts his weight and turns his head to look up at me while he continues stirring.

"Just wondering." I open my bottle of water and chug nearly half of it out of nervousness.

"Everything alright with you?" He asks.

"Yeah, fine. Just tired, so I think I'm going to crash early tonight."

"Before you do, want some food? I made enough for both of us?" He asks and lifts up the pan to show me what he's making. *Oh yum. Breakfast potatoes.* I used to love whenever he would make breakfast potatoes. He'd usually leave me a plate in the microwave when he did, but he never made them for breakfast; it was always at night when he would be out late and come home acting like he was starving and hadn't eaten all day.

"No. I'm good, thanks. I'm beat. I think I'm just going to go to bed." I tell him as I start to head back out of the kitchen door.

"Wait Jo…just so you know…Jeff isn't here." He says hesitantly and looks at me instead of the hot pan he has in his hands.

"Oh. Okay. Um…where is he?" I say, not that I really care. I'm just glad he hasn't shown his face here in a while. I repeatedly twist the cap on my water bottle while I wait for his answer. It's nice to know he's not here, but when he's coming back is the thing that I'm worried about.

"I don't know. He just never came home the other day after work, and his boss called here looking for him today. Said he hasn't shown up in a while. If you remember, he's done this before when he went on a bender. He'll mostly be gone for a couple of weeks. I just thought I'd tell you so maybe you could, um, maybe you could get some sleep tonight knowing that." I do feel a little better knowing the house is possibly going to be quiet and peaceful for the next little while. It hasn't been like that since the last time Jeff took off. Nate is becoming more and more thoughtful lately. I know he's worried about a lot of things and rightly so because Jeff makes it anything but easy around here. I just wish I wasn't one to add to the things he needs to be worried about.

"Thanks, Nate." I push the door open and turn my head back to look at him. "You're a good brother." I tell him before I walk out and head back to my room.

Hunter

I have to call for a Lyft to go back and get my car from Coaver Park. I fucking hated leaving it there, especially now since I have to go all the way back there to pick it up before I can see my girl. It's been a long day dealing with idiots. Between meeting up with Cam to getting, I don't know, *'fake arrested'* I guess, to being questioned and finally let go to have to walk and meet my Lyft driver because he's too much of a wanker to pull up in front of the police station. *I left Jo today for this shit?*

I get in the car and tell the driver where I need to go. He grumbles out how far of a drive that is from here for this late at night but he puts the car in gear anyway and proceeds in the direction I told him to go. I close my eyes for a second and lean my head against the chilled glass. The coolness is nice on my sweaty forehead. After the day I had, I'm grateful that it wasn't any worse, when it definitely seemed to be heading that way.

About twenty minutes later the driver pulls into the parking lot. I tell him to pull over to the side of the café where my car is as I pull out a twenty-dollar bill from my wallet and hand it to him over the seat to him as a tip.

"Thanks, mate." I tell him and I step out into the pouring rain. I run over to my door and unlock it before I propel myself inside. Sometimes I wish my car had remote entry for times like this. But it's a classic, and I'm not willing to trade it in for such a trivial luxury.

It takes forever to get to Jo's house. It's not that long of a drive, but of course when I crave seeing her; it seems to take a lifetime to get there. I pull up along the curb a few houses down from Jo's and sit in my car for a few minutes to see if anyone is home. It's late, so she has to be home by now. I went past the bookstore and all the lights were off except for the security ones. I didn't expect them to still be there anyway, but I had to drive past it just to make sure. I get out of my car and quietly walk up to the side of the house. The garage door is shut, so I make my way over to Jo's window and look inside to see if she's even in there. *There's my girl.* She's on her bed with a blanket wrapped tightly around her body, just like when she fell asleep in my bed the first time. I look over to make sure her bedroom door is shut before I check the window to see if it's un-locked. Sure enough, it is, so I push my hands against it and slide it open all the way. It's hardly a large window, but I can still fit through it easily enough. I climb in, trying to make as little noise as possible, and turn around to shut the window and close her curtains.

Jo hasn't moved an inch since I came in, so she must be exhausted if she can sleep through me moving around in her room. My clothes are soaking wet so I take off my jacket and shirt and lay them over her desk chair before nearing the edge of her bed again. I sit down softly enough, hopefully not to wake her just yet since she looks so comfortable lying there under the protective layer of warmth. There's not a hint of stress or worry to speak of, she just looks so peaceful and I would happily stay awake all night just to watch her sleep.

59
Hunter

I kick my muddy boots off and shove them away as I carefully make my way onto the narrow bed. Jo's hand peeks out from under the blanket so I caress the back of it and lean down to leave a small kiss in the center of her palm. As I look up at her sweet face, her lashes begin to softly flutter open, revealing those brilliant emerald grays. *Beautiful.* Tightening her hand around mine, she finally focuses on me sitting next to her and a sleepy smile appears on her lips.

"Mmm, hi." She whispers.

"Hi." I murmur back.

"You're here." An excited glint sparkles in her gaze, and it warms my soul to be the cause of such a genuine expression.

"Yeah, sorry I'm late." I whisper an apology. She's still half asleep so she struggling to keep her eyes open.

"It's okay." She says, as her eyes close and she brings my hand closer to her and holds it tight like she's giving it a bear hug. I lean closer and whisper her name in her ear.

"Jo…." She scrunches down into her pillow without letting go of my hand.

"Mmm…hmmm?" She answers with a soft moan.

"Can I stay with you?" I ask. After the words leave my mouth, I almost regret letting myself ask such a thing. That is until she opens her eyes again and tells me yes.

"You're sure?" I don't want her to feel pressured into letting me stay. But I'm elated that she said yes because I don't know if I was going to be able to pull myself away from her if she told me no. Jo lets go of my hand and slides over to make room for me without saying a word. She moves her extra pillow to my side of the bed as I crawl in next to her and she unfolds herself from her only blanket. I think I still make her nervous because she deliberately turns away and stares up at the ceiling; avoiding all eye contact as I lie down. I'm about to ask her if she would rather that I sleep on the floor, but as I peer over at her gorgeous face, I see her smile just before she pulls the top of the blanket up to hide her face.

I love that she's smiling right now. The fact that I get to be next to her and she looks perfectly content is an unexplainable feeling. I've never felt this before, with anyone. To be next to such a beautiful and shockingly different girl without any expectations is new to me, so I'm beside myself to know what to do. So, I take in the moment and savor every second of being with my girl.

I soak in the way her body moves as she takes in each breath. Her hair gently blowing in the breeze of the fan; wafting her delicious bouquet towards me. It's all over every surface in this room and its's the strongest right here on her pillow, so I fight with myself to keep to my side of the small bed without wanting to experience more with her until I can fall asleep.

Josephine

I can't fall asleep even as tired as I am, I just can't. My brain will not shut off. I want to look at Hunter, to see if he's asleep, maybe if he's still awake we can talk until my nerves calm down. But before I get the chance, any words that were about to pass my lips slip away when I feel the light tickle of his fingers trailing along my arm. I keep my eyes closed, and enjoy his touch as he smooths his hand down my arm until he reaches the exposed skin that's peeking out from under my shirt. Feeling the weight of his hand on me sends my breathing into a jittery mess; clueing him in that I am in fact still awake. I let the feeling take over and let out a silent giggle before I open my eyes and turn my head sideways to look at him. He's looking at his hand that's still on my stomach, slowly tracing the waistband of my shorts, and then his eyes suddenly dart up to look at me. He meets my gaze and I see so much want, in his expression. The weight of his hand almost becomes too much and I want to pull away, but I don't, not yet. I want to feel like this a little longer, being wanted and touched by someone without it coming from anger. I close my eyes and take in a deep breath as Hunter slowly grazes the skin just below my belly button with his thumb, gently rubbing circles as his hand inches further inside the material.

"Hunter…" I moan his name, not meaning for my words to come out sounding needy, but the feel of his hand is making my head a little fuzzy.

"Mmm…hmm….?" He hums without taking his eyes off of me. He hasn't done anything but touch my skin and he's already gotten me in such a state that I'm considering letting him continue. "Jo?" He says as his hand stops to rest on my stomach. His breathy voice is now in my ear as he wriggles closer to me. "Can I kiss you?" He finally asks. His eyes are buzzing as they try to focus, but they keep flickering to my lips that I now realize I'm biting, to try and keep myself from blurting out an eager yes. I so badly want him to kiss me and let his hands roam freely wherever he chooses to put them. I don't answer his question with words; they wouldn't make any sense anyway so I lean into him and nod ever so slightly, granting him permission.

60
Hunter

My hands have a mind of their own as they roam the curves of Jo's body. The tiny little goosebumps that appear all along her arms tells me that she's surely enjoying this as much as I am. *Her body feels incredible.* Getting to taste those irresistible lips of hers again sends the most thrilling shockwaves through me, making me crave more and more of her. The way her waist dips makes me crazy just before my hand runs along her hip to pull her further into my grasp. I can't seem to get her close enough; I want all of her right now, and its torture trying to hold myself back from letting go and ravishing her right this second.

I pebble little kisses over Jo's lips, along her jaw, and finally… finally getting to run my lips over her the seductively delicate skin of her neck. I nuzzle her neck and bury my face in her hair, exactly how I wanted to earlier at the bookshop and deeply inhale her delectable essence. I move my hand to her waist, up the back of her shirt and I can feel the sudden goose bumps start to prickle along her bare back, while I tangle my other hand in her hair to pull her lips to mine once more.

Josephine

This moment, right here as I let Hunter consume me, is euphoric. The way he busies his hands along my skin, lightly trailing his fingers up and down my spine; it's giving me the best kind of goose bumps all over my body. He keeps pulling me closer, holding me tight as he kisses me. I can feel my lips swell as he nibbles on them before sliding his tongue across, asking for entry. I eagerly part them and let Hunter devour me whole.

Hunter

Damn her body is fucking incredible! I feel Jo's hands slowly working their way down my torso and under my shirt; her fingers grip at the material and she starts tugging up at the sides, lifting it further up. I unwillingly pull away to sit up and pull my shirt off, quickly tossing it to the floor. I carefully crawl over and rest my elbows on either side of her torso, bringing my body to lie on top of her. Her breathing increasingly becoming more erratic as I gently slide my knees up to part her legs and rest between them. I stare into her eyes when she finally looks at me and I run my hand along her flushed cheek before she closes them and smiles into my hand like she's done every other time I have caressed her beautiful face. My only wish would be to have her like this, in my arms every single night from now on. *Only it would be in My bed.* She may not realize it, but holy fuck she's messing with my head, and I wouldn't want it any other way.

Josephine

I open my eyes to find Hunter staring at me with a smile on his face. His pupils are blown out; making his eyes look so much darker compared to the unmistakable hazel that they usually are. I can feel his chest move against mine with heavy breaths while his body hovers over me, his legs resting comfortably between my thighs. Suddenly his lips pull away and he moves his head lower to just under my chin, kissing and sucking the skin there. The wetness from his tongue makes my skin cool as he pulls his heated lips away and dares to move lower to another spot on my chest. His tongue starts to move in tiny little circles at first and then as I take in another quick breath, he starts drawing a straight line further down, leading to my breasts; pulling me further into a state of bliss.

Hunter

The skin of Jo's chest is silk beneath my tongue. I'm having a difficult time containing the urge to just rip off her top and toss it to the floor. I'm battling with myself to take things slower with her. She's not just some door prize to be won over just for one night of fun. She means so much more than that to me. I lean up slightly and run my fingers over the buttons that run along the neckline of her shirt. I hear Jo take in a gasp of air as I pop them open one by one, and kiss her bare skin after I unbutton each one of them. I lay my other hand on her stomach, slowly moving it further under her shirt and caressing the parts of her skin that I still have yet to see.

Sliding further down her body, my lips trail kisses over her clothing, stopping when I get to the end of the material and when I do; I lift her shirt, exposing her beautiful midsection that lightly glistens with nervous sweat. My lips tease their way around her belly button and she surprises me by bucking her hips at the same time that she lets out an undeniably pleasurable moan. *That's what does it for me.* I grip her left hip tightly in my hand and slide her down so that her mouth is level with mine again and press my lips to hers. I can feel the want in her movements; how she lets her body grind against mine in all the right places, it's making my brain utterly useless.

Josephine

What the hell am I doing? "Hunter…wait, wait, stop." I whisper. *I don't want him to stop, but I can't do this right now…I don't think I'm ready to do this yet.*

"What, what's wrong? Are you okay? I didn't hurt you, did I?" He asks franticly as his hands come to an abrupt halt on my body. His eyes are laced with concern as he stares down at me and I can't seem to answer him, because I don't know what to say. "Jo…did I do something wrong?" He asks and starts to take his hands off of me, but the absence of his touch makes me want to rewind and pretend that I had never asked him to stop in the first place. I grip his hand so he can't move and I look up at him to try to explain. “Hunter, I’m sorry. I’m…I’m just not…” I can’t bring myself to say it. Not after I feel like I’ve led him on that this is what it was going to turn into tonight. I can’t believe I let it get as far as it did. I hear Hunter let out the biggest sigh as he drops his forehead against mine and I feel his entire body relax.

“Jo.” He sighs, before lifting his head to look at me. “I can’t tell you how relieved I am to hear you say that.” He takes in another throaty breath. “I thought I hurt you. I wouldn’t be able to live with myself if I did.” He clarifies before leaning down and quickly kisses my closed lips. He sits up and slides the covers up over my legs then gets off the bed to pick up his shirt.

“Hunter I’m sorry.” I apologize again but he quickly walks back over to me as he slides his arms through his shirt and pulls it down over his delicious abs.

“No…don’t do that. Don’t apologize remember.” He reminds me as he sits on the edge of my bed and takes my face into his hand, tilting my chin up to meet his eyes. “I shouldn’t have let it go that far.” He sighs before he rubs his thumb along the bottom of my jaw and lifts his head to kiss where he just touched. “You should get some sleep.” He tells me. But I don’t want him to leave. I want him to stay here with me tonight, and fall asleep in his arms again. So, I decide to do something I never thought I would have the guts to do. I ask him to stay the night this time.

“Hunter?” Right away he looks up from having his eyes closed as his strong hands’ stroke my left cheek. “Will you stay with me tonight?” I ask quietly. I usually lack the confidence that it just took to ask such a question, but I’ve noticed from the day I met Hunter, that being around him, has begun to bring me out of myself and act like I know what I’m doing. It’s made me start going after what I want, and right now…I want him.

Hunter

After Jo asked me to stay the night, I couldn’t bring myself to leave like I probably should have. I don’t want me being here getting her into any trouble. She doesn’t need that. But my brain justifies my selfishness as being protective; because if I'm here, then I don't have to worry like I would be if I were away from her.

Jo's sleeping peacefully beside me but I'm struggling to fall asleep because I'm thinking of all the ways that I could possibly screw this up. She's curled up in the crook of my arm, her head resting on my chest and our legs are comfortably tangled together under the blanket. Before I met Jo, I would just end up drinking myself stupid until I passed out next to some girl that I knew nothing about, and later I would wake up alone, or having to make up some excuse as to why I wouldn't want her to stay the night. I wasn't a total dick at least. I would always call them a ride home or pay for a Lyft when I had enough of her. I regret ever treating any of those girls poorly; because I would kill anyone if they ever treated Jo that way. I would never even think about treating Josephine less than what she deserves.

61
Hunter

The last few weeks since I had the pleasure of falling asleep with Jo in my arms, we have hardly spent a moment apart; aside from those pesky times when we absolutely can't be together, like when she's at work or in the shower before she comes to bed. Every night since then, I wait patiently for her until I hear her light footsteps creak as she comes down the stairs and opens the door to her room. She always smells of fresh rain and coconut. *My favorite.*

The scent wafting around the small room just about kills me when she walks past me to her closet. Swaying those beautiful curvy hips side to side makes me want to ravage her where she stands. The long dark strands of her hair still wet from her shower, trickle water down her bare shoulders making them glisten in the soft light from the lamp. I take in a sharp breath and hold it in as I sit on her bed and watch her calculated steps. I try and fight the need that I have to run my hands over every inch of her body as she walks back and forth and puts her things away.

"Jo, if you keep teasing me like that, I'm going to have to take a cold shower tonight!" I warn her. She knows I won't push anything. I'm happy to wait until she's ready to let things go any further between us, but fuck, her body is driving me mad.

"Teasing?" She questions while giving me a coy grin. She very well knows what she's doing, and I love the fact that she's doing it on purpose.

"Yeah, teasing." I echo and as I approach her, look her in the eye and quickly wrap my arms around her tiny waist, bringing her into my arms and she giggles as she thumps against my chest. With Jo wrapped in my arms, I let my fingers trace the band on her shorts that sit low on her hips, and I run my fingers just inside of the material to make her body react to my touch and I softly kiss the top of her head. "You know what you do to me, Jo. It's why I can never keep my hands off of you." I admit as I quicken the pace of my thumb that's drawing little circles on her hips, and I run my other hand up her side and then to the back of her head as she stands on her tiptoes to reach up and kiss me. Our lips urgently come together and my hands suddenly have a mind of their own as they run along the inside of her shorts. I force my hand to stay still for a moment, trying to give myself time to think about what I'm doing, but then Jo pushes her groin into me and moans into my mouth. *Fucking Hell!*

That little movement does me in. I take both my hands as we kiss and grip her hips to lifting her off the floor. She swings her legs around my waist, bringing every sensitive part of her body in contact with mine and our mouths never come apart. I walk over to the bed as she clings to me and I lean down, guiding her onto the cushy surface. She gently falls back and I slowly move over her, keeping my weight on my hands so that I can enjoy the vison of her staring up at me.

The tiny little shorts she's sporting, ride up her thighs as she crawls back onto her pillows. Her silky-smooth skin calls to me, begging for contact as my lips brush along the lines of her shoulders, feeling her pulse quicken the closer I come to my favorite spot. I gently suck and leave little pink bite marks along her neck as I twirl my tongue in circles and enjoy the sounds of her soft little moans.

Josephine

The familiar feeling of letting go, starts to creep up on me again and I feel like I'm back in the exact same situation that I was weeks ago, when I found myself wrapped up in Hunter, allowing him to grab hold and devour every part of me. But this time, my feelings for him have evolved into something far more complicated and I don't want to drown out my feelings for him just yet, so I won't do something that I might regret later. I just want to share this moment with him and let every single sensation running through me right now completely consume me.

I find my hands running up along the ripped muscular contours of Hunter's torso. His body is flushed and warm to the touch and I want nothing more than for him to kiss me again. I meet him halfway before he can pin me underneath him and I smash my lips against his as my hands continue to explore his body.

Hunter's hand is tangled in my hair as he trails kisses up and down stomach as my hands search for the button on his pants. He somewhat pulls away and glances up at me, our foreheads still touching and our breath labored. Hunter quickly moves his hand to mine to stop me from undoing the button that's keeping his pants around his hips.

"Jo…?" He questions. I know what he's going to say, so I interrupt before he can talk me out of it.

"I'm sure." I flash a smile and nob my head to make sure that he knows I'm serious. Before I know it, his lips are back on mine and his hands are desperately searching for the bottom of my shirt. He grasps it as I unbutton his pants, and he pulls my top over my head, sending it to the floor next to his. Our bodies are a labyrinth of emotions and hands and sweat and lips. An all-consuming dance between the two of us has us both reveling in the desire that is this moment. *I wish this didn't have to end.*

62
Hunter

Jo is fast asleep already; spent from a night of exchanging ravenous energy. I have never felt more content, but the guilt of taking something so fragile from Jo is eating away at me already. I don't want her to wake up in the morning, regretting the decision she made to give herself to me.

My thoughts are getting the best of me while I lie here next to her, thinking about how magnificent her body is. Of all the nights I have spent in her bed, I always managed to restrain myself from losing all control with her. But tonight, was without a doubt, profoundly different. There was such an ease about being with her that I had never felt before. Any other time she always seemed to be on edge, like she was waiting for some drastic change to happen so she was never able to let herself go and relax to fully enjoy being with me.

Her mind would seem to occasionally wander away from the present moment, leaving me to try and figure out what was making her so discontent about whatever it was that she was thinking about. Always brushing it off like she was just daydreaming, but most of the time I knew she wouldn't want to talk about it, so I would never force it. I wanted her to come to me when she felt ready.

Tonight, Jo was calm and happy as she moved around her room, walking back and forth in front of me with a new brightness in her smile, like the weight of the world had been lifted from her shoulders, finally letting her true self come through and being absolutely comfortable in her own skin. I watched her body sway with confidence as I sat on her bed, letting her drive me mad with that tight little body of hers in the least amount of clothing I have ever seen her in.

The room suddenly feels hot and I can feel the sweat starting to bead along my forehead as I lie here thinking about our time together. The fan in the corner hums as it sends a gentle breeze throughout the room, but it does very little to distract me from my thoughts enough to fall asleep for a few hours. I decide to get up and go to the kitchen for a drink, hoping the short walk will help clear my head before Jo wakes up in a few hours. I reach my hand onto the floor to feel around for my pants and boxers as I swing my legs out from under the blanket and onto the creaky wooden floor. I slide my clothes on and zip my pants up before I grab my shirt from the pile and pull it over my head. Before I leave, I lean my knee on the bed and bend down to leave a light kiss on Jo's forehead. She doesn't stir at all, telling me she's in a deep, peaceful sleep.

I walk out of the room and quietly shut the door before I head into the kitchen. The house is quiet, the only sounds I hear are from the humming of the refrigerator and outside. The window is open but there's no breeze to speak of, just stale humid air.

I take two bottles of water from the fridge and down both of them in mere seconds. Since I greedily drank the bottle that I was going to bring back to the room for Jo, I open up the fridge again and grab another bottle for her. When I walk back out of the kitchen, I hear heavy footsteps coming toward me from the living room. A glowing red cherry from a lit cigarette is all I see in dark hallway as the footsteps come to a halt in front of me.

"Hey man." I hear Nate say. I'm relieved it's him, but Jo never mentioned he would be home tonight. I feel like I've been caught with my hand in the cookie jar, but I much rather deal with Nate than her stepdad after hearing about what kind of person he is.

"Nate." My one word, response. He takes a few steps towards me as he inhales again.

"Where's Jo?" He asks.

"She's sleeping." I tell him and point to her bedroom door.

"Good. Is she okay?" The darkness of the hallway leaves the expression on his face a mystery, but I can hear the concern in his voice.

"She's fine. Why? Everything alright mate?"

"Yeah… all good. But look." He says and pinches the cherry of his cigarette between his fingers. "Just be careful with her, okay? You seem like a good guy. I wouldn't want to have to kick your ass. So don't even think about hurting her." His tone is serious when he gives me the warning. *'don't even think about hurting her'*. I would never hurt Jo. Nate and I may not know each other very well, but he has to know that Jo's smart enough that she would never let someone into her life that's going to hurt her again, especially since it's ultimately her decision to keep me around in the first place.

"Hey, no, I would never hurt her, Nate. Believe me. You don't ever have to worry about that." I assure him.

"Good. She's been put through enough. I've let her down enough by not looking out for her the way I should have from the beginning, and she doesn't need any more of that shit coming from someone she seems to actually care about." He warns me. The hurt in his tone is evident and his words are dripping with guilt. I'm shocked that Nate would tell me this. He doesn't act like the type to do anything other than use his fists to solve a problem, much like myself. Lucky for me I have Jo; her mere presence helps me keep my hot temper at bay.

"Hey man, like I said, I'm grateful she even wants me around. I wouldn't do anything to screw that up." I remind him.

"Alright then." He says and pushes open the kitchen door pausing just before he disappears behind it. "Yo…feel free to use the door next time." He tells me and walks into the kitchen.

I don't want to wake Jo, but as I turn around from trying to sneak in, I see her sitting up in bed with her knees pulled up under the blanket to her chest.

"Hey." She whispers and lets out a sleepy yawn.

"Hey. Sorry if I woke you. I was just getting some water." I hold the bottle up and walk over to the bed, handing it to her and she gratefully takes it out of my hand and immediately drinks about half of it almost as fast as I had.

"Thirsty?" I question and she nods her head while she downs the rest.

"Yeah…I was. Thank you." She caps the bottle and leans over to set it on her nightstand next to her lamp and then pulls the cover off of her legs, crossing them in front of her.

"I thought you might have left." She says while looking down at her hands. I follow her gaze and notice her nervously rubbing her thumb into her palm. I hate when she does this because every time, I know that she's feeling insecure, and right now that's the last thing I want her to feel about us. I'm quick to reassure her that I wasn't going anywhere by gripping her chin delicately with my fingers and guiding her eyes up to look at me. Her gaze doesn't lock on mine but restlessly shifts between my eyes and my lips. "I'm here, Jo. I would never just leave you, not after a night like that." I grin. "You hear me? You can't get rid of me."

63

Josephine

It's finally lunch-time and I am starving. The three of us decided to go off-campus and to grab a bite to eat at the diner today since the weather has finally begun to feel like spring. It's been warm for a couple of weeks, making me wish we had air conditioning at home; but at least Hunter has it in his car. That's one thing he said he had to build from scratch when he restored his car because of the year it was built in. I'm so grateful he put it in, because if he didn't; being in this dress would have my thighs sticking to the leather seats today for sure.

I walk out of the side doors that face the senior parking area, looking for Hunter's car. I quickly spot it since it's literally the only one of its kind in our small town. Everyone else has these heinous-looking bubbles that have absolutely no room. Hunter's car is huge, so it's not difficult to spot from across the lot. The color of it is as dark as the forest is at midnight. Hunter says it fits his personality rather well. I don't ever see that side of him, I only see how sweet and caring he is for the people in his life.

Hunter's back is towards me as I walk over to them so he doesn't see me right away. Kyle is sitting in the passenger seat and looks up suddenly when he notices me and his eyes quickly dart back up to Hunter, almost like he's warning that I'm behind him. He turns around to greet me; a semi worried look creases his forehead but it swiftly disappears as we get closer and leans down to kiss my neck. Taking my bag from my shoulder, he guides me toward the car.

"Hey babe, you ready to go to lunch? I'd understand if you changed your mind; considering this dipshit is tagging along again." Hunter smirks and looks at Kyle to see the hilarious pout on his face and I let out a giggle, knowing he's only messing around. The look on Kyle's face is priceless, but then he opens his mouth and all hope is lost. "Hey man.

That's harsh. I just wanted to go see my girlfriend, she is working you know, so if you maybe stop being a dick, she might be nice enough to give you some free pie." Kyle bellows over the hood of the car.

"Yeah, yeah, I knew that's why you suggested we go to 'Jo's favorite place' right?" Hunter says making air quotes to mock Kyle.

"What can I say? Kimberly loves my ass, so she gives me free pie to get her squeezes in." He says this out loud so I'm pretty sure the entire school has heard every word. Now the look on Hunter's face holds the prize for most disgusted as he desperately tries not to picture his best friend getting man-handled by the diner waitress that also serves the food we eat.

"Alright…now that I've lost my appetite." Hunter pulls the driver seat forward. "Just get in the car, jackass." He quips and Kyle walks over to his side and plops himself in the backseat, with a proud smirk on his face knowing he just burned a horrible image into his best mate's brain forever.

When we get to the diner, we notice that it's a lot busier than usual so we have to park down the block. Hoping to still get our favorite booth in the back, we walk in and see that there aren't many tables open. I have never seen it this full before. That's one reason why I like this place so much. Hunter takes my hand in his and carefully walks past everyone to get to our booth. We never sit anywhere else, it's always this one. Except when we see that it's already taken, he stops and I almost bump into his back, but after a second, he walks over to the table exuding such confidence and starts to speak to the couple that's sitting there while Kyle and I stay back and look around for another table. I see Hunter lean on the edge of the table, talking to the people sitting there and a minute later the couple looks over at me and then back at Hunter, nodding their head before getting up and taking their plates with them to another table that a waitress just cleaned off. Hunter waves me and Kyle over while he starts to wipe up the fallen crumbs with a napkin.

"What did you say to them?" I ask curiously. I know Hunter has a sense of authority about him, but I can't picture someone just moving from a table just because he asked nicely.

"I told them it was your birthday and that you come here every year and sit in this exact spot to celebrate with your favorite dessert. I told them I didn't want to break your tradition and end up disappointing you; given the fact that it's your first birthday that we get to celebrate as a couple."

I can't believe he did that so we could have our same booth all to ourselves. Well of course with Kyle tagging along as Hunter put it.

I sit down and slide in toward the window. Hunter sits down next to me and Kyle thumps himself across from us on the other side. It's how it's always been since the first day Kyle started coming here with us. I don't mind it. Kyle is a really sweet guy under all that male bravado; and now that he's dating Kimberly, this is the only place he ever wants to eat. Fine with me, since it is my favorite place, Kyle wasn't wrong about that. The reason isn't because of the food; even though it is really delicious. It's because this is the first place I had come to where I felt safe after having my world fall apart on me. Suzie was a kind face. She was nice to me and didn't make me feel like she pitied me because of the state I was in at the time.

"You're such a kiss ass man." Kyle cackles.

"Yeah well, at least I'm not whipped like you mate." Hunter bites. This back and forth between these two never seems to get old to me. I love the fact that they can be insulting each other all the time, and still be best friends.

"Yeah, well…ah screw it, I got nothing. I admit it, I'm whipped, but she's hot, what can I say?" Kyle concedes, throwing his hands in the air before lightly slapping them back on the table.

"Speaking of, where the hell is that sweet little ass of hers anyway?" He says as he looks around the diner for Kimberly. Hunter rolls his eyes and then picks up a menu and throws it at Kyle while he's distracted. It hits him in the chest and lands on the table in front of him. He just gives Hunter a dirty look before picking it up and dramatically wiggling the paper it in front of his face, making unnecessary noise.

Hunter

"So, what was the serious face about earlier?" Jo asks as I wave over to Suzie letting her know we're ready to order.

"What do you mean? What face?" I ask her. I honestly don't have a clue.

"When you and Kyle were talking by your car outside of school, is everything okay? You seemed kind of agitated?" Now I know what

She means. I don't want to tell her, because I know that's she's going to side with Kyle on this one, but now that she's asked, I don't want to lie to her. Kyle will most likely open his big fat mouth anyway.

"Kyle wants to go out tonight and celebrate." I say, annoyed that she knew I was in a foul mood about it. I'm not even remotely interested in going out. I'm over the parties and waking up with a hangover. Besides, I have better things to do with my time, now that I have Jo to keep me company.

"Celebrate?" She asks curiously.

"Yeah, uh, remember when I told you that I had some things to figure out a while back? And those things kind of involved what happened with my sister. Well, Kyle and I settled everything and he wants to go out and celebrate our new found freedom." I explain, using Kyle's choice of words when he tried talking me into it earlier.

"Oh. That's really great. What, you don't want to go or…?" She asks. Thinking I would automatically want to, I guess.

"It's not that I don't want to, it's that I don't want to be away from you." I admit. As sappy as it sounds coming from my mouth, I don't regret telling her; even if Kyle hears me and decides to make it a big deal from now on.

"No, you should totally go." She tells me. And don't I know it, that Kyle would butt into our conversation with his two cents.

"Yeah Hunter, you should. See, even Jo agrees with me!!" He gestures to Jo with a long look on his face waiting for me to agree, even if it is to get him to shut the hell up and stop pestering me about it. After a few nudging looks from Jo I finally give in.

"Alright!" I say a little louder than I think I needed to. "Fine! I'll go, I'll go. Now can we drop it?" I request. The look on Kyle's face says it all. Now he knows if he can get Jo on board with any number of his dumb ideas, then I'll have no choice but to cave. Let's face it; I would do absolutely anything for this girl.

64
Josephine

Hey guys, what can I get you? Sorry for the wait by the way. I've never seen this place so busy." Kimberly says. Taking her by surprise, Kyle sweeps her off her feet, (*literally)* and plants what looks to be a nice wet kiss on her lips as she plops down on his lap. She doesn't seem to mind, but after Kyle removes his lips with a loud smack and helps her stand upright again, I can see the blush in her cheeks rise as she notices almost everyone staring at her. *Poor girl, she has no idea what she has gotten herself into.*

"Hey babe, can I get the special today, please?" Kyle begs, staring up at Kimberly like a little puppy dog begging for a biscuit. It's adorable. I know Hunter could do without seeing his best friend being such a softy but I know he thinks they're good for each other.

"Sure babe. And for you two, would you like your usual?" It's nice to have a 'usual'. We come here so often and it's the only thing Hunter and I ever order any more. Hot cocoa, with cinnamon and blueberry pancakes with a side of extra crispy hash browns.

"Yeah, that would be great, thank, Kim." Hunter says and Kimberly quickly gives eyes to Kyle.

"Behave yourself mister," she tells him. "Or there's no free pie for you today." She playfully threatens. Kyle's face drops, exaggerating the frown on his face so Kimberly doesn't deny him his free dessert. She walks away to go behind the counter and Kyle watches her every move. It looks like he has drool dripping down the corner of his mouth as he stares at her. He really seems to like Kim and she may be just the type of girl to keep his mischievous ways from getting him into any more trouble. He kind of needs it.

"So, Kyle!" I say suddenly to try and get his attention before he creates a puddle of drool all over the table. "What?" He asks startled out of his trance from gawking at his girlfriend.

"Hey man, you got a little something right here." Hunter tells him as he points to the corner of his own mouth, showing Kyle where to mop up the streak of drool. Kyle takes his sleeve and swipes it across his face, giving Hunter the stink eye; warning him to keep his comments to himself.

"Not a word from either of you." He demands. And we both just laugh a little at his embarrassment, because it's cute that he now knows we can make fun of him for being 'whipped' as he put it, just like he said Hunter is.

"What are you guys going to do to celebrate tonight?" I ask. I'm excited for them, and I want them to have a good time.

"Honestly, I have no idea, Kyle is the one that usually makes up these hair brain schemes and I just go along with them." Hunter claims.

"Yeah well, my ideas are way better than your lame ones. You would just stay home with Jo and suck face all night. Ah…no offense Jo." Kyle adds and his shoulders shrink back when he looks over at me.

"Yeah, and you shouldn't have a problem with that, you were just making out with your girlfriend in the middle of a diner!" Hunter quips back. And Kyle opens his mouth to say something, but his usual quick comebacks are halted as he looks over to Kim and then back at us.

"Fair point." He plainly says as he tilts his head.

"Listen, Jo. Why don't you come with us? I don't have a clue what this douche has in mind." Hunter nods across the table to Kyle. "But I'm sure it would be way more fun with you there." He whispers in my ear. Whenever Hunter gets close to me and I can feel his tickling breath on my neck, I love all the little shivering goosebumps that prickle up along my skin. I let out a low giggle as he nudges his nose into my collar bone and leaves a peck on the side of my jaw before slowly pulling away.

"Um…" I say, breaking the haze around my head from his touch. "No, it's okay. You two go and have fun. I have to study for the PSAT's. I'm really far behind."

"Ah, come on Jo, come with us, I promise it will be fun, Kim's going to be there, you girls can talk and do all that girly stuff you girls do." Kyle trails off; probably because he just realized how dumb that sentence sounded.

"No, it's okay. I really do need to study."

"Are you sure? Maybe just an hour, I promise I'll show you a good time babe." Hunter says in that low sexy voice that he knows usually works on me. I can't help it, he knows how to be irresistible, but I really have to stand my ground. Otherwise, I am never going to pass my junior year.

"Yeah, you know I would love to go with you guys, but I really can't. I hope you understand." I say regretfully.

"I know. I was just hoping to spend some more time with my girl this weekend." He tells me as he takes my hand and places it between both of his and plants a kiss on the tips of my fingers.

"Here is everyone's food." Kimberly calls out as she sets our plates down in front of us. "Enjoy guys, and let me know if you need anything else, okay?"

"Thanks, Kim." Hunter and I say in unison.

"Thanks, babe." Kyle says as he starts to dig in.

Hunter

Kyle left school early today to be dragged by his mom to another follow up doctors' appointment. Of course, he's been healed for a while and he's functioning normally again, but his mom is so overprotective, I think he's probably gonna have to endure a few more appointments like this just to make her happy. I'm not complaining because now I can just be alone with Jo the entire evening.

I sit in my car and play around with my pack of cigarettes that I had stuffed in the glove compartment. There's still a few left, but I can't remember the last time I actually bought a new pack. I guess since being around Jo, I haven't had too many, she doesn't like them; and I don't like smelling like a dirty ashtray from a bar top. So, I shove them back in the glove compartment and push it shut.

We stopped by the bookstore for a couple of hours so Jo could help Honey clean up after a kid's story time thing or something. There were juice boxes and snack wrappers and little humans running around everywhere. It was chaotic, to say the least, but Jo being so amazing, she handled everything so well like she always does; even when one of the little creatures threw up all over the floor and almost got it all over her shoes. "You know, I'm going to miss you the entire time I'm gone tonight, right?"

"Yes. I know. You always do." She answers with a side-eye grin playing on her lips.

"You're sure you can't come out at all? I can help you study later when we get back." I tell her and see her thinking before she answers.

"You know that's not going to work, right?" Every time I try to study, you somehow manage to distract me long enough to make me forget what I'm trying to study for." She says.

"I know, I'm sorry. You just, those lips of yours do something to me. I can't control myself when I'm around you." I admit and I see Jo's cheeks turn a rosy pink, followed by yet another adorable smile, and then she leans over and kisses me on the cheek as I pull up outside her house.

After I make us something to eat, we go back to her room and watch a movie on my laptop until I have to leave to go pick up Kyle. I've left some of my things here in her room since I stay over so often. It's been nice to just be able to exist in our own little space together and not have to go home and be without her for an entire night. She makes me happy and it's been a really long time since I've felt this way.

My phone quickly beeps three times before I even think to reach for it. Signaling the impatience of whoever is interrupting my time with my girl. I unlock it and see Kyle's name. *Damn, already?* Jo walks over to me with some drinks and gives me a sad look. She most likely knows that it's Kyle wondering where I am, so I get up off her bed and walk over to her. I take the drinks out of her hand and set them on her dresser before wrapping her up in my arms, holding her close to me in a tight hug.

Josephine

"Was that Kyle?" I ask. Even though I know it is. I'm just hoping that maybe he changed his mind about dragging Hunter out tonight.

"Yeah, he's waiting for me at his house. Said he found a place to go where they don't ID anyone." He adds. That sentence sends a queasiness to my stomach after I realize what he means by it. My shoulders slump in Hunter's arms and I push my forehead into his chest, taking in his enticing scent.

"I'm not going to drink, if that's what you're worried about shortcake." He says as he lifts my chin to meet his eyes. I can tell it's the truth, so it makes me feel a little better knowing he'll be safe. "I won't be gone long. I can't stand to think about you falling asleep alone after all that studying that you have to do." He says while rubbing his thumb along my jaw. His gentle touch feels so good. I feel his other hand slowly crawl to the small of my back, pulling me even closer to him and I have to stand up on my toes to meet him-half-way for a kiss.

65
Josephine

I walk Hunter to the front door and he turns to plant one last kiss on my lips before he opens it to leave. We walk out onto the porch; my hand still gently snuggled into his grip as he tries to walk me out to his car. I know he wants me to come with them, but he needs time to hang out with his mate without having to worry about dragging me along or getting me home in time to get enough sleep for tomorrow. He's always so worried about me, it's time he focuses on himself; at least for a night.

"Hey. What's going on with you two?" Nate asks as he leisurely strolls across the grass towards the steps and up onto the porch. He stops just before the front door and looks at us as he takes the last drag of his cigarette and flicks the butt across the lawn.

"Not much." Hunter replies. "What are you up to?"

"Same shit, different day." Nate says as he grips the door handle.

"Hey man." Hunter calls before Nate steps inside.

"What's up?" Nate doesn't sound as irritated as he usually does after work, which is surprising and he looks like he's in a pretty decent mood for once.

"You want to go for a beer?" Hunter offers, surprising me that he would ask my step brother to hang out. They barely know each other. The most I knew that they talked was when they ran into each other in the hallway. Before that, they had maybe said ten words to each other the day my mom showed up out of nowhere.

"Yeah…sure, I could go for a beer. I'll be right out." Nate says and then he walks inside the house.

"Are you sure you won't come with?" Hunter asks looking up at me with puppy dog eyes as he wraps his hand around my waist and pulls me to him. I rest my hands on his shoulders and lean down to kiss him on the nose. "Yes, I'm sure. Now go have a great time. I'll see you later." I playfully shove him, but he hops back up on the step with his feet placed on either side of mine, closing me in his arms, and kisses the top of my head before he jumps back off and lands on the path.

"Alright fine, I'll go, but I'm not happy about it." He clarifies as he sulks towards his car. Nate comes out of the house as I walk up the steps about to go inside when he stops and turns around to face me.

"Jo? Are you cool with this?" He asks and it catches me a little bit off guard because all of my attention is focused on Hunter looking sexy as usual behind the wheel of his car.

"What? Oh yeah. It's fine. I hope you guys have fun." I tell him. I don't have the slightest idea how the night is going to turn out, but I think we're safe as long as no one pisses either of them off.

The guys have only been gone a half-hour and I'm already bored out of my mind. Since Hunter has been staying over every night for the last few weeks, I would always have someone to talk to and share movie snacks with. It's been such a nice change from consistently being alone for so long. To get my mind off of whether or not everything will turn out, I decide to go for a quick run and get my mind off of things for a while.

As soon as I get close enough to be able to smell the ocean, I spot dark heavy rain clouds above my head and decide to turn back towards the house so I don't get caught in what looks like a storm. Just before I turn the corner onto my street, the skies open up with a summer night downpour, drenching me from head to toe. *Awesome.*

The rain is soothing against my sweaty forehead and it helps to cool me off as I walk the last few feet to my house. The sensation of it running down my body is relaxing, but I'm very much looking forward to a nice hot shower when I get inside.

After having to talk myself into getting out of the shower, I decide now is as good a time as ever to start studying. I start reading about the French revolution and then move on after a short time to calculus before I get too tired and the numbers start to jumble themselves together. I keep checking the time on my phone since it's getting late, and figured I can call it a night on this god-awful chapter since this was the last subject that I needed to cover. I throw my books off to the side of my bed and decide to listen to the rest of the playlist Hunter made me. He isn't back yet, so they must be having a good time. I haven't tried texting him even though I would like to. I just don't want to be one of those girlfriends that nag their boyfriends whenever they go somewhere without them.

I'M JOSTLED AWAKE when I think I heard a loud noise. I still have my headphones in and the music has skipped to the next playlist on my phone so I have no idea what the heck I'm listening to, the volume is harsh on my ears especially for just waking up. I pull the one side of my headphones out of my ear and listen for the noise again but I don't hear anything unusual, so I figure it's just from the music being too loud and messing with my dreams while I was asleep. I guess I wasn't asleep for long though because the time only says it's just after midnight and I stopped studying around eleven. I figure since I'm already awake I'll get up to wait for Hunter to get here. I check my phone for any messages and see my battery is basically dead again and to my disappointment, there are no new messages either. I throw my phone on the charger and grab a hoodie before going to get a snack.

Hunter and I had an early dinner before he left but the anxiousness is making me hungry, so I rummage through the fridge and the cabinets until I finally make up my mind and pour some cheddar popcorn into a bowl. *I wish it was buttered popcorn. Hunter makes it so good.* Hopefully, he will be back soon so we can share it and watch a movie together.

I push the kitchen door open with my elbow since my hands are full and before I even get to my bedroom door, I hear a loud crash coming from inside my room. The sudden noise startles me and I end up dropping the bowl of popcorn and it scatters across the floor as my glass of soda splatters up the old peeling wallpaper, staining it a sticky dark brown. My throat is tight as I stand still and hold my breath. I'm trying not to make any sound, so I can listen for any sort of movement. It's quiet for just a second longer until I hear footsteps shuffling around again. As quietly as I can, I run down the narrow hallway on my tip toes and hide behind the wall in the living room. That's when I see the mess of furniture rearranged and almost everything in here is lying broken on the floor. *What the hell?*

I slowly turn my head as I push my back into the wall and see the table that use to be next to Jeff's recliner is now lying on its side, the lamp that was sitting on it is smashed to bits on the floor near the wall across the room. All I can think is that someone had broken into the house while I was gone. Or maybe while I was in the shower and I couldn't hear anything because my music was too loud.

I freeze in the middle of the living room, too afraid to move because I might make too much noise and the person that did this would know where I am. I hear another loud crash coming from my room and it makes me jump while simultaneously letting out a startled squeal. I immediately raise my hands to my mouth, desperate to muffle the sound, but it's too late. Whoever is still in here must have heard me; because the commotion suddenly comes to a halt, making the house shutter back into silence.

I push my body up against the wall again; standing as still as I possibly can and I have to keep my hand over my mouth to make sure that I don't involuntarily make another sound. I can feel my body shake as I hear my door open and the sounds of heavy boots creaking across the hardwood floor at an angry unsteady pace. They stomp around and whoever it is; lets out a deep groan as they slide all the clutter from the hallway table onto the floor. Even though my eyes well up with silent tears I don't dare let another frightened sound escape from my lips. I can feel the vibrations from their footsteps getting closer to me, but I don't dare try to move until I know I can safely getaway.

I quietly back up further into the living room and head for the doorway that leads into the kitchen, since the person is inching their way closer to me. Just as I see the toe of a dirty work boot come into view, I hastily turn around before I see the person's face and run in the opposite direction of them.

I don't notice that Jeff's chair is blocking the doorway at first because I step onto the broken glass from the lamp that's scattered all over the floor and I stumble to the ground as the shards puncture the bottom of my foot. I yell out a pained cry and grab my foot as I fall to the floor, but I quickly push myself up and get to my feet again. I try my best to ignore the pain as I lift my injured foot over the chair to hop over, but I'm too late. I can feel myself being pulled back by my hair and then slammed hard to the ground as my scalp screams from the sting of being ripped away from my skull.

I think I must have blacked out for a few seconds because when I open my eyes, I see a blurry figure towering over me; the faint echo of their voice spitting vile sounds into my ears as I lie on the floor in agony beneath their feet. I hold my hands to the back of my head to relieve some of the throbbing on my scalp and I have to blink a few times before my eyes completely focus. When I finally recognize the nightmare that is hovering above me; I'm up and running for my life.

66
Hunter

We've been at this club for almost two hours and all I've done is sit here on this massively uncomfortable lounge…thing, and watch Kyle stick his tongue down Kimberly's throat. I can't say I blame the guy since he seems to have found someone who isn't completely insane like his ex, Miranda was but if I have to sit and watch them dry hump each other any longer, I swear I'm going to gouge my own eyes out with that damn umbrella from Kimberly's drink.

Nate seemed to be getting on just fine the second we walked in the door. We hadn't sat down for more than a minute and he had already attracted the eyes of some blonde sitting at the bar in a dark, skin tight dress. He quickly excused himself, leaving me to be the third wheel at our table while he went off. I assume to get her number. Kyle didn't waste any time either after taking a seat and pulling Kim onto his lap; they immediately started petting each other as soon as they sat down on the oversized white marshmallow of a chair, directly across from me. I'm pretty sure it's only meant for one, but they obviously don't seem to care.

I pull my phone out to see if Jo had text, maybe wondering when I'll be back, but I unlock my phone to find no new messages from her. I feel my hopeful expression dwindle, turning sour from the lack of contact. I thought about texting her earlier, in fact as soon as we got here, I wanted to leave, but I didn't want to distract her while she was studying. *I've done that enough times already.*

I'm sitting here alone, not enjoying myself at all without Jo, so I try to think of a good excuse to get the hell out of here and head back to see my girl. I don't think Kyle will miss me and Nate I'm sure is otherwise occupied. I can't think of anything that won't make me sound like a total dick for wanting to leave but right now I don't really give a shit, I have to get out of here before I go insane. The smacking sounds coming from Kyle's side of the table makes me want to chuck my phone at his head while he's distracted by Kim's mouth so he can't deflect the blow, but I decide against it because I wouldn't want to hit a girl, even accidentally; but the sounds they are creating are making me want to vomit. How can they be so loud in a place that's blaring music from a million different speakers at once?

I slide my phone in my pocket, drink the rest of my water, and stand up to lean over the table to get Kyle's attention.

"Hey man. I'll be right back." I yell loud enough over the music and he acknowledges that he heard me by waving his hand in the air at my face, all while never removing his lips from Kim's exposed neck. They're acting as if there will never be another opportunity to kiss each other as long as they live. I roll my eyes as I slide out between the table and the seat I was sitting on and make my way to the front entrance of the club.

Speed dialing Jo's number as I step out into the muggy air, I contemplate for another five minutes if I should text her or not. It's after midnight so I would think that she would be done studying for tonight anyway. The phone rings three times before she picks up, but all I hear is a rustling sound from her end.

"Jo? Are you there?" I question, trying hard to listen, I look at my screen and see that the call is still active, and when I put it to my ear again, I hear a weak whimper coming from her end of the call. "JO! JO. Answer me, are you alright?" I scream into the phone with a noticeable shudder in my voice. I'm outside and there are people all around me, staring at me as I lose my mind with worry. I listen harder but all I can hear are her hurt cries bleeding into the speaker. Then without warning, her startled screams come through again followed by a deep muffled growl.

My heart brutally thumps harder and harder in my chest as I stand helplessly on the street, listening to the dreaded sounds that I can't bear to hear. *I have to get to her!* "JO! GOD DAMIT JO!" I scream one last time and then a crashing sound blares its way into my ear just before the line finally goes dead.

I run back into the club and head straight for Kyle but the table we were at now sits empty. I don't see anyone anywhere as I look around and the sheer panic is starting to take over and get the best of me. Luckily, I spot Kim a few seconds later across the way, talking to a girl near the bar so I don't waste any time before I run-up to her to find out where the fuck Kyle took off too.

"Hey, Kim!" I say out of breath. "Where the hell is Kyle?" I demand. She looks at me with wide eyes and opens her mouth to speak before pointing behind me.

"Over there, he went to the bathroom." I look over my shoulder and see Kyle walking out, wiping his hands on the thighs of his jeans.

"Hunter what's wrong?" I hear Kim ask and I don't mean to ignore her but I don't have an answer for her. I just need to get to Jo.

"Kyle…where the fuck is Nate?" I howl over the music as I approach him.

"What? I don't know. I haven't seen him in over an hour, what the hell is going on?" He asks as the worry slips out with his words.

"I have to go. There's something wrong with Jo. I heard her screaming over the phone." I say in a panic, my words spewing their way out of me. "Find Nate and tell him to get the fuck back to the house as soon as possible alright!" I angrily demand; clearly pissed, to say the least, that Nate is nowhere to be found. *I could really use his fucking help about now!*

"Alright, I'll find him and be right behind you." He assures me as I start making my way out towards the exit. I have to push my way through the crowd, anxiously staggering between sweaty bodies that seem to be trying to keep me from getting back to my girl.

I get to my car and throw it in reverse to peel out of the parking lot, past the line of people still waiting to get into the club. They back up as my tires squeal on the blacktop and I leave a trail of burnt rubber and smoke behind me as I accelerate down the street.

I'm coming baby!

67
Josephine

I stumble out of the living room and race across the hall as fast as my body will let me. My eyes whirl around from the dizziness taking hold but I make my way to the front door. I slip along the hardwood floor again and again as the blood rushes out of the cut on my foot. *Oh god please!* I pray I can get it open before he reaches me. My foot painfully shifts my weight and I almost fall to my knees as I reach for the door handle; forgetting about the deadbolt. Just as I reach to unlock it, I feel Jeff's thunderous footsteps behind me and I turn around just in time to move out of the way as he throws his fist at my head. His knuckles make a deafening crackle when they make contact with the door and I scramble to my feet, limping down the hallway to my room without looking behind me.

I manage to get inside and start moving my dresser in front of the door but I'm too late to block it; Jeff is too fast. He pushes all his body weight into the door, shoving my dresser across the floor and into my shins.

"What the fuck do you think you're doing? You trying to keep me out of my own house?" He bellows as he stands in the doorway, eyeing me as I cower on the floor. My body is frozen, terrified of moving, like the prey that senses his predator near-by. Somehow, I find the courage to glance up, praying that he may show me mercy if he sees how afraid I am. *He likes when I'm afraid.* But all that stares back are the lifeless eyes of a cold- blooded monster; and I am *his* prey.

"I leave for a while and already you have some…some fucking piece of garbage living in my god damn house!" He spits. I don't know what he's talking about. I crawl backward on my hands as he steals a few slow steps closer to me. I don't want him anywhere near me and I'll do anything I can to keep him at a distance, so I keep trying to slowly back up without him noticing. "No, I don't know what you're talking about. I haven't done anything!" I cry. My voice comes out weaker than I intended it to this time but I'm afraid of what he'll do if I challenge him. *Will it be worse than last time like he promised?*

"You know what you fucking did you little whore. I found the evidence myself." He seethes. His voice is lower, mocking me as he pulls something shiny out of his pocket and bends down a little closer to shove it in front of my face. "Is this what you want huh? To be some little slut like your mother!" He stands up in a hurry and starts pacing back and forth in front of me waving around the condom wrapper from last night. I pull my legs up into a ball, slowly sliding behind my bed as he screams his shrill words in the tiny space of my room. "That's why your bitch mother never came back for you. You're a disgusting little slut; that needs to be taught a lesson!" The tone of his voice is nauseating as he snarls the vulgar words, that I'm sure he's been saving for me since day one and the sheer volume of his growl paralyzes my own vocal cords, preventing me from being able to distract him, or apologize to get him to leave me alone.

I slide myself further back towards my bed and notice my phone lying on the floor next to my sneakers. It must have fallen off my nightstand when Jeff was in here trashing my room and going through my things. I reach behind my back for it while I stare up at Jeff, desperate to make sure he doesn't see me with it. I discretely unlock it and slide over to Hunter's contact and press send. I don't recognize the sounds that are coming out of me as I pray and wait for Hunter to pick up. The room suddenly goes silent and I slowly lift my eyes to see that Jeff has stopped pacing and his eyes are fixed directly on me as I press the speaker on my phone.

Hunter answered and all I could do was try to catch my breath to scream for help, but all that came out were scared little sobs from a pathetic weak little girl. I grip my phone and try to scramble away from Jeff as he lunges for it, but he grabs me by my waist and I let out a painful scream as he slams me down on the bed. My phone is knocked out of my hand, so as I lean down to reach for it and Jeff strongly backhands me across the face, and I instantly see a flash of white blur my vision.

I lie on my bed in the fetal position with my hands shielding my face, scrunched tightly in a defensive little ball, hoping to avoid another painful blow to my body. Everything is so quiet and still for a second right before I hear something shatter on the floor. I regrettably jump, sitting up on my bed to see Jeff looking down at my phone that he just smashed on the floor and an evil grin is smeared across his putrefied mouth and he seems completely satisfied with himself for doing it.

I can't help the flood of tears that are now flowing down my cheeks as I stare at Jeff standing so very still in the middle of my room. I position myself to get ready to run and that's when Jeff brings his attention back to me, but I'm up on my feet and already off the edge of the bed. I start hobbling towards my door, and just before I reach the opening, I feel his bulky arms grab me around my shoulders and whip me back on the mattress, so hard in fact that I actually bounce back up before he throws himself on top of me, painfully pinning my wrists down above my head.

He puts all of his weight on me as he breathes heavily against my cheek. The smell of scotch and cigarettes on his breath makes me want to gag as the intense burning of bile slithers its way up my throat while I squirm beneath him

"Jeff, you're hurting me! Get off of me!" I whimper. His weight is crushing and it's hard to take in enough air to force my words out loud enough for anyone to hear. He quickly runs his face up and down my neck as he inhales me into his disgusting mouth, sucking a breath through gritted teeth. I wriggle my arms and his grip loosens enough for me to get one of my hands free, so I whack him across the face as hard as I can. The shock of it makes him lock eyes with me. The anger and spiteful hate are clear as day on his face. If I wasn't afraid of what he was going to do to me before; I certainly am now.

"You stupid little bitch!" He screams and jerks his head up while raising a fist at me and punches me in the ribs. I let out the most intense wail as I dry heave in the middle of my bed and clutch at my stomach, the second he takes his weight off of me. "You see, if you would just listen for once, I wouldn't have to do any of this to you, little bean." I hear him cheaply use the nickname my mom used to call me. It makes me realize, even more so now, that this is never going to get any better. "Hell, if you're whore of a mother would have taken you with her when she decided to cheat on me, maybe you wouldn't be at the mercy of me, right now?" His words are knives, stabbing and twisting into my gut. Every word that crawls out of him kills me more and more, the longer I lay here listening to everything that I should have realized for myself a long time ago. My mother never cared about me. If she did, she wouldn't have left me here with someone like Jeff. She had to have known what he was like if she chose to leave and selfishly only save herself.

Jeff roughly grabs my arms and breaks them free from around my ribs. The pain is excruciating as I struggle to catch my breath when he gave me one swift blow to the stomach and knocked the wind right out of me. He creepily leans on me, again pinning me in place, not needing much strength to do so since I'm already so weak. *I just want it to stop*. He takes his hand and pinches my mouth between his fingers to force me to look up at him while he runs his other hand up my leg. My stomach wrenches when I feel his hands crawl up my thigh and slither their way under my shirt. I know I can't do anything about it except maybe plead with him to stop because I have no strength left to fight him anymore.

"Stop, please stop." I quietly weep. The tears roll down the sides of my face as I squeeze my eyes shut, some fall into my ears muffling the sounds of Jeff breathing, others I can feel slide down the side of my neck. I'm so tired I just want to fall asleep. I want this to end.

"You really should have listened to me, Josephine." I can't handle looking into his eyes as he does this to me. I don't want to witness the satisfaction it brings him. I feel his hot breath on my skin as he licks the side of my face, lapping up the fallen tears from my cheek.

"No one's coming back for you, and you have nowhere else to go because no one is ever going to want you once I'm done with you!" He finally reveals. The pure evil in his words sends a horrid chill through me, thankfully provoking the last bit of energy I can muster up to fight back.

"Fuck you, Jeff!" I scream in his face before I try and push him off of me. I slide my arm up and shove his face to the side, but he comes back and slaps me so hard I feel a shocking pain rip through the side of my face. But I don't stop. I struggle until I get my knees up in between us and thrust forward, but he's far too strong and he overpowers me. He yanks my legs out of the way and collapses his heavy torso in between them as he claws at my shirt, ripping it to shreds and exposing my chest, trying to get it off of me. I fight as hard as I possibly can to make sure he doesn't get to touch me without putting up one hell of a fight.

As I scrap and kick and tussle with him, I frantically search my room for anything I can use against him, anything that will give me a slight advantage. Out of the corner of my eye, I notice on my nightstand that my lamp is teetering on the edge, about to fall off. I grab my pillow as Jeff continues to pull at my clothes and I swipe at my lamp to get it to fall on my bed. The third time I hit it, it tumbles off the table and lands to the right of my head onto my pillow. I quickly grab hold and raise it over Jeff's head and forcefully bring it down on top of his skull. I hear the light bulb pop as it shatters and sparks flicker, lighting up like fourth of July sparklers, and then the entire thing explodes, sending pieces of broken glass all over the both of us. I quickly shut my eyes as the glass scratches at my skin and I feel Jeff go limp just before he slides off of me and lands with a loud thud as he hits the floor.

I lay still for a while with my eyes tightly pinched shut, covered in glass and blood and completely exhausted. I'm too frightened to move. I don't even want to look over the edge to see if Jeff is still there. *Please be gone. Please be gone.* I cry. I can feel myself slipping into a deep sleep and everything being drained out of me. I could have been lying here for hours already and I wouldn't be able to tell. I feel like I just need to sleep, and maybe when I wake up everything will be okay.

A loud groaning followed by shuffling brings me out of my exhausted state as I lie on top of my bed. My body is in too much pain, or maybe its shock, to bother looking. I open my eyes just enough to peek through my wet lashes. When I do I see Jeff hunched over by my chair, using it to try and steady himself on his feet. He stumbles and has to catch his balance but he manages to stand up. His hand is holding the side of his head as he stalks towards the door. Suddenly stopping in the middle of my room, he pulls his hand away and looks at it for a second then leans down and picks up one of my shirts from the floor and presses it to the side of his head. He trips and stumbles over the broken chair leg as he makes his way to the door but catches himself before he falls. I tightly close my eyes and let out a shaky breath as he disappears.

68
Josephine

My body violently jerks as I lie in the middle of my bed with my hands over my mouth, trying to silence my sobs like a coward. I cradle my aching body in my arms, wanting desperately to block out what just happened; but the images of Jeff's predatory snarl flash behind my tired swollen eyelids, over and over making my stomach violently twist itself into knots. I can still feel his nails where they dug into my skin every time he pawed at me, and everywhere his rough dirty claws slithered over me, still burns like he had dragged hot iron across my flesh as his weight pressed me further into the mattress. The vile acid from his breath felt like it was suffocating me as I struggled beneath him.

The feeling instantly causes the bile to surge up into my throat again making me jolt up on my knees and dry heave over the side of the bed, but nothing comes out except the stifled screams of a broken little girl that nobody will ever want when they find out what happened. Just the thought of anyone knowing sends a humiliating shiver through me and the tears break free once again.

My drained body collapses heavily onto the floor as I slide off the edge of the bed. Using it as a shield, I press my back up against the frame and blankly stare past my curtains into the darkness outside the open window. I feel the cool wet breeze on my face as the wind blows the rain inside and it splatters onto my floor and kicks up water droplets onto my feet. It feels good and for a brief moment, the feeling distracts me from the invasive thoughts that will forever haunt me.

I lazily bring my hand up to wipe away the tears that are staining my cheeks after I finally stop crying and I feel something scratch my raw skin. As I pull my hand away, I'm surprised to see blood trickling down my palm and a long splinter of glass sticking in the fleshy part of my hand. *I didn't feel it.* I scan the floor and notice the broken lamp that is now scattered around me. Grasping the shard of glass in my hand, I slowly pull it out, feeling the sting as it slides free and I drop it beside me with the rest of the mess. The blood starts to trickle out of the cut and I suddenly get a familiar sense of relief for just a brief moment. But the feeling doesn't last but a few seconds before leaving me all too aware of my reality.

I don't want to feel like this anymore. The memories I will have from this night are too much, and I just wish, it would fuckin end. I've tried to glue the shattered pieces of my life back together far too many times and I'm exhausted. I have nothing left. *I have no one.* No one is going to look at me without seeing the fractured shell of a girl that has been torn apart by the awful circumstances, life has thrown at her and knowing that she was too weak to do anything about it.

My knees are pulled tightly against my chest as the rain creeps along my floor, inching closer and closer, threatening to soak me if I sit here any longer. I couldn't care less about the cold, or if everything I own were to be ruined by the unforgiving storm raging outside, so I let my legs stretch out in front of me as my feet slide over the broken glass and I feel every single jagged edge scrape across my bare legs.

A large, shiny piece of glass lay on the floor next to my thigh, tempting me to pick it up as I glare at it and remember the feeling that I had the first time I was in control of the pain I felt. The welcoming relief it gave me was unexpectedly comforting.

I lean up and my fingers automatically wrap around the piece of glass and I clutch it securely in my hand. I take in a deep breath and hold the rough edge to my wrist and quickly swipe it across the pale blue ribbons peeking out from under my flesh. A meager whimper escapes me, but I bite down and stifle it just to go back and open another angry gash on my arm. My resolve quickly weakens as the searing pain sends an unbearable burning to my core and I let the glass drop to the floor as a painful wail emerges from deep within me.

I wrap my fingers around my wrist and clutch my arm to my chest while the tears rush out of me as I sit here trying to keep the whimpers at bay. I can feel the wetness spilling through my fingers as I concentrate on taking in a few slow breaths. *I'm okay, I'm fine…*I slowly open my eyes and hesitantly look down. My hand is covered in my blood and it only continues to flow freely through the cracks between my fingers, allowing all the pain and disgust and bullshit to ooze out of me and finally be forgotten. The dizzying fog from opening my flesh has finally started to settle in and take over, making everything slow down, amplifying the sounds buzzing around my head. The curtains flow elegantly in the breeze that's drifting through my window. The rain splashing onto my bare toes seems to freeze in mid-air before I feel the warmth of it on my skin. I notice even the pounding in my head has grown tired and finally given me the reprieve I've begged it for. So, I let my head fall back again as I relax into the most peaceful moment that I have been awarded and I can feel all my muscles let go all at once as my knuckles make the faintest of knocking sounds on the hard wooden floor as my arms fall to my sides.

A soft smile grows on my lips as the heaviness leaves my body drained and exhausted and I finally get to welcome the quiet slumber that my soul has been craving for months.

I let my eyes flutter closed and the sound of the relentless rain has all since been silenced and replaced by the sound of my slowing heartbeat. I can feel myself slipping, letting the heavy sleep take over…forever.

69
Hunter

I try calling Jo's phone for the fifth time as I recklessly drive down the damp streets towards her house. The route seems to take a lot longer than it should; making my anxious heart, beat out of my chest. My rage pushes me to drive faster while the sounds of Jo's agonizing cries replay over and over in my head as I draw closer. I senselessly push harder on the gas and try my best not to get caught up in any traffic as I take the least busy streets, trying to avoid as many red lights as possible, even if I have to go through them. After the sixth time trying to get through to her, I end the last call and toss my phone next to me. I'm almost to her house as I pull around the corner and finally turn into the driveway. The wet pavement makes my tires slide and come to a screeching halt as I slam on the breaks just before hitting the garage door with the front end of my car.

I smack my car in park, snatch my phone off the passenger seat and jump out without turning off the engine and I leave the door open as I run around the bumper and head for the back of the house. Just as I get to the side of the back porch, I see the screen door swing open, and hear it slam violently against the house; the sound of it stopping me dead in my tracks. A tall figure stumbles out of the opening, activating the motion light behind them and they flop themself down on the first step. *Jeff?!*

He hasn't noticed me standing here in the dark, staring at him as he holds what looks like a small piece of cloth to his head. He pulls it away and lazily glances at it. The porch light highlights the dark red stain on it and he winces and lets out a groan when he touches the material to the side of his head again. I stalk my way around the overgrown hedges that surround the porch and stop in front of him at the bottom of the steps. "Where is Jo?" I demand before he can even lift his head to look me in the eye. The warning in my tone is clear, but I'm afraid of what he will say and what I might do if he gives me the wrong answer.

"Who the fuck, are you?" He roars as he lifts his head and tilts it to the side, giving me a sideways glare. His lips curl up into a grimace, bearing the yellow stains across his teeth as recognition crosses his expression. Before I get to ask again, he stands up, trying to intimidate me by quickly forcing his feet down the steps. He removes and lowers his hand from his head, dropping it down to his side, and pushes himself forward, stopping on the last step so that he still towers over my head, thinking it will give him an advantage over me.

"I know who you are!" He snarls. "You're the little boyfriend, aren't you?" He questions while he tries to hold his posture and has to grip the railing beside him before leaning over and spitting a mouth full of blood into the bushes. I can smell the vile aroma of alcohol on his breath, which mixed with the scent of fresh blood, sends a queasiness to my gut. He's plastered and my patience is quickly dissipating.

"Where the fuck is Jo?" I bark. Never even acknowledging what he said. My knuckles are tightly fisted at my sides and my blunt nails dig into my palms, ready to swing if he comes any closer.

"Why should I tell you? You don't belong here, so you better leave before I call the police on your ass." He spits the words in my face but all I can think about is finding Jo and getting her away from this piece of shit before I end up doing something, I'm not so sure I'll regret. I notice him look down and sway from side to side again as he lifts his head up. He holds out a hand and stiffly pokes a finger into my chest.

"Hey, I told you to leave!" He quickly repeats. I shove his hand away with little effort and it almost knocks him off his feet. *Pathetic!*

"I'm not fucking leaving without Jo, now tell me where she is, or I'll go find her myself!" I urge. My breathing picks up pace as he tests my patience and I force myself to hold back on pummeling him into the ground, at least until I see that Jo is alright.

"Don't worry. You're not going to want her after what I did. Little bitch finally got what she deserved!" Those last words that leave his putrid mouth trigger my pent-up rage that I've been desperately trying to restrain as I stand here questioning him. Without warning I feel my body lunging forward and my hands stretch out in front of me, reaching for his throat. Jeff stumbles backward and falls hard, hitting his back on the steps and letting out a stifled grunt as I land on top of him, pressing all of my weight down on his neck.

"WHAT DID YOU DO TO HER? WHERE THE HELL IS SHE?" I shout at him and clench my teeth so hard I can feel my jaw tense as I press my forearm even harder into his throat. But before I give him a chance to answer I grip at the collar of his shirt and slightly lift his shoulders off the porch as he grabs hold of my hand that's still around his neck. I let go of his shirt and pull a clenched fist back and drive it into the side of his jaw. His head bounces off the porch and his eyes roll back into his head.

"Fuck you!" He groans as he tries to buck me off to the side and I hit him again before I stand up and drag him to his feet, pushing him up against the back door with all my strength, wanting to snap his neck in two. I could do it too. It wouldn't take much effort on my part. I'm almost at the point of no return. I pin him in place with my weight so that we're eye level and he can't maneuver away from me.

"If you hurt her, I promise I'll fucking kill you!" I warn and I land one last massive blow to his ribs, making him retch forward and heave for air. I shove him out of the way of the door and he falls back against the house and cowers to a hunched-over position. I reach for the handle to the screen door and swing it open and run inside.

"JO! JO! Where are you?" I yell to my girl as I make my way through the house. I hurry over to the kitchen door that leads closest to Jo's room and try to push it but it doesn't budge as if something is blocking it. So, I go around to the doorway that leads into the living room and notice the broken recliner lying in the middle if the doorway. I hop over it and land on some broken glass, grinding it further into the floor as I make my way around to the front hall. Every piece of furniture is tipped over and the hallway is littered with glass, mail, and a mess of odd trinkets that were once sitting on the table that rested up against the wall.

"JO!" I cry out for her as I make my way down the hall, stepping over whatever is in my way. I glance at the kitchen door as I jog towards Jo's bedroom and see a wrought iron fire poker wedged up against the handle easily preventing it from being opened from the other side. The worry I had, has suddenly turned into a sic, heart wrenching feeling that what I might find beyond the hallway will rip my heart wide open. I can't handle the thought of Jo being hurt, but by the looks of the house, the evidence is enough to make me think the worst has already happened, and I should have been here to stop it.

My feet hesitate for a split second when I spot a bloody handprint on the white doorframe leading into Jo's room. My breathing hitches in my throat as I call out for her; praying that she answers.

"Jo? Baby?" I call out to her again and will my feet forward, pushing my way past the dresser that's blocking my view of her bed. I carefully shove the door open when I hear crackling beneath my boots. I stop and look down to see more glass on the floor and quickly scan her room. Her clothes are scattered everywhere, torn from the hangers from inside her closet. The spine of her favorite books, are shredded and tossed all over the floor. Even her lamp from her nightstand lies shattered at the foot of her bed.

The panic rises in my chest as I search the closet for my girl and it becomes almost unbearable when I don't find her hiding in there. I stumble over her things with weak legs as I make my way further into her room towards her window. *Please be outside Jo.* I start to walk over to the window but when I look down to move what's left of her desk chair out of the way, I see her feet peeking out from the other side of her bed.

"Oh my god baby, I was so scared he had…" I pause when I look at Jo's face and see that her eyes are closed. My only thinking is that she's sleeping. I touch her gently on the arm to try and wake her. S*he's sleeping. She's okay. She's going to be okay.*

"Jo? Jo, wake up, it's me. Everything's okay, I'm here." I assure her. But she doesn't move. "Baby, come on, wake up!" I say louder, more forcefully, and shake her shoulders again. I'm at a loss as to why she won't wake up, she looks so peaceful, not at all like she's hurt. My head isn't thinking logically as the memories of my sister come barreling full force into my brain. The heartbreak I felt when I lost her hits me hard as I try and snap out of the horrible memory, willing for the outcome to be different for Jo than it had been for Maci.

I lean in to wrap my arms around her body and pick her up, but when I do my hand touches something warm and wet on the other side of her. I raise my hand to my face to try and see through the darkness that has overtaken the small space and realize what the liquid is that coats my left hand. *Blood?* "NO! This isn't happening again, you're going to be okay, I got you baby, I'm going to get you help, I promise!" The words rapidly leave me, hoping that if I say them out loud, they will come true. I can't lose her! I can't lose Jo. If I do, it will be the end of me.

70
Hunter

I hold my hands to Jo's face and quickly peck her lips and it shocks me with how cold they feel against my own. I place the tip of my fingers to her neck to check for a pulse but with my heart rapidly beating painfully in my chest I can't tell if what I feel is her heart beating or if it's mine.

My hands reach in my pocket for my phone and I use it to search Jo's body for where the blood might be coming from. I scan the light over her and see the dark red liquid on both of her hands.

"Oh my god, what the fuck?" I yell out. "God damn it what the fuck did he do to you baby?" I hover over her still body and grab her arm as gently as I can. Both her hands are covered in blood and her shirt is drenched on her left side and I see that her wrist has two long angry, jagged cuts. There's so much blood I can't believe I didn't see it sooner.

My phone drops to the floor with a smack and I reach across the bed and snag a pair of her pajama pants that she wore to bed the other night. I slip it under her arm and tie it tightly around her wrist to try and stop the bleeding. I expected the sudden tightening around such an awful wound to cause an unwelcome amount of pain and startle her awake but she doesn't flinch and that scares the hell out of me.

I reach for my phone again and dial 911. I put the phone to my ear while I anxiously wait the five seconds before they respond. Holding Jo closely to my chest to make sure that I can still feel her heart beating while I wail into the phone where we are and how the love of my life is bleeding out in front of my eyes.

"Please don't leave me Jo! I won't let you. I just got you!" I cry heavy sobs into her hair as I pull her in to feel her breathing. "I fucking love you Jo!" I tell her for the first time as I desperately cling to her limp body. I hope she can hear me and that my words will get her to wake up and tell me that she loves me back.

I can't stop the flow of tears that are spewing out of me. My chest heaves heavy painful sobs as I cradle her in my arms and then the person on the other line says the next most awful words I could ever hear.

"The paramedics are seventeen minutes away. I'm afraid they can't get there any sooner so…" I can't understand anything else the person says to me, I just drop my phone in Jo's lap and scoop her up in my arms, not wasting another fucking second by sitting here to wait for her to slip away from me.

I run out the front door to my car. Jo is cradled in my arms as I open the passenger side and slide her in the front seat; buckling the seatbelt around her body. I notice after finally seeing her in the light how pale her skin is and I can feel my heart starting to give way and crack. I don't even seem to recognize her even though she's right in front of me. My angel is cold and lifeless as she lies limp against the front seat and I know I don't have much time left to get her help.

I run to the driver's side of the car and put it in drive even before I get my door fully shut when I see headlights pulling up in front of the house. I still pull out of the driveway though and almost hit someone as they run-up to the side of my car.

"Holy fuck Hunter, what the hell is going…" Kyle's eyes dart past me to the other side of the car and his mouth drops open and he stops mid-sentence. I follow his stare and look over to my girl. Her head hangs to the side, her eyes lids are a dark purple and her bloody arm rests heavily in her lap. I can't stand to see her like this. I need to get her help.

"Is that Jo? What the fuck happened?" He shrieks at me as he points to her before I can get one word to properly form. I don't have time to explain but I can't forget that Jeff was the one to do this to her and I can't let him get away with it. He needs to fucking pay for what he's done to.

"Look, she's hurt… badly. I need to get her to the hospital alright. Stay here… wait where the fuck is Nate?" I question because I didn't notice him getting out of the car behind me.

"He ran inside, why didn't you call 911?" He asks as he fumbles with his phone and starts to dial. The panic breaks his voice at the end while he stares down at his screen.

"It was the first thing I fucking did man! Look, I don't have time for this." I get Kyle's attention away from the phone. I need his help. "Stay here and help Nate and make sure Jeff doesn't take off." I instruct and given the look on Kyle's face, he knows it's worse than he can tell and I have to leave now!

"Alright yeah, yeah I'll stay, don't worry, just go take care of your girl." He says and he takes off towards the house to help Nate as I let off the brake and hurry to get Jo to a hospital.

I speed down the street, avoiding every possible thing in my way. If I had waited for the ambulance to show up, we would still be wasting precious minutes I'm afraid she doesn't have.

"Just hold on baby, we're almost there, okay? Hold on." My voice is a hopeless whimper as I try to convince myself that we'll make it there in time. I have to believe everything will be okay. But even I can tell by the way her head slowly sways as I turn the corners that she's slipping further and further away from me. I feel utterly helpless as I have to keep my attention on the road, I just want to pull over and hold her in my arms until she wakes up. I need to feel her, to know that she's still with me. I reach over and clutch her hand. Her skin is getting colder with each minute that passes, but to my relief, I finally see the bright lights of the hospital just ahead.

I pull around the corner into the emergency lane in front of the sliding doors and carefully place my hand on Jo's chest to keep her from lurching forward as the car comes to a quick stop. I throw it in park and turn off the engine before yanking my keys out of the ignition and throw open my door before I take them out. I scream for someone to help as the emergency doors open and I run around to Jo's side and quickly yank her door open to get to her. I pick her up bridal style and jog over to the doors as three people with a gurney coming barreling through and meet me halfway. I place her quickly, but ever so gently on the gurney and they whisk her away from me faster than I can comprehend.

I follow behind them, keeping my eyes on my girl the whole time as we all hurry down the short hallway. I don't even get any words out to tell them what happened before one of the doctors hops up on the gurney and hovers over Jo and starts pressing on her chest. The other two doctors continue to wheel her towards the metal doors, that are all too familiar to me. The twist in my gut makes my feet hesitate for only a second as the shiny metal comes into view and the doors open up as they push Jo in that direction. I try to follow but someone steps in front of me, trying to tell me something, but I can't hear them. My only focus is my girl, and I can't let her out of my sight. "Where are you taking her?" I scream as I try to push the person off of me. "I need to know she's going to be okay!

Please!" My rough voice pleads with them to let me back there. I try to push past them to follow behind, but the echoes of someone yelling at me are getting louder in my ears. I shove a hand off of my chest and rip my hand away as I try to jaunt forward towards the doors, but then I feel another set of hands grab me around my wrist as I stare in front of me until she disappears down the hallway, the doors closing only seconds later, keeping me from being able to get to her.

I feel my body being pushed to the ground, and this time I don't fight it. I know the doors are locked, so I couldn't get through them even if I wasn't pinned to the floor right now.

"Please, tell me she's going to be alright! Hey, listen. Please help her, help her, she doesn't deserve this. I can't lose her!" My distressed screaming echoes into the openness of the waiting room and my chest is burning with every desperate plea to get them to listen.

I have to take in a deep breath and I can feel the rawness ripping away at my throat from yelling so much. The slick tile floor is cool against my cheek as I lie here, waiting for whoever is holding me down to get the fuck off of me. I know the longer I fight, the worse it will be and they won't let me back to see Jo at all.

So, I stop struggling to get free and let my body go limp and take in another much-needed gasp of oxygen while I press my face into the floor and let the exhaustion seep into my muscles. I can feel the person that's got me restrained slightly loosen their grip on my arms and just let their hands rest on my back. My body aches. It physically hurts me to be away from Jo, especially at a time like this. Not knowing if she's okay or if she can feel the pain that was wrongly inflicted on her. *I need to be with her.*

I won't let this be another time where someone I love slips through my fingers. I can't let her go, I won't! I refuse to live this life without her!

71
Hunter

My head hangs low in my hands while I restlessly sit and wait in the lobby for anyone to come and tell me what's going on. I couldn't be around all those people in the waiting room. There were too many eyes gawking at me, probably waiting for me to lose it again, I'm sure.

Kyle is behind me, driving me nuts asking me if I need anything almost every half hour like clock-work. I know he means well, but I just can't do anything until I know Jo is going to be okay. Fucking doctors haven't even come out once to tell me anything, and I'm about to lose it if they don't tell me something soon. Nate has been back and forth trying to get any kind of update, but they tell him the same thing, even though he's family. They don't know anything yet. That's all they fucking tell him, and I'm sick of hearing it.

"Hey man?" Kyle sounds like he's currently questioning my state of mind. I haven't moved the slightest bit in so long, my arms are starting to go numb from bearing the weight of holding my head up. My elbows press firmly into my knees as I grip at the ends of my hair and pull out it of frustration, knowing I have to eventually say something to him. I draw in a heavy breath and sit up and lean my head back against the wall behind me with my eyes still closed.

"What?" I sigh. Kyle nudges my arm.

"Someone's walking over here, maybe it's about Jo." He says. My eyes spring open as I vault up from the chair and lock eyes with Bethany from the front desk. I'm quick on my feet and reach her in three short paces, eager to hear good news; but from the expression on her face as she looks up from the clipboard in her hands, something tells me I'm not going to like what she has to say.

"Mr. Scott." She says before taking in a shallow breath. She pauses. "Could you come with me for a moment? The doctor would like to speak with you." She says shortly. I look back to where Kyle and Nate are standing a few feet behind me, the concern evident in their expression. Of course, they're adamant to find out what's going on, but they stay back to let me handle this on my own.

I'm without words as Bethany leads me into a small office and tells me to have a seat. I don't want to have a seat. I've been sitting for what feels like fucking days, while everyone in this place keeps me from the one and only person, I care about seeing right now. A few seconds after I grudgingly sit down in front of a large lavish desk, a man in black scrubs walks in and takes a seat behind it. His sorrowful eyes reveal more than his words can in the few seconds he's glanced at me since sitting down. I lean forward in the cushioned chair and brace myself for the next words that hesitantly escape from his throat.

"Mr. Scott. We have some news for you. We want you to know that we have done all we can, for Miss Michaels but…"

"Jo." I interrupt.

"Sorry?" The doctor questions.

"Her name is Jo." I correct him quickly and don't hesitate to speak my peace to him. "Please. Please tell me she's okay, I can't lose her. She means everything to me…" A squelched sob emerges from deep in my throat as I speak and I lower my head, waiting for him to crush me with his news.

"Apologies." He says and I can tell he's sincere. That's what makes it so much worse because I would recognize that pitiful apologetic tone in anyone's voice from a mile away. It's the same one that made me feel like I was suffocating when they spoke to me a year ago and told me that my sister didn't make it; that I would never see her again. The realization only hitting me when I saw her with my own eyes; I just couldn't bring myself to believe their awful words. Now I find myself having to face the same thing again. But this time I'm sure it's going to kill me.

"Mr. Scott." I hear him clear his throat, getting my attention. "She's stable." I pick my head up and lock eyes with the doctor, noticing that his expression has shifted. His sullen frown is subtle but with something of a hopeful blip hiding behind his expression. "I know some of this is difficult to hear, but we do have hope, that she will make a full recovery." He explains. With those words finally being spoken into existence, the crushing pressure in my chest that was seconds away from destroying everything that was keeping me alive, slowly starts to lift away. "But…" I hear him continue. And the feeling hastily makes itself known once again, with no reprieve. I brace myself in the chair, gripping the armrest until my knuckles have surely turned white and start to tingle. "You should know that we had to put her into a medically induced coma for the time being. Her injuries were severe enough in the sense that if she were awake, we were afraid that she may not take to healing quite as easily after being through so much trauma; and we didn't want to put any more stress on her body." He pauses for a moment and the room is so silent with just the three of us in here that I can distinctly hear the difference in our breathing. Mine has almost stopped completely as I absorb this new information. I understand what he's saying, I just can't wrap my head around what could have happened to put her in such an awful state. *Did I not notice if she was hurt somewhere else and I made it worse by moving her?* "Just know, son, that by you getting her here when you did, you saved her life. Any longer and she would be much worse off at the moment. I couldn't be sure what kind of outcome it would be instead." I hear the good doctor assure me. After a minute, I pick my tired head up and stare past him. The thick haze that swarms my head is draining the last bit of energy that I have and all I can think about now, is going to be by Jo's side.

"Can I see her?" I ask, hopeful that his answer will be yes.

"Of course, I'll have Bethany here take you to her room." He motions to Bethany standing timidly in the corner. I glance over to her and see her fingers tighten slightly around the clipboard she's still holding. The subtle gesture adds to my tension, thinking maybe they're not telling me something, but I won't ask, not right now. The only thing I'm focused on is going to see my girl.

My limbs are tired. The weight of so many hours that have passed since I've seen Jo has taken its toll on my body and I have to force myself to unravel my tight grip from around the armrests and get off the chair that I've sunken into. I pause before walking out the door, letting Bethany through first to lead the way.

I drag my sorry ass across the floor of the lobby and follow Bethany through the metal doors; feeling my muscles tightly tense as they shut with an audible click behind us. We walk past so many empty rooms down the white sterile hallway and I can feel the eyes of two people on me after their conversation comes to a halt, when Bethany and I stop in front of a door across from where they're standing and she turns towards me before opening it. "Here you are, Hunter." She says quietly. She clicks the handle and gently nudges the door with her foot, propping it open a crack. "I hear that when loved ones speak to someone in…" She pauses and quietly clears her throat. "…this condition, that there's a good chance they can hear you. It seems to make all the difference in their recovery." She tells me and gently squeezes my shoulder as I push my hand against the door and walk into the room. "Call me if you need anything." I hear her say, so I nod my head in thanks and shut the door behind me.

72
Hunter

I stand inside facing the door with my forehead pressed firmly against the smooth surface. Thump, thump, thump. I wrap my fist on it and it makes a dull thud each time my fist makes contact. I tightly close my eyes and lean into my throbbing hand. I'll admit right now that I'm not so sure I'll be able to look at my girl when I finally force myself to turn around. I had seen her hours ago and mostly in the dim light on a dark street. Her wounds that plague her alluring skin were still so fresh; they didn't have time to fully surface and reveal the brutality that she had endured.

The machines make themselves known with a relentless and irritating beeping. I try to catch my breath but I'm struggling to hold back from choking up painful sobs when I finally get the nerve to turn around. I push off the door and stand up straight to face her but then I quickly look down at the floor as I shuffle my feet closer to the bed. *I'm such a fucking coward.* I think as I slowly raise my gaze just enough to see the white sheet on the end of the bed and I suddenly have to fight the bile that rises in my throat at the thought of seeing her lying there helpless. The sick feeling in my gut tells me to pick my head up and look at what I let happen to her, so I raise my head again and I come face to face with an agonizing reality.

"Oh my god baby no…no, no, no, no!" My legs suddenly go weak and give out under the weight of my body and I collapse onto my knees. The oxygen has been forcefully sucked out of the room, causing my head to spin. Heaving breaths violently jerk my body forward as I let out the most distressing whimpers and I can feel a black hole start to form inside my chest. I've never felt absolute devastation before. I thought I had when I had lost Maci last year. But this feeling, this all-consuming hell that has taken a liking to ripping my heart from my chest and incinerating the cavity that once held it; gives an entirely new meaning to the words. *'There are worse things than death.'*

"Jo." I cry out to her as I drag myself over to the side of the bed and glide my hand over the material that covers her fragile body until I finally feel her hand beneath mine. My hand searches through the wires and tubes piercing her skin and it makes it difficult to be able to feel the unforgettable softness I remember. I've missed the feeling so much more than I knew was possible, especially after I thought I would never get to feel the warmth of her touch again. I gently take her hand and slowly bring my lips to kiss her knuckles and relief washes over me because I can feel the warmth slowly breathing life back into her. I lean my head down against Jo's hand whilst I kneel next to her, and let the copious number of tears steadily fall between us.

After some time kneeling by my girl's side and willing any kind of strength back into my body, I manage to get my legs under me again and stand up so I can take in the sight of my beautiful angel. I stare at her full lips, high cheekbones, and her soft pale skin, but all I can see are the bruises that discolor her face and the many tiny little red scratches that mask her true beauty. I notice that one of her eyebrows still has some dried blood on it, so I gently wipe it away by brushing my thumb across it and leave a small kiss there, before I leave another kiss on my favorite spot on her forehead. A few tears fall from my eyes and wet the side of her cheek as I pull away and I watch them slide their way down her face and disappear into the pillow.

When I lean down and lightly nuzzle my nose against her cheek, I'm so grateful for the warmth I feel against my skin as I whisper her name.

"Jo…" I have to swallow the lump of nails that are caught up in the back of my throat before I'm able to continue. "I love you Jo…come back to me."

IT'S BEEN TWO days since the doctors removed the breathing tube and stopped the medication that was keeping Jo sedated. I haven't left her side in over a week and I don't plan on it either. The damn doctors keep telling me she should wake up soon, but she hasn't shown any signs of making me believe that. I have sat in this chair next to her every single second I could, since they allowed me in the room to see her, and I haven't so much as noticed any changes that I would consider positive.

The doctors still don't know exactly what happened to her besides what they could tell from her injuries because that fucker Jeff wouldn't say anything about what he had done. *Of course. He wouldn't want to incriminate himself now, would he?* All I can do is wait…the rest is out of my hands until Jo wakes up, and when she does, I hope she puts him away for life.

"Good morning, Hunter. How is she doing today?" A nurse asks as she walks in the room past me and straight over to Jo.

"No change Summer, just like yesterday." I mumble as I stand up and move out of her way.

"Well, her vitals are strong as always. She sounds really good." Summer says after a few minutes of checking all the monitors and refilling the IV connected to Jo's hand. I can tell she's smiling by the way her voice sounds and it gives me some temporary comfort. Every day she comes in to check on Jo and she's in a good mood. I don't see how that's possible when everyone she takes care of seems like hollow shells of the people they once were. That has to be an awful thing to wake up for every day.

Summer starts to fold the blanket down from around Jo and tenderly lifts her bandaged arm up to place on a disposable cloth. I can see where Jeff had grabbed her by the black and blue finger-shaped bruises he left along her arms. The dark-colored handprints *'his handprints'* are painted all over her body. Every time I have to see them, I think about demanding Nate to tell me exactly where Jeff is, so I can find him and fucking kill him. But then I think in order to do that, I would have to risk Jo waking up alone with no one to reassure her that she's somewhere safe and that Jeff can't hurt her anymore. I have to be here for her. I promised I would keep her safe, and I will be trying to make it up to her for the rest of my life for breaking that promise.

"I'll be back later on. You call me if you need anything at all." She tells me. I nod my head to her and slowly walk back to sit down next to Jo. The door handle clicks and then the room is silent once again.

"HEY MATE." I hear a voice say behind me. A second later the door softly clicks shut and I turn around to see Kyle and Nate standing on the other side of the room. Nate has three cups of coffee in his hand and Kyle holds what I'm assuming to be Jo's favorite pastries from the look of the bag, but I don't move from my chair to get up and greet them. After I turn back to watch over my girl, I hear their heavy footsteps as they walk over to us.

Nate walks up to the opposite side of the bed and places the drinks on the table as Kyle sits up on the window ledge and sets the pastries down on the other table that currently holds the last two bags of food that I never touched. Nate slowly leans down and leaves a kiss on Jo's hair. A gesture I've come to be a little more comfortable with now than when he had done it the first time a few days earlier. I know he cares for Jo as more than just a step-sister because he acts like a real brother would to her. He reminds me a little of how I was with my sister, with small caring gestures like that.

The conversation Nate and I had a couple days ago about him telling me how their home life was far from normal or pleasant in any way and that he regrets not noticing sooner how Jeff treated her. It's opened my eyes to more of the unpleasant things that Jo has had to deal with. Nate said when he confronted his dad about hurting her, he wanted to kill him, but he never thought it could have ever gotten to the point of her ending up in the hospital because of him. If it weren't for not wanting to go to jail and leave Jo alone, he probably would have killed him. I know I'd like nothing more than to watch Jeff suffer by my own two hands for what he's done to her, so I understand where he's coming from.

I've come to respect Nate for being so honest about everything, and I'm grateful she has him in her life. Jo needs as much support as she can get right now; and when she finally wakes up, she's going to need all of us.

"Have they said anything more about how she's doing? Any updates at all?" Nate asks, hopeful. I stop the nervous picking at my finger to look up at him and shake my head.

"No…nothing new...they tell me the same thing every day." I say dejected.

"Hunter. I hate to say it man. But…you look like utter shit!" Kyle announces out of nowhere. Serious is never a word I would associate with Kyle. He's always got some snide smart-ass remark he spats just to get a rise out of people. But this time he sounds as serious as someone could when he tells me how awfully shit, I look.

"Yeah well…" I don't bother with a coherent response and just shrug my shoulders. I'm currently not up for bullshit chit chat or being distracted from the reality of the situation. I just want to be left alone.

"Have you even slept since…?" Kyle asks, but trails off; leaving the open question to cut through the heavy feeling around us.

"I don't need to." I bite shortly.

"Nate and I can take shifts to watch over Jo. Why don't you go home and get some sleep?" Kyle assumes I would be open to that idea, but clearly, I'm not because I feel the panic rise in my chest and I defensively shoot out of my chair towards him without thinking.

"NO!" I growl. The word vibrates through my voice box and I realize by the look on their faces that I must resemble a cornered animal, fighting to protect its young. "Shit." I say under my breath. *I feel like a fucking asshole.* "Look, I'm sorry. I know you guys are only trying to help. I just…I can't leave her again." I stammer. *I never should have in the first place…*

My thoughts trail off when I'm distracted by the sound of the door being opened yet again. *Can no one leave us the fuck alone?* I'm still facing Kyle and about to say something to him, thinking it's just another nurse coming to check on Jo, but then I see Nate's fists visibly tense at his sides and his eyes increase to the size of dinner plates, so I hesitantly turn around and come face to face with yet another thorn in my side.

73
Hunter

"What the hell are you doing here, Lily? I thought I told you to leave." Nate says in a displeased, authoritative tone; a warning to Jo's mom for daring to step a foot inside the room.

"I just want to see my daughter Nate…" She says weakly. The few words come out sounding unsteady. I stand next to Kyle and watch the hateful exchange between Nate and Lily as she starts to walk towards Jo's bed. With how Nate is taking to Lily being here, it's like I'm about to watch another train wreck and I can't seem to move fast enough to push them both out of the way.

"Nate's right. You shouldn't be here, Lily." I interrupt. She stops in her tracks just before she reaches Jo's side, not quite within reach, but her hand is outstretched like she was just about to stroke the top of Jo's head. Her hand lowers and she clasp her fingers together in front of her before bringing them up to her mouth like she's trying to prevent herself from crying. Her intake of breath is long and drawn out before she exhales and drops her hands to the necklace she's wearing and nervously tangles her finger in the chain for a second before letting go.

"Please, Hunter…" She pleads and stares into my gaze as fresh warm tears spill from her watery eyes. "Please, let me stay. I'm not going to cause any trouble." She whimpers. I may not like what Lily has done. I may not even agree with her showing up here expecting to see her daughter only after she nearly lost her life. But I'd be lying if I said I didn't feel for her for what she may be going through right now. I had to witness what losing a child does to a mother. Losing Maci was devastating to my mom; it tore her apart for months and caused an unrepairable rift between us. My mom hasn't been the same ever since that night and I wouldn't wish that on anyone. Lily may not be the perfect mother or even a sufficient one, but I can't imagine what's going through her head, seeing her daughter in the conditions she's in.

It kills me to watch Jo lying there day after day, hoping that her next breath is when she will finally wake up and says my name, letting me know she's okay. When I look at Lily as she hopefully stares at her daughter, I can't help but share in her pain, so I decide to just let her stay.

"It's not about what you fucking want…this is about Jo, you need to leav…" Nate screams and I hear his boots thudding across the hard floor, inching closer to Lily.

"Enough!" I bellow. Nate freezes mid-step as I turn around and step in front of him after I look back at Jo. "I don't want this around Jo, Nate! If you two need to hash out whatever this is, that's between you and her; but don't do this in here." I look him directly in the eye and give him a hard stare that makes him go silent. I'm on His side, but I don't want to chance Jo waking up to all of this. She doesn't need this shit right now. "Nate it's fine." I say as calmly as I can. I take a breath and look over my shoulder at Lily. Tears are flowing freely down her cheeks as she stares directly at me with hope in her eyes. "She can stay." I say and I hear Nate huff under his breath.

"Then that's my cue to leave." Nate angrily pushes past me, nudging my shoulder out of the way and makes haste towards the door. But when he grabs the handle, he turns back and says, "I'll be back later. Let me know if anything changes, I won't be far." He opens the door and walks out, leaving the three of us staring at each other in strained silence. He's pissed. That much is clear, but I know for Jo's sake he will come around, even if he doesn't know it yet himself. Kyle clears his throat behind me. A second after I hear him smack his hands together and sigh out a heavy nervous breath.

"Alright so, I'm starving. I think I'm going to go grab some grub from the diner. You want anything?" Kyle asks, but I just shake my head no. "Okay then, I will leave you guys to it…I'll be back later too." He gives me a reassuring pat on the shoulder as he steps past me and heads in the direction of the door. I'm thankful for the peaceful silence that has finally fallen over the room. I don't think the painful throbbing in my head could have taken much more of the bickering. I feel guilty for Nate feeling like he had no choice but to leave. He has as much right to be here as I do, but I'm caught in the middle and I'm just trying to do what I think is best for Jo, right now. Nate and Lily need to grow up and handle their differences on their own time. I tread lightly over to the side of Jo's bed and pick the blanket up off the chair that I've been occupying for the last week now. The room has a chill to it from the window being scarcely cracked so I take the blanket and place it over Jo, careful not to catch up any of the wires. I lean over and gently stroke her hair before leaving a kiss on her forehead and then drop down into my chair next to the bed and sink my tender joints into the awkwardly firm cushion.

"Hunter…?" Lily draws out my name after a few quiet minutes.

"Yeah?" I question. Not knowing what else she could have to say to me.

"Thank you." She says lightly. "Thank you for letting me stay." She softly clears her throat. "I'll be in the lobby if you or…Josephine need anything?"

I'm glad she doesn't push to try and stay in here. I know I should maybe let her, or offer her the chance at least, but I'm far too selfish to actually go through with it. I don't even know her enough to trust her to be around Jo. And after the things Jo has told me about her mom, not to mention the way Nate reacts when she shows her face. I know I'm not too comfortable with her being here. Before she gets the chance to leave, I need to ask her the one question that has been nagging at me for weeks.

"Lily…this may not be any of my business, but can I ask why you left?" I turn in my chair and see her that her expression is vacant of any emotion but her lips part, like she's about to answer when I immediately spat out another question at her. "How could you just leave your daughter alone to live with a fucking monster? You didn't even have the decency to call and see how she was, did you? All of that time did you even think to see if she was okay?" My harsh words start soaring out of my mouth and I don't care to stop them. Lily needs to hear this. She needs to realize the damage she's done to her daughter because she doesn't seem to get it just by looking at her.

"I…I don't know, but I'm here now, doesn't that count for anything?" She sighs and starts sobbing again. I don't buy it. I'm actually so pissed off, now that I've had a little time to think about what it means for her to show up out of the blue. She should have stayed the last time she came barreling in the middle of Jo's life and made an effort to be a mother to her. This all could have been avoided if she had.

"Tell you the truth. I don't know. Jo is going to be the one to have to decide that. But whatever she chooses, you're just going to have to live with it, Lily. If you were my mom, I don't think I would ever be able to forgive you."

74
Hunter

I came back." Lily bawls, into her hands, sniffling as she reaches around her for her purse, sliding open the zipper to take out a tissue; using it to dry her tears.

"Yeah, you came back…but you didn't stay. You just left her again. Without so much as a goodbye. So, do you truly think that she's going to accept you coming back so easily? I question harshly.

"Hunter, can I please just explain?" She pleads with me. Her swollen red rimmed eyes rapidly blink more tears away as she looks up to meet my pessimistic glare.

"Alright then, go ahead…explain it to me. Explain why you abandon your daughter, not once, but twice. I'm all ears." I urge her as I cross my hands over my chest and take in a deep breath. I'm trying to hold off from just telling her to leave and never come back ever again. I so badly want to protect Jo from getting hurt by her again and if I have to be a dick to do it, I don't have a problem with that.

"I left to go back to rehab." She plainly says, her voice dripping with shame as she admits it and she looks me straight in the eye because she's telling the truth. "I was in a treatment facility for a few months before I decided to come back the last time. I was finally getting my life together and things were going really well. I had a sponsor and an apartment, so I thought that I would be able to come back and see Jo to ask her to move back with me. I wanted another chance to be a good mom to her."

"Then why couldn't you have just told her all this when you were here?" I ask her.

"Because, when I saw the way Jo looked at me, I knew she would just be disappointed in me again because I messed up. When I found out they moved I thought Jeff was keeping her from me out of spite after I left him. I searched for her everywhere. When I finally found out where they moved to, I called the school but they wouldn't let me see her or even talk to her. That's the day I showed up in the office. You remember, you were there." She points at me and shamefully looks away, knowing full well I would still remember that day.

"You should have talked to her Lily. She needed you. You left her with him and he was abusing her." My words hold bitterness that I have never tasted before until now, but she needs to hear the truth. "Did you see what he did to her? Did you really look to see what he did? Because I have! She could have died. Do you realize that? I could have lost her because of you!" I shout at her and the malicious words bolt out of my mouth while I let the animosity grow inside my chest and eat away at my will to keep a cool head.

I suddenly wince and snap my lips shut when I remember that Jo is only a few feet from where Lily and I are standing. Yet here I am shouting out the harsh reality of the situation, currently losing my mind and it's the exact thing I asked Nate to avoid before he left.

"Don't you think I see that? Hunter, I didn't know any of this was going on. I never thought he would hurt her. I wouldn't have left her with him if I did. I thought she was better off without me until I could get better. That's why I left. I needed to get help before I could be any kind of mother to her again." She confesses. The tears have stopped flowing from her bloodshot eyes, but they still unveil the sincerity of a mother's love for her child.

The realization is starting to hit me that maybe Lily is telling the truth about everything she's said. There's no way she should have left her only daughter with someone like Jeff, but I can't fault her for thinking it was the best she could have done at the time. Allowing her mom to stay is the least I can do, to allow them the opportunity to heal, but it's ultimately up to Jo to make that decision if she wants to let her mom back in her life. I can only hope for Jo's sake that Lily doesn't make her regret it if she does.

"Look…I'm sorry Lily. This is all gonna have to wait for now. I want to be alone with her." I say exhausted from the conversation. I turn away and hear Lily hiccup or maybe try to get another word in edgewise, but before she does, I look over my shoulder and say, "As I said before…you can stay. I'm not going to make you leave and have to worry about your daughter, but it's not up to me if you get to see her when she wakes up."

Her eyes grow wide as she nods her head in agreement. "I understand, thank you, Hunter. You have no idea what that means to me." She whispers. “Look, here…” She starts digging through her oversized bag that’s crossed over her shoulder and pulls out a crinkled piece of paper and a pen, and hastily scribbles something down. “Here…this is where I’m staying for now and my cell number in case-in case you need…I mean if I can do anything for either of you, just please call.” She says, and she hands me the paper. I take it from her and she quickly leaves without another word while I stand in the middle of the room staring at the words scrawled across the paper. I notice her handwriting just then. It looks so similar to Jo’s. The memory of watching Jo scribble in her notebook at lunch or study hall, makes me miss her that much more. I wish she would have shared all those thoughts with me that she would always hide away. I only hope that she still gets a chance to share them with me one day.

75
Josephine

I wiggle my toes and point them towards the end of my bed to allow my legs the pleasure of stretching out the dreadful stiffness. I went for a run, but I don't remember being out so long that my body would be this tired and sore afterward. A hushed yawn escapes me as I bring my hands up to erase the sleep from my eyes, but when I lift my left arm and it brushes against something soft, I sleepily open them and look down at my side, surprised to see that Hunter is fast asleep in the chair next to me. His head is resting on top of his arm that rest against my thigh and his other hand is lightly draped over my torso. The warmth of his body feels good against me. It must still be late if he hasn't gotten into bed yet. *I wonder when he got back?* I wish Hunter would have woken me up when he came in, but he's here now so that's all that matters to me.

A smile creeps across my lips as I move my hand into his hair and I notice that it's slightly shaggier and in desperate need of a trim, as I lovingly tug at the ends. He doesn't move, so he must have had a long eventful night while out with Nate and Kyle. I'm almost afraid to ask what trouble they possibly got into while I was asleep; I just hope they all had a good time.

I would like to watch him sleep a little longer with how adorable he looks but I missed him and if he sleeps in that position any longer, he's going to regret it in the morning, so I decide to wake him by delicately brushing my finger across his temple and down the bridge of his nose a couple of times until he lets out a soft groan and rubs his forehead into the crook of his arm. Not even a second passes before his head suddenly shoots up and his eyes dart to look at me. Shock falls upon his gorgeous features as he anxiously and carefully grabs hold of my hand, like it's a life preserver and gives it that reassuring squeeze I'm always so grateful for; but this time it feels more like he's begging me for comfort, instead of offering it. Hunter is silent as his eyes burn with the fire that I know is inside of him, eagerly demanding my attention as he stares into my eyes. I feel like he's looking at me as if he doesn't believe I'm real and it has me awfully confused. He quickly leans down and gingerly places his palm against my cheek as he presses his forehead to mine, allowing me to inhale his impeccable essence that I am completely addicted to. I'm smiling at his reaction to seeing me, but why do I feel like there's a hidden sadness behind that cryptic smile?

Hunter

Oh my god! Is this real? Is she really awake? Please don't let me be dreaming...please!

I feel the warmth of Jo's skin as the blush rises in her cheeks and the soothing sound of her breathing falling in sync with mine is the most brilliant thing I could be experiencing at this very moment. The gorgeous color of her eyes staring up at me, and her full pouty lips that finally have her unique shade of pink back in them is more than I could have asked for today as I hold her in my arms and think to myself what a lucky bastard I am, to have found her and how grateful I am that she came back to me.

"Jo...Jo, you're alright." I whimper into her ear as my lips softly graze her cheek. I feel her stiffen under me and shortly pull back and look up at me as she slides my hand off of her cheek, holding onto it tightly.

"What? Hunter, of course, I'm okay...why wouldn't I be?" She asks. She looks at me and her eyes dart back and forth, searching for the reason for my acting so strange. I hold onto her hands and sit down in the chair next to her when I see that her eyes start to inspect our surroundings.

"Hunter...? Where are...wait is this...are we in a hospital?" She stutters and lets out a short breath, not finishing the first two questions she was going to ask. She doesn't seem scared, just...confused really over the fact that we're sitting in this room and everything is quiet around us. Her eyes stop searching and quickly land back on me, waiting for an answer. I'm ignorant as to what I should tell her because it seems like she genuinely has no clue, why we would be in a hospital and she hasn't even seemed to notice the painful-looking stitches in her arm that I am currently trying to shield from her sight by holding her hand close to my chest.

"Baby…you don't remember what happened? Do you remember, anything?" I carefully question to see if there's any kind of recognition in her eyes.

"No…I mean. I know you went out last night with Kyle, and that you invited Nate along. Wait, why? Did something happen, are you guys all okay? No one got into like a fight or an accident or anything, right?" She anxiously asks me so fast the words clumsily tumble out of her mouth while she looks me over for any evidence of being injured. All the concern is for me and she's not understanding that she's the one in the hospital bed.

"No, no. We're all okay. None of us got hurt." I reassure her in a monotone so I can try and keep the stress from coming out in my voice, and she seems to relax a little.

"Then what's going on…I don't understand." There's the sound of worry in her voice that I was waiting for and very much dreading. I knew I would have to tell her what happened eventually when she woke up, but I'm not even sure what to tell her, considering I have not a damn clue the extent of what Jeff put her through before I got there. She still thinks that it's the same night I left to go out with Kyle. Little does she know, so many things have happened, and I can't find it in me to explain a single one of them to her.

I lay my head on our intertwined fingers, holding them close to me. I can feel her pulling away to get me to look up at her, so I quickly pick my head up to meet her eyes and tell her what's going on. But before I can, tears start to well up in her eyes. She's uncertain of what I might say to her, but I can tell that she can sense it's something she doesn't quite want to hear.

"Hunter, you're scaring me. Please tell me what's wrong. Is it my mom, did she come back again?" She asks as panic strains her voice and the tears fall from her misty eyes onto her flushed cheeks.

"No baby, no. Look, there's something I have to tell you, and it's going to be really hard to hear, but you have to trust me that it's all going to be okay." My voice betrays me while I choke out the words to her. "Jo, it's not the same night you remember. It's actually been almost two weeks since then and…" I start to explain but she cries out to me. "What do you mean?" She whimpers at me with glassy eyes. I instantly move from the chair to sit on the bed next to her and wrap her snuggly in my arms. I feel like someone is twisting a knife in my gut while I think about what I'm about to tell her. If I could only have one thing to protect her from, I would choose this moment. I would choose to never have to tell her the awful truth I know and I would keep it a secret forever if it meant that she would be okay.

"Jeff came back that night." I finally spit out his spiteful name and her body immediately tenses in my arms at the sound of it, but she stays quiet, so I resentfully continue. "I saw him coming out the back door of your house when I showed up. I didn't know it was him at first. You called me screaming into the phone and it scared the hell out of me, so I came back as fast as I could, I tried to get to you sooner baby, but I was too late, he had already hurt you so badly." I can feel her body trembling, but she doesn't make a sound as I reveal one painful truth after another.

"I found you in your room…you were unconscious, so I put you in my car and drove here as fast as I possibly could. You didn't deserve what he did to you and I couldn't lose you too Jo. You mean everything to me." I assure her. I place my lips on the top of her head, feeling her soft hair against them, and leave her a comforting kiss. Jo is far to upset, to continue telling her anything else tonight. I can't let her pull away from me and go back to hiding inside herself. She may think that it's her only option right now, but I know I can help her through this. Whatever it takes, I will be here for her.

"I'm sorry, baby. I'm so, so sorry. I should have been there!" I quietly sob into her hair as I sit and rock her back and forth on the bed as she clutches her hands around my waist like she's holding on with her life. I don't know if telling her anything was the right thing to do, especially so soon, but she had to hear it from me. Not some stranger, not Nate, and certainly not her mother if she were, to come back anytime soon. It kills me to see her like this. But I know she can get through this because I know how strong she is. I've witnessed it.

As the exhaustion sets into our limbs and the long night hours slowly pass by, Jo's cries eventually soften and grow weaker as her body sinks further into mine. I listen as her breathing evens into a gentle rhythm, letting me know she's finally asleep and I lie awake until the early hours of the morning just so I can watch over her. I just wish when we wake up that this could all be nothing but a horrible nightmare.

76
Josephine

Hunter is still sleeping peacefully beside me as I sit here and contemplate how today might possibly go. The new scruffy look he's got going on is kind of cute and I have to say I'm not hating the rough look at all on him; he could make anything look good without even trying. I again noticed that his hair has grown out recently. Not too much but just enough, so a few small strands of hair fall onto his forehead and curl slightly at the ends. When I look at the elongated strands, I guess the length does show that some time has passed and it's a little unsettling that I wasn't aware of it.

I look out the window and notice the sun is just starting to barely peek up over the mountains far off in the distance. The bright orange hues have such a warming glow to them and it makes me remember the day Hunter had brought me up there to show me his favorite place that he shared with his sister. That was one of the best days I have had in my entire life, and Hunter gave me that wonderful memory to cherish for the rest of my life. When I think back throughout the last few months, he's been the only constant reason I've had so many unforgettable moments, and I certainly hope that he wants to be a part of more.

I look down at my arm again as the need to scratch at the surrounding skin near my stitches becomes unbearably irritating. The cuts look like they're healed enough, so I'm hoping to get these awful things out soon because the itching is driving me nuts. Movement from the other side of the bed pulls my attention towards Hunter as he shifts his body on the stiff mattress. This is one of the worst beds I have ever slept on, so I can't imagine that he was too comfortable last night having so little space to share.

"You're awake." He says in a surprised sleepy murmur. *He's adorable when he wakes up.* I watch him smooth his hand through his hair and roughly rub at his face with the heel of his hand before sitting up and sliding closer to me. He stares directly into my eyes and doesn't waste any time before gently gripping my chin and pulling me toward him to leave a light peck on my lips.

"Hey." He whispers after his lips leave mine and he tenderly strokes my jaw with his thumb as his eyes question how I'm currently feeling after last night. I can tell he doesn't want to bring it up, but I know he needs some reassurance from me that I'm not going to implode, the very second, I go to open my mouth.

"Hey." I answer him quietly and close my eyes as I enjoy the feeling of his soft touch on my face.

"How are you feeling?" He delicately asks as he tries to camouflage the worried look on his face.

"I'm okay." I say truthfully. And I am; at least for now.

"You're sure? Do you need anything? I can go get a doctor, they should know you're awake, I'm sure you're going to need…" Hunter starts to ramble so I grasp his hand tighter to stop him before he manages to slip off the bed.

"Hunter, I'm okay, really." I assure him quickly. "Please can I just have some time before everyone starts coming in here asking me all kinds of questions? I don't really want to deal with all that right now. Not yet."

Hunter

I awkwardly stand still for a minute, and I feel Jo tighten her delicate fingers around my rough hand to stop me from going to let the doctors know she's awake. I should have gotten someone last night when she woke up, but the overwhelming feeling of just needing to hold her as her mind absorbs everything that I had to tell her, hindered my better judgment and I ended up falling asleep with her in my arms. But if she needs this time alone before whatever is to come next, I want to be able to give that to her for as long as I can, so I sit back down on the bed and lovingly wrap her back up in my arms.

I HEAR TWO quick taps on the door just before someone turns the handle and walks in while Jo and I are sitting on the bed facing each other. My back is to the door, while Jo faces it head-on. Her eyes grow slightly in size as she eyes the person that just came in and I see an excited grin on her face before I turn around to see Kyle with his face buried in a pastry bag. Again.

"Hey man, they didn't have those new pastries you like today, so I got…" Kyle looks up and immediately stops talking. It's an unusual sight to see him lost for words, but he just stands a few feet from the end of the bed with his hand still stuck in the white bakery bag. I think something has finally been able to make him shut his big fat mouth for more than thirty seconds. I look back to Jo and she's already getting up off the bed. I hop off on her side and get behind her to help in case she still feels weak. She's been up and moving around a couple of times when the nurses came in to check on her. They have also run every test I can think of before she finally that said she didn't want to be bothered anymore this morning. So, for the last hour or so we have had the room all to ourselves.

"Kyle!" Jo says excitedly as she stiffly walks up to him and throws her arms around his neck to hug him. He just stands there a second with the bag still in his hand, looking to me to see if he's allowed to hug her back. He knows how protective I am of Jo, but I nod my head, and he lets out a breath before wrapping his arms around her to hug her back.

"Hey Jo, you're awake." Kyle greets her as she unwraps her arms from around his neck and before either of them can say another word Nate walks up behind Kyle and his mouth almost drops to the floor as soon as his eyes land on his sister. I guess none of us were paying attention to the door too well, because none of us even heard it open.

"Jo…oh my god you're okay." Nate says. He walks from behind Kyle, leans down, and gently puts his arms around Jo's waist, carefully giving her a brotherly hug.

"Yeah, I don't know why you're all so surprised, it's not like I came back from the dead, but you're all sure as hell acting like it." She belts out sounding pissed, but then she quickly smiles and shatters the awkward silence as she grants my ears with the pleasure of hearing her intoxicating laugh.

"Come on guys, lighten up. I'm fine, okay?" She tells us. "Doctors have checked me over and everything. No need to worry." She adds. "Yeah, alright. Great." Kyle says as he starts to dig in the bag again and takes out the biggest croissant I have ever seen in my life and hands it over to Jo. Her face lights up when she takes it from him and she squeals with joy when she sees that it's filled with Nutella.

"Oh my god Kyle, you are the best." She says and takes a colossal size bite off the end and closes her eyes while she enjoys the very first bite of her favorite dessert.

77
Josephine

Nate and Kyle stayed for a while before my nurse had to kick them out since it was after visiting hours. The hospital staff still allows Hunter to stay with me thankfully because he has been here the entire time I had been recovering. Summer, my favorite nurse, informed me that Hunter hasn't left my side once since they allowed him back to see me, and even if they wanted to, she said she knew they would have never been able to drag him out the room unless they hogtied him. And even then, she was sure he would find his way back here.

The thought of Hunter being here the whole time gives me mixed feelings. I'm so grateful that he stayed, but I also feel guilty that he's probably missed out on so much. Comfort for one. He hasn't even slept in a real bed in over two weeks until the night I fell asleep in his arms.

"Hey, babe." Hunter says as he walks back in the room with a to-go cup in each hand, distracting me from my thoughts as he sits down on the edge of the bed. He hands me the hot cup and I instantly smell the wonderful aroma of my favorite hot cocoa with cinnamon.

"Mmmm...oh god, this smells so good." I say as I inhale the chocolate-ty aroma before taking a sip and letting the warm liquid slide down my throat to warm my belly. "Thank you." I say to Hunter as he takes a few hot gulps from his cup before nodding.

"Of course, anything for my girl. You should know that already." He tells me and he slightly smirks behind the lid of his cup as he takes another sip.

"I know." I say shyly.

Hunter

I stare at Jo over the lid of my cup and feel a smirk creep up onto my lips while I watch her thoroughly enjoy her cup of cocoa. I've been debating on whether or not I should tell her about something that I've been working on for a few days and I'm surprised she hasn't caught me talking about it yet whenever she would wake up and I was on the phone with Honey. Luckily Nate was cool enough to help me out with a few things that I couldn't manage to do from the hospital, and with any hope, the stress of trying to figure everything out will all be worth it when I do tell her.

"Baby, can I ask you something?" I look at her and watch her eyes brighten at the sound of my voice. I take my drink and set it on the table next to the bed, and then carefully reach over to take Jo's cup out of her hand to set next to mine. I don't want any distractions and I certainly don't want to burn either one of us with scalding liquid. She doesn't say anything as I move closer to her and reach for her hand as I stare into those beautiful emerald gray eyes. "I've needed to tell you something for what feels like an eternity, Jo. I didn't have the nerve to say it before, but after I thought I had lost you…" I pause and swallow a lump that's suddenly caught in my throat as I think back to that brutally dreadful night and I hear Jo take in a quick, shallow breath like she wants to speak. "Please baby, let me get this out." I gently plead and she squeezes my hand before I continue. "I never thought when we met, that you coming into my life would change it from being this meaningless destructive mess, to being something that made me not want to miss out on a single second of living." I gently brush the back of my hand across her cheek and she lovingly, leans into me and closes her eyes, letting a single tear fall from her lashes. "So, when I found you that night in your room, I thought I had missed my chance to tell you how much you meant to me, it nearly killed me, Jo. I couldn't lose you, not then, not now, not ever. I can't ever lose you." I repeat and I see her eyes fill with tears as she looks at me.

Then all at once, without warning, she frees her hand from mine and pounces on top of me, pressing her luscious body into me until I'm lying flat on the bed with her in my arms. Her mouth makes full contact with my lips and her hands roam through my hair. She tugs at the ends as my hands feather down her arms and find their way to her hips. *I want this. I want her, again.* But when she starts to grind her hips against me, I can't help but think I might hurt her, so I take my hand off of her thigh and gently place it on the back of her head and reluctantly pull my lips away from hers.

"Baby…baby…hey. We can't do this yet." I breathlessly voice into her ear and she lifts her head up to look at me before letting her forehead drop to touch mine. *I am such a moron.* I want this with her, I really do, but I can't take it any further and risk hurting her. It's only been a few days since she's been cleared from having to be monitored every single second of the day but she's not out of the hospital yet, so I doubt her doctor will be okay with her taking up extracurricular activities anytime soon. Jo's breathing starts to normalize and she slowly crawls off of me and sits down on her heels.

"I know. I'm sorry." She whispers and a glimpse of shame shows on her face as she looks away from me. I sit up and grasp her chin between my thumb and forefinger, gently forcing her eyes to settle on my face so I can reassure her that she has nothing to be sorry for.

"Don't be sorry." I remind her as I concentrate on her eyes and pull her lips to meet mine. I drop tender kisses all along her jaw and then she crawls onto my lap and wraps her arms around my neck. "Jo." I hiss her name through my teeth as I try to control the urge to ravish her incredible body. "Jo." This time the tone of my voice demands her attention and she promptly, gives it to me.

My breathing matches the rigidness of her exhales. The sweet minty scent of her makes me salivate at the thought of tasting her again, but not before I get to tell her…

"I love you, Jo!" I'm finally able to say those words to her again and even better that I get to witness her reaction to hearing them. I can see the intensity in her eyes as she takes in what I just said and there's not a hint of regret as I sit here and hold her to me, while I wait for her response.

"I love you too." She says. Finally, Jo utters the four most pleasing words to me in the entire English language. I don't think it could get any better than this and I couldn't be any happier than I am in this moment.

"As long as I'm alive you will never be alone, and I will make sure that you never doubt how much I love you."

Epilogue
Josephine

Are you ready?" Hunter asks me as I try to fix my hair at the last minute in the mirror that hangs on the back of our bedroom door. He sneaks his hands around my waist and plants a small kiss on my neck before looking at me in the reflection of the glass. Without warning, he grips my hips between his fingers and gives them both a nice squeeze that forces a surprised squeak from me. It makes me lurch forward to avoid being tickled and I turn around as fast as I can to try and swat his ass with my hair brush; but he sidesteps out of the way and avoids it without effort.

"You look beautiful babe." Hunter smirks over his shoulder at me and twirls his car keys around his finger while he slowly walks down the hall. "And hurry up; we're going to be late…again."

ACKNOWLEDGEMENTS

To my Husband, thank you for encouraging me every step of the way and truly believing in me that I can achieve whatever I desire. All your input is deeply valued and appreciated and I couldn't have done it without you. You are the love of my life and getting to create something so special to me is the best feeling in the world, I loved every minute of it. And to my sweet little ones, thank you for being so patient with me as I learn the ropes of being a writer. There is so much more to publishing than I thought and learning it all takes a lot of time. You are the best little versions of me and I hope I can inspire you to make your own dreams come true.

I want to thank my author friends (Jensen Kristyne, Hannah Cowen and Holly Hamilton) that have helped me in navigating this lovely chaotic world of writing and publishing. Without you, I would be forever elbow deep in You-tube videos.

To my favorite Authors, (Monica James and Willow Winters), thank you for being so incredible and opening my eyes up to entirely different worlds than what I was used to. Your writing has inspired me to embrace the Damaged, the tragic and the Dark Depth of Romance. No one does Dark Romance better.

About the author

Autumn Rivers spent her childhood devouring such books by Stephen King and J.K Rowling. When she is not writing, she's either enjoying family time out in nature, even though she is not a true outdoor type of girl, or you can find her by an open window reading books by her favorite authors. She has an entrepreneurial spirit and is always looking for ways to inspire her family to be more self-sufficient and making sure they have the opportunities to embrace their own passions.

Her obsessions include, collecting books, owning a farm, and getting to travel to the birthplaces of her ancestors.

Connect with
AUTUMN RIVERS

***Goodreads:* AutumnRivers**
https://www.goodreads.com/user/show/119347481-autumn-tessie-rivers

***Instagram:* @Short_cake17**
https://www.instagram.com/short_cake17/

***Wattpad:* pseudonymLove**
https://www.wattpad.com/user/pseudonymLove

***Inkitt:* AutumnRiversAuthor**
https://www.inkitt.com/AutumnRiversAuthor

Website:
https://autumnriversauthor.wixsite.com/autumnriversauthor

Linktree:
Https://linktr.ee/autumnriversauthor

www.ingramcontent.com/pod-product-compliance
Lightning Source LLC
LaVergne TN
LVHW020530100826
845148LV00010B/1410